W9-BUJ-802

As Night Falls

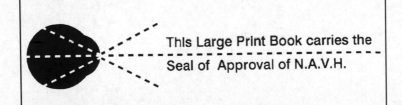

This Large Print Book carries the
Seal of Approval of N.A.V.H.

AS NIGHT FALLS

JENNY MILCHMAN

WHEELER PUBLISHING
A part of Gale, Cengage Learning

GALE
CENGAGE Learning·

Farmington Hills, Mich • San Francisco • New York • Waterville, Maine
Meriden, Conn • Mason, Ohio • Chicago

GALE
CENGAGE Learning®

LIBRARY OF CONGRESS CATALOGING-IN-PUBLICATION DATA

Milchman, Jenny.
    As night falls / by Jenny Milchman. — Large print edition.
      pages cm. — (Wheeler Publishing large print hardcover)
    ISBN 978-1-4104-8337-9 (hardcover) — ISBN 1-4104-8337-1 (hardcover)
    1. Escaped prisoners—Fiction. 2. Brothers and sisters—Fiction. 3. Family secrets—Fiction. 4. Hostages—Fiction. 5. Psychological fiction. 6. Large type book. I. Title.
    PS3613.I47555A9 2015b
    813'.6—dc23   2015022920

Published in 2015 by arrangement with Ballantine Books, an imprint of Random House, a division of Penguin Random House LLC

Printed in Mexico
1 2 3 4 5 6 7 19 18 17 16 15

This one is for three magnificent women without whom this story would not be. First, my editor, Linda Marrow, whose keen insight, wisdom, and heart enable me to write the books I always dreamed of. My agent, Julia Kenny, has dedication, passion, and perspective enough for the hundred books I hope we get to share. And finally, Nancy Pickard is a masterful writer, literary angel, and someone I treasure in my life.

CHAPTER ONE

Sandy Tremont stood at her kitchen island, staring out the window at a jagged run of mountains, and stirring a pot on the stove. Some dish she didn't remember making. Only when the sauce began to burp and Sandy smelled tomatoes did she recall her decision to serve spaghetti tonight. She shook her head, blinking away the view before her. Sandy would sometimes find herself reaching into a drawer and have no idea what she'd opened it for. She needed to try some of the mindfulness techniques she used with her patients.

The window ran the length of the wall beyond the island, her favorite part of this room. At the right time of the season, the mountains were the same color blue as the sky. And even now, in the dreariest portion of a waning year, there were beautiful things to see. Way out toward the back of their property, a creek galloped by, water leaping and rolling over rocks. The temperature must be dropping, for the flow had thickened and turned black, a sludgy, tarry brew. Sandy switched her gaze just long enough to lower the flame beneath her sauce.

When his father died, after a lengthy illness, and left them a healthy inheritance, her husband had decided to build their dream house. It was actually more Ben's dream than hers; Sandy had been concerned about a new house being too showy for the neighbors, people in town, her patients. Sandy didn't like to stand out. But Ben had assuaged her fears by finding a remote piece of property. It suited Sandy, the privacy that bordered on reclusion. If you looked down the hill when the trees were bare you caught sight of a rim of roof, which belonged to the nearest full-time resident. And there was the remains of an old Adirondack great camp to the left, an amputated parcel of land. The acreage Sandy and Ben now owned had once been part of this spread, which still boasted a stick-and-beam structure kept shambling along by infrequent injections of cement to the stone foundation, a fresh coat of paint over the splintery wood.

The isolation never made Sandy nervous.

Her job — even though it was only part time — wielded a stranglehold of people with needs that tended not to stay in neat hourly boxes. It was good to get home and really set things aside, feel as if she were truly away.

Sandy allowed herself a small smile. Most days she couldn't believe that this house, draped in peace and serenity, was the place she got to live. She wished Ben were home right now so she could tell him how glad she was he'd urged the move. Sandy gave the pot another stir, breathing in deeply. The sauce smelled spicy, fragrant. She turned away from the stovetop, glancing at the clock whose digital display blared a warning. Time for the daily countdown to begin. Ivy had fifteen minutes till she usually got home from school. And less than an hour until, if she wasn't home, Ben would know about it.

Sandy felt a furry twining at her knees and lowered her hand. "Hiya, Mac, you good boy."

The dog gave a yip of agreement, flank rising and falling as Sandy stroked him. There were a few burrs in his coat from their afternoon walk. Sandy's fingers pulled and sorted, removing the gristly spurs along with a clump of milkweed fur. Mac was a

9

blend of breeds, nothing very clear, although he had to have some Husky in him somewhere. He had one startlingly blue eye, while the other was brown, and perfectly pointed ears. It was more than those features, though. Something wolfish lived deep within Mac, a touch of the wild that hadn't been stirred for some time.

"Gonna have to give you a bath," Sandy said, and this time there was no assenting yip.

Instead, Mac's furry brow signaled his displeasure. He turned and trotted toward the sitting area of the kitchen, the farthest away he would stray on his own. The dog lay down on the rug in front of an upholstered loveseat.

Westward-facing glass doors formed the wall behind the sitting area. They framed a pale expanse of sky canopying starkness all around. Stripped trees and fields of brittle grasses: a landscape the color of potato peelings. It was the end of a dying year, with a seemingly infinite stretch of bleakness before it, yet Sandy loved this face of the countryside, too.

She walked back to flick off the burner. The sauce was done, and a lid over the pasta water would keep it hot for later. The salad sat in the fridge in a bowl covered by a paper towel. She'd even sliced the bread. Tasks had always had a way of flitting away from Sandy, which was why she liked to get a jump-start on dinner, as if she were lining airplanes up for takeoff instead of preparing a meal for her family of three.

With nothing left to do, Sandy picked up the phone to call in to work, catching a glimpse of turquoise numbers on the clock.

Three-forty.

Despite uncountable reminders and remonstrations to come straight home from school, or at least call with an alternate plan, Ivy was now inarguably late.

Sandy sighed, and Mac got up and stalked back over. He didn't like his family to be worried or annoyed or upset. He was like Sandy in that sense, she thought, watching the dog make his way across the room. Mac wasn't as limber as he used to be, she realized with an internal flinch. It was impossible to believe that a day would come when Mac wouldn't be here. He had grown up alongside Ivy.

Wedeskyull Community Hospital had recently installed a telecom system that, as far as everyone could tell, had only resulted in alienating the patients and annoying the employees. The automated welcome came on as Sandy pressed the cordless to her ear.

11

If you would like to speak with someone in the Emergency Department, please press 1. If you would like to speak with someone in the — Sandy hit 4 before she had to listen to the rest of the menu.

"Mental health services, this is Gloria, how may I help you?"

"At ease," Sandy said in response to the perky tone. "Anything?"

"Oh, Ms. Tremont, hi," Gloria said, her voice returning to a more natural state of deflation. "Not really, it's been pretty you-know-what so far today." Uttering the word *quiet* was a jinx. Everyone who worked in a hospital knew that.

Sandy caught a rustle of papers over the line. Million-dollar system or no, WCH still operated mostly as it had for over a century, eschewing paperless replacements for treatment plans and notes and charts.

"Madeline Jennings put in a call," Gloria said. "But only one. I'd say we're doing well."

Sandy allowed herself a brief, invisible nod of acknowledgment. On the days Sandy didn't see patients, Madeline sometimes called as many as five or six times. "What did she say?"

"She asked if she could give you a call at home," Gloria replied. "I offered to beep

12

you, but then she said she was all right."

It was something of a ruse, having patients phone the hospital so that their therapist could be beeped. Therapists were supposed to block their number before calling back, but technology wasn't advanced enough in these parts for that to be a foregone conclusion. Often you were lucky to be able to place a call at all.

"Whatever *all right* means with that one," Gloria went on.

Sandy didn't echo the administrator's chuckle. Gallows humor was the method of choice for many in their professions, a way of coping with exposure to the mental health ills of a population who lived in stark, often savage circumstances. But Sandy couldn't look down, even undetected, on these people who eked out a living at the edge of great wilderness. And Madeline was a patient she particularly liked. A young mother dealing with the triple whammy of grief, post-traumatic stress, and what appeared to be an absolutely bizarre childhood.

Gloria relented. "I'm only kidding. If anyone can help that girl, it's you, Ms. Tremont."

"Thanks, Gloria," Sandy said. "I'm thinking you-know-what thoughts for this evening."

"Don't even say it," Gloria responded darkly.

Sandy hung up, checking the phone to be sure she hadn't missed any calls. Madeline was in a special live-to-work program on an organic farm where they de-emphasized technology. Landlines were about as modern as they got.

She replaced the cordless and went to peek through a narrow column of window by the front door, Mac trailing her. He was a rescue who couldn't bear to be alone, his first year or so of life too painful to contemplate, although Mac was the sweetest and most compliant pet you could imagine so long as he had company. On Sandy's hospital days, Mac went in with Ben to work, although the arrangement struck Sandy for the first time as finite. What if Ben scheduled a trip and Mac could no longer keep up the pace? Maybe he could start accompanying Sandy instead. Mac's gentle nature would make him a good therapy dog.

Although she couldn't see the twists and turns at the bottom of the road from this vantage point, every foot of the mile-long trip up their drive was visible. Sandy wouldn't be able to miss whichever car was chauffeuring Ivy, nor could she avoid spotting Ben's arrival. It seemed like a wacky game of chicken: which set of headlights would appear first? The familiar circles on their Jeep or some unknown pair?

If Ben arrived before their daughter, Sandy wouldn't be able to conceal another flouted arrival, a kindness she was usually willing to extend to Ivy, who'd been engaging in typical teenage displays lately, but was overall quite a good kid. Ben butted heads with Ivy more than Sandy did, and Sandy didn't want the night to devolve into an ensnarement of accusations and flared tempers.

She let the strip of curtain fall back, obscuring the driveway.

Mac whined high in his throat.

"It's all right, Mackie," Sandy said reassuringly. But she was stroking the snail shell of scar on her wrist, while chiding herself for her nerves. A teenager home late? Imagine that.

From outside came the rumble of an engine, smoother and more sedate than their Jeep.

Sandy felt a flicker of relief, or something close, while Mac let out a delighted yelp. Sandy pulled at the hasp on their front door, reminding herself not to scold.

The door of an overlarge SUV swung open.

EARNED

It was so quiet outside you could hear the rasp of leaves, but as soon as the prison door clanged shut behind him, Nick might as well have been stepping outside into a carnival. Sunlight flaring, colors barking, air so clear it felt like glass upon his skin. He had to blink and shade his eyes as the scene before him resolved. There was asphalt and drab cement, a faraway circle of trees, already winter-brown, and one lone decommissioned school bus, painted white.

They were headed toward the bus, Nick last man out, his preferred position now. On line for chow or the shower or the yard — last was just fine by him. You saw more that way.

He took a look around.

After three o'clock, and a hard frost still lingered on the ground, feathering the pavement. They had been issued jackets — thick, ugly brown things to wear over their greens

— and the feel was foreign, as if Nick had been transformed into some bulky alien life-form.

So many things to observe out here, and so many that weren't demanding the usual attention. Barely buried tempers, cattle calls from the guards that signaled chow, change of shift, med dispersal, quiet time. But you never got silence, not really. There was the continual spatter of piss from four men sharing a john. The sound the clicker made during counts and recounts, each man accounted for like a box on a pallet. And talking, of course. Constant mutters, chatter, screams. Cries for Mama, even in the middle of the night.

The prison sat on a carved-up plot of land. Trees had been hulled out and the ground shorn of grasses, paved over for visitor parking, and so the guards could have a clear line of sight. They were far enough away from the nearest town that there was no place to run, and the only cars that drove by went at a pretty good clip, warned by road signs not to stop. There hadn't been a successful prison break since 1961, although a story was habitually trundled out about a more recent attempt, with the inmate rounded up in the adjacent woods hours later, never having even made it off the

18

grounds. There'd been no escape attempt during Nick's twenty-four years of incarceration as far as he knew. That tale was a composite, a patchwork stitching of every desperate man who had the thought to leave, meant to serve as a deterrent for anybody foolish enough to harbor such hope still.

But today it didn't matter how isolated they were or how unlikely was escape.

Nick had a plan.

Harlan took up most of a seat at the back of the bus, and Nick positioned himself across the aisle from him. Two other inmates sat just ahead, with the guard up front.

Rear position. Nick was pleased. He wondered if Harlan sensed his preference, and had deliberately set up the seating. Probably it'd just been luck. Harlan wasn't much for organization.

They'd been cellies since a few years after Nick had gone in, which meant that by now Harlan was completely exposed to him. Nick knew the mutters Harlan made while sleeping, how he shuddered after taking a piss, that Harlan had been paid only one visit his entire time inside. But by the same token, Nick didn't know Harlan at all, not his age, or why he'd gotten life when he hadn't laid a hand on anybody, or even who'd come to see him that time.

Nick slid his palm across the green vinyl seat. He hadn't felt this pebbly texture in years.

"Listen up," the guard said. He touched the rifle slung low by his side.

This guard was in his forties or fifties, a long time on the job. But today his voice held a note that was different from its usual ring of command.

On the other side of the bus, Harlan's face appeared bland and unchanging, his features lumpy. Harlan hadn't heard the same thing Nick had, but that didn't mean much. Harlan was loyal, better than any man inside, but still, his brains were made of paste, and no amount of heart could change that.

The guard sounded off-kilter. Outside on his own with four men was a change from the usual day-to-day. Nick felt a small sizzle of satisfaction.

"We got blacktopping on a bridge," the guard said. "You'll work in teams of two."

Information inside was strictly on a need-to-know. You had to qualify to earn a stint on the outs — even just for a two- or three-hour job — and that had taken Nick a while. The first job he could've worked had

20

been scheduled in August, and that timing would've been a whole lot better considering what he had planned. But the job kept getting postponed — cutbacks probably — until a day sheet stuck between the bars told Nick he'd be riding out today. Nick didn't tend to be a take-what-he-could-get kind of guy, but he had learned a thing or two since going inside. A better chance might not come along.

It had cost him two packs and four shots to get details on the job. He tended to be well supplied, but that trade had wiped him out. If he went back in, he'd be jittery as hell, with a mean clamp of a headache, out of smokes and juice for a week.

He wasn't going back in.

"All you got to do is set down cones," the guard continued. He reached up to scrub the gray spikes of his crew cut. "Simple as that. Start a quarter mile before the bridge, go a quarter mile after it lets out. Make a nice, generous curve to guide 'em along. We don't want anybody not knowing they don't got two lanes."

Nick saw Harlan's brow furrowing; he wasn't great with anything beyond simple instructions. And he didn't like guards, especially the older, more experienced ones. Harlan's fists would roll into masses the size of wasp nests, his blank eyes would smolder, whenever he was confronted by a guard.

Before coming up with this idea, Nick had considered simply ordering Harlan to take out the guards who stood in their way; escaping by brute force. But, in addition to the relatively slim chance of that working, it wouldn't have got them where they needed to be.

The driver lurched the bus into gear, rolled out of the lot, and through the gates. Then they were on the road — a real road again, smooth as a woman's ass — and headed north.

They reached old Route 9. Setup looked just about like he'd pictured it. Nick blew out a breath of relief. The intel he'd stripped his stash for had been right.

The bus lumbered over to the side of the road. Cresting it was a hump of hill that let out onto a bridge, only one lane of which was open. The other was newly paved, shiny as sealskin.

A temporary stoplight flared red in the low afternoon light, making sure that cars didn't meet coming over the single lane of the impaired bridge. Visible through the bus window was a pickup parked at a sharp angle. The truck's bed held nested stacks of orange cones.

Harlan began straining to get a look, misting Nick's face with his breath.

"Cut it out," Nick said, and Harlan lowered his big body back down, biting his lip with piano key teeth.

"Ready?" the guard asked, unease still alive in his tone. "Out of your seats."

The convict in front of Nick stood up. Small — by prison measures anyway — and dark-skinned, with wiry white coils of hair receding on his scalp.

He took a look through the window at the road.

This particular inmate was of the old school variety, locked up before Nick was even born. Old-School was a rampart, a foundation of the prison who helped keep eight hundred men from battering it apart. Prison lore had it that he was the one who'd helped with the escape more than fifty years ago, but Nick had never been able to buy that. The story had the feel of a tall tale. Why wouldn't Old-School have gotten out himself?

The newer guys used the fathomless measures of time inside to beef up, Nick included, but Old-School had long since passed that mark, allowing himself to shrink and shrivel over the years. Still, he had a commanding dignity about him. The twitchy alertness new guys wore, always on the watch, looking out, had been worn away, smudged like the charcoal of Old-School's skin. He still took everything in — you didn't survive inside if you stopped paying attention — but Old-School did it with a studied breed of acceptance. Even this has its limits, he said with every slow blink of his eyes. Everything does.

"We going to have trouble with that light?" Old-School asked, his eyes still on the road. "Cars barreling through, hitting our cones?"

"We're not going to have trouble so long as you don't make any," the guard said.

Nick watched the square off, monitoring it for signs of combustion. He'd been planning for too long to let anything go wrong now. Figuring out what was likely to bring them down, coming up with workarounds. Learning how the world had changed since he'd gone in. And, of course, securing this stint on the outs. That had been the toughest part. To everyone else, Nick probably seemed like just another jailhouse convert, finally come to see the light and the error of his ways. In fact, the good behavior had nearly killed him — holding himself in check whenever anybody crossed him or tried to piss him off. For Harlan, good

24

behavior came easy; he was slow to act on his own volition. But Nick had earned every oxygen-rich breath he took out here, and no wizened old con was going to mess with the scenario he was banking on.

A blink. "You don't got to worry about me," Old-School said.

Nick took another deep, heady breath.

The guard handed out jerseys, slick with orange reflective tape. "Then get off the bus."

Harlan's girth caused each step to heave as Nick followed him down. A chill sun shone through the naked spires of trees. In concert he and Harlan approached the pickup, so in sync they glided. Harlan hoisted up a batch of cones, taking the bulky rubber tower into his arms as if it were a toddler. Old-School and the other inmate wrestled their own stack down.

A sick, eerie light descended, and Nick looked up to see the temporary stoplight turn green. A late model sedan shot across the bridge, its driver clearly pissed off by the delay.

Timing was going to be key.

Old-School and the other inmate made it to the far end of the bridge, probably thinking that haste had bought them the choice position, farthest away from the guard and the bus. But Nick was glad again to be last. He watched both men walk on — a quarter mile looked about right — before Old-School took the first cone out of the other inmate's arms and set it down, his placement as precise as if decided by instrument.

The guard jerked his chin toward Nick and Harlan, indicating that they should get a move on. The guard's gaze was targeted and direct, switching back and forth between the woods, the adjacent fields, the thin skin of the river itself. Only last did he scan the long, empty road, where a body would be seen instantly, a fool's choice of escape.

Nick led Harlan along the asphalt, gauging the distance till they'd gone about fifteen hundred feet, just like the guard had specified. Then Nick held up a barricading hand, stopping Harlan, and reached for a cone. Harlan had to stoop way down for Nick to take it.

Nick placed the orange dunce cap on the road, then took a few steps in the direction of the bridge. Harlan trod after him, and they repeated the sequence.

Nick touched a spot on his leg before tackling the next cone. Weather coming in. He could feel it, even if the sky was still clear, and for a second the privilege he'd

26

fought so hard to win turned nasty, useless, something to stomp into the ground. Bring inmates in at the tail end of the day so the fewest number of cars would be coming over that bridge. It wasn't like there was rush hour out here. Schedule the job in November instead of the summer due to someone's budgetary screwup. Nick felt a dagger of resentment toward the powers that be, not to mention the citizens who were able not only to drive around freely, but be protected as they did it.

Harlan began shifting his burden of cones from one arm to the other while Nick tried to wrestle his anger down. It was a trick he'd learned in mandated counseling, to picture a mental scabbard and thrust his fury into it. Nick had dutifully attended one idiotic session each week all year. Now he breathed in air so fresh it tasted like menthol. Never again was he going to take a whiff of the stale, recirculated air inside. The sensation in his leg was sometimes misleading, and in this case, it'd better be.

A car streaked by, its cloud of exhaust smelling like freedom. The light changed to red, and Nick stilled with a cone in his arms.

He began to count.

The car cooled its wheels, forced to wait at the bridge. It occurred to Nick that these drivers weren't so free themselves, and he felt a swell of satisfaction build.

He swiveled to share it with Harlan, then scowled. Nick had been keeping track of how long the light stayed red, maintaining a beat in his head. But he could see Harlan's lips visibly moving, expelling white puffs into the frigid air. If the guard were any closer — and could lip-read — he might've seen that Harlan was counting.

"Quit it!" Nick ordered, low.

The stack of cones Harlan was hugging to his chest pitched sideways, off balance.

Nick reached over to steady them, cuffing Harlan on his coat sleeve as he did.

It was like hitting a girder.

The light changed and the car moved on across the bridge. The driver gave Old-School and the other inmate a wide berth on the opposite side.

Harlan's mouth stilled and so did the count in Nick's head.

He'd gotten to ninety. A minute and a half.

They would enter at the seventy-five-second mark. That would give them fifteen seconds more for maneuvering, the inevitable balking and surprise.

The road behind them was empty now, a faded gray strand in contrast to the new lane they were approaching on the bridge.

Nick didn't want to risk looking too long in this direction — the guard was headed back their way — but he would've felt a whole lot better if he could've seen another car. This road was supposed to be decently trafficked for these parts, but here was that end-of-the-day thing again, poking up its ugly snout.

The light went through another cycle with no car appearing. Harlan struggled with his armful of cones, and Nick reached for a few more, lightening Harlan's load. They were getting close to the bridge.

A car sped by, braking hard when the stoplight flashed red.

Nick and Harlan weren't ready for it. They weren't quite there yet; maybe five or six more cones to go. Nick juggled possibilities. He could speed up to ensure they made the next red — although getting Harlan to move faster was like shoving water — but if a car wasn't there for that light change, then they would have to change course and find a way to stall. Nick supposed they could literally reverse, walk back up the road and make sure their cones formed the nice, smooth curve the guard had asked for. But even though Nick tended to like things tidy since his I'm-a-changed-man conversion inside, straightening cones at a work site might look a bit suspicious.

On the opposite side of the bridge, Old-School and the other inmate were moving slowly, enjoying their freedom. Nick focused so hard, it felt like a string was about to snap in his head. He tried to match Old-School and the other inmate's pace.

The light switched to green, and the waiting car drove off.

Nick eased a cone out of Harlan's arms, lining it up with the one that'd come before.

The guard reached Nick and Harlan's side of the bridge, nodding at them and pivoting before crossing back over the creek that swelled beneath.

No car.

The long, waving road was empty.

Everything inside Nick seized up. His lungs felt like a solid mass of concrete, his veins a web of cement. The thick orange rubber of the cone buckled in his grip.

And then, as if he'd willed them into existence, two cars appeared over the rise.

Nick kept his gaze aimed down. If either driver saw him as they passed, they would read the glee in his eyes. Everything always worked out for Nick. Things fell into place where he was concerned as if they'd been ordained, as if *he'd* been ordained.

Harlan was regarding both vehicles with

interest. Did Harlan remember what they were doing here? That would be something — Harlan's memory was usually for shit. For a second it occurred to Nick to wonder whether Harlan even wanted to live on the outs. Or could he just not stand to go back inside if Nick wasn't there? Nick needed Harlan for obvious reasons. His size, his ability to intimidate. But in a way, Harlan seemed to need him, too. The awareness gave Nick a strange feeling; that and the presence of the cars made him send Harlan a brief, approving nod.

Harlan's broad brow creased.

Nick drew as close as he dared to the temporary light. It was a metal thing on stalks, like some kind of massive heron or stork.

Harlan trudged over beside him, his shoes throwing up clods of dirt.

Nick stooped to set a cone down, at the same time taking a quick glance through the window of the first car. Its driver was young, his head bobbing back and forth, although Nick couldn't hear any music playing.

Perfect.

A teenager who didn't know anything, and would be overpowered in a cinch.

The light hadn't changed — by Nick's

mental timer, it still had forty-five seconds to go — but the kid was already pulling forward, like choking up on a bat. He was trying to shave seconds off his waiting time without having any idea what that would do to Nick.

Then the kid turned his head sideways, and his eyes caught Nick's.

The guard began making his return trip over the bridge. His usual militaristic march had come back, firm and in control. "Jesus," he said as he drew near. "He looks even bigger out in the open, don't he?"

Harlan's cheeks stained red, a wide swath of terrain. His golf ball–sized Adam's apple gave a jump, propelled by a rumble too low to hear.

The second car — a big, fancy SUV — remained in place, not rolling forward like the other one. Through the windshield, Nick spied a lone female driver, looking down, studying her nails.

The light was going to go green in thirty seconds.

The kid's impatience could be an asset: he would be gone by the time Nick forced the woman in the second car to drive off.

Nick started to assemble a smile for the guard. "Yessir."

The guard aimed a crisp gaze at him.

"Don't 'sir' me," he said, that earlier hum of nerves erased from his voice.

Nick crushed his smile.

Twenty-five seconds.

The light glowed like a ruddy burn, SUV stalled just before it, first car already moving on. Lucky there were no traffic cops out here, Nick thought, quashing another grin. He hoped the kid did jump the red.

Old-School crossed back over the bridge, coming up behind them. "We all done on our half of the bridge. Want us to get started here?"

The guard rotated slowly. "You questioning my instructions?"

"No, I am not," Old-School said, standing there in his dignified way.

The other inmate walked across the bridge, joining them.

The guard let out a scoff of dismissal. "Back on the bus. You two —" He swung around in Nick and Harlan's direction. "— finish up this section. And make it fast."

Old-School let the other inmate head off first.

The SUV inched forward, readying itself for the light change.

CHAPTER TWO

Sandy didn't recognize the SUV that had pulled up in their drive. She tried to get a glimpse inside, but couldn't see through the tinted windows. She wasn't even sure whether it was a girl at the wheel, or a boy. She made a mental note to ask Ivy later who her chauffeur had been.

The passenger door nudged open a few more notches — they made them so heavy these days, and designed to swing back — and Sandy watched her daughter climb out.

Ivy had an August birthday and thus was the youngest in her class. Most of her classmates had begun driving already. Sandy and Ben had discussed the idea of keeping Ivy out of her friends' cars, but it proved contentious. The kids were moving on, entering that fuzzy realm between childhood and maturity, and holding Ivy back would only make her rebel. It wasn't her fault that she was fifteen to everyone else's sixteen or seventeen.

Whoever the friend had been began to execute a careful exit, taking the SUV around the half-moon of gravel, then driving off at a reasonable pace.

Sandy watched her daughter flounce up the wide stone steps, newly rounded hips twitching. Probably a boy in the car, then. Mac stepped forward and Ivy graced him with a pat. Mac panted, his tongue lolling out, and Ivy pinched the tiny bud of her nose. How pretty her daughter had become — transformed from merely cute — seemingly overnight.

"Your breath stinks, Mackie," Ivy said.

The dog's regal shoulders sloped. He turned around in a circle, sticking close to Ivy. Sandy reached out and touched Ivy's arm as the girl went by. Ivy glanced back in passing.

"No hello?" Sandy asked lightly.

"Hello," Ivy said.

These days, her daughter could make obedience sound like defiance.

Sandy made sure the porch lantern was turned on against the waning light. How had the rest of the afternoon slipped away? Not only Ivy: Ben too was late today.

Sandy drew the front door shut, listening for the catch of the handle — firm, somehow reassuring, although of course nobody locked their doors way out here — then looked over her shoulder. Ivy had already disappeared into the house.

Banging in the kitchen beckoned. Sandy followed the sounds to the center island, where Ivy was arranging a motley array of condiments: mayonnaise, mustard, something spicy in a jar that had probably expired months ago.

"I made dinner," Sandy informed her daughter. "Spaghetti and tomato sauce. No meat."

Ivy slapped two pieces of bread onto the bare counter and added cheese.

Here's where you say, *But you prefer Bolognese, Mom,* and I reply, *It's no problem, I'm happy to accommodate.* Sandy went on, conversing with Ivy in her head, which is where the two of them seemed to have their best discussions these days, when she realized that Ivy had also placed a piece of paper down on the counter, a greasy slick of mayo now staining it.

Sandy looked while Ivy raised her sloppy sandwich to her mouth and took a bite.

The paper on display appeared to be a history test, although it was hard to tell from all the stark red slashes across it. Three of those slashes made things clearer, though.

36

"An F, Ive?" Sandy said, truly shocked.

Ivy shrugged. She took another bite.

Mac lowered himself down beside Ivy's feet, ignoring a comet trail of crumbs on the floor. They'd worked hard to train him not to scavenge, not that Mac had put up much of a fight. Their dog didn't really fight about anything. Sandy watched her daughter rip off a clump of crust from her sandwich, dangle it by her fingers, then drop it deliberately. Mac hesitated before tonguing up the tidbit, swallowing with a grateful gulp.

Never mind, Mackie, Sandy thought, upon seeing his remorseful glance. *In a war of wills with a teenage girl, even a dog can't win.*

She found room on Ivy's test to sign, then took one of her daughter's hands off the sandwich and folded the page into it. It was a treat to touch Ivy, even like this. "Why don't you put this away?" Sandy said. "We can tell Dad about it some other time."

Ivy stowed the paper in her knapsack. When she straightened up, she was looking at Sandy. "That's it?"

"What do you mean, 'that's it'?" Sandy echoed.

Ivy glared at her.

Sandy blinked. "Ivy, look, I signed your test. I'm not punishing you. I'm not even insisting we tell Dad yet and you're —"

Ivy spoke over her. "Are we ever going to tell him?"

"What?"

Ivy shoved the remainder of her snack into her mouth, speaking in a garble. "You heard me. Are we ever going to tell Dad? About my test?"

Sandy sighed. "Why are you doing this? It's like you're looking for trouble." It occurred to Sandy that that wasn't exactly the right explanation. But, like reaching for an object in the dark, she couldn't quite grasp what was correct either.

Ivy wiped her hands off on her jeans, which clung in a way her clothes never used to.

"You know why," she said.

Sandy shook her head. "I really don't."

Ivy stared at her.

Sandy knew better than to engage in a blinking contest with a fifteen-year-old. She turned to busy herself with kitchen tasks, speaking over her shoulder.

"Look, honey, why don't you finish your homework? Then you'll be ready to come down and sit with us at dinner, even if you're not hungry."

Ivy picked up her knapsack. As she headed toward the kitchen archway, she turned back and said, "Who said I wouldn't be hungry?"

Sandy took this as the peace offering it seemed to be. "Well, good. I made a salad, too. All the vegetables you could want tonight."

"Did you get the dressing I like? That really good kind, with basil?"

Sandy nodded. "Mmm, and the sesame. I love it, too."

For a moment, they traded smiles, and it was like having the old Ivy back. The one who'd been so interwoven into Sandy's days that for a long time she had worried Ivy would never find her own independent sense of self. Ivy had already turned eleven — a tween, especially by the standards of her older friends — when they'd begun to rehab their old house in town with the help of a local historic restoration specialist. Ivy had been as interested in the wallpaper swatches and discussion of finishes as Sandy herself. She'd foregone birthday parties, and trips downstate with her best friend, to join Sandy at the lumberyard, pricing scallops and gingerbread trim.

Then they'd gone and sold that house, and now Sandy had the uneasy sense, like the first twinges of a coming illness, that she and Ivy had lost something far more

39

precious. Not just a piece of her childhood, but the whole loving tenor of it.

"Mom?" Ivy said.

Sandy nodded, bearing down so as to be able to face whatever Ivy was about to bring up — her grades, school, the move maybe. Sandy would confront whatever it was with honesty instead of parental sleight of hand. "Yes, honey?"

"Would it be too big of a hassle for you to make garlic bread tonight?"

Sandy bit her bottom lip, masking a smile. "Already on it."

"Oh good." Ivy walked through the archway, Mac at her heels. "It fills me up a lot more than just plain pasta."

Sandy felt like she'd been given a governor's pardon. She suppressed the urge to offer one final homework reminder, unwilling to disturb this jumpy, fragile rapprochement, like the first skin on a mold. But she knew how annoyed Ben would be if Ivy's homework wasn't started by the time he got home. Her husband was the ultimate worker ant, believing nothing should be done later that could be tackled now.

"I'll heat up a whole loaf," Sandy said, then added, "but go do your homework, okay?"

"I don't have any."

Sandy had begun searching the depths of the mammoth fridge for butter; now she lifted her head. "You sure? Because this would be the first time since middle school that you didn't."

"I did it with Cory," Ivy said. "The guy who brought me home."

"Ivy —" Sandy knew Ivy was lying, but she had no idea why. First the test, now this. Although her daughter's grades had dipped a bit this year, it hadn't been that big a deal because Ivy had started out so high, with a 4.5 GPA in mostly honors and AP's. But that Ivy was shape-shifting lately, morphing from one creature into another mysterious, unknowable one.

"What?" her daughter said, brazenly. "You want to check? Look through my things?"

Fights with Ivy never fully went out these days. They were like a fire whose bed of embers always lay ready to spark. Sandy's patients had shared stories of their own teenagers, so she knew that this was normal. But that didn't make it any more enjoyable, especially for someone who had always craved peace, built her entire family around it.

"What I *want*," Sandy said, moving a little closer to her daughter, "is for you to go upstairs, finish your homework, then come

41

down and join Dad and me for dinner. What I want is for us all to have a nice meal. What I want —"

A flicker of emotion changed the set of Ivy's mouth. "Are you calling me a liar?" she cut in.

"No," Sandy said. "I'm not. I'm just saying that I'm pretty sure you do have homework. I have no idea why you would say that you didn't."

"Good," Ivy replied, and at first the reply sounded nonsensical. "Because you're the liar."

The accusation hit Sandy like a club. "What?" She stepped forward, surprised when Ivy shrank. "What are you talking about? When have I ever lied to you?"

Suddenly, shockingly, Ivy was crying. She swiped at her face, transferring a beige smear of mustard from her hand to her cheek so that her face was for a moment that of the little girl she had been, oh, five minutes ago.

"I don't know, Mom," Ivy said, and sniffled.

Sandy took another step, thinking to comfort her daughter, but Ivy turned away. All the pepper and posturing of a teenager was gone, replaced by a child's despondent shuffle. Mac matched Ivy's pace out of the room.

At the border between the dining and living areas of the big, open space beside the kitchen, they both paused.

Sandy looked down. Mac was watching her with one dark, trembly eye and one bright blue one.

"I don't know when or why or what you're lying about, Mom." Ivy took in a breath deep enough to make her chest swell. "I just know that you are."

ESCAPE

Nick edged through a scatter of dry leaves. The sound was whisper-light, yet it had the force of buildings toppling. He could see the road unspooling before them. He put down a last cone without considering its placement. This was pure charade now; soon Harlan would toss aside the few he still held, and then he and Nick would be gone.

Instead of dropping the cones though, upset bloomed on Harlan's face. His faulty memory had kicked in, and now he was watching his only friend walk away from him, with no idea why. A full second ticked by as Nick weighed the risk of trying to hiss a reminder in Harlan's cabbage leaf ear — which he would have trouble reaching — versus waiting for him to remember the plan.

Understanding dawned and Harlan moved over alongside Nick. They stood beside a pack of trees bordering the bridge.

The guard's back was turned as he observed the fourth inmate board the bus, moving slowly, enjoying the last remnants of his freedom. Old-School must've already given up on his. Nick could picture the ancient inmate selecting a seat and sitting down, silent and resigned.

In just five seconds — not as many as Nick had wanted; the teenage driver had introduced infuriating delay — the light was going to change and both cars would take off. The driver of the SUV didn't appear to be as impatient, but that didn't mean she'd stick around.

Nick seized the handle on the rear door. He knew it wouldn't be locked — cars here never were — but Nick's heart still pulsed until he felt a reassuring give.

This vehicle might wind up being even better than the kid's. Its windows had that nice tinting that had become standard while Nick was inside. He'd seen the evolution take place on TV ads and cop shows.

Harlan crowded close, bumping into Nick, and their entrance was clumsy.

The driver twisted around. She sucked in one quick breath — it made a *click* in her throat — at the sight of Harlan filling the plank of seat behind her, his head pressed up against the roof. Harlan barely got his legs out of the way before Nick let the door swing shut. He heard a second thud that he couldn't account for.

"Drive," Nick said conversationally. "And we'll let you live."

The guard was just beginning to frown as he surveyed the suddenly transformed makeup of his work crew.

The car in front of them drove off slightly ahead of the green.

A bullet rang out, fired up at the gray, featureless sky. A warning shot, an alert, or perhaps simply sheer futile fury on the part of the guard.

"Drive!" Nick roared.

Harlan cringed, curling in on himself, the massive vehicle shaking with the movement of his body.

The light changed and the SUV rocketed through.

This car was as nice as someone's living room, provided that living room was inhabited by a half-dozen teenagers. The floor was covered with wrappers and stray cosmetics and bits of food, the seat ridged with something sticky. Nick saw a flurry of white that resembled dandruff. A wink of silver in the low light made him realize that the dust was actually nail filings. Quick as a snake's tongue his hand shot out, closing over a slim, sandpapery blade that had gotten wedged between the door and the seat.

He refocused on the woman in front. Her grip on the wheel was unsteady, and the great vehicle gyrated as it drove forward.

"Give me your phone," Nick said, back to his original friendly tone. There wouldn't be a signal out here, but he wasn't taking any chances. He had spent months going over each of the changes that had taken place during his twenty-four years inside, and pondering their effects. His escape wouldn't be felled by the widespread use of computers or the arrival of 911 in the area.

He became aware of Harlan breathing hard beside him, his body giving off heat in waves now that they'd hit the high-octane warmth of the car.

The woman fumbled with something on the seat beside her, and Nick's heart had a second to flare. She had a CB radio, or a relative on the job; maybe she was a cop herself. But then the woman dropped her pocketbook over the seat, and a useless fluster of things came tumbling out, along with her wallet and cell phone.

Nick emptied the wallet of cash, then examined the phone. There was a casing with a seam along it; when he picked at the opening, the plastic popped up. Inside sat the strange-looking battery that powered the device. Nick removed it. Now the phone could no longer serve to establish the woman's whereabouts to this point. Just a few of the facts he'd learned: that everyone had one of these mechanized insects now, and they could do a lot more than dial a call.

"What do you want?" the woman asked. But there was no heft to her question, or expectation of being answered. Her tone was whimpery and weak.

Nick reached for the lever to roll down the window, then quickly corrected himself. He found the button that did the job now, and pushed it, but nothing happened. He jabbed at it again.

"What the hell?" he said to Harlan, low.

Harlan reached out a hand. It covered the whole ledge on the side of the door.

Childproof locks, Nick realized. When he twisted around, he glimpsed special seats with straps and harnesses, in a third row that looked a whole acre away. There were humps back there, boxes maybe, a jam-up of shapes impossible to make out.

"Roll down this window," Nick growled.

The woman jumped and let out a little

cry. She began stabbing at buttons. Nick almost laughed at the sheer number of them.

"Want me to come up there and help?" he said, beginning to rise from his seat.

Harlan laid a hand on Nick's arm, which Nick shucked off with some effort.

"No, no —" the woman cried. She kept flailing around. Smacking sounds, whirrs, from up front until his window finally dropped down.

Nick sent the pieces of her phone sailing out into the frigid remainder of the day.

"Now," he said, friendly-like again. "I want you to get off 9 and head toward Wedeskyull. You know where that is?"

"Yes," the woman whispered. "I live in town."

"Ah," Nick said. "All the better. Except we're not going to town. We're going somewhere outside. Long Hill Road. You know it?"

"Yes, I know it," the woman said, sounding oddly pleased, as if they'd discovered common ground.

Nick looked at the trees whipping by, their bare branches lashing.

Long Hill Road.

Just the name in his head had become the purest drug during the last year he'd spent preparing. Long Hill Road was where he would find what he needed to get away, not only from prison, but from a life that had inexplicably succeeded in dragging him down. On Long Hill Road, Nick could take a brief pause, gather breath for the final push that would enable him to lose himself forever. Reach a place where he'd never be found.

"Good," Nick said. "Then hurry."

In the end, the woman turned out to be a good little getaway driver. Her foot pressed hard on the gas, and she didn't slow down even on the twists and ells and curves.

But a stop sign beside the broad flank of a field finally brought her to a halt.

Nick sensed the possibility a moment before it occurred to the woman. His mother always said how smart he was, but prison had shown him that even more than brains, Nick had great instincts. He knew whenever somebody was getting ready to piss him off, buck him or thwart him. Sometimes he knew before they knew it themselves.

Now he started to climb into the front. From this position he could see how lovely the woman was, although not young, with a silver sheen to her otherwise brown hair, and bottle-green eyes behind eyeglass

50

frames. She had taken off her coat in defer-
ence to the cranked-up heat in the car, and
her breasts swelled beneath a clingy top.

Nick paused. It had been more than
twenty years since he'd felt the warmth of a
woman beside him, let her scent fill his
nose. Nick fingered the catch on the
woman's pants, some kind of smooth hook
contraption he'd never seen before, and the
woman shrank away from him, her body
becoming an inviting curve against the back
of the roomy seat.

Harlan's hand dropped over the seat; he
didn't have to stretch to do it. That hand
was like a sandbag, and it held Nick down
for a crucial strike of a second.

They didn't have time anyway. Once Nick
would've indulged, taken what he wanted
without thinking about the repercussions,
or what would happen next. But prison had
poured a smooth, hard shell over that part
of him, taught him to take a more
considered approach.

He wrenched himself around toward the
rear. He could make out the sound of
labored breathing, loud even for Harlan.
Was it the woman breathing so raspily?

"Get off me," Nick commanded, his gaze
flitting between shadowed spaces.

Harlan looked down at his hand as if it

didn't belong to him.

The woman released her seatbelt and scrabbled at the door handle. The door flew open on its hinges, almost slamming shut again and sending the woman back onto the seat. But she was able to slip through a gash of space before the door closed itself. She took off at a run across the field, awkward in high-heeled boots.

Harlan finally lifted his hand, and Nick uttered an order, thrusting the nail file at him. The file was only insurance; Harlan wouldn't need any weapon besides his fist or foot or fingers.

"No," Harlan said, starting to shake his head. "I don't want to."

Nick squinted out into the gathering twilight. The woman had made enough headway — although there didn't seem to be any place she could really go — that Harlan would have the best chance of catching up to her. Harlan wasn't agile or graceful, but sheer size would allow him to cover more of the space that lay between the woman and the road.

"Nick," Harlan said, the skin around his eyes forming valleys. "Please. She's leaving."

Nick slapped the dash. "And you think she's just going to let us take this baby?"

52

Harlan began kneading his fingers, knuckles popping in distinct detonations.

"Besides, she knows where we're headed."

Harlan's eyebrows lay like a cattail across his forehead. They rose as one when Nick's gaze met his. Harlan had always been able to read Nick; that ability had latched them together from the start. He knew that Nick wouldn't let up till this was done.

"You want to be free, don't you, Harlan?"

Harlan's head moved in a nod.

"I don't just mean free of prison," Nick went on. "I mean that once we're out, for good, you never have to listen to anyone you don't want to again. You don't even have to see that person again. That's a whole other kind of freedom."

He'd pieced it together from Harlan's mutters and murmurs in the middle of the night. There was someone Harlan hated with an intensity that threatened to crash his bunk, rattle their whole block. Somebody had screwed Harlan over, cheated him of everything he deserved.

Nick saw the jolt his words delivered, but uncharacteristically, Harlan didn't jump to carry out the act he'd been tasked with.

The woman's stumbling progress across the field was starting to irritate Nick. He'd had enough of reasoning and cajoling. Nick could feel a thick sludge all around him now; something bad would happen if Harlan didn't snap to.

"I'm telling you what to do," Nick said. "And you'd better do it."

Harlan moved like he'd been yanked. He snatched the file out of Nick's hand, his thick fingers surprisingly dexterous. Harlan got out of the car as if hypnotized. He emerged on the wrong side, and a car sheared around him, horn wailing its reproach. Harlan appeared unfazed as he lumbered off across the field.

The woman put on a burst of speed, headed for trees at the faraway edge of the field. If she reached them, she would be lost amongst the slashes of trunks and the coming night.

But Harlan caught up to her and grabbed her from behind, wheeling her around with the butt of one hand. Nick was still far enough away that Harlan had to shout to be heard.

"She doesn't even have her coat on! I don't have to do nothing — she'll just freeze out here by herself!" He twisted his head to look in Nick's direction.

Nick strode forward, the message in his eyes unchanged. His breath condensed into white clouds as he began to jog. It cast a haze over what Harlan had been told to do.

"No," the woman cried. "Please don't. I won't tell anyone. You can have the car —"

Harlan raised his arm, blotting out the sight of the woman's body and the sky. Her disembodied voice released a cascading wail that sent a flock of birds wheeling.

"Please, no! No! I have children!"

Harlan drove the file into the woman's neck. The noise it made as it entered sounded like sawing steak.

The woman walked forward as if nothing had happened. After a second or two, she took a skip-step, like it still might be possible to jump out of the path of the blade. Then she fell, facedown on the flat, level plane of the field.

Nick arrived at the place where she had dropped. Time was of the essence now, they had to get away from the body. Still he stood, staring down at a sight that sent him reeling backwards more than twenty years. The rush of blood from the woman's neck was beautiful against the barren landscape. Dimly, Nick registered the thud of Harlan retreating.

When at last Nick turned, he jumped. Harlan had come back, and he stood so tall that he blocked out the remaining light. Filled with regret and remorse — whatever he'd done to earn his time, Harlan wasn't a killer — he was going to rebel, and Nick had an image of the two of them tangling. Mind control would be no match for the force Harlan could apply without even trying.

But Harlan only bent down and draped the coat he'd retrieved over the woman's fallen form.

Back in the car, Nick sat and stared at the dashboard. It was like looking at a flight deck. He couldn't find a key, or the silver slit into which it should be inserted. He kept checking the road, expecting to see a cop pull up behind him in the deepening dusk. He told himself that they'd driven some distance, and the guard hadn't seen which car they'd gotten into. There was no reason for anyone to be suspicious of a luxury SUV stopped at the side of the road. Folks would think the rich lady inside was just handing out those pouches of juice to her brats in their fancy additional seats, like one upholstered throne wasn't enough for a five-year-old.

After a minute or two it occurred to Nick that the car had never been turned off. He tested the gas pedal, which indeed emitted a rush, the engine straining against being set in Park. The motor purred so gently, Nick hadn't even realized it was on. Only then did he spot a round glowing button. Cars turned on without a key now. Did they drive themselves, too?

He shifted into gear. The car took off like an arrow instead of something made of two tons of steel.

"How come?" Harlan asked miserably as Nick adjusted to the easy, seamless spin of the wheel. "How come we're going to that hill — that road — that Long Hill Road?"

Nick glanced over at him, surprised. Harlan wasn't usually one for questions.

He took his time before returning his gaze to the road. This thing really did practically drive itself. "I told you already. To get some things we're going to need."

Harlan's face pocked with confusion.

"You escape from prison in two parts," Nick explained for the fifth time. He should know better than to trust Harlan's memory. "First you have to get out. Then you have to stay out."

Harlan still didn't appear to understand, but the mention of their former residence made him fold in on himself, his body dwarfing the wide leather seat.

Nick took a right onto a closely coiled road. Switchbacks, turns, drop-offs into a

57

rounded bowl of forest. Trees like a million skewers down there.

"Nick?" Harlan said, and snuffed in deep.

"Yeah?"

"No more, okay?"

The SUV clung to the edge of the road as if glued. "Sure, Harlan."

Harlan extended his fist, settling it around Nick's upper arm. His thumb met his fingertips on the other side of Nick's biceps. Nick tried to shake him off, but he didn't stand a chance.

It had never really occurred to him before, what would happen if Harlan turned his might against Nick, instead of allowing Nick to use it. The thought was so surprising that even as Harlan bore down, Nick didn't feel any anger mounting. That horizon lay far off in the distance, enabling him to focus on the matter at hand.

So long as their goals stayed aligned, everything would be fine. He and Harlan both wanted to get away. No more and no less.

The car swerved, difficult to maneuver while thus encumbered. Dirt and dry leaf matter skittered under the tires, and the SUV lurched dangerously close to a sheer drop into the valley.

Nick braked. He let his gaze meet

Harlan's, tilting up his neck.

"Yeah, okay," he said. He would've agreed to just about anything so long as it brought Harlan back in line. Whether he meant it or not. "I promise. No more."

Harlan released him and settled back in his seat, making the whole car rock.

"Now come on," Nick said, rubbing his arm. "Help me look."

Harlan turned his head. "Look for what?"

Nick spotted lights shining from a house of wood and glass that sat high on a rise. He braked, then let the SUV roll back, coming to a stop behind an overhang of sweeping fir boughs. Nick made sure the vehicle was completely concealed. Then he peered out between the branches, watching as the house gazed back at him.

"That," Nick said.

CHAPTER THREE

Sandy poured herself a cup of coffee from the pot she'd brewed earlier, aware that her hand was shaking. The coffee was dark and dense from sitting too long. It would probably only worsen her nerves. She pushed the cup away, sloshing black liquid onto the counter.

Where had Ivy's accusation come from? It had been like lying on a tropical beach, then all of a sudden getting hit by a tsunami. The one thing Sandy prided herself on and relied upon was the harmony of her family. Even the sudden onslaught of teenage moodiness consisted mostly of Ivy sequestering herself away in her room under a sullen cloud that never quite burst.

It was a precarious way to live, Sandy realized. Pending storms eventually arrived.

But the charge Ivy had hurled was absurd. Sandy had treasured her daughter from the moment she was born, and worked hard to weave closeness between the two of them. She'd never lied to Ivy — not even taking advantage of the shortcuts all parents used: substituting a *maybe* when the answer was clearly *no way,* or promising that the goldfish was going to live.

Now Sandy was glad that Ben wasn't home yet, caught up with some last minute booking probably. She wouldn't have wanted him here for what had just taken place.

Sandy got down off the stool she'd been perched on, and glanced upward at the ceiling. It was quiet up there, just the slow breathing of an occupied house. Sandy could picture Ivy stretched out on her bed, earbuds inserted, Mac lying below her on the floor since he was no longer able to clamber up. She turned toward the wide set of glass doors. A sinking orange globule of sun trembled on the horizon.

Sandy's breath began to level out. Storms came, yes, but they also blew over.

She heard the grit of wheels on gravel and went out to greet Ben.

Stepping outside was like a plunge into cold water. Sandy wrapped her arms around herself. "It must've dropped fifteen degrees today," she called to Ben.

Even after twenty years, the sight of her husband still made her smile. For a moment the dusk turned warm, and Sandy started to walk forward.

Ben slammed the door of the Jeep, looking up at the sky. "I just booked the first skiers of the season backcountry. There's going to be at least two feet by tomorrow."

Ben ran an outfit called Off Road Adventures, which catered to weekend warriors coming up to the Adirondacks for a taste of adventure along with a well-contained dash of risk. Ben occasionally scoffed at his clients' approach to sport — *when you don't have any real danger in your life, why not scale a cliff to add some* — but it was a bit hypocritical, since his veins too pumped with forced adrenaline. Ben had pursued adventure sports for decades, artificially inflating the level of peril in his life until he was expert enough to help the novices.

Sandy used to accompany him on these journeys: free-climbing, biking, and skiing off-trail. But once Ivy came along any such activity was difficult to schedule, and Sandy couldn't justify the hazards. Ben craved challenge; Sandy had accepted that when she married him. But Ivy needed at least one parent who stayed on the ground.

She followed Ben's gaze to a sky smeared with pasty clouds. "Looks like it."

Ben closed the distance between them, mounting the stone steps of the porch. He reached out and their cold fingers tangled in greeting. "How are things at the ranch?"

"Had to do a little rustling today, cowboy," Sandy said.

"Bad?" Ben said with a look that could've been a grimace or a grin.

Sandy shrugged. "Ivy's in one of her moods." A pinch of tears surprised her. Sandy couldn't remember the last time she had cried, and knowing not to get rattled by a teenager's mood swings wasn't exactly something for which you needed a degree in psychology. She looked away, hoping Ben would assume that her eyes were just stinging from the cold. "Come on," she said, adding a deliberate shiver. "Let's go in."

Ben was facing their driveway again.

"Honey?" Sandy said.

"Did the Macmillans come up for the weekend?"

"What?" Sandy asked. She glanced toward what Ben called the no-longer-so-great camp. "Hmmm, I don't know. No one's been by."

"Never mind." Ben ringed her waist with one arm. "Thought I saw something moving around in there."

"Probably just the wind," Sandy said, and shivered again, this time for real.

In the kitchen, Sandy turned the stove light on, bringing the water back to bubbling. She held her hands near the flame for a moment, warming them. Then she went to raise the heat in the rest of the house.

"Give me a sec and I'll start a fire," Ben said.

He reached into the fridge, snapping the tab on a can of Red Bull. Ben could drink three of them, or down a whole pot of coffee, and still sleep like a baby. Sandy figured it went along with his choice of career. Her husband could tolerate more stimulation than most people. In fact, he seemed to require it.

He went out onto the side porch, and after a moment Sandy heard the *thunk* of the ax as it sliced into the wood stump Ben used for cutting. He liked to split logs himself, refusing to have a cord of firewood delivered at the start of the season. Ben didn't come from around here, but in many ways he seemed to. Self-reliance was the anthem of the Adirondack old-timers.

Ben staggered back into the kitchen underneath an armload of wood, then crouched by the stove. "Think Ivy would mind fetching me a little kindling?"

Sandy let out a snort and turned to leave the room. "I'll go."

Ben called, "Hey, San?"

She rummaged around in the closet they used for outerwear; no more impromptu trips outside coatless for the next five or six months. "What?" she asked, walking back to Ben while pulling on a pair of gloves.

"Tell Ivy to do it, huh?"

"Honey . . ." Sandy was torn. If she said she didn't think Ivy would do it, then she'd reveal just how recalcitrant their daughter had become, the extent of which she'd kept hidden from Ben. But if she asked Ivy to take on the task, the same thing would become apparent, and there'd probably be a big battle, to boot.

Ben dropped a match into the pile he'd constructed, shutting the stove door with an iron *thud,* and propping up the poker in its slot on an ornate stand. "Never mind. I have enough for now. Why don't we just eat?"

Sandy shot him a fast, grateful glance. She wondered if he knew any of what had been running through her head, or if he'd simply decided to wait a little while before sending Ivy out.

Either way, best to begin dinner.

Sandy left Ben setting the table, and went upstairs to fetch Ivy.

Her daughter was lying just as Sandy had pictured, stomach-down, her calves in skinny jeans at a right angle in the air. Red licorice wires dangled around her neck and her head bobbed in time to a silent beat.

Sandy said Ivy's name loud enough to be heard over the song that was playing, and Ivy twisted around. Mac, lying on the rainbow-patterned rug beside the bed, opened one eye without getting up.

"Dad just got home," Sandy said. "Want to come down for dinner?"

Ivy ripped the wires from her ears and tinny music entered the room. "This is unreal."

Sure. Do you need any help? Sandy heard in her head. Once that would've been Ivy's response. Not all that long ago even.

"Yeah," Sandy said. "I know. It is a bit late for him."

Ivy bit back a smile.

Encouraged, Sandy dropped down on the bed.

"Get up, Mom," Ivy said. "It wasn't that good a joke."

Sandy laughed. "Scooch," she said, and Ivy shifted, making room.

After a moment Sandy asked, "Paper or

66

plastic?" It was a game they'd played in one form or another practically since Ivy could talk. One of them would give the other a set of choices, always pertaining to some relatively inconsequential matter. Sometimes the game led to discussion, sometimes to debate, occasionally just to giggling. Sandy figured it could serve as both icebreaker and peace treaty now.

"Paper," Ivy said. "It's greener."

Sandy nodded. "Of course."

Mac's furry side rose and fell as he panted on the rug. Ivy was right: the dog's breath did smell. Of old, tired, closed-in spaces. The next time she was in town, Sandy would get some of those rock-hard biscuits from the Blue Chair bakery. Her dog-owning patients swore by them.

"Hot or iced?" Ivy asked.

"Hot," Sandy replied, indicating the weather outside. "Self-explanatory."

It was Ivy's turn to nod. Then she got herself into a sitting position, and laid her head on Sandy's shoulder. She began to thread long, looping strands of her own hair through her fingers as she rested there.

Sandy felt herself holding her breath. The mingled scents of Ivy's shampoo and breath and sweat entered her nose, the silky feel of her daughter's cheek caressed the skin on her neck. Sandy wished the spell would last forever, that she and Ivy could stay like this, no push/pull, in exquisite balance, one atop the other. The moment swelled, a balloon consuming air until it threatened to pop.

"Upstairs or down?" Sandy said at last.

There was a pause.

"Are we just going to eat dinner and pretend like nothing happened?" Ivy blew out a breath, lifting her head. "Like I didn't say anything?"

So the storm hadn't passed. Here it was back to catch Ben up in its rush of hurled debris. But here also was her little girl, so vulnerable just a moment ago in her splayed-out position, smiling and playing their shared game. And Sandy had to try to protect her, too.

Ivy read her dilemma, challenging Sandy with a gaze that also beseeched.

Sandy's finger wandered to the spot on her wrist before she could stop it. "Honey," she said, aiming for a return to levity, "if I responded to every single thing you chose to say these days, I would be all talked out. I'd have no words left."

A curtain came down and Ivy's eyes went dull and gray. "Okay, Mom," she said. "Okay. I'd better let you save your breath. I'm not hungry anyway."

Sandy shut her own eyes for a moment. There were things she should do right now — she could feel them brushing against her like underwater fronds — but Sandy couldn't settle on a single one. She pushed herself up off the bed.

Ivy stood also, shifting Mac's body over with her foot, and walked to the door. She held it ajar, gesturing for Sandy to leave.

Sandy obeyed the invitation extended by her daughter's outstretched arm, wondering how an open door could feel so much more final than a closed one.

In the hall, Sandy paused by a stack of clean folded towels that hadn't made it to the linen closet. She chose to put the towels away mostly to allow herself one last peek at Ivy. These upstairs closets were connected by a run of narrow passages — Ben's clever idea for extra storage space — and since Ivy's own closet door usually stood ajar, Sandy could see into her room.

Ivy didn't seem to be reconsidering her dinner boycott. She'd flopped back down on her bed, reinserted her earbuds, and looked permanently affixed, like some kind of art installation. *Teenage girl, sulking.* She hadn't turned on any lights, and the only illumination came from the roving dot of

69

Ivy's cell phone as she tapped out a text. After a moment or two, perhaps sensing Sandy's presence, Ivy got up and closed her closet door with a firm *click.*

Sandy went back down the broad-planked staircase, hand trailing along the single spear of railing, to join Ben in the kitchen. He had drained the pasta, begun to heat up the sauce.

Sandy lowered the flame, and Ben came up behind her. She could smell ash from the now crackling fire, feel the smoke of his breath.

"Dinner for two tonight?" he said.

Sandy turned around. "Well, Ivy does have a lot of homework —"

"Hey," Ben said, and she stopped.

"What?"

"Don't do that."

Sandy frowned at him. "Don't do what?"

"Make excuses for her. She's fifteen. She's in a snit. Big deal. She'll probably be in some mood or other for the next three years." Ben leaned forward, cupping Sandy's hand on the wooden spoon so he could sample its contents. "That is some sauce."

Sandy spoke dryly. "Tomato. I'm creative, I know."

She checked around for Mac, but he had stayed upstairs with Ivy. They'd always been

70

diligent about not feeding him from the table, so mealtimes didn't provide any particular lure.

Ben took the spoon and laid it in the pot.

"Ivy will be fine," he said. "And you and Ivy will be fine, too. The two of you have always been close." Only for a moment did Ben look away, past the shiny stainless appliances, the copper pot ring overhead, beyond the walls even, and out into the darkening night. "You know, I used to be jealous."

"What?" Sandy asked, though she thought she knew what he meant.

Can't we try for one more? Ben used to say, over and over, during the years when Ivy was little. *It doesn't matter what we get. I don't even care if it's a son.* And with that relinquishment, Sandy's last excuse evaporated. Before that she'd been able to hold Ben off, take birth control pills with the fervor of an addict, saying that she knew he wanted a boy, and what if they didn't have one? A boy would've completed their unit. Two matched sets, one parent to tag-team each child in public restrooms, during weekend sports and Scouts. But then Ben decided that what he really wanted was a second to raise, for Ivy not to be an only. While Sandy wouldn't have had another

71

baby unless a gun had been pressed to her head, and possibly not even then. She knew how hard it could be for parents to love more than one child.

Ben was still talking. "Not because Ivy loved you more — I figured that was normal for a daughter. But because *you* loved *her* so much." He leaned forward, toying with Sandy's hair in a way that sent shivers down her back. "I'm just saying that it might not be such a bad thing if we got some alone time for a while." He touched the knob of her neck, igniting another rain of shivers. "You know, we used to be pretty good at this."

Sandy looked up at him. "This?"

Ben extended his arms, taking in the whole of the sprawling kitchen. "This. Just the two of us. Dinner. Conversation. A little music maybe."

Sandy glanced at the table, and Ben bounded away, scooping up the third place setting and depositing it back on a cabinet shelf. So much was contained in the swift ballet of motions that Sandy's heart seized. Love. Understanding of how Ivy's empty place would strike Sandy. Her husband's own penchant for thoroughness, how he would never leave so much as a plate out. Perhaps the greatest demonstration of all was in Ben's willingness not to delve into whatever had happened, the nature of the conflict with Ivy. He let Sandy have her silence and always had, as if there were some smooth, invisible repellant around her.

"Ivy can fix herself a plate later," Ben said. "Won't hurt her to eat alone."

Sandy tilted her head. All was quiet upstairs.

Ben took a step toward her.

Then his chest was pressed against hers, and Sandy couldn't tell whose heart was beating like that, so fast and so strong. Ben leaned down, roaming her mouth with his.

"As for us," he said, leaving Sandy with cutoff breath, her body straining to find his, "maybe we'll also do a little of that."

ENTRANCE

It was cold in the SUV; the temperature had fallen while the sky thickened. Nick could feel it now for sure in his leg. He hadn't wanted to give any hint of their presence, not even a plume of vapor from the tailpipe, so he'd turned the engine off.

"Nick?" Harlan said.

"What?" Nick asked. No snap to his tone, although his nerves were on edge. As many preparations as he had made in advance — and there was a limit to what could be done inside — there was still so much that could go wrong.

The weather being number one.

He'd meant for them to be in and out and on their way with everything they needed. Speed meant safety. The hunt for two escaped cons was on, and staying put would be risky, even in a spot as out of the way and remote as this one. While where Nick had them going was unsearchable. He and

Harlan would never be found so long as they kept moving.

But if they had to remain here longer, pinned in place by a storm? Nick looked up at the hill, considering.

"Nick?" Harlan said again.

Something must've shown in Nick's face because Harlan recoiled, or tried to. There wasn't anyplace for his massive body to go, despite the roominess of the car.

"Forget it," Harlan muttered. Then, "It's just that it's cold out. I'm cold, Nick."

Harlan should've known better than to complain, but nothing was normal about tonight. The rules had all changed, and though Nick wouldn't have thought that he'd miss them, there was a frenzied whirl of emptiness inside him, like he'd fallen into outer space.

"Yeah," Nick said. "I am, too. Just give me a second to think."

They could stay in the car a little while longer before making their entrance. Limit their exposure and the potential for complications inside. But that was a temporary solution given the temperature. Might be better just to make their presence known and deal with the repercussions right off.

Harlan spoke up again. "Nick?"

75

"Goddamnit!" Nick roared, and Harlan jumped, his head grinding against the roof. Nick lowered his voice. "I said, give me some time to think. I just need to think."

Harlan stared at him for long enough that Nick broke their silent exchange. If another man had looked at him like that, Nick would've broken something a lot worse than a glare. But Harlan had always been different. He didn't anger Nick the way other people did. Also, there wasn't much to argue with behind his eyes.

Not a blink of awareness of what might be coming.

Snow would slash their chances at survival. Distort things, blind them, freeze.

Of course, it would also make the search for them more difficult. And it might help in another way, too. Since Nick had gone inside, ways to summon help had multiplied like rabbits. He couldn't believe there was cellular signal up here on the mountain, but if there was, it would likely be compromised by the weather.

Cell signal wasn't the only kind he had to worry about, though. There was something called Wi-Fi, which rich people used to make their useless computers run faster and to watch TV. Nick was forced to pay cash for this bit of recon — the new guy who'd informed him was some kind of religious nut, didn't smoke or even drink coffee. But it'd been worth it to find out about the existence of a junction box through which all sorts of cables would run.

"Like a fuse box?" Nick had said in the yard, lowering his barbell.

His cult case informant had also been lifting: squatting, heaving, standing.

Nick's moves were smoother. His arms made winged patterns in the air.

The kid grinned between huffed breaths. "Not quite like that, old man."

In the midst of his set, Nick cocked his head, watching the kid raise his own weight. He wondered how much force it would take to smash the kid's skull with the iron disk, given that gravity would be on his side. That was the kind of computation someone smart would think of. All this kid had going for him was that he'd been born a little later.

"This thing is gonna look space age," the kid said, grunting with effort. "Probably be in the basement."

He'd told Nick a few more things then, throwing them in for free and soothing Nick's rage. GPS, satellites. People could watch things from the sky, or from objects small enough to fit in a pocket. Their possessions. Their children. Themselves.

The whole goddamn world had changed.

Nick was finally out in that world. He had actually pulled this off, back to the kind of success he was meant for. Things were proceeding according to plan, and now Nick had to focus on the next phase.

Having made it here, he had hoped to accumulate some old-fashioned intel on the house, the kind you picked up with your eyes and ears. But this place was even more secluded than he'd been led to believe. Two hands again; one good, one bad. The isolation would work in their favor, especially if this driveway became impassable. It wasn't like the man of the house would be getting out to plow tonight, not till Nick had finished with him anyway.

He felt a smile grow, then wither.

But because of the emptiness, Nick couldn't get close enough to a window to peer inside, determine who was home. He might be walking into a happy family talky-do, or he could have minutes on his side to secure things.

Finally there was Harlan. Harlan who could make someone jump just by looking at him, who would keep order without even trying, but who also impeded things by not understanding, or misremembering, especially if he didn't like what he was being told to do.

Nick's tolerant direction usually did the trick against the outstretched palm of Harlan's obstinacy, but he just wasn't feeling all that patient right now. And he'd sensed earlier what might happen if a rare instance of Harlan's opposition met rising mercury inside Nick.

He looked across to the other seat.

Harlan was inhaling and exhaling heavily, his breaths loud enough to fill the whole car.

Nick took a look around the vehicle — Christ, he was on edge — before holding out his hand. Nodding understanding, Harlan removed the sole from his shoe. He took a homegrown smoke, a combination of road kill tobacco and toilet paper wrapping, and laid it on Nick's hand.

"Harlan?" Nick said. Back to patient.

"Yeah?"

"Aren't you forgetting something?"

Harlan studied the cig. Finally his eyes cleared — great furrows smoothing out on his forehead — and he reached for his shoe again. He shook out a match, the colored tip of which had nearly all been worn away. Harlan had to strike it against his bared heel to get a spark.

Nick sucked nicotine in — paltry, pitiful

stuff, the shreds of someone's nearly finished smoke — trying to quiet his nerves.

Stupid. Pointless. There were too many unknowns up in that house. Nick wouldn't be able to calm down till they had truly escaped, not just reached this way station.

He cracked the door and flicked the smoldering butt onto the ground. Cold punched him. They hadn't been issued any gloves or hats, just the coats. It wasn't freezing like this when they'd bussed out a few hours ago. That moment already felt like a full sentence served. Time moved fast outside.

Nick zipped up his coat, and watched Harlan try to do the same, but Harlan's coat was too small. The sleeves only made it to his forearms, and the zipper couldn't close over his chest.

Harlan gave up. "Hey, Nick, we don't have any masks."

Nick's mouth made a thin, bleak line. "We don't need any."

Harlan looked at him. "We don't?"

"No," Nick said. "These people are going to know who we are."

He opened the car door, ducking to avoid the branches that hung over the car. Harlan came out, hunching even lower to get beneath the stalks. Needles and twigs flew off as he shouldered his way through.

They concealed themselves behind the firs that lined the drive as they walked steadily uphill. At a certain point, there were no more trees and they had to step out into the open, just the descending night for cover. The rush of a nearby creek camouflaged any noise they might make, but nothing could be done about Harlan's enormous, lurching form or the dash of Nick's body against the dark.

A series of precisely pinpointed floodlights came on, and Nick ducked, shoving Harlan to make him do the same. He barely budged Harlan's bulk, although momentum did carry him a little ways out of sight.

This place was lit up like a painting in a goddamn museum. There must be motion sensors on the lights. Nick stepped out of a cone of white, pulling Harlan along with him. It was like trying to tow a barge. They stood in place, both of them breathing hard, until the lights turned themselves off.

Nick edged forward, coming to face a wide sweep of porch with pillars on either side of the staircase. The house seemed to grow out of the landscape: huge boulders giving rise to stone siding, windows that looked clear through from front to back, sloping roof backed by a cup of valley.

Get in, get what you need, get out.

Nick stood there, staring, until the words became a tuneless ditty in his head.

Get in, get it, get out.

His mother used to tell him that he had musical talent. Nick would be banging a knife on the counter while his sister did the clearing up, and his mother would compliment his drumming.

But while Nick had once been content to fool himself, going along with such grand ideas, the years inside had cured him of that. You didn't get what you wanted — truly achieve greatness — if you settled for empty visions of glory. There was reality, and then there was every crap promise and proclamation about him his mother had ever made.

The temperature had finally leveled out — the twinge in Nick's leg was letting up — but that was only because snow was getting ready to fall. The sky was laden with it, big-bellied and full. Nick hadn't had to figure in the weather for twenty-plus years, but he'd grown up in the north country, and the instinct came back. They had some time yet, but not much. He and Harlan needed to be lost to search efforts, able to crawl into a shelter and wait out the storm in some distant place soon. Getting there depended on things going smoothly inside.

Behind him, Harlan shifted on his feet.

They were surrounded by wilderness. In a half hour or so, weather permitting, they would walk off into it, never to be seen on a single stretch of road. That was the bolt of genius that had come to Nick just before he pulled the road crew assignment.

No manhunt could cover the great swaths of land between here and his destination.

Nick turned back to the house. Through a wide wall of glass, he could see into a lit-up room. The kitchen spotlighted the whole first floor, while the second level was dark and empty, nobody moving around up there. The occupants were about to eat dinner downstairs, two places set, two chairs pulled out.

It was going to be a short meal.

Nick's boots thudded onto stone, while Harlan started heavily forward as well. He caught up just as Nick brought his hand down on the door.

AUGUST 1, 1975

Barbara stood in a cold draft from the refrigerator, despairing as she studied the shelves. No milk, no butter, no eggs. No orange juice, which of course boded trouble, and how was she going to fix a side dish or vegetable for dinner tonight? They were out of just about everything except for a freezer half-full of the game Gordon had hunted last fall, processed for them by Thiele down the road, and neatly wrapped in yellow paper by Thiele's wife.

Barbara hadn't figured out the trick other mothers seemed to have for getting errands done with their children. All the constant needs and demands, plus the ever-present threat of a tantrum. People had started to talk when Barbara was out and about in town; she knew they had. And she couldn't stand to give them additional fodder for gossip, nor let them look at her beloved little boy in that way. He had been the most adorable baby, always drawing attention for his looks; and as he learned to talk, his precocious vocabulary. But once he turned two, the reactions had started to change.

He toddled in now, surer on his feet every day. He'd been small as an infant — although darkly beautiful, as if to make up for his size — but he seemed to be growing now. Barbara didn't really know any other children his age to compare him to. She could see that he was skinny; the doctor had advised adding a raw egg to milkshakes in the hopes of plumping him up a bit. But how could you worry about straw-like limbs or the knobs on his back when you saw those thickly lashed eyes and thick, droopy curls?

Every day, Barbara marveled at the miracle of this child who'd gone from beetle-helpless, flat on his back, to scooting around, then walking, and running. The boy hadn't even turned three yet, but he was as agile as an athlete. And his speech! Barbara was constantly suggesting to Gordon that they consider starting their son in school early, though she knew she'd have trouble letting him go when the time came.

She turned and shut the refrigerator door with her hand behind her.

The cold air settled, and for a second all

was still.

"Want orange juice."

Barbara took a moment to treasure the pronunciation. *Owange.* Then she felt her eyes flutter shut. "I'm sorry, dear. We're all out."

"No orange juice?"

Barbara shook her head. "No, Nicky. We don't have any —"

He started to wail. "Orange juice! Want orange . . ."

Barbara glanced around as if some of those townsfolk might be peering in right now. They weren't, of course, and thank God Gordon was gone, too. Lord knew what her husband would do if he ever had to witness one of these tantrums, let alone handle it.

Gordon was a good man, loving and kind, but he didn't have the will their son did. Gordon accepted things; he was an able provider. But Nicholas, even at this young age, bristled against whatever bothered him or held him back. Her son had a brute strength that staggered Barbara. One day, he was going to make his mark on the world.

The little boy marched toward the refrigerator and began tugging at the silver handle. He wasn't strong enough to open it yet, or at least he never had been, but as

Barbara looked on, she heard the suck of the seal breaking and watched the door release. Nicholas shot backward, landing on the floor halfway across the room.

Barbara waited for a yowl, but instantly the boy was on his feet again, surging forward with an intent expression on his face.

"Orange juice," he said decidedly, then leaned his little body inside the refrigerator.

Not the refrigerator. Nicholas had accidentally opened the freezer side.

Barbara stared with a mix of admiration and disbelief. A thought seized her — *what if the door swung shut right now* — followed by a queasy pang. She began pulling on her son, trying to get him out, but he was fighting her, not registering the cold until his little shrimp fingers curled around the metal rim of a shelf and stuck there.

The howls started then.

Barbara left her son and ran for a cup of warm water. She poured the liquid over the frosty shelf, soaking Nicholas' wrists through his pajamas while his screams climbed in volume. Finally his hold loosened, and she was able to drag him out.

Nicholas' arms were as strong as cables when Barbara turned them over to check for damage. The flesh on his fingertips had pinkened, but looked intact, nothing peeling away. Something in Barbara's stomach lurched, and she pressed her hand over her mouth.

She began stroking her son's hot, wet cheeks, his whole body vibrating against hers as he continued to cry. Barbara got up and pawed through the trash. She found the empty orange juice carton and poured the remnants into a cup, diluting them with water from the tap.

She handed the concoction to Nicholas, who downed it thirstily.

Blessed silence filled the room.

Barbara fisted her hands on her hips and smiled down at her son. "Now. Shall we go to the store for some more?"

Nicholas looked up at her. "Orange juice? In the store?"

"Can you be good in the car?"

He nodded, three rapid jerks of his head. His curls flew. One day, she was going to have to trim them.

Love seized her, warm and glowing. She bent to scoop up the little boy in a hug.

"Why don't you put that carton in the trash for me," she suggested, pointing. "While I get us some clothes?"

Nicholas walked in the direction she'd indicated. For just a second, he wasn't a toddler anymore, but a growing, competent child, completing a task. Barbara bent over, feeling herself grow short of breath, as if she were being compressed in some creature's great fist. How had no one ever told her what it felt like to be a mother, the way it robbed you of air and light and nourishment, but you didn't care, didn't even notice, because in exchange you were given this one consuming focus and it was all you'd ever need again?

Barbara turned and left the room to fetch an outfit for her son and a fresh dress for herself, assuming she could find one. In addition to errands, it was hard to make time to iron and do laundry these days as well.

Gordon had purchased a station wagon just before Nicholas was born, which turned out to be a bit of an indulgence given how rarely Barbara ventured out. But she was grateful for the new car now, complete with air-conditioning, which she'd never used. She reached across the generous front seat and buckled Nicholas in. She slipped the shoulder strap behind his back, leaving just the lap belt.

Nicholas started to twist and churn. "No buckle."

Barbara turned the key in the ignition,

speaking lightly as the engine rumbled to life. "Then no orange juice."

She wasn't sure she'd have the strength to carry out this threat if Nicholas continued to protest. He could move into the back where you didn't have to worry about seatbelts. But the little boy settled down, looking out his window.

Barbara rolled hers open. It only got good and hot for a month or so in Cold Kettle, but this was the month. A breeze fanned them both as Barbara drove along Crook Road.

The back of her dress grew clammy, sticking to the seat. Maybe she *should* turn on the air-conditioning. She checked the rearview mirror and saw that her face was flushed. From the fracas before? Nicholas' response had been understandable. Barbara served him orange juice every morning and he'd come to expect it.

She checked her son, sitting there solemnly, watching meadows and pens and barns roll by outside. He looked as still and cool as stone.

Barbara wiped off her face with one of Gordon's handkerchiefs, left behind in the glove compartment. She imagined Mr. Mackey would have the fans turned on in the grocery store. She didn't usually react to the heat this way, and it was a little disturbing. Barbara made a turn onto Main Street, angling the wagon into a vacant parking spot.

"Come, Nicky," she said, an idea striking her. "We'll buy you an ice cream cone after we get our groceries. Would you like that?"

Nicholas was already pushing at the door. He tumbled out onto the sidewalk, but righted himself swiftly and took off. Barbara got out, too. She paused for a moment, placing one hand on the flank of the car and jerking back at the metallic burn. Then she noticed Nicholas looking over his shoulder at her, his little sneakered foot poised above the curb. Barbara felt too queasy to give chase. But Nicholas stepped into the street then, which did necessitate a run.

It took forty-five minutes to load the cart, so sluggishly was she moving. Nicholas kept seeing items and demanding that they be added. The total was going to be high, and Barbara nervously fingered the fold of bills in her purse.

"Want orange juice," Nicholas said, twisting around in the high-up seat.

It was an unfortunate echo of this morning. Barbara gave her son a wan smile.

"When we get home, okay?" she said. "You can have a nice big glass."

Maybe she would have one, too. With ice.

Nicholas leaned over the metal lattice separating him from the groceries, and stretched out his arm. Unable to reach down far enough into the cart, he stood up on unstable legs.

Barbara wasn't sure what to do. If she took him out, Nicholas was likely to throw another fit. But the chances of him successfully climbing into the cart were low. And what would he do even if he made it? Guzzle juice straight out of the carton?

She realized her son was likely to do exactly that, and the thought of the sticky mess he'd make caused her stomach to lift.

Nicholas stood teetering on the seat. There was a gasp from a woman standing by the pyramid of soup cans beside the cart, and the next thing Barbara knew, her son was in the woman's arms. The woman turned toward Barbara, who was leaning against the red-and-white cardboard Campbell's sign.

"Oh, Mrs. Burgess," said the pastor's wife.

Barbara felt grateful that if anybody was going to observe what was about to happen, it would be a woman of God.

"I didn't see you there. You must keep an

eye on your little boy now that he's so mobile."

As if on cue, Nicholas bucked against the woman. "Down! I want to go down!"

Glenda Williams cocked a brow at Barbara. "Mind your *p*'s and *q*'s, then," she said.

But Nicholas continued to writhe in the woman's arms until Barbara reached for him.

Glenda gave a quick shake of her head, keeping Barbara at bay. "Should I count?" she asked Nicholas. "By three you're going to be nice and still. All right? One, two . . ."

Nicholas quieted, and Glenda set him down on the floor.

She aimed a smile at Barbara. "Always worked like a charm with mine," she said. "And what a smart boy to know his numbers already."

Barbara fingered the chain that lay in a damp hollow at her neck. She made her tone modest. "He hasn't even begun school yet."

As if knowing he was being talked about, Nicholas took off in the direction of the dairy section. Barbara heaved a sigh and started after him.

Glenda trailed along behind, still murmuring. "My boys didn't get so . . . willful until they were older."

The comment was charitable. The Williams boys were shining examples of the community, one with his own farm, two studying downstate, the youngest planning one day to assume his daddy's pulpit.

A thick, wet *thud* came from the rear of the store. Barbara abandoned her cart, purse slapping against her arm as she hurried forward.

Nicholas was sitting in a puddle of orange juice. A carton had fallen onto the floor. Barbara had no idea how Nicholas had gotten a hold of it; he must've climbed into the refrigerated case.

He was trying to scoop up a handful of liquid, slicked with gray dirt from the floor. Barbara went to Nicholas, taking care not to skid. He screamed as she stooped down beside him.

"Mama! No pick me up! Want juice!"

He beat his sticky fists against Barbara's chest — the only clean dress she had left — and one found its way into her mouth. She tasted grit and syrupy sweet citrus and the combination was too much for her stomach, which had been so fragile all morning.

It lifted, disgorging its contents to mix with the juice, and as Barbara leaned over, wiping her mouth with the back of her hand, she suddenly remembered the last time she had felt this hot and nauseous and tired all at once.

It had nothing to do with the weather, or her boisterous little boy.

Glenda Williams appeared, towing Mr. Mackey alongside her, and Barbara let out a lone, solitary howl of protest that joined her son's.

Glenda scooped Nicholas out of the mess on the floor, directing a hapless Mr. Mackey to unlock the washroom door, and carrying the boy inside. Nicholas' protests didn't abate; the little room rocked with their force.

But as Barbara leaned against the refrigerated section, fanning herself and trying to rid her mouth of its vile taste, things did begin to quiet down. Eventually Glenda emerged, plunking Nicholas on the floor with a little pat to his bottom. The boy smiled up at her. His chocolaty curls were slicked down and his face looked clean, though the bottom of his shorts was still stained orange. Laundry on a live, yelling child in a washroom was beyond even Glenda Williams.

Barbara tried to muster words.

"Mama?" said Nicholas.

Barbara gathered breath for her reply.

"Yes, angel?"

"I want ice cream," he said.

Glenda let out a rather heretical snort.

Barbara looked at her.

"Please tell me you're not going to give this child a treat," Glenda said.

Barbara opened her mouth to explain. "He's stormy by nature. Sensitive, really. He takes things so hard —"

"Mama! You said ice cream!"

Glenda spoke over the cry. "Barbara Burgess, stop making excuses. For yourself and for the boy. He won't listen because he's not in the habit of listening."

Barbara stared at her.

"Ma-ma! I — want — ice cream!"

But Nicholas' heart clearly wasn't in it anymore. His throat sounded hoarse, and his cries were croggy. The boy had tired himself out; his small body appeared to be wilting.

It was one way to end a tantrum, Barbara supposed. Just outlast it.

"I thought about spanking him myself," Glenda said, turning briskly. "There's nothing wrong with this child that a little discipline won't cure." She paused, then swiveled back, a note of portent in her voice. "Not now there isn't. Where he'll be in a year or two," she added darkly, "I couldn't say."

She didn't walk off, but continued standing there, quietly observing. Barbara was left with no choice but to lift Nicholas into her arms and leave the store. She got them both into the car, whose internal temperature had risen to a baking heat. It was only once she'd twisted the key in the ignition that Barbara realized she had left all her groceries back in the store.

They suddenly seemed of the utmost unimportance. Barbara couldn't recall why she had ever thought to venture out today.

She turned to look beside her. Nicholas was fast asleep already, his small body slumped over on the seat like a dead thing.

On the way home, Barbara stopped by Dr. Benedict's office, grateful when she entered the cool chambers. She'd left Nicholas in the car, rolling down a window to make sure the little boy would have enough air. Last time Nicholas had been here, the nasty nurse kept trying to get him to stop touching things, which had been a burden on the little boy's creative, curious spirit.

The nurse led Barbara back to an examining room.

"You seem a little calmer today, Mrs. Burgess," the nurse said as they walked. "No child with you?"

"No," Barbara replied. *See what all your bossing did,* she added in her head. *Now you don't get to see Nicholas.* "No child."

Barbara got up on the table, paper sheet crinkling beneath her.

"Well," the nurse said, smiling as she readied the things for the test. "I suppose we're going to see about that."

The double meaning hit Barbara, and the nurse recoiled a bit when Barbara lifted her gaze and met hers. The needle snagged before plunging deeply into Barbara's arm, but Barbara refused to give the nurse the satisfaction of wincing.

She tried to read the result in the inscrutable stream of blood that rose inside the syringe.

CHAPTER FOUR

Ivy lay on her bed in her darkening room, scrolling through updates on Facebook, and madly posting comments in the hopes that someone would respond. She wanted to talk and the sad truth was that she had a better chance of doing so with somebody ten or twenty or forty miles away than with her mom or dad, who were in the same house.

She had gotten one text from Melissa — at dereks game cant talk u kno the rule — which was true, Ivy did know, though she'd forgotten that Melissa's brother had a game tonight. After that she texted a few other people — friends who didn't quite click or get her the way Melissa did — but two of them didn't even reply. Which was part of what Ivy was talking about.

Darcy did text back, but when Ivy suggested she come over to work on their world history study guide, due tomorrow, or their algebra two problem set, also due, Darcy wrote: cant get the car my parents say weathers coming in

bummer Ivy typed, then dropped her phone onto the bed.

On the floor below, Mackie let out a snuffle.

Ivy extended her hand. Mac didn't jump onto the bed — he hadn't done that in almost a year; Ivy could remember the exact last time — but tonight he also failed to give her fingers a lick. Ivy felt a clamp in her chest that was familiar. The clamp took hold whenever she saw Mackie these days, or even thought about him. Her dog that she kind of sort of named and couldn't remember a day of her life without. McLean was his whole name, which they'd had to keep because after they brought him home from the shelter, only hearing his name yelled really loud would make him come. But after a long, long, long time, Ivy had started to say Mac, then Mackie, until those started to work, too.

Mac thumped his tail in slumber. It didn't have the heft it once had, when Mackie could make her floorboards shake with doggie enthusiasm.

He wasn't the dog he used to be.

Ivy knew it, even if her mother would never admit it in a million years. Which, as

100

with everything else bad in her life, meant that Ivy was alone.

Her mom didn't do too well with *bad*.

She had called her mom a liar, but even as she said the word, Ivy knew she'd never be able to explain it. Even if her mother asked, which of course she wouldn't. Ivy was starting to understand something about her mom, and it put so much space between them that she wondered how she would ever feel close to her again.

Ivy kicked her legs with all the vigor Mackie lacked, scattering papers at the bottom of her bed. She had been planning to do her study guide, and the problem set, too. She didn't know why she'd said different during the fight. The non-fight. Like everything else that seemed to be happening lately, it had been an impulse that snuck up from behind, caught her by surprise. Ivy opened her mouth and words came out that she hadn't planned. She sat down at her desk at school and wrote answers that she knew were wrong.

Same thing now. Ivy wasn't sure where the urge to slither onto the floor came from, except that it allowed her to bury her face in Mackie's fur. He hardly even lifted his head, just gave another soft snort as Ivy cried and cried against him.

■ ■ ■ ■

Her phone buzzed, but Ivy ignored it. Just Darcy probably, texting back to say something lame like *yeah* to Ivy's equally lame *bummer* comment. Ivy wiped her nose, keeping her face buried in Mackie's flank, which rose and fell at a pace as comforting as the tides. Her phone gave another insistent rotation and Ivy finally reached up to grab it off her bed. Maybe the game had finished early and Melissa was going to come over after all.

whats up read the words on the screen.

She glanced down at the number, unfamiliar at first, before realizing who it must be.

He'd given her a ride earlier, after Melissa was stuck in detention and her other friends lamed out.

Ivy's whole face heated. She stared at the message, thumbs hovering.

not much she typed, hearing Darcy cackle in her head. *Can't you come up with anything better than that?*

u? Ivy added, Darcy laughing all the harder.

same came Cory's reply. want to do something?

102

i thought a storm is coming? can u get ur car?

i can always get the car

my parents might not want me to go out Ivy typed, which wasn't a lie, although she had the scary, perilous sense that she might be able to get around the rules just by threatening another outburst, or launching a camouflaged exit strategy.

Cory's reply appeared on her screen.

dude, did you see how slow i drove when i dropped you off? ur parents would probably let me take u to burning man if i asked

Ivy wasn't sure what he meant, but the message sent a thrill down her shoulders. She leaned over and squeezed Mackie, muffling her squeal in his coat.

The front door banged downstairs. Hard. It made the wall in her bedroom, which was right above the entryway, vibrate. Ivy's dad always yelled at her for being careless with the door. "Hypocrite," she said out loud, the word a surprising, bitter tablet on her tongue. Plus now her dad would probably be buffing out the mark on the wall when Cory arrived.

Her phone trembled in her hand and Ivy looked at it again.

so what do u say

Ivy glanced out into the hall. She typed

swiftly, before she could change her mind.

sure come on over

There came the sound of twin thuds then
— hard to place, different from the door —
and Ivy set her phone aside.

"Mom?" she called out. "Dad?"

CHAPTER FIVE

Sandy surprised herself by cleaning her plate. Pasta, salad, bread, all gone. A balloon of red wine drunk even. By dinnertime, she wasn't usually all that hungry; actually, Sandy had never been the biggest eater. But tonight Ben had awakened all sorts of appetites, and Sandy felt a slow, grateful burn as she looked across the table to him.

"This was nice," she said softly.

He gestured to the plates. "Great meal."

"Great lots of things," she said, and he reached out, closing her fingers up in his.

"Not much left to clean," Ben remarked as they stood. He surveyed the lone pot on the stove, the sparse place settings required by just the two of them.

"We could even leave it for tomorrow," Sandy teased. She could no sooner imagine her husband putting off chores than she could see him resisting the challenge of a climb.

But Ben surprised her, appearing to consider the idea before glancing at the clock. "It's early," he said, and it was, just a few minutes after seven. "I'll finish up. Meet you upstairs."

A long, luxurious night stretched ahead. Sandy decided she would fill the oversized tub in the master bath, big enough for two, although they almost never used it. Maybe she'd even light a few candles, put on one of the CDs Ben had reminded her they used to enjoy.

Sandy smiled at her husband. "Let me fix a dish for Ivy before you put that away." She began to fill a bowl from the serving platter in the middle of the table.

She was reaching for a chunk of garlic bread when the front door slammed against the entryway wall and a blast of cold air shot in.

Ben frowned. "Did Ivy go out?"

"She'd better not have . . ." Sandy began.

The fact that it wasn't Ivy registered in some low column of her brain. An oozing, primordial cluster of cells that lay beneath thought, beneath sensory input even. Long before Sandy heard the two sets of footsteps thudding toward their kitchen — and parsed that they were too heavy for Ivy or even some male friend of hers — she knew they were in danger.

Sandy lifted her head. It felt as if she did it slowly, in discrete steps. First her eyes came off the bread plate with its gloss of butter upon the china. Her gaze sought out Ben, finding him by the fridge. And only then did she take in the two bodies that suddenly occupied her home.

In truth, mere seconds must have passed, for both men were moving fast, one knocking over a chair with the bulk of his hip before the other appeared from behind.

Everything inside Sandy came to a stop. Her blood turned to sludge in her body; her eyes were unable to blink. The muted light of the kitchen showered sparks across her line of vision. When she could finally see again, the second man was staring in her direction. His gaze pierced her like a spear. Then something came down in her mind — a garage door rumbling shut — and Sandy was able to turn away.

A forest now filled her kitchen — brown stumps and green stalks — the color of the intruders' clothes. Plus a strange, shocking slash, appropriate to autumn woods. Fierce scarlet painted across one of the coats, still tacky and glistening.

Blood, recently spilled.

Dimly, Sandy registered the fact that Ben hadn't wasted a moment on any of the things people usually did when faced with a reality they couldn't process. There was no protest or denial. Not a single *who the hell are you* or *what are you doing in my house* came from her husband's lips. Instead he seized the closest weapon at hand, a bread knife lying on the counter, and leapt forward.

The man he was trying to jump was enormous, but Ben had intuited the physics of the situation. He thrust the serrated edge of the blade out at a sharp angle, arm raised high above his head.

The big man leaned down and wrapped his fist around the knife's handle, stopping it in midair. In the next instant, the knife was in the big man's hand and Ben was looking down at his crumpled fist. He didn't seem able to open it, to uncurl any of his fingers. Ben bit back the howl that must've been building, but his eyes had gone muddy with pain. Sandy could see her husband suffering, and it made her want to weep.

She started forward and the second man turned.

His eyes were like bits of ash, cold and dead and gray. They were the eyes of a nightmare from which you never woke up.

Sandy's step faltered and her vision wavered, along with her hold on place and time. This couldn't be the year 2015, and she couldn't be a grown wife and mother, in the kitchen of her recently completed home, a house built with so much love and devotion by Ben for his family. A place to grow old in, to finish raising their child.

Ivy.

Sandy felt a fizzing in her hands, her wrists, an itchy sensation she almost remembered for a second, then just as suddenly was gone. She whirled around, Ben coming into sight. He ignored his injured hand to face off with both men.

Sandy had the mad idea to pretend she simply didn't see them. Maybe she and Ben could make it to the second floor, still have their night together. Unlike Ben, who had adapted so instantly to their new circumstances and acted so fast, Sandy was unable to resolve the place they had been moments before with where they were now. One part of her recognized her dissociation, but elsewhere images swarmed. Of Ben kneeing open their bedroom door, Sandy going for one of her prettier nightgowns, Ben remarking that she didn't need to wear anything at all. She wanted this other version of the night so badly that she swayed.

Her daughter's name arrowed into her brain again, obliterating everything else. What was Ivy doing? Had she heard the commotion downstairs? Sandy couldn't let Ivy walk into this blind.

Her gaze spun, seeking Ben amidst the madness that had come.

Her husband had positioned himself on the opposite side of the table. He crouched low, a fighter's stance, although Sandy took in the sheer impossibility of the task even if Ben couldn't see it in his adrenaline-charged state. The man she'd been thinking of as the big one was more than big. He was an ogre, less human than creature from lore. He looked as if he would crush Ben beneath the sole of his shoe if he came around the table. En route, without even trying, simply by taking his next step.

Except that Ben clearly had an idea, some sort of plan in mind. It moved behind his eyes, like a ticker scrolling across a screen. Although Ben's gaze was aimed straight ahead, he looked as if he were considering something in their surroundings.

What was it? Sandy's gaze shot around the kitchen before the knowledge that Ivy was still unaccounted for slammed back into her consciousness. Thank God for earbuds and texting.

Texting.

Ivy might be able to summon help if she determined that something was wrong, and figured out not to come down. It was a lot to hope for from a fifteen-year-old, but Ivy had always been smart. Not only smart — capable, too.

Thinking about Ivy, Sandy was assailed by one irrefutable thought. She could not, would not let these men near her child. Especially not the one with flinty eyes.

Sandy shuddered.

She had to assist Ben. She couldn't just stand here, helpless. Options came at her like darts. Another knife, a different utensil from one of the drawers, some sort of lethal kitchen spray, maybe cleanser with bleach. Which would be closest at hand? Sandy turned around.

The intruders began to circle the table, Ben waiting in place, motionless.

Only her husband's eyes moved. Back and forth, between the two men, assessing the risks and dangers with laser precision, his gaze coming to settle on the enormous one. Which made sense. If he took out the threat who had twelve inches and a hundred pounds on him, that would even the odds dramatically. But Ben didn't know what

111

Sandy did, he hadn't seen what she had in the other man's eyes.

Sandy tore her focus off her husband, and looked upward. The rack with its ring of copper pots hung above the island. Not two feet from where she stood.

She took a sideways step, unobserved. Brought her hand up from its position by her thigh. At hip-level now. Then over her head, reaching, stretching, as she rose on tiptoes to touch one of the handles. The column of metal felt long and lean in her grasp, the welded-on pot heavy enough to require a second hand as she unhooked it and lifted it free.

Bring it down on his head. The command was a horn blast in her mind. The second man was within her sights, then within her reach as he moved around the table, closing in on Ben. Each bristly hair upon his scalp grew magnified, a forest of buzz-cut splinters.

Sandy honed in on her target.

In an instant he was at her side, as if he had sensed her intent all along.

The pot dropped with a *thunk,* denting the floorboards. At the same time, the man's knee slammed into Sandy's stomach and sent her flying backwards. She landed squarely on the chair behind her, as if the whole sequence had been choreographed.

Ben saw the violence with which she had been struck, and fury arced from his eyes like electrical current. Sandy was surprised that the force of it wasn't enough to flatten the man now holding her in place. Ben didn't roar with rage, nor make a single sound that would've warned he was coming. At least, Sandy didn't think he did; she was having trouble hearing over the buzz in her ears, and a sick thrum in the place where she'd been kneed. She felt as if she was going to throw up. Through blurred eyes, she tracked Ben's movements. He had made his way over to the woodstove. The poker was on the far side, tucked into its tricky, notched stand. Ben bent down and picked up a log that was closer at hand.

Sandy gasped to regain breath while Ben crossed the floor, silently, stealthily, the man pinning Sandy to the chair in his sights.

The man turned around, still guarding Sandy. His fists were held up to block and parry a blow, and if Ben had already raised the log, the two men would've gone down in a clash of wood and limbs. But Ben was smarter than that.

Without lifting his weapon more than a few inches off the floor, he drove it down punishingly onto the man's foot.

A great gust of time seemed to pass.

The man didn't double over, or make so much as a move. For a moment it seemed as if his foot hadn't just received a shattering blow. Ben raised his arms, readying the log for a killing strike at the man's head.

There was a bellow, a wounded animal's bleat of pain — "Harlan!" — and the big man jerked to.

Ben hoisted the log higher to adapt to the new threat, and swung in a wild trajectory. Ben was an athlete though, well conditioned and strong, and for a moment it looked as if the wood — good, hard, seasoned oak — was going to make contact with the big man's neck.

Then the big man got up on tiptoes so that when the log struck, it hit his upper arm. An arm that was wider around than the piece of wood, and possibly as strong. The man straightened, rubbing his biceps as if he'd been bitten by an insect. He reached out and took the log out of Ben's hand, a mere matchstick in his grasp. The man threw the piece of wood across the room; it landed on the loveseat with enough force that the small couch tipped over backward and fell.

The other man stood over Sandy, his face chalky. "Harlan, take him out."

There was resignation in his tone. Whatever was coming, he hadn't meant for it to happen, at least not right now. What would it be? What did *take him out* mean? Sandy had an image of Ben being released into the outdoors.

The big man seemed as confused as she.

They were both idiots.

"I said, hit him," the other clarified.

The growl that came in response was more vibration than sound. It seemed to shake the whole room. "Okay," Harlan said, and lifted his football-sized fist.

Ben spun to find Sandy, opening his mouth. An idea, a command that he never got a chance to say. Harlan's club of a hand came down on the back of Ben's head, and Ben struck the floor face-first.

CHAPTER SIX

Ivy got down off her bed, setting both feet on the floor with a stealth that almost made her laugh out loud. *Stealth* had been a vocabulary word last week. She was like a character in a video game, or in one of the old movies she and Melissa liked to stream. If Darcy could see her now, Ivy would never live it down. It'd be all, *Who do you think you are, that dumb girl from* Scream? for the rest of time.

Mac was standing, blue eye and brown eye both narrowed and alert. He didn't make a sound — Mac wasn't a barker — but Ivy knew what her dog was telling her. No way would he stay behind while she went to scope things out. From the time Mackie had come to them, the one thing he could never stand was being alone. The guy at the shelter told her parents it was a reaction to trauma, but Ivy had never wanted to know too much about that. Anyway, she

116

could see the effects. Being without one of them nearby was impossible for Mac.

Solitude was his Kryptonite.

Ivy liked superhero movies more than horror flicks. The old ones, not the glitzed-up new versions. How wrong the *Green Lantern* was had been the first conversation she and Cory ever had.

Maybe Cory had come over. Could he be the one who'd made those loud noises downstairs? But Cory hadn't had enough time to get here since Ivy sent her last text. He would've had to have just been sitting at the bottom of Long Hill Road or something, trusting that she would say *yes.* Which, Ivy realized, wasn't as far-fetched as all that. Cory was one of the guys at school she and Melissa called sleek. They had sleek cars. Sleek, muscled bodies. Sleek lives. Cory was probably one hundred percent convinced that Ivy would invite him over when he asked. Who turned Cory Gresham down?

He might also have banged the front door that carelessly, and then, oh, would he be off to a bad start with her father.

Ivy entered the hall, speeding up to run interference with her dad. He and Cory should get along well; they were a lot alike. Athletic — no, outdoorsy — and both so easy and confident, as if they were certain

117

that everything was always going to go their way in life.

Ivy herself had never believed anything like that.

Mac treaded along at her side, his flank pressed to her thigh as if held there by a magnet. His tail pointed straight down at the floor. Another sign of age — losing his jaunty wagging — or an indication that Mac was disturbed about something? For a second, Ivy wished he would growl. She and her dad used to joke about getting a kitten so that they would have a better watchdog. It was sad, though, really. Part of Mac had been buried during the first year of his life.

Ivy squinted straight ahead. The hall to the stairway seemed endless when she wanted to fix herself a snack late at night, or had the idea to sneak out, even if she hadn't done it yet.

Mac sort of sniffed and jumped forward — a momentary leap back to puppyhood — before retreating and sticking himself to Ivy again.

Ivy found herself whispering, even though she knew they wouldn't be heard.

"Something's weird down there, right?" She felt it, too. She hadn't just been watching too many movies, and it didn't even matter if Darcy laughed.

She and Mac reached the staircase, which seemed to float in place, no wall on either side, only a slender branch of railing to hold on to. When you were on the steps, it felt as if you were suspended high up in the air. A masterpiece, the builder had called it, after finally succeeding in bringing her father's design to life. Ivy herself hated the staircase, hated this whole enormous house, in fact. She missed their old one, a cozy Victorian back in town, painted the prettiest shades of pale green and lilac. Ivy and her mom had labored over those colors, going outside again and again, holding up sheet after sheet of tiny colorful squares. They'd been accompanied by some woman with a black Lab who was in charge of the whole fixing-up process — the woman, not the dog — and who swore that she loved this stuff, Ivy and her mom could take as long as they liked choosing.

But then her dad had decided that their house — Ivy's childhood home — was too small for them, not to mention too old-fashioned, and began creating this one from scratch. It was big enough that it couldn't be in town, and the new school bus driver complained every single day about making the trip out here. Felt like a long haul trucker, he said. Her old school bus driver never would've complained. But Earl had retired, just one more piece of Ivy's childhood gone.

She stepped onto the top stair, Mac squeezing himself down beside her. She peered over the side, perplexed.

Through the empty air to her right, Ivy could see that it wasn't only the front door that had been treated with careless abandon. A chair was also overturned. And no way, even if Cory had gone and done something bizarre like that, would her father have just left it there. He liked his furniture — made by some master craftsman in Ohio and shipped all the way out here — almost as much as he liked this precious house.

Ivy stopped her foot from reaching for the next step. She paused in place, motionless on the level plank of wood. Then, soundlessly, she began to back up.

She needed a few moments to think. Mac padded along toward Ivy's bedroom in his own position of consideration, or relief.

Another thing about this house, it was virtually soundproof. Ivy hated that, too. Someone could be practically on top of her before she heard them. Her mother, she'd always been able to feel somehow, at least know when she was around. It was like the two of them were connected by a sheer, invisible thread, something spun by an insect. Although lately that thread seemed to have gotten snipped. But with her father, Ivy might be lost in a homework assignment, or a conversation with Melissa, only to look up and see him looming in her doorway.

Point was, she had no way of telling what might be going on downstairs, not by overhearing anything anyway. She couldn't imagine any scenario that would result in a chair being overturned, but whatever it was, it must entail some degree of confrontation, right? Like, a scuffle or something?

The idea of her family scuffling made Ivy almost laugh out loud. But there was a deeper place inside her, pinprick-sized, and that place wasn't laughing. It felt cold and hollow and scared.

If Cory had gotten here, her mother would've come up and told her. She didn't stay mad at Ivy for long, never really got mad at her at all, in fact. And she would know what a big thing it was for Ivy to invite a boy over. Something that had never happened before actually.

There was no use calling out; she wouldn't be heard. And if she went downstairs, then that would rule out any other option or plan. She'd be a part of whatever was going on down there, and something told Ivy that might not be such a good idea.

Was the fight between her parents? The idea was almost laughable. Ivy's mom and dad didn't even snipe at each other much, let alone throw chairs.

Outside, the wind was blowing hard enough that a faint whistle made its way into her room. The last leaves were being sheared off the trees. Ivy could see them; brown, jagged flying things, propelled through the air. She retrieved her cell phone — maybe Cory had texted — and wasn't surprised to see two words in the status bar. No signal. Her phone was basically as useless to her now as a lump of rock. Happened all the time up here. The signal went out in town too, just not as much. Another thing to hate about this place.

Ivy heaved a sigh and tossed the phone onto her bed.

Only what had she been thinking to do? Call 911? Say that a chair had fallen over?

She glanced at her laptop, humming contentedly away in hibernation on her desk. She realized she didn't have to call 911 — which was like a crime if there wasn't a really good reason; the chief of police had come to their class last year and explained it. But the Wi-Fi always worked even if their phones didn't. Ivy could message Melissa, say that something weird was going on. They could decide together what to do about it.

She was just about to cross to her desk when it hit her. Who must be here.

It wasn't Cory, and Ivy heaved a sigh of relief. She looked at Mac, who hadn't lain back down, but was standing in place, claws digging into the rug as he watched her.

"It's okay, Mackie. I figured it out. You know who's come over? To stir up trouble again?"

Her dog gazed up at her, all the trust in the world in his eyes, so that for a second, Ivy had the crazy impulse to cry.

"You're right," she said, stroking the silky fur on Mac's ears. "It's those icky Nelsons."

Ivy started for the bathroom, shaking her head at the positively bizarre level of paranoia she'd reached tonight, and untangling wisps of hair with her fingers. She wanted to change her shirt, just quickly, then check the mirror, make sure she looked okay before she went down. Cory would be here any minute.

The Nelsons were their only neighbors, if *neighbor* was the right word for people who

123

lived a workout-length jog away. There was a house a little closer, but it was falling down and no one lived there anymore, especially not in the wintertime.

There was another reason not to think of the Nelsons as neighborly, and that was because they hated her parents. Probably Ivy too, for all she knew.

It had gotten ugly as soon as this house started to go up. At first Ivy had been neutral when her parents traded stories — all wide-eyed shock at how some people could act — but even though she basically agreed with the Nelsons, if their point was *go back where you came from,* she had to admit to being kind of shocked at how they behaved. The Nelsons had dammed a part of the creek so that the banks flooded onto Ivy's parents' new land. They blocked the road from being extended with a whole bunch of logs. And when none of that worked, and construction went on ahead anyway, the Nelsons had thrown a bucket of paint across the boards her dad had made a big deal of *not* painting, only staining, an application he said would allow for almost no maintenance in years to come. Something like that anyway.

Just after the outside walls had gone up, her dad and mom had forced Ivy to make the trip out here, believing she'd feel better — start to *adjust* — once she saw how the place was coming along. Well, fat chance of that, but even Ivy had to feel sorry for her parents when they got there. Red splotches all over their velvety new boards, like the house was one huge Jackson Pollock canvas or whatever.

The Nelsons. Their name came to be uttered like Lord Voldemort's around here.

They thought the new house was outsized — *true* — that they'd lost their precious privacy — *ick, privacy for what* — and that their view would be cut off. Ivy had no clue what they were talking about with that one. There were views everywhere you looked around here. This whole place was a view.

After the paint incident, the police had been called, and Ivy's mom floated the idea that maybe they shouldn't move out to the middle of absolutely nowhere. Ivy had wanted to sing with relief. She'd hugged her mom unasked for the first time in months.

But her dad had gotten really mad. It'd been the only time Ivy could remember her parents having a real life, honest-to-God argument, with yelling, and awkward silences that lasted days instead of immediately being dusted up and cleared away

125

by Ivy's mom.

"What do you want to do, just slink off with our tails between our legs?" her dad had demanded. "You don't back down at the first sign of a fight."

Which was pretty hypocritical on her dad's part, since of course that was exactly what he wanted Ivy's mom to do at the first sign of any fight with *him*.

Okay, honey, you're right, we'll move, her mom had finally said. Something like that.

And they had. Construction had continued, and maybe it was the police, maybe something else, but the Nelsons had pretty much left them alone after that.

Until tonight.

Ivy wondered what had caused things to fire up again.

She took a last look in the mirror, running a wand of pink gloss over her lips. Maybe her parents would be so distracted, they wouldn't even notice she was wearing makeup.

Ivy raced down the stairs, her feet pounding. Mac huffed as he fought to keep up.

She was most of the way to the kitchen, skidding round the bend that divided the living and dining rooms from it, when she suddenly reared back. Mac halted too, his body thrumming like a guitar string against her. He didn't make a sound, none of his little yelps or whimpers, but Ivy knew her dog was scared.

Whoever had come, it wasn't the Nelsons.

CHAPTER SEVEN

Sandy's gaze slid away from the man who stood with his back to her, close enough to make her gag. At one point he reached behind him, feeling to make sure she remained in the chair, and there was an intimacy, a familiarity to the blindly delivered touch that sent ripples of disgust throughout her whole body.

The skin on her hands was itching again in a way that couldn't be scratched.

The kitchen clock caught her eye. The last time she'd looked at this clock, back when Ben had declared the night early yet, the slashes of numbers had read 7:04.

Which meant the intruders had been inside her house for less than three minutes.

How long ago had it been when Ivy accused Sandy of lying, her tone like a toxin? Even the sulkiest version of Ivy had never dripped contempt like that before. Now this man had come to flay their lives. He couldn't. Not before Sandy and Ivy had a chance to make it through the bombed-out years of adolescence, cross over to the peacetime eras mothers and daughters inhabited on the other side.

"Where's your medicine cabinet?" the man demanded.

"What?" Sandy asked.

He started to twist around, and Sandy responded before he could turn fully. "In the powder room. There." She pointed.

"Harlan," the man ordered. "Get me some aspirin."

The goliath returned with a bottle of Advil.

The man stood with his leg thrust into the space between Sandy's knees, one arm barricading her body in the chair.

"Empty the drawers," he ordered the big man. He fumbled with the cap on the bottle, shaking out a handful of pills onto his palm, then crunching them up.

Sandy wondered what kind of damage Ben had inflicted on his foot.

Ben.

A sob rose up, blocking her airway.

"Empty them into what?" The big man had a voice to match his body: its rumble so deep that it was hard to parse into distinct words.

"Look underneath the sink for some trash bags. And Harlan?"

The big man lifted his head.

"Clear this rack." The man with the cold eyes pointed.

Harlan swept the pots off the rack in a jingling clatter, hardly having to reach over his head to do it. Then he pounded over to the rows of drawers, huge mitts of hands yanking each one out, graceless fingers combining the contents into the gaping maw of a black garbage bag. Sandy's brand-new drawers, which slid so smoothly on their tracks, now rattled like a drum kit.

She was thinking about cabinetry.

When she needed to fight, to check on Ben, to rouse him.

No, she had to go after Ivy, somehow defying detection.

Thoughts circled around in her mind, like water going down a drain.

Sandy opened her mouth and let air into her lungs, her bruised chest cramping.

The man blocking her looked down, sensing something. The minute, almost imperceptible way she drew back, readying herself to spring forward.

He gave her a knowing glance before something puckered between his brows.

Sandy switched her gaze so fast her head

cramped. Her hands bore down on the arms of the chair. She was starting to rise without having any idea she'd meant to do so.

In an instant the man's hand was around her throat, five splayed fingers bracing it till her breath was reduced to a thin whistling stream.

His coat gapped, revealing a dark stenciling of tattoos around the stem of his neck. He was small compared to the other man, but thickly muscled. His wrist felt like it was made out of cast iron.

"Don't even think about it," he said.

His voice made her want to puncture her own eardrums. Sandy fought to get away from his touch, the branding of her flesh with his eyes. Time slowed to a syrupy swirl. Finally Sandy stopped struggling, her body curling over. Her back was a carapace, the only protection she had.

The man's fingers slowly loosened, granting air.

"You have no idea what I'm thinking," she said as soon as she could speak.

Across the room, the big man was still raking out cabinets. He'd just discovered an old pencil case of Ivy's. Sandy hadn't seen the thing in years — she couldn't believe it had survived the move — but at her captor's behest, Harlan began emptying its contents.

Pens whose potential as daggers Sandy only now realized; a small blade contained in the blue plastic housing of a crayon sharpener.

She was going to be left without so much as a toothpick for a weapon.

Sandy looked across the room to Ben, still lying on the floor, and her heart twisted. She could see the rise and fall of her husband's back. He was alive.

The pyramid of wood he'd stacked earlier had been taken apart.

The big man dragged a fistful of logs and his sack full of kitchen contraband across the floor. The load was cumbersome even for him; all the bits and pieces, the many objects that made up their lives.

The big man headed to the sliding glass doors. He elbowed them open as if they'd been greased, doors weighty enough that Sandy and Ivy always fought with them. Harlan heaved everything out into the yard, far enough away that the pieces couldn't be heard when they came down. Sandy tried to envision their distant destination. She had loved all the space upon moving up here; now she feared and loathed it.

"Does your husband have a gun?" the man with the lightless eyes asked. He was breathing easier now, color returning to his face.

She'd actually forgotten him for a moment, so focused had she been on the dismantling of the kitchen. It used to be an ability Sandy was grateful for: the laser pinpoint she could apply with her mind, while other parts broke and splintered off, never to be looked at again. Now that tendency had nearly made her miss something essential.

"What?" she said.

"Sure he does." The man looked down and Sandy twisted away from him in the chair. "Where is it?"

A belch of bile rose, burning, in Sandy's throat as options skittered through her mind. Could she come up with something to throw the man off, preserving the guns for later use? Simple refutation maybe, the ostrich-like denial of a five-year-old? No, sorry, we don't own a gun. But it wasn't as if things would stop there, her word for it simply taken. Perhaps she could send the man on a wild goose chase, someplace far away from Ivy. Give Ben a chance to come to — and come up with something.

She looked up, daring the dark pits of the man's eyes, and saw in them patience, and just the slightest shading of mirth. As if he was utterly certain that she would tell him whatever he wanted to know.

133

The prospect of defying him suffused her with a never-before-felt warmth.

And suddenly it occurred to Sandy how she could accomplish two things. Create a needed delay and save her husband by placing a value on his life.

"The guns are in a safe down in the basement," Sandy said. "But it's kept locked. And I don't know the combination."

"Guns," the man said. "Plural. Well, well. You country folk are well armed."

Sandy didn't respond.

"In a safe in the basement," the man went on, gazing down at her. "And unfortunately you can't open it." He paused. "So near and yet so far."

Sandy held his stare. It took all the strength she had to do it.

"I'm surprised," the man added, "that it wouldn't have occurred to you that one day you might need to shoot someone."

Sandy's gaze trembled and finally fell. She stared off at the stripped-bare kitchen, cabinet doors opening onto empty shelves, drawers lolling out like tongues. Taunting her with everything she'd had, and lost. Or everything she'd never really had at all.

"It's your husband who knows how to get at them," the man said, in that musing tone.

Sandy forced a nod.

The man crouched before her, so close she could see bits of beard growing underneath the pale skin on his jaw. They matched the stubble across his scalp. "Was that a *yes?*"

Sandy nodded again. When the man didn't move away, she said it out loud. "Yes."

He duplicated her nod. "Well, that only leaves me a couple of options." He twisted behind him to where the big man stood, absolutely still, casting a shadow across the floor. "I could ask Harlan to do me the honor of making sure you really can't get at that combination." He aimed a smile at her, empty as a sunny sky. "Harlan has a way of helping people remember things they think they forgot."

Sandy pressed her lips together.

"Harlan."

Harlan took a few halting steps forward.

The man nodded sagely at the other's slow progress. "This will be easier than the alternative . . ."

Instantly, Sandy knew which alternative he meant. It was carried by the dark gleam in his eyes, a tilt of his lips that said he had a taste for destruction. And so Sandy also knew that she couldn't allow this idea — which was going to involve searching the house for the combination to the safe — to be fully formulated. Because somehow, through intuition or smarts or sheer blind luck, Ivy had so far kept her presence unknown. These men didn't know about her. Ivy must have Mac with her, too; their dog would never have remained on his own. Which meant there was a chance that both Sandy's daughter and their dog would find something in the house to help them. Maybe they'd even get out.

Any bravery she had felt receded in a wave.

Sandy had no problem looking terrified as Harlan covered the distance to her, even though it wasn't the prospect of his information extraction skills that scared her.

She hardly felt her hands wrapping around the legs of the chair; sensation had been blocked as if by a trivet or thick gloves. Her fingers dug into the wood and she calmly registered the split of a splinter.

At any second Ivy would realize she was hungry or bored or, God help her, sorry about before. And then she would bound downstairs and —

The ceiling over Sandy's head, the floor that lay between her and her daughter, felt like it contained fathoms of water, its pressure unbearable.

"Zero-zero, seventy-six, seventy-four," she burst out.

The man raised one hand, and Harlan stopped walking. The floorboards vibrated, accepting his weight.

The other man leaned close.

He was going to make sense of those numbers, Sandy thought with a lightning strike of fear. The combination was their birth years — it occurred to her only now how startlingly, appallingly unoriginal that was of them — and so this man would realize there must be another member of the family. Sandy's whole world, everything she loved, contained in a measly handful of digits.

But the man merely rose from his crouch. "I'll get the guns," he said. "Harlan will never be able to remember the combination."

Sandy sat back, her breath coming in a ragged hitch.

The man added something as he reached the basement door, and it made the big man start forward again. "Harlan can decide what to do about your lying."

CHAPTER EIGHT

The first thing Ivy did was look around for Mac. She knew he wouldn't have gone far, but she had lost sight of him in the immediate aftermath of her fright.

As soon as she spotted her dog, Ivy set to work on her next task. Wheeling around, ever-so-carefully, a centimeter at a time, so that her back was to the wall instead of the opening into the kitchen. She didn't think she had been seen. Seen by who? A giant had come to their house, for reasons Ivy couldn't imagine, but one thing she felt sure of: it had nothing to do with her. The scary-big guy seemed totally focused on her mother.

Mommy.

The word was a whimper in her head, bitten back, swallowed down, a cry that would make Darcy laugh for sure, although even she would have to admit that Ivy had been right to skulk around her house like a character out of a movie.

Thank God she hadn't just run downstairs and barreled into the kitchen.

Ivy reached out a hand, placing it on Mac's furry head. The dog stayed as still and silent as she. Of course, making noise had never been what Mac was known for.

Still, Ivy mouthed, *Good boy,* the praise rolling up her throat on a sob, threatening to make a noise in the hushed cavern of the house.

Mac blinked, holding his place like a soldier on stakeout. As long as Mac had his family, he was all right. But still, her dog was Ivy's biggest problem right now.

He wouldn't attack anyone, even a menacing growl was above Mac's pay grade, as her dad liked to put it, but Mac wouldn't let Ivy out of his sight either. If not for that one aspect of his personality, which had never presented a problem before for Ivy — she actually found it kind of sweet — she could've snuck out. Gone somewhere to get help fighting the intruder.

Not with Mac, though. Ivy couldn't trust him to get out of the house unnoticed. His claws would click once they moved off these boards and onto the slate part of the floor. The cold, hard part Ivy hadn't liked from the moment they moved in, and now hated for a really good reason. Mac didn't do it as often these days, but he might even give a happy yelp upon catching a whiff of the outdoors.

Although the look in Mac's eyes told Ivy he wouldn't do that. He knew something was wrong, even if he couldn't do anything about it.

Another stupid sob, louder this time. Ivy put her hand over her mouth.

What a crazy idea, needing her dog to defend them. Of all the complaints Ivy had, things that ticked her off about living here, some horror movie scenario that depended on isolation had never occurred to her. Ivy realized, with a perspective that felt altogether new, that she didn't come from a scared family, nor a particularly imaginative one either. Neither of her parents had ever laid out far-fetched scenarios for Ivy to worry about. Or made up rules about stranger danger like other kids were taught. Ivy's mom was calm, capable, and confident. And her dad? He was just plain strong.

Ivy couldn't believe it had taken her this long to realize.

Where was her dad?

He'd only be doing nothing while some huge guy stood over her mother if he'd already been outmatched. Which Ivy once would've had trouble believing, except now fairy tales had turned real in one blink of an eye, and almost any possibility seemed likely. Even something happening to her father.

She gagged, harsh and sour.

If she could just get out, she'd go get help, drive for a working phone, or for the police. Ivy hadn't started really practicing yet, just loops up and down their long driveway, but she'd watched enough of her friends. First step, find the keys to one of the cars.

Her mom's purse would be upstairs.

And so was Ivy's sleek, gleaming, always connected computer.

She looked down at Mac. For years he had been like an extension of her own body, and when Ivy started to move, so did he.

They crept back up to the second floor, Ivy glad for once to have the muffling acoustics of this house on her side.

The hall that led past the bedrooms felt longer than ever. She and Mac wouldn't be heard downstairs, footfalls overhead, but what if the big guy decided to come up?

Ivy inched her head around, taking a look over her shoulder.

Shadows fell in a way they never had

before, cast down from the ceiling fixtures and lying low on the floor. There were cones of light on the smooth gray walls, and the photos her mom collected, nature shots mostly, seemed to leap out of their frames, coming crazily to life. A snowy tip of mountaintop looked like a single extracted tooth. Branches stirred, scissoring the sky. An alpine lake lay as unblinking as an eye.

Ivy shivered in her thin top. It was her favorite, but it seemed worse than silly to have chosen this one now that she'd have to go outside without a chance to find her coat.

She didn't have to make it far. She could blast the heat in the car.

Mac pushed forward a step, moving through air as if it were solid, and his boldness freed Ivy's gaze. She bent over her dog, rumpling his fur with quaking hands. Mac nudged her with his nose, cold and wet, and Ivy began to move on.

Was that a hump of shoulder appearing over the rise of the stairway?

She was stuck again, her feet planted, and this time even Mac couldn't budge her. If the man came up, she wouldn't be able to think of one more thing to do. Possibilities hovered just out of reach, like answers on a test, but Ivy couldn't conceive of anything right now. Her brain hurt, throbbed in its

142

canister as if she had worn it out, studying too hard.

The hall closet lay ahead — that would be a good place to hide. Or should she go backwards? If the big guy was on the stairs — that open run of wood — and Ivy came at him, she might just be able to push him over, gigantic or not.

She had to act, had to do *something.*

In the end, though she cursed herself for being one of those silly girls in the movies, not clever or brave at all, Ivy simply ran. Full out, Mac loping along beside her, past her own room, the guest rooms, headed for her parents' bedroom. If they were being chased, Ivy couldn't hear it, whether because of the soundproofing or the buzzing in her ears. It didn't matter; she hadn't been stopped. No hand came down on her shoulder. There was the doorway just ahead. Ivy put on a burst of speed, and so did Mac. They reached the door and fairly fell against the long, lean boards, bursting inside.

Mac pushed past her to go in first, and then Ivy entered, easing the door shut.

She squinted into the bedroom's dark nooks and crannies. A sitting area, the place where a TV came down from the ceiling, the opening to a bathroom that was more like a spa.

143

A crazy thought beckoned, comforting as a cup of hot cocoa. Maybe her dad didn't know what had happened yet. Maybe he was just being his usual out-of-it self, lost in a river map, or marking up a new trail to a summit, while her mother struggled downstairs with a super-huge foe.

They'd been studying antagonists in English class.

What if Ivy flicked on the bank of lights, only to see her dad lying back on the king-sized bed, against a swirly mound of pillows, hiking boots on — her mom would be annoyed about that, even though she'd never say anything. He'd grin at her, and Ivy would let out a rush of words, and her dad would take in her story before rising and racing downstairs.

To save the day.

Mac nosed her, and as a cold bath of air descended — neither of her parents having turned on the zoned heating for the night — Ivy let the image roll away like a ball down a street.

She knew she and Mac were on their own.

Ivy was smart enough not to go for the light switches. For all she knew the big guy had left, and Ivy didn't want him summoned back by the flash of a bulb from the second floor. She moved around the bedroom by feel, finding her mom's purse on a hook in the walk-in closet. She was tempted to run right then, but she didn't want to be fumbling around as she tried to make her exit. Ivy pawed through the contents of the purse until she located the keys.

As she pulled them out, she couldn't help but pause.

The key chain her mom used was ten years old. Ivy had made it in first grade — a tiny shrunken piece of plastic with a photo of her and her mom somehow mounted inside. In the picture, her mom's arms were flung around Ivy. A hundred photos like that had probably been snapped, but it was the raw emotion in this one that fixed Ivy's gaze. She couldn't believe she had let her teacher — her whole class — in on this moment of such pure and sublime joy. Actually, she couldn't believe she and her mom had taken that kind of happiness in each other's embrace. They might as well have been captured naked. Right there and then, with the home invader below and a car she didn't know how to drive waiting outside, Ivy cringed, as if Darcy had been looking over her shoulder and laughing.

Mac poked her with his snout.

Ivy looked down. "I know, Mackie," she

whispered. She folded up the keys in her hand, then jammed them into her pocket. "Let's go."

The house was dead quiet as they reversed their trip along the hall.

Mac paused outside Ivy's bedroom, and Ivy looked at it, torn. It was worth a minute's delay to check her phone again, turn on her computer. She could tell Melissa via Facebook to send the police to her house. Blast the whole school, for that matter. Ivy leaned against her door with her shoulder, pushing it open before crossing to her bed in three long steps.

The screen on her phone stared back at her, dark as a lake bottom.

NO SIGNAL it taunted when she fired it up.

Ivy stuck the phone in the pocket of her jeans, then ran to her desk and lifted the lid on her laptop. The screen saver imploded to a pinprick of red before disappearing altogether. Ivy madly typed in her password and hit Enter.

A message she'd never seen before appeared on the screen.

NO CONNECTION TO THE SERVER.

With TRY AGAIN below.

Ivy clicked the button, and got the same implacable message.

Her dad had promised when they moved. Wi-Fi meant that she would have all the connectivity she'd had in town. No matter what, she could always chat with her friends.

Ivy didn't try again.

Instead she backed soundlessly away from her useless, voided computer, and she and Mac began to descend the stairs.

She questioned herself the whole way down. Ivy couldn't have seen what she'd thought she had, could she? It was crazy. But if everything was normal tonight, then where were her parents right now? And what explained her computer, the soundless bubble she now inhabited?

Ivy swallowed, letting her foot reach for another step. Darkness yawned on both sides. Ivy clung tight to a clump of Mac's fur instead of the twig railing, and her dog didn't protest. They kept to the middle of each step, avoiding the precipices, because a fall of some sort seemed destined. Ivy couldn't believe that what she was planning would actually work, that she might be able to save her family.

She dared a peek toward the kitchen. It was silent, and dark. Whatever the man was doing in there, it couldn't be that bad. Unless it *had* been that bad — and was already over.

Ivy's heart bucked in her chest. She stumbled, and Mac sidestepped, barricading her body with his. Reflexes like he'd had as a pup. Ivy gazed down at her dog, her throat solid.

It occurred to her when they reached the bottom step.

They couldn't just leave through the front door, go out as if Ivy were running for the school bus in the morning. Opening the door would let in cold air, and night noises, making what she was up to altogether apparent.

She congratulated herself on keeping her wits together enough to understand that. Ivy gave Mac a nod, jerking her chin in a different direction.

Her plan might have a few holes in it — Ivy wasn't that great a driver yet, hardly a driver at all — but she couldn't think of a better one right now. At least this approach would get them outside, and let Ivy send help back. Bottom line, now that trouble had come to these mountains, the only place she could think to head was home.

There was a door from which she and Mac could make a camouflaged getaway, where even a startled whine from her dog wouldn't matter. The motion detectors would help them. It got so dark out here that without light you could stumble around for a while, trying to find your car. And Ivy didn't have time for wandering.

She and Mac would leave through the basement.

CHAPTER NINE

Harlan stood over the chair, looking down at Sandy from his great height.

With the other man in the basement, Sandy's heart stopped gonging; her palms lay flat on her lap. For the first time since the sun had fallen that night, taking along with it her life, Sandy felt able to pause for a moment, assess and regroup.

Harlan's brows drew into a fat, fuzzy vee.

And then Sandy's heart did start ponging lightly, because there was an opportunity here. She sensed it the same way she did whenever a new client walked into her office.

How much time did Sandy have before the man with the terrible eyes returned? Thinking about him sent a spike through her brain, so she simply stopped. Only — what relationship did he have with Harlan? Why had they come here? If Sandy knew that, then she might be able to figure something out. But it was like there was a wall inside her head, one that would have to be dismantled brick by brick, mortar scraped at, hard pieces of baked earth clawed out.

Sandy didn't have time for that now. She had minutes at most.

Four or five for the other man to locate the safe — their basement was big — another few for him to fiddle with the combination, one or two more to remove the weapons.

Weapons they owned, but had never anticipated any need of using for protection.

Sandy had stepped into a different way of life when she married Ben, and a more different one yet when they moved up from town. Not that Sandy's hometown was any sort of metropolis; actually Cold Kettle was even smaller than Wedeskyull. But Sandy's mother had lived differently from those around her, reading books instead of turning on the TV, talking about careers and being an artist and going to college. She'd also bucked several customs of the town, right down to a paranoid locking of the door every night to keep whatever was outside from getting in. Her mother had always been scared of the wrong things.

151

One of Ben's guns was a rifle. His outfit didn't offer hunting expeditions, but Ben sometimes went out during buck season with friends. The other was a decent-sized pistol, although Ben had said Sandy would be able to hold it comfortably. She'd just never had any interest in trying. Violence was something she'd always intended to avoid.

Harlan's form blocked the light as he peered down at her. Sandy felt stunned by the sheer size of him; up close he was even bigger than he appeared from a few feet away. The idea of thwarting him by force was laughable; she might as well have tried to break apart a cliff with her bare hands. Could she get past him, though? Harlan's body was like a building, his chest the high outer wall, peaked rooftop shoulders overhanging. Sandy had no hope of pushing him over, but she wondered whether down might provide a way out. If she slumped suddenly in her seat, Harlan wouldn't expect that. She could slip through the space between his legs.

And if he brought them together, he would crush her.

Therapists didn't use physical means to encourage people. They had other techniques.

Sandy glanced over at Ben just long enough to see his back form a slight hump before leveling out as he lay prone on the floor.

Then she looked up, high enough to put a crick in her neck.

Harlan had a face to match the rest of his body. His nose resembled some sort of rodent, loosely formed and plunked down in the middle. His eyes also lacked precision and fine-honing, round as half-dollars. His mouth was like the bend in a creek, curving and wide, although unsmiling. There was no emotion in his face, and the constellation of his features appeared only loosely related to whatever he might be feeling.

Sandy sat on her hands to quiet the itch, then forced herself to begin, just as if there was no demon about to make his way back upstairs, as if they had all the time in the world, or at least fifty minutes of it.

"Rough night," she said.

Harlan continued to loom over her, unresponsive.

"Tonight, I mean. It's been rough."

Harlan's expression didn't change. "What?"

IQ of seventy-five, Sandy thought

shrewdly upon hearing the thickness in Harlan's voice. Eighty tops. Fastest WAIS-IV ever administered.

She shrugged. "Coming all the way out here. On such a cold night."

Harlan turned away, considering the moonless expanse through the window. "It's okay. We'll be out of here soon."

Sandy's thoughts scrambled to keep up. They were planning to leave. Why, then, had they come? "Right," she said. "I know. I just meant that you'll probably be glad to go."

Harlan's face did amass something of a frown then. "You know?"

She'd been trying to shield her reaction to that welcome piece of news, act as if it were expected. Now she sensed a mistake. "Well, I mean, I guessed," she said, backtracking. "Why would you want to stay here?"

Harlan's head swiveled slowly, taking in the kitchen appliances, the glass-walled sitting area, the salvaged wood archway that led into the rest of the house. "Right," he said. "Why would we want to stay here?"

Sandy felt an uncomfortable swirl start in her stomach. She couldn't tell if Harlan was toying with her, being ironic, or if he meant what he'd said, but she added ten points to the IQ score she'd given him simply for the ambiguity.

At a loss, she waited for him to say something else, but Harlan didn't seem the type to speak unprompted. Sandy's mind flashed to the way she got the most difficult patients in the world to open up: recalcitrant teenagers dragged in by their parents. She did it by subtly aligning herself with them, instead of with the people who held all the power.

Harlan clearly didn't hold much power. So far, his friend had given the orders while Harlan carried them out.

"He's pretty bossy," Sandy remarked. Talking about the other man threatened to slow her thoughts like freezing water, but she forced herself through the sludge in her mind. "Just decides what to do and does it."

Harlan turned back to her. "He does?"

Or had it been, "*He* does?" There was irony in Harlan's response that time. For sure.

Sandy emitted a feeble laugh. "Right. I mean, you do."

No answer.

"You do all the hard parts, right?" Sandy went on, forcing out another husk of a laugh.

It happened then, the way it did sometimes during the exhuming that was therapy. You reached a level of truth — skipping over years of explanation and recounting — because knowledge between therapist and client was forged out of a connection deeper than words.

"Yeah," Harlan said in his deep rumble. "He makes me do a lot of things."

Sandy looked over at Ben, lying on the floor, still motionless. As Harlan tracked her gaze, some feeling finally sparked on his face.

"He shouldn't've tried to hurt me," he said. "Then I wouldn't've had to hit him."

Sandy nodded, making sense. "Okay. Yes. I got it."

Harlan aimed his bland, sandy gaze at her.

"If we don't fight you, then you'll just leave. Like you said. Right?"

Harlan gave a single nod.

The unlatched door to the basement had stayed open, and a wedge of light shone up from below. Sandy felt a frantic impulse to grab this fragile soap bubble of communication, snatch it up and force it to solidify. But the process didn't work that way.

"Is there something you want first?" Sandy asked, speaking slowly and quietly. "Some reason why you came here?"

Harlan lowered himself into a squat, his thighs a tabletop before him. He continued to regard her, and Sandy saw that his eyes weren't as empty as she'd thought when she peered upwards. The orbs twitched and moved, like newborn, mewling creatures.

"Don't you know?" he said. "I mean, you seem like you know so much."

Something sour and scared curled in her gut again. She had been coasting along, as sure of her conclusion as any diagnosis she'd ever made. But this wasn't a therapy session at the hospital. She was in her own house, trying to interpret the words and behaviors of a home invader who had only failed to torture her because his partner had changed the command.

Harlan began to move his block of a neck, then each shoulder, rolling the logs of his arms around. It was like watching a machine start up, the sight alarming in its power.

He was hot, she realized.

Harlan's coat was thick, and densely padded, and the heat in this house could be intense once the stove got going efficiently. On a normal night, Ben would've fiddled with something by now, opened or shut a vent —

Ben.

She looked.

He was still breathing, slowly and rhythmically. If he hadn't been sprawled out on the kitchen floor, with Sandy in a chair guarded by an oversized stranger, Ben might've looked as if he were fast asleep for the night.

Harlan scrubbed at a slick of sweat on his forehead.

"You should take off your coat," Sandy said.

The speed with which the coat came off, falling like a canopy to the floor, was astonishing. The suggestion had scarcely left Sandy's mouth before it was obeyed.

What lay beneath the coat made the first of the bricks in her mind start to crumble.

If she thought about this now, she wouldn't be able to stop. She'd simply sink down into a murky bog and never climb out. Sandy turned away from the sight of the green jumpsuit, and forced herself to focus on what she'd learned about Harlan.

He didn't want to hurt them. And he had a tendency to follow orders, including Sandy's. Maybe she could build up to a more important command.

She was just starting to chart a course in her head when something snagged her gaze.

Across the room, Ben was trying to stand up.

AUGUST 15, 1975

Barbara sat on the couch in her living room, staring at the sun coming through the blinds until her eyes watered.

After six o'clock in the evening, and the sun was still this high. The heat hadn't broken; it'd been weeks now. Barbara had sweated all day long, running after Nicholas, her face damp and armpits trickling. But she welcomed the temperature. The heat felt so toxic and punishing that it gave her cause to hope her body might rid itself of the contents it carried.

The call had come this afternoon, with Barbara listening into the earpiece, as stunned as if a dart had hit her. Although she'd known, hadn't she? Since that day they'd run out of juice.

She looked down at the album spread across her lap.

There weren't many photos in it, but she liked studying the few there were. The first ones especially, when her mother had still looked into the lens with a faint glow. Later, you could see the march of children and the years palpably on her face. Barbara was the oldest, and by the time her first sister had come along, lines were already being drawn. By the third, wings had been etched beside each of her mother's eyes, and her mouth was pulled in like a purse. After the fourth, Barbara's father had taken no pictures at all.

Barbara let the album cover fall shut. She glanced toward the dooryard, listening for the rumble of Gordon's truck; she cocked her ear toward the stairs, making sure all was quiet.

Nicholas had gone to sleep already, worn out by the exertions of the day, and also by a cold he was fighting off.

"Do you have a tickle in your throat?" Barbara had asked the little boy at lunch, while he was eating his third helping of ice cream. It was so hot out, surely a cold treat was in order. Plus, there was the need to put weight on the little boy. Barbara's own body was going to balloon, which would make Nicholas look all the skinnier. "Your voice sounds funny."

Nicholas glanced up, his mouth wreathed in pink.

"Give a little cough," Barbara had urged. "Let me listen." She'd put her ear to Nicholas' thin chest. It sounded perfectly clear, but just in case she'd administered a dollop of cough medicine before bedtime. "Come on," she'd coaxed. "Strawberry. Like the ice cream."

"No more pink," Nicholas had grumbled. "My tummy hurts."

But Barbara couldn't have Nicholas coming downstairs tonight for his usual multitude of trips, which protracted bedtime by an hour. He wanted water, he needed to use the potty, could he have another kiss? What mother would refuse her child a kiss? And yes, Nicholas had already gone potty, once, twice, three times. But how badly would Barbara feel if he wet the bed because she refused to let him try again? They had struggled with training; Nicholas used to soil the linens and his clothes, seeming to take a strange sort of glee in the activity, which Barbara was glad about on the whole. She wouldn't have wanted her child to feel ashamed.

Tonight, though, she needed Gordon alone, with her own attention undivided. The need was pressing enough that when Barbara saw a full-scale protest begin to boil in Nicholas, she leaned forward and pinched her son's adorable little nose between her fingers. Nicholas' eyes widened, and he wagged his head wildly back and forth, curls flying. Finally he went still. His mouth popped open, and Barbara poured the fruity stream down his throat. She let go of his nose as soon as he'd swallowed, giving the kitteny tip a stroke to wipe away any redness.

"See?" she said. "Wasn't that yummy? And now I bet you won't even come down with that cold at all."

She lay a sheet over Nicholas. It was so hot out that just the one layer dampened with the little boy's perspiration. She sat beside her son, looping her fingers through his dark hair to detangle it, and singing his favorites, one after another, softly, robotically, so that he wouldn't get up. Nicholas' gaze soon grew groggy and his lids fell as if weighted.

Barbara went downstairs to wait for Gordon.

She'd only been back to the market once since that dreadful visit two weeks ago, and so she had trouble finding in the sparse wares of the kitchen an evening appetizer to prepare for Gordon. She settled on squeezing lemons for lemonade. It was so hot out, a body couldn't think of eating much that was solid anyway. Barbara herself had hardly taken a bite in weeks.

The lemon juice ran down her fingers, stinging like a swarm of bees. She had torn her nails down to their beds. Her hands looked as ugly as her whole body soon would.

Earlier in the day, Nicholas had upended one of the living room chairs with a crash that shook the house. Barbara hardly noticed. Nicholas had torn a cushion, reaching in and scooping out handfuls of stuffing for snow, spattering his head and hers, while Barbara sat there and tried to imagine the future.

She wasn't stupid, and as old-fashioned as their life might seem to some, Barbara considered herself a modern woman. She had subscriptions not just to *Good House-keeping,* but also *Ladies Home Journal* and *Redbook,* and she took out books the librarian recommended, by female writers like Doris Lessing and even that horrible Erica Jong, although Barbara had returned that one before the due date. Barbara believed that women who wanted to should work, although she herself couldn't imagine spending that much time away from her son.

And she knew that far away, in the nation's

capital, a battle had been waged and won, or lost, depending on who you asked. But the effects of that war hadn't made their way to Cold Kettle, and Barbara couldn't see how they helped her. The idea of traveling with Nicholas to Albany — or worse, Manhattan — then actually undergoing such a procedure, was laughable. She might as well have planned a trip to the moon.

Plus, Gordon would never allow it. She wouldn't have to tell him, she supposed. But that still left the problem of Nicholas.

A stinging droplet of sweat entered her eyes, and Barbara licked away the film above her lip. Her sweet boy wasn't a problem. This new factor that had caused Barbara to judge him thus made her look down now, seized by an internal hatred so fiery, the temperature without felt chill.

The front door opened and Gordon stepped in.

"Whew," he said, pulling his shirt out of his waistband and using it to fan his belly. "Beastly out. You've kept it nice and cool in here."

"I didn't open the blinds all day," Barbara said, her mouth numb. She forced her hands, which had made their way into small, knotted fists, to uncurl.

Gordon set down his toolbox and sniffed

the air. "Dinner almost ready?"

Barbara's legs straightened and she stood up. It felt as if the movement were accomplished at someone else's behest. "How about some lemonade first?" Her voice came out smooth, lacking intonation.

Gordon went to settle down in his chair, then stopped with a frown. "What happened?"

Barbara spoke over her shoulder as she entered the kitchen. "Nicholas had a marvelous idea for a game. I'll sew the cushion tomorrow."

"Looks like more than a mending will be needed," Gordon said. "This is my favorite chair."

"Don't scold," Barbara called automatically. "Your son is creative, and that's important, especially for boys." She brought back a glass freckled with condensation and handed it to Gordon.

He took it, drank, then said, "Does creative have to mean destructive?"

Barbara stared at him. "Why don't you leave the care and keeping of Nicholas to me, and you can tend to whatever goes on at the shop?"

Gordon's features bunched and his grip tightened on the slick glass. Barbara took it out of his hand. "Go," she urged. "Sit in my

165

chair tonight."

After a moment, Gordon allowed her to scoot him in the right direction. "I guess I will," he said, a note of confusion in his voice. "You're sure doing something right, Barb. Only —" He glanced at his wrist. "— seven o'clock and you've gotten him to sleep already."

Barbara started to look up at the ceiling, but ducked her head so as not to jinx things. She didn't see how she could dose Nicholas again with her husband at home. He wasn't as observant a parent as she, and might not register the incipient signs of a summer cold. Those could be such a misery. Barbara sat down on the couch in front of Gordon.

He frowned again. "Shouldn't you be seeing to supper?"

"Gordon," Barbara said.

He leaned back, flattening his palms on his thighs. "It's hot, all right, but I've still got the appetite of a crocodile." He wrinkled his nose. "What's cooking?"

"Gordon," she said again.

He shook his head. "Can't really smell it yet. Maybe you need to turn the oven up? Or are we having one of your salads?"

"Gordon?"

He gave her a smile. "Never could see how a bowl of rabbit feed equals dinner, but I'm so hungry, I'll eat anything by this point —"

"Gordon!" Barbara shrieked, so loudly she was sure she'd break through Nicholas' medicine-induced haze, send the little boy running downstairs, and lose this last chance she had. "The doctor called today. We have —" The words were some kind of bracing fluid on her tongue, like lye or bleach. She spat them out disgustedly. "— another on the way."

Gordon's whole face went red. It was alarming in this heat. Her husband rose, he stumbled. "Darling," he said, crouching down before her. "That's why —" He broke off to nod. "You've been acting so strangely." He placed a hand on her stomach, then snatched it back, staring wonderingly at his palm as if it had touched God.

Barbara felt a tickle of nausea inside her. "We can't have this —" She stopped. "We can't have it, Gordon."

It took him a moment to respond, and when he finally did, it was with a smile. "Not much choice in the matter now, is there? But don't you worry. I'm making good money."

Barbara shook her head. She caught her husband's hand in hers, then dropped it as if it singed, this object that had touched her belly. "No," she said again. "I can't be a mother to two children. Nicholas — he's so smart, so energetic, he takes up all of my time. I can't give him what he needs if there's another —" Again she broke off. "— if I have to think about anyone else."

An expression that Barbara couldn't read crossed her husband's face. Just as quickly it was gone, and Gordon let out a chuckle.

"Don't be silly," he said. "You're a wonderful mother."

Barbara bowed her head. Was that perspiration or tears striking the floor? In a short time, all sorts of emissions would be coming from her body. Barbara used the pointed toe of her shoe to wipe the wood clean.

"This is good news," Gordon said, touching her again, although this time on her shoulder. His hand seemed to clench with a terrible, thieving grasp. "And anyway, it's a little late for second thoughts, isn't it?" Letting go, he gave a ringing clap of his hands, while Barbara cast an alarmed look up at the second floor.

"Now," Gordon went on, "I think I'm going to fix you a little supper for a change."

CHAPTER TEN

The entrance to the basement lay just outside the kitchen. Ivy might get a chance to catch a glimpse of her mother — or the man.

She looked down at Mac. *Quiet,* she mouthed.

The dog aimed his snout at the floor in what looked like a nod.

Ivy felt a charge inside her. They could do this. They *were* doing this. She walked forward, Mac beside her.

As she drew close to the kitchen, Ivy heard a sound so familiar she nearly dropped all attempt at concealment and rushed into the room. It was the murmur of her mother's voice, low and understanding. When Ivy had to hang out at the hospital, waiting outside her mother's office for a ride, this was the voice that drifted through the door. She couldn't hear specific words, of course, just the low cadence of comfort. It was the same tone her mother had used when Ivy was little, a lullaby of long ago.

Mac's body trembled, giving off a doggie scent. Then he began walking, not exactly toward the basement, but definitely away from where Ivy had been headed, lured by the sound of her mother's voice. Ivy should be smart enough to recognize when her dog was leading her. She squared her shoulders, turned, and followed.

Ivy kept her back to the living and dining area walls so that she wouldn't be visible to anybody in the kitchen. They were going to have to slip through the basement door, though, and during that moment, either her mother or the big guy might see them. Ivy would just have to hope for a little bit of luck.

As the flight of stairs came into view — these just normal compared to the ones that led to the second floor — Ivy saw that she and Mac had indeed gotten lucky. A light was on, so their way downstairs would be illuminated. She set her foot on the first step as quietly as she could, then descended two more quickly. Mac hesitated for a fraction of a second, but Ivy knew there was no real debate. She could've been walking into a snake pit and Mackie would've followed, rather than stay up there without her.

The basement was enormous. It ran underneath the whole house, although the space was mostly empty. It consisted of smooth, gray concrete walls and floors, with hidden systems here and there that resembled the cockpit of an airplane or something, and which only her dad knew how to use. Plus thin, looping pipes — those were the radiant heating — air transfer somethings because the house was way well sealed, propane tanks, and a hot water heater that never ran out no matter how long Ivy showered.

In a far off corner, their mountain bikes and her dad's kayak were stored. Ivy caught a glimpse of shadowed frames, the dolphin hump of the overturned boat, and blinked. Her hand reached down to stroke Mac. They used to explore trails in a blotchy, uneven line, the four of them. Her dad ahead, her mom keeping pace with Ivy, and Mac running back and forth between. They didn't do things like that anymore; her dad took clients out instead. How long had it been?

Taking a trip down memory lane, Darcy scoffed. *When you're supposed to be escaping.*

Ivy's hand left Mac to begin rooting around in her pocket. She pulled the keys out, not taking care to stifle their jingle. If nothing could be heard from room to room upstairs, down here was like a full-fledged bunker or something. Her dad joked that if the apocalypse came, they would be able to ride it out quite nicely in the basement.

Ivy set off across the football field–sized floor, Mac's claws ticking beside her. She walked at her usual pace, confident and brisk, and it felt good. It had been hard to creep around upstairs, trying to be quiet.

There was a gift-wrapping station down here, a long, broad table and shelves filled with rolls of colorful paper. Ribbon too, in the sheerest, prettiest gold. Her mom was gearing up for Christmas, and the thought gave Ivy a pang, then made her lift her chin.

She and Mac passed a stack of bins that contained old clothes, toys Ivy used to play with, and picture books. She should look through these things. Not now, of course, although the doll-sized outfits did beckon. Neatly folded, laid flat, with no person inside to give them form and life. As soon as this was over — whatever *this* was — Ivy was going to make a point of coming down here. Read the books. Ask her mom to tell her which dresses Ivy had worn to what.

She walked past two barrels where her dad was aging some kind of nasty liquor even the most daring of her friends probably wouldn't touch, then caught a glimpse of the outside door. Cold air breathed from around its frame.

Ivy paused a moment to picture their route. This exit led out to the side of the property: fields, then the creek, woods that climbed a mountainside. The circular driveway in front of their house wouldn't take long to reach at a run. If both cars were here, and her mom's happened to be behind her dad's, Ivy would have to pull around the Jeep since she didn't think she could handle reverse very well. The long road down would be a breeze, though, she promised herself and also Mac, whose tongue lolled as he brushed up against her. They would stop at the icky Nelsons' first. Maybe their phone would work. Or else the Nelsons could come up here and help.

Help how? a small voice inside her asked, but she ignored it just like she tried to do with Darcy. Ivy needed to get some grown-ups involved. Then everything would be all right.

She tugged at Mac and they crossed the remaining space to the door.

Mac started to whimper.

The sound was startling in the huge space. Aside from the white noise of the systems down here, it was totally quiet. Even though she knew Mac couldn't be heard back upstairs, a rush of chemicals coursed through Ivy's body, making her heart leap and her limbs feel shaky.

Plus, Mac was still doing it.

"Shh," Ivy begged, but Mac only yelped louder.

Ivy placed her hand on the exterior doorknob. It was freezing cold, and she could just imagine what it was going to feel like outside. She looked down at her dog.

Maybe he didn't want to leave her parents alone. Her mom anyway; her dad must've gone out somewhere. That was the only explanation for his ongoing absence. And then a man had come, and was doing who-knew-what to her mom. Except her mom was talking, using her therapy voice, so things had to be basically okay, didn't they?

She got down beside Mac. "It's all right. We're just going to go and get some help."

Mac buried his snout in her shirt, the fabric going sheer beneath his nose and tongue. Ivy gave his head a pat, then twisted the doorknob and stepped outdoors into the frigid air.

Mac lingered behind in the heated confines of the house.

Ivy started in surprise. "Really, Mackie?

You're going to stay there without me?"

It was darker out here than she'd pictured; the sky moonless and starless. The first of the motion sensitive lights hadn't come on yet. Ivy actually found herself glad for once that her dog had his phobia. Even though Mac wasn't much of a protector, she wouldn't have wanted to go any farther without him.

Mac seemed to come to his senses then, taking two loping steps to catch up.

Ivy scrubbed his head again. "Don't get me wrong," she said as they began to walk. The driveway lay some distance to the right. "I would've been very proud of you if you'd decided to stay by yourself. It would've been so" — she had to hunt for the word — "*evolved.* But I love you, Mackie, don't you know that?" Another pat, though her fingers felt stiff and numb as she delivered it. She was starting to shiver, tremors that slowed her down. "Just the way you are."

Now that they were outside, whatever she'd left behind in the house didn't seem quite real. It was more like she'd imagined there being a problem. Except that Mac was still whining. He hadn't let up since they'd crossed over the basement threshold. Other than that, Ivy might've simply been going over to Melissa's, just like any other night.

Without your coat in November? Darcy's voice jabbed her, and then the enveloping darkness assailed her, too. Where were those lights? It was so quiet out here, a pressing, crushing silence. Ivy broke into a run that felt a little flailing, almost panic-stricken. She yanked on Mackie's collar, and he started to trot.

It was hard to make out shapes in the dark, but she thought that was her mom's car, in front of the Jeep. At first Ivy felt only relief: she wasn't going to have to reverse. But then it hit her. Her dad's car was here. There were definitely two hulking shapes, including the higher outline of the Jeep. Her dad hadn't gone out. So why was he leaving her mother alone to talk to that horrible man?

And why weren't the damn motion sensitive lights her dad was so proud of coming on? In addition to feeling assaulted by the cold, Ivy realized that her nerves were absolutely frizzled, contributing to the shakes that now had hold of her body.

Not to mention the fact that Mac was still whining, high in his throat, which was starting to bug Ivy.

"Shh," she hissed. The admonishing pat she gave him was clumsy, even a bit rough. The car keys bit into her hand, so hard was she clenching them.

The first of the lights flared on — *finally* — just as Mac's whines exploded to a completely unfamiliar lone bark.

Ivy came to an abrupt halt, brought up short by her dog before her feet registered the danger, and dug into the earth.

Illuminated in the center of the bright cone of light was the utterly still figure of a second man.

The sky pressed down, a suffocating layer of gray.

The man faced her, blocking Ivy's path to both cars.

She gave several rapid blinks of her eyes, trying to adjust her vision to the sudden onslaught of light.

The man's coat was unzipped and he wore the weirdest green outfit underneath. Other than that, he was actually kind of good-looking, in a bad boy sort of way. Old, though, like at least forty. His hair was buzzed, and he had some tats that started at his throat and traveled down beneath the collar of his shirt. He looked muscular, like he worked out a lot. Way too strong for Ivy to be alone with out here.

She had her dog. She wasn't alone.

Mac had already let out a loud *woof.* Only

one, but Ivy hadn't known her dog was capable of making such a sound. Now he seemed back to his old self though, shrinking against Ivy, black lips pulled over the pointed tips of his teeth.

"Keep a grip on your dog," the man said flatly, "or I'll shoot him."

Mac's throat trembled with a dying rumble beneath Ivy's hand.

Ivy's fingers dug into his fur; they hooked around his collar. But when her voice came out, it sounded surprisingly normal. Or not normal for her actually — more like Darcy's perpetual jeer. "Mac? He's not going to hurt a fly. Can't you tell that?"

The man lifted a gun almost lazily, and Ivy took an instant, twisted step back. She'd never had a gun held on her before. *Shocking,* Darcy intoned. *Most kids have by this age.* It looked just like in the movies.

"You might as well learn now that there's no place for you to go," the man said. "Don't try something like this again. If you do, I'll get there before you. Every single time."

How long had the man been standing here, just waiting for Ivy to make a run for one of the cars? Couldn't be too long; he didn't look cold. He must've been watching her the whole time she was walking through the basement, and slipped out just before she did.

Ivy's skin, already raised and warty, broke into a million stinging bumps.

"Who — are you?" she asked stupidly.

Stupid because it was a dumb thing to do, just ask the bad guy for his name.

There were two of them, she realized. The big dude plus this guy.

Ding, ding, ding, Darcy said inside her head.

And stupid also because she knew who he was. Sort of.

He looked like an older celebrity or something, like the guy who played James Bond in the movies. Super buff. Maybe he was part of some hipster band her parents listened to? Somebody recognizable anyway. He could almost have been someone's hottie dad, the kind that made you a little bit psyched when you had to babysit his kid. Like Emily Randall's husband. One way or another, this guy looked familiar. The only weird part — totally out there strange actually — was that he was at her house.

The man thrust the gun in her direction. "Back inside."

Ivy hesitated. If she made a run for the car, he would outpace her, especially given Ivy's unfamiliarity with driving. It would take a little while for her to start the engine and get going. Unless Mac interfered, let out another uncharacteristic bark, maybe even worse than that. But Ivy couldn't count on such a thing from her pet, and anyway, what if the man really was willing to shoot Mac? She couldn't imagine anybody hurting an animal, but Mackie's early life proved there were people who would.

The man took a menacing step in her direction, gesturing for Ivy to go ahead.

Better to wait, see what he wanted, look for a less risky way out.

Silently in the dark, Ivy stuffed the keys back into the pocket of her jeans.

CHAPTER ELEVEN

The lights in the basement came on when they reentered, bulbs embedded in the ceiling. With just a few of them shining, weird shadows were cast: great wings flung out across the walls. Ivy felt dumb — Darcy would definitely say that she was — because she hadn't thought to wonder why the lights had been on when she and Mac first came down from upstairs.

The man had set them off. He'd been here, following their progress toward the door.

Ivy went on thinking, so hard that it hurt.

Then he'd gone outside to hide in the dark, await her arrival with Mac. Without even getting a chance to zip up his coat first. But if he'd wanted to hurt Ivy, he could've just grabbed her in here. It was like he was trying to prove a point by getting to the cars before they did, demonstrate who was in charge. Which maybe meant that he didn't intend to hurt them.

He hadn't laid a hand on Ivy so far.

She was still shivering, way too under-dressed for the temperature, but her heart started to chug a little less violently.

Against a near wall stood the junction box, its door hanging open. Her dad called this his command station, and it did look like something out of a dystopian movie, all blue lights and sheathed wires. Only not right now. The box was half-darkened, and wires poked out stiffly at odd angles, like miniature elephant trunks.

Which, Ivy supposed, explained the Wi-Fi.

She gulped around a clump of something in her throat. She felt as if the controls had died while she was on a chairlift. Here she and Mac and her mom and dad were, dangling in midair, cut off from everyone and everything.

Ivy hunched over, aware of the man's presence behind her as she and Mac walked across the vast space. She pulled her dog close, wanting the feel of his warm flank against her leg.

Her dad's other gun, a rifle, had been taken out of the safe and was lying on the floor. A whole bunch of stuff was arranged there. Ivy took everything in with a confused blur. A rough, thready webbing of rope; then a brighter coil, which her dad used for climbing, along with their carabineers; a roll of silver tape, dirt encrusting its sticky sides; a knotted chain; gleaming metal tools with hooked heads and jagged edges like fangs.

Mac let out a series of high, hysterical yips.

"You're going to lock up that dog," the man said. He pointed to a room where Ivy's dad kept bottles of wine.

Ivy began to shake her head. "No," she said. "You don't understand. I can't. He can't —"

"Doesn't matter if I understand," the guy said, hard and fast.

He looked a lot less attractive now, illuminated by the light inside. His buzz was too short, probably camouflaging gray, and his tat wasn't cool or artistic, just kind of dark and blotchy. He wasn't anybody famous. Who did he look like, then?

"Please," Ivy said, a totally alien warble in her voice. "Mac's a rescue dog. He was traumatized — we don't know how exactly — but anyway, he wouldn't hurt a bug on the ground."

Mac rubbed against her, as if corroborating the point.

"Please," Ivy said again, detesting the strange croak in her voice. "He's not any

183

kind of watch dog."

"Save your sob story, or your dog's going to die." The guy twirled the gun so it wound up pointing in Mac's direction. "Do *you* understand?"

Ivy looked down at Mac. She nodded.

"Good," the man said. "Then do what I said."

Ivy began walking Mac toward the wine cellar. She turned back once, picturing letting Mac go, the leap he might make for the guy's throat. But more likely was that he wouldn't know how to do it, or be able to even if he did.

The gun stayed aimed at Mac's head. More effective than if it had been pointed at Ivy's.

They reached the little room and Ivy twisted the knob.

Mac stopped walking. He became a lean, pointed dart of pure muscle, unwilling to be budged.

Ivy bent down and wreathed her dog's neck with her arms. "I know, Mackie." She was crying, stinging pellets on her cheeks. "I know." She caressed the soft fur on his legs. How much bonier those legs felt since the days when she used to pet them all the time. "But please go, Mac. Please. You'll be safer this way."

Mac started that high yipping again.

"Mac," Ivy said, sniffing in a long, rattling chain. "I'll come back for you. I promise —"

When the safety came off, it made a noise like a detonation. Ivy ducked, expecting everything around her to explode.

She turned, and saw the man curl his finger around the trigger.

"Please," Ivy said in a calm, level tone. She knew Mac wasn't fooled, could smell the fear inside her. But maybe he also scented the sense of her words. "It's just a little while in a nice, quiet room. I'll turn on the light." Her dad hardly ever used it, just ducked inside to grab the bottle he wanted. Ivy found the switch and flicked it. "And I'll come back. Just like I said."

She went on, varying the repeated re-assurances, stringing them together like beads. She didn't hurry, even though she had no clue what might be going on behind her, where that gun was trained and when the guy might fire it.

The slow drum of her words finally took effect, and Mac began to move. Backing up, he entered the room, holding Ivy's gaze.

"Good boy," she said in the same voice.

It sounded like the one that came out of her mother's mouth. Ivy listened to its echo and despite everything going on around her, a distant memory came into her head. Two winters ago, her jacket had gotten soaked when she'd gone sledding. Ivy had forgotten to put it in the dryer and when it came time to leave for school the next day, her mother went and found one of her own coats instead of scolding Ivy about *responsibilities* and how could she be so *forgetful.* Ivy had expected the coat to billow, for her arms to be lost in its sleeves, but when she slipped it on, it almost fit. When she got compliments during the day, she'd replied casually, "Thanks, it's my mom's," and the words had felt natural, too.

At a certain point that connection had been lost, like a dropped call. Lately, the last thing Ivy had wanted was to be like her mom.

Mac turned in a slow circle, then lay down on the floor and wound his tail around him.

He looked at Ivy, and she expected the room to be shook by another volley of yelps, for the wine bottles to shatter from Mac's high weeping, which she knew she had heard even if everyone said that dogs couldn't cry.

But Mac only closed his eyes, and Ivy was able to shut the door.

It had just latched when the man came up

from behind and grabbed her around the waist.

He tilted her backward until Ivy's feet left the floor. His arm felt like an iron band.

Ivy wrenched and twisted the top half of her body, one hand clawing at his face.

The man grunted, reaching for Ivy's arms, and succeeding in clamping one of them. But the man had use of only one hand — he was holding on to something with the other — and so Ivy was able to keep her left arm free. She used it like a lever, throwing it upwards and making contact again with the man's face.

He roared at a volume that in any other house would've carried, brought Ivy's parents dashing downstairs to see what was the matter. Tears of sheer, hopeless rage blistered in Ivy's eyes. In any other house, at any other time, her parents would've come running.

She kept pinwheeling her arm around, hitting the man, hitting herself, until the man hurled whatever he'd been holding. It spun through the air, coming to a stop when its snub metal end hit the cement wall. A volcano of dust erupted, then the object dropped. A hammer.

The man had both arms available now,

and he used them to try and wrestle Ivy still, but Ivy kept fighting. He almost had her, though. She was no match for those humps of muscle, which ground against her with lethal force. But just at the moment that Ivy was about to wilt in his hold, the man let out an enraged shout, and threw her down onto the concrete floor.

Ivy landed with a *thud* that jarred her, kept her from getting to her feet. All she could manage was her knees, which ached, every part of her now ached, and tears began to fall as she tried to crawl.

She tore a look back over her shoulder — oh, how it hurt her neck to do that; Ivy felt like an eighty-year-old woman — as she lurched forward.

The man reached for her, and now he appeared totally different. No longer a hot older guy; in fact, hardly a man at all. More like one of the boys in Ivy's school when they lost a game, or even one of the kids she babysat for, red hot and tantruming over something they'd smashed.

Ivy began scrambling faster, and the man grabbed her leg, pulling her backward.

She screamed, loud and long.

He dragged her like a sack behind him, headed in the direction of that awful array of items, rifle and rope and tape and tools.

Lengths of wood, too; Ivy saw two-by-fours her dad had never gotten around to using. Ivy kept screaming the whole way, until finally the man whipped his body around, maintaining his hold on her leg so that it twisted at a pain-splitting angle. He dropped her just before the bone would've cracked, but Ivy's sudden freedom meant nothing. Her leg throbbed so badly, it might as well have been broken. She couldn't scream anymore; she could hardly even whimper.

The man lunged toward the pile on the floor. Then he came for Ivy.

Chapter Twelve

Not a second passed between the moment Sandy registered the bud of Ben's recovery and the time when her gaze shot back to Harlan, to her lap, anywhere but the other side of the room. It was as instantaneous as fire igniting. She had to keep Harlan distracted so that Ben would be able to take him from behind. If he acted quickly, her husband would have the advantage of surprise this time. Or would it be better for him to simply run out of the house, go and get help?

Ben would never run.

It occurred to Sandy that it was taking an awfully long time for Harlan's companion to return from the basement, and just as swiftly followed an explanation as to why.

Maybe he'd found Ivy.

Sandy suppressed the idea before it could take hold of her. Time got distorted during crises, slowed and pulled like rubber cement, or hastened to the speed of a lightning strike. It was possible that far less had passed than it seemed.

More than likely, Ivy was still upstairs, blithely texting away and hanging out online. Her daughter could spend an entire night this way, even if she hadn't been trying to prove a point by not joining her parents for dinner.

Sandy took another look at Ben.

Her husband wasn't going to be able to act fast.

He had risen to his feet, but barely, bracing the overturned chair with both hands for assistance. His legs wobbled as he tried to take a step toward Harlan.

A megaphone seemed to magnify each noise Ben made as he stumbled, although Harlan appeared ignorant, focused on whatever Sandy had unleashed inside him during their talk.

She had to keep him occupied, give Ben time to recover. Sandy opened her mouth, and the question that came out had been rising inside her ever since Harlan took off his coat.

"Why did you get sent to prison?" she whispered. Making Harlan lean down, get closer to her.

"Armed robbery," he said. No pause, as if

191

a question required a response whether Harlan liked it or not. "I'm a bandit," he added with a slower bloom of pride.

Sandy nodded, hardly hearing. Ben was walking on his own now, but wavering, as if someone were tugging at him. His vision looked unfocused; a starfish of red floated in one eye.

Sandy clutched at something else to say. "How much time did you serve?"

Harlan's features bunched. "Enough with the questions."

Ben took another step before his knees buckled and he went down. His flattened hands hit the floor, which at least spared his head.

Harlan began to turn around, his body moving slowly, like the barrel of a cement mixer, and Sandy lashed out for something, anything that would summon him back.

"Sorry. Stupid question," she said.

Harlan gave her a nod, then began to frown.

"I mean, you escaped," Sandy offered casually. "So what does it matter what your sentence was supposed to be?"

Harlan bent down, and Sandy got a whiff of the threat he could apply without even intending to. His torso was so big, it overtook her own. Harlan could cut off air, constrict her like a python, just by leaning in too close.

Ben got back to his feet. He pressed both temples so hard that it looked as if his fingertips would penetrate his skull. Then he gave a hard shake of his head, wincing with pain.

"It's okay," Sandy said wildly, speaking as much to her husband as to Harlan. "I don't care if you escaped. I'm not going to tell anyone."

Mollified, Harlan straightened.

Sandy slid her chair forward, trying to shift Harlan within reach of Ben. Harlan took a step back when the wooden seat touched his shins, and Sandy went on, gathering words that were sure to please, the reflecting phase of therapy where you didn't challenge a thing. "Sounds like you were right to escape. I mean, robbery isn't such a bad crime."

"That's what my daddy says," Harlan replied.

It took Sandy a moment to parse that. "Is your father a rob— a bandit, too?"

Harlan's fists began to knot, great coils of roped fingers. "How do you know so much?"

"I just like to talk to you," Sandy said. Another few inches with the chair, another few steps backwards on Harlan's part. "You're interesting to talk to."

No longer any kind of therapy; this was sheer, blunt flattery.

"Me?" Harlan said.

Despite everything, Sandy felt a bolt of sorrow at how completely he seemed to doubt it.

Ben took a look around the kitchen, flinching with pain as his neck and shoulders swiveled. Ben had been knocked out for the part where Harlan had rid the room of anything remotely resembling a weapon. Now he bent down, as slowly as an old man, and tried to hoist the only object left, one of the chairs.

"Yes!" Sandy said, though she was no longer sure what she was responding to. The cry was both an answer to Harlan and a cheer for Ben.

She scooted her chair a final few inches forward. Harlan stepped back, clumsy but unresisting, as if getting moved around was the condition of his life.

The chair leg pitched forward in Ben's trembling grasp. It was going to drop, alerting Harlan, surely, maybe even reverberating all the way down to the basement.

An idea slammed into Sandy.

Harlan followed instructions. Yet there was

one he had failed to heed.

"You were supposed to decide," she said, in a tone of command.

Harlan's gaze traveled a long way down. "What?"

"You were supposed to decide what to do about my lying," she said. "Remember? That's what your —" She broke off, swallowed. "— friend said before he left."

With quivering arms, Ben lifted the chair into the air. Not high enough. It would splinter against the massive wall of Harlan's back. Ben needed to go for the soft spot just below Harlan's skull. But any blow would be better than none, at least catch Harlan off guard.

Her husband's biceps shook as he sought altitude.

"You'd better do it now!" Sandy shouted, the message applying to both men.

Harlan gazed down at her, unaware of the missile level with his shoulders.

Sandy could see her husband's chest heaving. His vision still appeared cloudy and unfocused, but luckily his target was huge, not requiring precision.

"I did decide," Harlan said. His mouth lifted in a rusty smile.

Ben gained a final margin of height.

The movement of his body changed subtly

though detectably then, at least to Sandy, who sat forward in her own chair, clenching its lifeless wooden sides.

"Don't make me change my mind," Harlan added, but his words sounded listless. Harlan appeared to be somewhere far away, carried there on the wings of what had transpired between him and Sandy, a brute misuse of her training.

Ben started to bring the chair down. Arms still wobbly, shaking, but gaining strength as gravity aided his swing.

At the moment Ben began to attack, the flinty-eyed guy entered the kitchen. His timing was pinprick accurate, as if he had been standing nearby for a while, allowing Ben to struggle, and for Sandy's hopes to rise. One hand was twisted behind his back, its contents concealed by the pantry door. The other swung the butt of the gun in a high, arcing trajectory through the air, knocking the chair out of Ben's hands, and breaking a bone in his wrist with a firecracker snap.

Ben appeared to consider his useless right arm for less than a second, a field examination when the conditions that had led to the injury continued to pose a threat. Then he wheeled around, lingering unsteadiness gone, and slammed his fist into the other man's firing hand before the man was able to pirouette the gun into position.

The gun flew across the room, landing with a metal *thwack.*

The man had been slowed because he was still one-armed, keeping hold of something at an odd angle, by the pantry. Sandy made out a slash of red across his cheek. He'd gotten cut.

Harlan would be distracted now, awaiting his orders.

Sandy assimilated all of this in the cluster of seconds it took for her to stand up. It felt as if she'd spent her whole life yoked to that chair. Freedom beckoned, but like any longtime prisoner, she was at first unable to conceive what to do with it.

The gun. She had to get the gun.

She raced forward, but skidded to a halt when she heard a second crash. She tore a look over her shoulder.

Ben had gone down, stumbling as he aimed for one of the wooden daggers on the floor, pieces of the broken chair. He got up, right arm hanging by his side while the other wielded the makeshift weapon. Ben lashed out with the piece of wood just as the tattooed man yanked hard and brought out what he'd kept hidden.

Sandy whipped around, fast as the strike

of a snake, all thoughts of the gun instantly expunged from her mind.

"Ben! Stop!" A paralyzing shriek, sufficient to freeze everyone in the room.

But Ben had a plan to pursue, and the enemy in sight. In the wake of Sandy's cry, he lifted the spike of wood and drove it forward.

There came a ferocious shout — "Take her!" — and the call to action animated Harlan.

Then the man with the deadened eyes spun around, and Ben tripped as his spear met air instead of a body. The wood left his weakened grasp like a bar in a relay race, winding up in the other man's stronghold.

Sandy scarcely registered the smooth exchange because her gaze was pinned to Harlan, who had reached down to pick up Ivy as if he were plucking a weed out of the ground.

CHAPTER THIRTEEN

Her daughter let out a yelp, muffled by a slash of silver duct tape, and Sandy blinked away the afterimage of the gun lying on the floor across the room. Too late to try and get it now; Sandy needed to concentrate on her child. Ivy had twisted to get a look at the enormous man holding her aloft. Harlan frowned upon seeing the tape. With the fingers of his free hand, he nudged the tape loose, pulling it off as gently as if he were peeling a slice of fruit.

Sandy felt a pulse of bitter, throbbing regret. Ivy never should have had to face this. If there was one thing Sandy would've wanted for her daughter, it was to preserve her from this.

What kind of denial had she been in to imagine Ivy tucked away in her room this whole time? Sandy helped her patients dismantle walls in therapy every day, yet she herself had bricks enough to fortify a whole city. How stupid was she, picturing Ivy upstairs, doing what? Playing with dolls? While her parents were taken prisoner below. Did Sandy even know her own daughter anymore? Ivy would never be so out-of-it, so unknowing. Ben, yes. Sandy herself maybe. But not Ivy.

A sob crawled up Sandy's throat as her gaze roved over Ivy's dangling form. Sandy knew every inch of her daughter. Had watched her go from a round nugget of baby to a teetering toddler; grow from a coltish, overlong little girl into a lithesome teenager. She'd noticed the changes, seen them coming before anyone else — before Ivy herself did.

And so she saw what was different about Ivy, what hadn't been there when her daughter flopped down on her bed earlier that night. There were red streaks on Ivy's fingertips, muddy half-moons beneath her nails.

Sandy's gaze traveled to the cut on the other man's face.

Ivy had fought.

It explained the strange way her daughter held herself as she hung from Harlan's hand. Cradling one arm, keeping her legs from swinging. She looked stiff, as if she'd taken too challenging a yoga class, or gone

200

on too long a run. Or as if someone had hurt her.

Sandy felt a searing, sucking pain in her chest. A heart attack, an attack on the heart.

Ben stood nearby. She saw him looking at the floor, scouring it for new shears of wood. And mixed with love and admiration for her husband's strength came a poisonous rinse of rage. Sandy had always counted on Ben to guide and steer things, allowed him to at least, but now those traits were putting them all in danger. The loss of her reliance on him was as vast a shift as any she'd had to make since the intruders had entered her house.

"Ben!" Sandy screamed. "Stop! Don't you see?"

The cry had a cruelty to it because Sandy realized that Ben really might not be able to make sense of this situation. He was acting on instinct — fight not flight was Ben's way — but that sparkler of red persisted in his eye.

Now he executed a wobbling turn, and Sandy pointed to Ivy.

Ivy went still, her legs dangling eight inches above the floor. Harlan held her by the scruff of her shirt like a kitten.

Ben's good hand rolled into a fist again, and Sandy suppressed a shriek. But Ben just stood there, blinking up at Ivy, as dazed and disbelieving as Sandy.

The other man had been eyeing them both. Now he bent to shove the gun into his sock, and crossed the room in a few swift strides. Something seemed to make him flinch; he looked down at his foot. Then he swept up the pieces of chair with a clatter. Using the sole of his left shoe, he broke the wood into shorter lengths, one dry, bone-cracking split after another. The stove let out a baked gust of breath, greedily gobbling the fresh fuel as the man fed it.

Sandy watched the blue-green flames shoot out, reaching for the air beyond the door.

Ben readopted his defiant stance, thighs slightly bent, good arm raised, panting as he confronted Harlan.

"Ben," Sandy pleaded. "Stop. Just stop fighting and see what they want." They had to want something, right? Harlan had said they planned to leave soon.

The other man kicked the stove door shut with a *thud.* "I would listen to the lady," he drawled. "She sounds pretty smart." He made no move for the gun he had stashed. He didn't consider Ben a threat, or perhaps he simply knew that Harlan could handle any threat.

"If I tell Harlan to dislocate one of your daughter's arms, he will do it," the man went on, in a voice flat as an untouched sea. Numbingly cold, depthless, devoid of any emotion. "If I tell him to dislocate the other one just to make it match, Harlan will do that, too. If I instruct him to break your daughter's neck . . ." The man stooped for a final shard of wood, snapping it in half to demonstrate. ". . . no problem. Are you getting the pattern here?"

Any lingering trace of defiance left Ivy's face, and her body went rigid in Harlan's grasp.

Sandy reached in her direction. "No, honey, it's okay —" Laughable words, ridiculous, to tell her daughter all was well while she dangled from King Kong's fist.

"Ah-ah." The other man held up a hand. "I'd really prefer that everyone stay right where they are until we get things straight between us."

Sandy stopped. Better to be still anyhow. So that she could hear, and figure out what needed to be done to save her family.

"Listen," the man went on brightly. "This is a good-news/bad-news kind of thing. If I don't tell Harlan to act, he won't. And that means that your precious princess should be all right, so long as the two of you cooperate."

Ben turned slightly, settling narrowed eyes on the man.

"Would you like a demonstration?" the man asked.

Sandy instantly swung back around. "What?" she said, an awful whisper, alive and frantic. "No, please —"

"Harlan," the man said. "Let go of her."

Harlan's huge hand opened, and Ivy tumbled from his grasp.

As soon as she was on the floor, Ivy scooted backward as far as she could go. Her back banged against the kitchen wall, and Ivy hunched over, trying to catch her breath. She gingerly felt for her shoulder, then her leg. A small whimper left her mouth.

The tattooed man looked down at her. "Quit complaining."

Sandy needed his eyes off her daughter. "What is it that you want from us?"

He turned in her direction. "Too bad you didn't ask that an hour ago. Then maybe all of this —" He wafted an arm out over Ivy on the floor, Ben's pain-bent form, and the destruction of the kitchen. "— could've been avoided."

"What do you want?" Sandy repeated, enunciating each word.

The man pointed to Ivy on the floor. "Make sure she stays there, Harlan."

Harlan got down beside Ivy, carefully lowering his big body. Still, the room trembled when he sat, and Ivy curled into a smaller ball. She was moving more ably already. The resiliency of youth. But Sandy knew that things had happened tonight from which her daughter wouldn't rebound so readily.

Sandy could at least cap it at this. She clenched her hands, awaiting the man's response.

He regarded her. "Well," he said, the same empty brightness in his tone. "You've probably already figured out that we — Harlan and me, that is — have got ourselves a bit of a situation. Kind that says we can't stay around too long."

Sandy glanced at Harlan. Seated on the floor, his eyes met hers straight on. His cheeks looked swollen and flushed; he didn't like this topic.

"So we came here for some help," the other man went on. "Equipment. A little route-planning. Due north should do it."

So Sandy needn't have bothered pretending she didn't know the combination to the safe. Ben had the knowledge these men required to complete their escape. Sandy's family might have gotten out of this without a scratch if only Ben had been less of a combatant.

The realization was a slug to the chest.

She lifted her chin, emboldened by the role her husband was to play. "I need to treat his arm before anything else," she said. "Splint it, I guess. He's in a lot of pain."

The man widened his eyes. "You some kind of nurse?" he said in a tone that told her he knew exactly what she was, and wasn't.

"I work in a hospital," Sandy replied curtly. "I'll figure it out."

"Eyes," Ben said, the *s* drawn out into a leaf's autumn rasp.

"Eyes?" Sandy echoed. "Honey, what do you mean?" She struggled to make sense of the word.

Not *eyes*. *Ice*. A bandage or splint wouldn't do much for Ben's fractured wrist, but the plum-sized swelling on his forehead, visible even through his hair? That had to be brought down fast, especially if Ben was to give these men what they needed, and make them go away.

"Ice," she told the other man, walking toward the freezer. He followed her, but even if he hadn't been standing right there, Sandy didn't bother to consider the clump of cubes in a towel as a potential weapon. The time for fighting was over. They never should've fought at all.

She walked back, applying the ice light as a whisper to the rising hump on Ben's brow.

Her husband didn't wince.

"Honey," Sandy said, "tell me what they need so I can go get it. I'll pack everything up, and then they can be on their way."

The man studying her gave a single nod.

Sandy switched her gaze to Ivy, still on the floor, Harlan a living, breathing mountain beside her. *Just a few more minutes, honey,* Sandy said, a silent message she hoped her daughter would pick up on. They used to communicate so seamlessly, the two of them, with smiles and raised eyebrows and head shakes. Words were all but superfluous. *Then they'll be gone and we can put all this behind us.*

Ben held his head perfectly still beneath the bundle of ice. Every now and then his eyes would close, more slowly than the usual reflexive blink, and a wash of tears would spill out.

Sandy suppressed a swell of nausea. She may not have worked on the medical side of the hospital, but still she knew Ben needed an ambulance. Now.

Her husband rallied, though, replacing

Sandy's hand with his own on the ice-filled cloth, and gingerly readjusting it to a spot on the back of his head. "Is she right?"

Ben didn't seem aware of how his words slurred — he'd dropped the last *t* in *right* — but the other man had no problem comprehending him.

"You give us the gear we need, map out a nice little route that will get us across the border," he said, shrugging. "That's all I want. Get us on our way and we'll be out of your hair. Out of this pretty house." He swung an arm around as if the place were his. "And you never hear from us again."

The man went over to the steps that led to the basement, bits of grit and shards of wood popping beneath his shoes. He squatted to pick up a bulbous roll of duct tape he'd brought from downstairs. "Harlan," the man said. "Tear this for me."

Sandy didn't even register the order Harlan had been given. As soon as he stood up, abandoning his post by Ivy, Sandy raced forward. She wrapped her daughter in her arms, Ivy's slight form quivering, her shirt scant wisps around her. Sandy buried her face in her daughter's hair, breathing in its elixir and letting the tangle of silky strands block out sight.

Harlan's voice was a rumble across the

room. "What next, Nick?"

Something began to break apart inside Sandy. Bricks crumbling red hot; she was choking on their dust. She let go of Ivy without feeling her daughter leave her grasp. The two men were occupied now, but Sandy felt drained, rid of all thought and action, as if a plug had been removed. Could she manage to drag Ivy out without attracting attention? Sandy's thoughts seized then, and her mind could move no more. It was a screw finally wound too tight, a lid impossible to turn.

The man — Nick — kicked Ben's ankles into place. Again, that passing wince, a certain constriction in his jaw. He dug the bottle of Advil out of his pocket, uncapping it and swallowing a few pills while Harlan tore piece after piece of duct tape, as steadily as a machine.

Nick pulled three strips off the bulb of Harlan's thumb, then yanked Ben's arms behind his back. He mummified Ben's wrists before setting to work on his ankles, bonding them while keeping Ben upright on the floor like a mannequin.

Nick ducked to test the seal around all four limbs.

"All righty," he said. "Let's get to work."

CHAPTER FOURTEEN

Ivy didn't look up at first because she didn't want to see what they were doing to her father. When she finally did lift her head, it turned out to be even worse than she'd feared. Her big, strong dad, who mounted summits and raked whitewater with a paddle, taped up like some kind of package. He stood in one spot, completely helpless to walk, or even crawl.

"So now you want your gear?" her mom said. "I'll go get it."

"Not you," said the man from the basement. Nick was his name. "Her." He pointed in Ivy's direction, then held up an admonishing finger. "Accompanied by Harlan."

The aches and pains Nick had inflicted upon Ivy were basically gone, and his hailstorm of temper seemed to have receded, too. After he had taped Ivy's mouth in the basement, Nick had gone to pick up the hammer he'd thrown, and used it to nail two-by-fours over the door that led outside. Ivy had sat there, fingering the lump of keys in her pocket, and watching this escape route disappear one board at a time. Now she looked at the scabbing-over cut she had managed to deliver to Nick's face, and refused to feel afraid.

"I have to hear what you tell him before they go," her mother said, words Ivy could make no sense of.

Nick walked over to Ivy's mom. "When you lied to me about the safe, it was for two reasons, right? To delay me, and to supply a reason for your husband to live."

Ivy had no clue what was going on, but her mother nodded.

"You can see now that deceit is unlikely to work," Nick continued. "Neither will giving me orders. Luckily you don't have to." He turned in Ivy's direction. "I have no desire to hurt any of you, or have Harlan do it either." When he smiled, there was a trace of that familiarity again. Ivy actually felt herself smiling back. "So why don't we just play this straight from now on?"

Ivy was trying to understand what Nick was saying when she saw her dad's bound form start to waver.

"Please," Ivy's mother said. "Can I help

my husband sit down?"

Nick blinked, a fake look of surprise. "Of course."

Ivy's mom led her dad over to the couch by the sliding glass doors. Ivy turned away, unable to tolerate the sight of her father looking like some handicapped person, or worse, really, really old.

"Nice," Nick said once Ivy's mom had gotten her dad settled. "You seem to have a pretty good hold over your husband. Which is why I want the pretty princess to go scavenger hunting while you stay here with us."

Ivy's mom looked at him.

"Don't worry," Nick went on, pointing to the floor. Dirt and woodchips from the stove were crumbled across it. "You'll have plenty to do." He gestured to a plastic dustpan and broom that had been in the pantry before their entire kitchen got thrown about. "Pick up the chairs when you finish." A pause, then: "Princess?"

Ivy looked up, slowly, effortfully.

"Think you can get us what we need?"

Ivy was about to reply when someone else spoke up.

"Eye . . . vee?"

Ivy had no idea who it was for a second, even though she had just seen her father sit down. His voice sounded strange, like an engine that couldn't get started. She ran for the couch and fell to her knees, placing her head on her father's shoulder. Where was he hurt? She didn't even know.

"Daddy?" Her own voice was also just shadings of its former self.

"Gore-Tex," he said, and Ivy looked at him and nodded.

"You won't have any outfits to fit him, though," she said, indicating Harlan.

"Next best."

After a moment, Ivy nodded rapidly. The next best thing would be wool and layers in as large a size as she could find. Her father brought extra clothes on expeditions for emergency changes, or for clients who arrived less than prepared.

"Matches, camel packs, filtration system, iodine tabs, dried food," she recited, sparing her father the effort. "Double socks, outerwear, poles."

Her dad didn't nod, but the look in his eyes was clearer than a *yes*. It said that Ivy was not only right in her listing, but also that she had replaced the terrible glisten of pain and something even worse — fear — in her dad's eyes. They now shone with pride.

Ivy felt her own eyes fill.

"Topo," her dad said.

"Maps," Ivy filled in. "And a pen so you can mark them."

That expression again. Ivy swiped at her face.

"Nav," her dad said, and Ivy nodded, understanding. The GPS. Maps would only go so far when these men entered the wilderness. But her dad seemed to be struggling to add something. "Get both . . . kinds of . . . devices."

Sweat had broken out on his forehead; it slid down in slimy streaks. After a second, Ivy realized that her dad couldn't wipe it.

"Hey," Nick said from behind. "Enough of the daddy's-little-girl crap."

Fresh tears started in Ivy's eyes as she dabbed at her father's face. She wanted to see that look of pride again so badly that her hands shook. But she had no idea what he was asking her to do.

"Harlan," Nick beckoned, and the big guy came to life. Ivy led him in the direction of her father's workshop, which was part of the garage. Just as Ivy opened the kitchen door to allow access, Nick called out casually, "Don't let her leave your side."

Her mother's voice rose in a completely un-mom-like shriek that made Ivy feel like a swimmer drifting out of sight of land. "Ivy! Don't try to get away from him! Not for one single second, do you hear?"

Ivy gave a tremulous nod and stepped through the doorway.

The temperature in the enclosed space was freezing; the heat hadn't been turned on for the season yet. Ivy wondered what it looked like outside, if ice had come to encase everything in marble. She maneuvered into her father's workshop, walking away from Harlan on wobbly legs.

Packs, food, water, clothes, outer gear. Most of the list was simple. Only, what had her father meant about two navigation devices?

A hand settled around her arm, although this didn't feel like a hand; it was altogether too big and strong for a body part. This was more like a piece of equipment, maybe something on a farm. It pulled her back, and Ivy's feet left the floor; she was airborne until she returned to earth on the spot she'd started walking from.

"Ow," Ivy said in a little squeak. She couldn't help it.

Harlan spoke so low she almost couldn't make it out. "Stay by my side, remember?"

Ivy imagined ways he would be able to keep her close. Harlan might break her arm or squeeze the life out of her simply by trying to restrain her.

"Okay," Ivy said softly. "I get it. I'll stay." She pointed into the dim recesses of the garage, where her dad had installed racks of shelving. Harlan would be able to reach the top shelves just by standing on tiptoes.

The two of them walked, Ivy taking three quick steps for each one of Harlan's.

Squatting and loading everything into two thick-skinned packs, compressing sleeping bags, balling up socks, Ivy felt as if she might've been preparing to go on a hike or a climb with her father, just like they'd always done.

Just like they'd do again so long as Ivy got her dad what he wanted.

She rolled one set of garments in a size XXXL and another from the stack of regular larges, also taking out a suit of Gore-Tex to be put on by Nick. Extra clothes were key. Ivy hadn't done many winter expeditions, but she knew from listening to her dad. The greatest risk was getting wet. Whether from falling snow or a slip off a mossy rock into a creek, clothes that were so much as damp had to be removed and exchanged right away.

She wondered why she was trying to protect these two men. Why not let them freeze to death once they were a few miles from their house?

Ivy carelessly scattered a handful of iodine tablets over the pouches of food she'd provided. She attached two camel packs to the side straps of the sacks, then opened a filing cabinet, and began to thumb through a folder of maps. Nick had said they were going north, which meant she had to look for Franklin County, southern Quebec, might as well throw in western Vermont for good measure. Then a Sharpie for marking and a Ziploc bag for storing. Harlan watched her preparations without questioning, or even seeming to register them. At last, Ivy rose and unlatched the lockbox.

There were different navigation devices in here, from a top-of-the-line GPS to less expensive ones with fewer features. Was that what her father wanted — to figure out the cheapest one he could get away with losing?

That seemed crazy. They stood to lose a lot more than a GPS.

Ivy cast her gaze up at Harlan, looming like a mountain above her; then she squinted into the deeper shadows of the garage.

Her dad hadn't said two nav devices, she realized. He'd said two *kinds* of devices. Ivy's gaze flicked back to the assortment contained in the box.

And she saw what her father wanted, and why.

CHAPTER FIFTEEN

Sandy stared at the sheets of paper Ben had covered with scrawl. There was a lot of information to convey, and Sandy had convinced Nick to loosen the tape so that Ben could write it all down. Ben's speech hadn't improved, but he still had perfect command of language, and his fine motor skills seemed all right, so long as he used his left hand.

When the door to the garage opened, Sandy felt relief rush over her. She ran to gather Ivy up in her arms, and Ivy clung to her so tightly it seemed they both might be swept away.

"Okay?" Sandy whispered.

"Okay," said Ivy.

Ivy wriggled free, dashing over to hand a stack of maps to her dad. Ben bent down and set to work, marking prospective routes. After a few minutes, with Sandy content to simply stand beside Ivy, Ben offered up the maps to Nick. They were folded imprecisely, lumpy and creased, either due to rage or to his injured right arm. But Sandy could make out the dark slashes of lines that would take these men out of their lives forever, and her need for them to go felt so urgent that the notes she'd been reading trembled in her grip like leaves in a strong wind.

Nick bound Ben's wrists tightly behind his back again, then turned around and said, "So. You have some things for us, princess?"

Ivy's slim back was trussed with one of Ben's backcountry packs, and Harlan wore one too, so small upon him that it looked more like a schoolchild's knapsack.

"Good," said Nick. "Let's see what we've got."

Both Ivy and Harlan shouldered off their packs, Harlan's making the long drop down from his shoulders to the floor and landing with a clang of equipment. The zipper whined as Ivy drew hers along its track, while Sandy held up the sheaf of papers and shook them straight.

Ivy got down on her knees to pull items out. Harlan sat on the floor beside her, awkwardly positioned like an overgrown lion, as Ivy exhibited things and Sandy read aloud, a duo in some gruesome game show.

Ben's notes covered a range of requirements: calorie minimums given energy expended, ounces of water per day for different conditions, the necessity of layers. Ivy continued to take pieces of gear out one by one, displaying each with a flourish.

"The biggest danger is getting wet," Sandy read from Ben's jerky, left-handed jottings. "Even from sweat. You can run out of food or even water, but if you get wet, hypothermia will set in and you'll die within hours." She saw Ben's fury in the words he had scrawled, dark slabs against the paper, and it shaded her intonation.

Nick made a hand-waving gesture. "Dry not wet. Got it."

Sandy looked down again. Ben had started to write another long bullet point, with the heading *Naismith's rule.* But he'd stopped in the middle to scribble a series of numbers. Sandy squinted to discern what was meant.

Nick took a step closer, and it was all the prompting Sandy needed.

"Figure a pace of four miles per hour because you'll be descending," she said, making sense of Ben's sums. "Five hours to the border, which will not be marked. Another forty miles to Montreal. Two-and-a-half-day hike approximately . . ."

It occurred to Sandy, as she continued to read, that this compliant, information-providing incarnation didn't sound like her fighter-by-nature husband. Sandy's voice began to trail off, the sound of a record slowing down.

He's a guide, she argued with herself. *And he's slipped into that mode to get us all out of this.* But the words sounded weak inside her own head, and her body felt as if it were filling with icy cold water.

Sandy looked down. Harlan was helping Ivy wrest items into place, his maneuvers clumsy and awkward beside Ivy's careful stacking.

Nick let the top of his jumpsuit fall to his waist, tugging a thin skin of Gore-Tex over his head. His chest was a graffiti wall of blue and black tattoos, delineating the muscles that reinforced his frame. Nick donned a second shirt, then bent and touched a spot on his leg before adding a third. Sandy pressed her eyes shut, hard enough to be headache-inducing. When she opened them again, Ivy was also averting her eyes, while Nick pulled on bottom layers. Clad, he used one foot to nudge a pile of clothing in Harlan's direction, issuing a command to get dressed.

"Wait," Ivy said. "Don't forget this." She took a black unit from a pocket on the pack, and held it up. "Mom? Did Dad write anything about this?"

Ben shifted forward on the couch, sitting on its edge.

Sandy looked down, frowning. She read a few lines at the bottom of the page. "You'll want a GPS. Topo maps are for emergency losses of charge, but this device will give you your location and get you where you need to go."

Harlan got to his feet, struggling to pull on a pair of pants that, though ballooning and expansive in their girth, fit like cling wrap around his legs and couldn't be buttoned over the waist.

"How do you use it?" Nick asked, taking the GPS and turning it over in his hand.

Ivy stood up and walked over to him. There was a sashay in her step that made Sandy cringe. Her legs looked long in their pasting of jeans, although they still brought the top of Ivy's head only to the height of Harlan's belly button. Her shimmery shirt was too low cut and sheer. Why was Ivy wearing that shirt to hang around the house on a school night?

"Simple," Ivy said, a shrug in her voice. She took the gadget out of Nick's hand and upended it. "Power here." She touched a button at the top. "This is us." She displayed the screen. "You can zoom out . . ." Her finger slid. "See? That's the house at the bottom of our hill."

Nick peered down at the miniature map as if Ivy had split an atom in front of him. "You're telling me we're looking at the place where we are right now?" He took a look around. "How is this thing finding us?"

Ivy frowned. "What?" She glanced over her shoulder. "I don't know what you mean."

Nick took the device out of Ivy's hand. She leaned close to him, and touched it again. "Anyway, you zoom in like this. And if you want to enter coordinates — tell it where you want to go instead of seeing where you are — you do this." A few final taps on the screen.

Nick crossed to the other side of the room, still holding the GPS. It had powered down, and he shook it before remembering the button at the top. After a few tries, he brought the device to life again. Nick looked at the screen, then through the sliding glass doors, from screen to doors, back and forth. Finally he pocketed the GPS, and pantomimed a soundless, exaggerated clap. "Quite a little tutorial. And I have to thank you for the use of such pricey gear. We'll be sure to return it."

On the couch, Ben's shoulders tensed and rose.

Nick grinned down at Ivy, who was back on the floor, loading everything up, and her daughter offered a smile back, flicking her sheet of hair over her shoulders.

Oh, honey. You shouldn't placate him. And you certainly shouldn't like *him.*

"Let me give you a hand there, princess," Nick said. He was visibly pleased. Sandy realized that he wanted to be out of here as much as they wanted him gone.

Nick got down on his knees and picked up several pouches of freeze-dried food from the floor, pulling one of the packs forward.

"It's okay," Ivy said. "I don't mind doing it —" She grabbed for the pack, flushing furiously as her hands glanced across Nick's.

Sandy felt her stomach give a sick roll at the sight of her flustered, blushing daughter.

But Nick ignored her, thrusting one arm into the open mouth of the pack. He drew his hand out slowly. "What's this?"

In his hand, a second black unit winked like a flirtatious eye.

"It's a GPS," Ivy said after a moment. "I just showed you."

Nick rose to standing above her. "Why do we need two?"

"Backup," Ivy said. "In case one loses charge."

"Loses what?" Nick asked.

Ivy looked at him.

Nick grinned. "I'm just kidding. I know they run on batteries. I was in prison, not the Middle Ages."

Ivy offered up an uncertain smile.

"So," Nick said, leaning close to her, "wouldn't it be simpler to give us a few extra double A's instead of a whole new machine?"

Ivy took a swift look over her shoulder at Ben, and when she did, a bolt of understanding hit Sandy. She couldn't have said exactly what this device did, but it had been hidden, buried in the pack, the one object not put on display. And she recalled the moments when Ben had spoken to Ivy, what he must've told her to do.

Ben, came a cry that split her head. *They were leaving. Oh, Ben, I told you to stop!*

She bit back a sour rush of fluid, stepping in front of her daughter to shield her from Nick.

Nick stared down at the piece of electronics, flipping it over in his hand. "This one doesn't look the same as the other." He glanced up. "I think it does something else."

"Then just take the one," Sandy said. "Or don't take either. You have everything you need to be on your way."

Harlan was ready, made wider around by the layers he'd swathed himself in, and seeming to finally grow a little impatient himself, shoes aimed in the direction of the door.

Nick nodded slowly, appearing to give the matter more thought. "We could do that. We could. But you see — while I haven't had access of late to the most recent developments, I did have a few interesting exchanges with a younger man who has. He gave me information. Facts I had to pay for, you understand. So I really wanted to make sure I understood everything he told me. Got my money's worth, so to speak."

Sandy suppressed a nod.

"And that's why I think that this particular item" — Nick palmed the small device — "might allow someone out there to know where we've gone. Maybe even where we are right at the moment. This thing, it tracks us." Nick brought the gadget up to his face, gave it a twirl. "Why, it's even turned on already. Isn't it, princess?"

Ivy's body quivered behind Sandy.

Nick shrugged. "That's okay. I don't really

227

need any confirmation. The only thing I'm wondering now is . . ." He peered around Sandy. ". . . who was responsible for this little plan. Did the princess have the idea when she went into the garage?"

Sandy felt Ivy's knees sag. She reached back to keep her daughter upright.

"Or was she instructed by Rocky over there to do it?"

Ben got into a standing position, using the edge of the couch to support the backs of his legs as he steadied himself. He took a twisting hop forward.

Watching the maneuver, Nick said, "I think you've answered my question. Unless you're just trying to protect your daughter from her own initiative." He paused. "That will stand the princess in good stead, assuming she lives long enough to use it. I hear initiative is in short supply these days."

"Please," Sandy said. "Just take the rest of the gear and go."

Nick went on as if she hadn't spoken. "But I'm going to choose to believe that the man of the house was responsible."

Sandy felt a trickle of relief — the amount of air someone in the early stages of anaphylaxis might take in — as Nick's attention coasted over Ivy.

He strode to Ben, pushing him in the

direction of the basement door.

"I think I like the downstairs part of your house best," he remarked. "It will be easy to keep you out of the way there."

A second slow drip of relief, liquid feeding into an IV bag one bead at a time. Ben could stay in the basement, no problem. Let Nick and Harlan resume getting ready, check that no other measures had been put into place, and that everything was to their liking. Once they left, Sandy could take an injured Ben out.

Nick came to a stop at the head of the flight, Ben propped up in front of him.

Ben twisted his head around, the look in his eyes lucid enough to call to mind years long gone, and days just past. His gaze sought out Sandy's and he mouthed, *I love you.*

Sandy's chest clenched. She felt for Ivy with knotted hands.

"Don't you want to say you love him back, Cass?" Nick asked, the words slow and syrupy.

Sandy jerked her head up.

Ben stood precariously over the top step. "Wha— ?" he began. There was a blur of uncertainty in his eyes.

Sandy spoke in the loudest voice she had mustered yet. "Don't call me that. That's not my name." The itch in her hands had returned, swelling to maddening intensity.

Nick rolled his neck around, gaze settling on her. "No? What should I call you, then?"

"Don't call me anything," Sandy said, marshaling scorn. "You don't know me, and you never will."

Her husband, looking so lost at the top of the stairs, managed to give her something like a smile.

Nick gathered the back of Ben's shirt into a twist in his hand. "Funny," he said. "You just sort of look like a Cass to me."

Deep wells appeared on Harlan's forehead. "I thought you said —"

Nick cut him off with a wave of his hand. Jerking Ben around by his balled-up shirt, Nick waggled his eyebrows and touched the tip of his tongue to his lip in a *watch this* kind of leer. Then he placed his foot on the small of Ben's back, and kicked him down the stairs.

CHAPTER SIXTEEN

Sandy felt as if she screamed forever. Her throat was a raw, red lava bed. Her screams crowded out the sound of Ben's body hitting stair after stair, his helpless, hopeless plunge.

Then, when he reached the bottom, silence more dreadful than any noise.

Sandy turned and faced Nick. He was reaching down, touching the top of his shoe and frowning. Inked symbols wreathed his neck, while light glinted off the steely brush of his close-cropped hair. Everything about him was metallic and hard.

"Okay," Sandy said, one muddy, boggy word. "You can go now."

Returning to the remaining items on the floor, Nick began stuffing them into the pack, as Harlan stared down at him.

Sandy went over to Ivy and touched her on the shoulder. "It's all right," she whispered, but Ivy flinched and turned away from her.

"It's not all right," she hissed fiercely. A spill of tears slipped out. "How can you say it's all right? Did you see what he did to Dad?"

Sandy recoiled as her daughter hunched over, hugging her arms around herself.

"You know how strong Dad is," Sandy said, needing to offer Ivy some semblance of reassurance. "He's going to be okay."

Ivy's shoulders sloped and she stared down at the floor. Sandy looked at the men, packs now hoisted, fitting fingers into gloves. She watched them head out of the kitchen. After a moment, as if by unspoken agreement, a mutual need to see, Sandy and Ivy traced their own path to the front door.

Nick drew it open.

As soon as Sandy got a glimpse, she knew.

The men weren't going to leave. Not now, and not anytime soon. And there wasn't much hope of help coming either.

Outside, everything was a whirling frenzy of white.

A cold and pelting snow had started to fall.

"This might work out even better," Sandy said through lips that felt thick and numb. The air rushing in had injected her with anesthetic. Her words came sluggishly; she couldn't feel Ivy standing beside her. "No one will be searching for you, they'll be too busy with the storm."

Nick let out a roar as if she hadn't spoken. "Goddamnit!" He slammed the door shut, but it banged against the frame and flew back open. Snow soared inside, a stinging wind. "Goddamn!"

"Nick," Harlan said. "We can walk in this." He stared at the snow in seeming wonder. "It's so beautiful."

A muscle jumped in Nick's neck as he forced his fists to unfurl. He took in a hissing breath. "Boots," he said tonelessly. "And galoshes."

Harlan's wooly eyebrows knit.

Nick turned to Ivy. "Your dad will have a pair that fit me," he said. "And galoshes can stretch over Harlan's shoes."

Ivy nodded.

"Go with the princess, Harlan," Nick instructed.

The two of them walked off, silhouetted side by side. Nick turned and headed over to the leather couches in the TV area. It was only then that Sandy registered the slight hitch in his step.

Nick removed a glove with his teeth, then stripped off the other one.

Ivy returned, letting Ben's pair of Hi-Tecs drop to the floor with a *thud.* Galoshes followed in a squashy heap of black.

Nick leaned down and pulled off his left shoe. He drew on the first of the boots, lacing it up snugly. Then he went to take off his other shoe, and they all saw.

The top of Nick's foot had swollen monstrously, a whale hump forcing up the cloth of his sock. There was no way he'd be able to stuff his foot into a boot — Sandy was amazed he was walking around at all. While they stared at him, Nick clawed out the bottle of Advil, opened it, and chewed the remaining pills. He tossed the empty bottle onto the couch cushion, before forcing his foot back into his shoe and removing the boot he'd put on already.

"You heard the man," Nick said, standing up. He licked white grit from the pills off his lips. "Our biggest risk is getting wet. I can't walk through this." He paused for a moment, appearing to wrestle some awareness down. "I mean, we'll have to wait out the storm."

Sandy felt her shoulders deflate. She could sense Ivy next to her again, and reached for her daughter's hand. Then the four of them turned and headed back to the kitchen as if it were some sort of base. Nick went last,

Harlan slowing his pace to shuffle along beside him.

They were all in this together now. Until they could get out.

"Nick?" Harlan mumbled. "Can I take these clothes off? They're too tight."

Nick gave a single nod.

There came a tearing sound, a harsh ripping of cloth. Then a pile of fabric sank to the floor like a parachute. Nick pulled his cap from his head and hung his coat on the back of a chair. Beneath the leg of his pants, the gun bulged.

Sandy fought to shuck off the resigned pall that had draped itself over her, and forced herself to think. She couldn't tell if Nick's foot was broken, or just badly bruised. Either way, nothing from Ben's store of first aid supplies, brace or splint or tape, would work a miracle cure.

Ivy sat down on the floor, her back against the wall, and her legs stretched out in a long triangular vee.

"Hey," Nick said, tracking Ivy's course. "Why the long face?"

Sandy looked at him, disbelieving.

He switched his gaze to her. "Nothing has to change really. We just get out of here a little later than I'd planned."

Sandy dropped her head, felt it shake back and forth.

"Just keep quiet, do what I say, and" — Nick let both fists fly open, making a *poof* with his mouth — "we'll be out of your hair and your house and your life in a few more hours." He gave a nod. "Really. Think of this as some kind of freaky slumber party."

Sandy reached down and pinched her arm where the skin itched madly. A droplet of blood welled up, and she studied it with cold appraisal.

"I would say we've got some housekeeping to do," said Nick. "Seeing as it looks like we'll be playing house for a little while."

Sandy stared at him with a hatred as icy and deep as the storm outside. The hatred was soothing. It cooled her throat and chilled her hands. She looked down and saw how dry and bone-sharp her fingers looked. Like tools.

"Careful," Nick remarked mildly. He reached down without taking his eyes off her and lifted the cuff on his pants to display the gun. Taking the weapon out, he placed it on the table.

It faced Sandy like a dare. She could imagine what would happen if she reached for it, how Nick's fingers would feel closing over hers, his serene tone of reproach hid-ing a wellspring of danger. "Please," she said. "I have to go check on my husband. He needs medical attention. And I work in a hospital. I might be able to do something."

Nick regarded her. "I thought we already established that your medical skills are less Marcus Welby, more Dr. Doolittle."

"Please," Sandy said stolidly. "At least let me check."

"Ask me one more time," Nick said. "And then *I* will go down. And if your husband isn't dead already, I'll finish the job." Amusement sparked on his features. "Unless there's a better way to stifle your infernal demands."

The words cast an eerie echo, and Sandy's belly went cold and vaporous.

Nick reached up to scrub the short stubs of his hair.

In a single svelte move, straight out of yoga or a long ago gymnastics class, Ivy lunged for the gun on the table, one arm extended, her back a flat, graceful plane.

Nick observed her, while Sandy moved as swiftly as her daughter had.

"Ivy! Give it to me!" Sandy shouted, and Ivy handed the gun over, fast, as if it burned.

Nick's arm came around Sandy like a seatbelt locking. Sandy used her free hand to try and prise Nick's fingers apart, but it was as if they'd been forged from steel. Even his hands were muscular; he must've spent hours practicing his grip. She writhed in his grasp.

"Let go. Please. Please! You can have the gun," she said and, satisfied, Nick released her.

He pulled at his sock. He scooped up a few metal oblongs, then let the bullets clatter out onto the floor. He'd just been toying with them; the gun wasn't even loaded.

"Scoop them up," Nick instructed Ivy.

Ivy crouched, no less nimble, but angry now at her mistake, her face red and fuming, breath coming audibly out of her nose.

Nick palmed the pistol as he waited for the bullets, then inserted each one calmly. "You guys just keep making things worse for yourselves. Bad things can happen with a loaded gun around, you know. How many times do I have to tell you that all I want to do is *get the hell out of this place*?"

The air seemed to ripple, as if Nick's shout had been a rock cast into the sea.

Sandy fought to take in breath, her ears ringing.

Nick spun the barrel of the gun. "All of this has got me a little tense," he said. For the first time, Sandy noticed faint lines across his face, etched by pain or the wear of the night. "I could use a smoke. In your room, princess?"

He looked to Ivy.

A wriggle of confusion appeared between her brows.

"Cigs," Nick said patiently. "Cigarettes. Coffin nails —"

Dismissal painted itself across Ivy's features. "I don't smoke."

Nick frowned at her. "What kind of teenager doesn't smoke?"

Sandy spoke up. "My husband," she said. "He'll have a few cigars."

Nick switched his focus to Sandy. "Nice," he said, sliding the gun back into his sock. "Two birds with one stone. We can tend to a few matters upstairs, and get me my smoke at the same time."

Faint hope lofted inside Sandy. Upstairs there might be chances.

September 8, 1976

Barbara stood at the stove, ignoring the chaos all around her. A drift of flour on the counter. Enough kitchen implements to fill the lower level of Swain's department store. The filet cut of venison searing in the pan, unleashing a meteor shower of grease.

Barbara was fiercely focused, intent on every moment of this meal preparation. It had been a long time since she'd cooked for Gordon, and he'd been so good to her lately, taking on household tasks, shortening his hours at the shop. For Nicholas, Barbara had pushed herself, fixing his favorites. But those were relatively easy. Grilled cheese, soup from a can, tuna noodle casserole. While Gordon loved fancy dishes and good cuts of meat — his own fresh kills especially — and Barbara had been unable to go anywhere near meat during the infernally long months of her pregnancy, nor her uneasy postpartum. Barbara had felt rather like a hunted animal herself for the last thirteen months in fact, surprised when her wounds didn't fell her.

She used a spatula to flip the piece of deer meat in the pan. *Joy of Cooking* lay open, pages floured and spine broken, near the stove. Barbara turned the flame down, then flicked aside the red ribbon that marked her recipe. She had to spread a mushroom mixture on the meat before somehow getting the whole thing inside a cloak of dough.

Pastry, Barbara corrected herself.

It was maddening to work with, but Barbara pushed on relentlessly, lip caught between her teeth, her still loose belly poofed out. She packed the slathered meat into its parcel, adhering sticky flaps of dough like pieces of wet cloth. Then she slid the whole mess into the oven. She brushed her hands back and forth, sending pills of dough onto the floor, before glancing at the hands on the wall clock. Time to get Nicholas up. Ever since he'd started nursery school — Gordon had arranged this, saying that Nicky should be around other children his age, and that Barbara could use the break — the little boy had begun taking naps for the first time in his life.

She unwound the strings of her apron and

tossed the garment at the disarray on the counter. The green-checked cloth fell next to the pan, which was smoking silently on the stove. She'd lowered the flame, but hadn't turned it off. Barbara shook her head, *tsk*ing herself. What a risk to take, almost setting the house afire with Nicholas asleep upstairs. She rotated the knob, then made a few halfhearted stabs at setting things to rights, letting the time idle by.

Kitchen matters attended to — a warm, buttery smell had started to drift from the oven — Barbara turned and mounted the steps to the second floor.

On the landing, she paused. There were sounds coming from the rear of the house, muted mews, and Barbara drew up her shoulders as if a mosquito had begun to whine by her ear. She went and closed the door to the spare room with a sharp *click*, and the cries were immediately damped. Barbara retraced her steps down the hall to Nicholas' bedroom.

It lay in a spill of afternoon gold, the walls as sunny as egg yolks. A bicentennial pennant was taped askew by one window. Nicholas had hung this up himself, enjoying the act of decorating his own room. He was turning out to have quite an artistic sensibility.

He lay sprawled across the top bunk, his curls forming rings on the pillow. Barbara had convinced Gordon to buy bunk beds when Nicholas moved out of his crib, citing slumber parties their son would have with friends. Now his skinny legs dangled over the side. Barbara worried that Nicholas would fall out, and he was so bony — a tumble from this height would be no joke, the thick carpet Barbara had convinced Gordon to lay notwithstanding. Especially because the boy had refused a bed rail. He'd called it a baby thing, and Barbara had applauded Nicholas' desire for maturity. Even Gordon had been impressed. He was the one who chided Nicholas for whining or throwing tantrums, both perfectly age-appropriate, but they bothered Gordon because his mother had made a big deal about the one she had witnessed. Nicholas just got frustrated. He wanted to accomplish more than a three-and-a-half-year-old really could. There was a parenting book out about gifted children, which Barbara had read, finding Nicholas on every page.

Still, this lying half out of bed wouldn't do. Barbara tiptoed across the floor and lifted Nicholas' legs onto the mattress, shifting his body. He was light enough that she was still able to move him, but gone were the days when she could just scoop him up. Barbara crossed her arms tightly over her chest. She had moved past the time for cradling her baby.

The sounds coming from the hall were growing louder. Barbara walked to Nicholas' door and pulled it shut, too. Another parenting book contained a chapter on the new cry-it-out method. Barbara hadn't spent much time on those pages, but she'd skimmed enough to know that sometimes a little crying was necessary for truly restful sleep.

She'd never had to let Nicholas cry, though.

Barbara had tried to close his door stealthily, but Nicholas began stirring. He sat upright, screwing his little fists into his eyes. Throwing one leg over the bed, he prepared to hop out, clearly forgetting that he was on the upper bunk.

Barbara could picture the impending plunge; Nicholas expecting the floor to be right beneath his feet. She was at his side in a flash, catching her little boy's slight body in the cradle of her arms as he dropped. An expression of surprise flashed across his face. Then Barbara sprawled out on the floor, Nicholas on top of her.

She'd come down hard, and something

twinged deep in her belly upon impact.

Nicholas began to giggle. "We went boom, Mama."

"Yes, we did."

Barbara was trying to determine how great the damage was. She hoped the bleeding, only recently stemmed, wouldn't start up again. She couldn't stand the thought of its ugly flocking on this new carpet. Plus, Barbara had already seen enough of Dr. Benedict, and though she now made sure to visit his office mornings when Nicholas was at school, the memory of that nurse getting near her son made Barbara's insides churn. Nicholas' regular checkup was long overdue.

"Again, Mama!" Nicholas ordered. "Let's do it again!"

Barbara fingered the little boy's glossy curls. "I have an idea for a game."

"A game?" he asked, interested.

Barbara nodded. Appealing to the boy's imagination was usually a wise approach. "It's about your bed."

"My bed?"

Another furious nod. "The bottom bunk is a boat. And the carpet is water, see? It's blue." She pointed. "And you have to stay in the boat because if you fell out, you'd get all cold and wet." She shivered dramatically. "Nasty."

A smile bloomed on the bow of Nicholas' mouth, entrancing Barbara. She reached to touch a pearly bead of spittle caught on the corner of his lip, like a drop of dew. Nicholas had slept deeply.

"All right?" she said after a long moment.

Nicholas looked at her. "What?"

"You'll sleep in the boat tonight? On the bottom bunk?"

Nicholas' features scrunched. "I wanna sleep on top."

"But only the bottom is a boat!" Barbara protested. She moved Nicholas off her, and stood up. "See? And all of this is the sea." She waved her arm.

"I know!" Nicholas announced. "The top can be the boat!"

Barbara shook her head, a little frantically. "The top is too high," she tried to explain over his rising cries.

Were his cries rising? Nicholas' mouth appeared to be closed. She couldn't tell where those cries were coming from. Barbara took a deep breath and continued to explain the game. "The water wouldn't be this far beneath."

But Nicholas was too smart; he knew it was just pretend. Either bunk could be a boat, and even in the midst of the escalating noise level, Barbara had to admire her son's logic. She went and crouched before him, detesting the flop of her belly over the rim of her panty-hose.

"The truth is, I'm scared, Nicky," she said. "In the night, you might forget you're high up, and roll over. I don't want you to fall. It was fine when I was there to catch you, but think about what it would feel like if you went all the way down by yourself. No Mama to go boom."

Her son stared at her, and Barbara offered him a smile.

Nicholas smiled back. Then he opened his mouth and screamed so loudly that the windows rattled in their panes.

"I wanna sleep —" He paused for air. "— on top! It's my top! My top! Mine!"

The force of his yell toppled him. Nicholas plunked down on the plush blue carpet, before raising his head and gathering breath to go on.

Barbara got onto the floor, swooping in before the developing bellow could take hold. "All right," she said. "All right, calm down! You can sleep on top, of course you can!" She had to yell herself now. "It is your bed, you're right!"

Nicholas smiled again. "My bed."

His bedroom door banged open, hitting the wall.

Barbara looked up to see Gordon standing there, holding something loud and squalling, rigid as a piece of barbed wire, its arms and legs thrust out of a twisted blanket that Barbara recognized from Nicholas' infant days.

"Gordon," Barbara said. "You're home early."

He looked at her and Nicholas on the floor, and his features settled weightily. He didn't offer a response; perhaps he couldn't hear what she'd said.

After a moment, he took a few steps closer.

"Barbara," he said, jiggling his body as he spoke. The noise at last began to wane. "We talked about this, remember? Barbara, honey, why didn't you go to the baby?" He gazed down at the bundle in his arms, trying to smooth the tangled folds of blanket. "Why are you in here with Nicholas when —"

Nicholas spoke up. "We were playing boat, Daddy!"

Gordon frowned. "Boat? When your sister was —"

All of a sudden, Barbara remembered, and she jumped up. "My Wellington!" She shrank from Gordon as she went by, refusing to brush against the burden in his arms. "I've made you the most wonderful dinner, darling," she said. "We'll eat on our own tonight, all right?"

The plates were empty, one thickly smeared with brown streaks. Nicholas hadn't liked the mushroom part, and had wiped the venison off with his fingers. The romantic dinner for two hadn't come to pass: Nicholas had insisted on joining them, and Barbara spoke up on behalf of their son's desire for time alone with his parents. She cited another book, all the adjustments Nicholas had had to make over the past several months. It was the same argument she mounted whenever Nicholas joined them in bed in the middle of the night, or refused to go to school.

Tonight, instead of saying that Nicholas didn't seem to be adjusting — that Barbara was behaving for all intents and purposes as if there were nothing for him to adjust *to* — Gordon simply acquiesced. He cleaned his plate, although he didn't say a word about the dish.

And she had worked so hard.

Barbara put Nicholas to bed. She tried to mound pillows along the side — a makeshift guardrail — but Nicholas knocked them all to the floor.

"It's a boat, Mama," he said. "Boats don't

have pillows."

Astounded again by his capacity for logic, Barbara left the pillows on the floor. At least they would provide a layer if he did fall.

She crept back downstairs to Gordon. Nicholas no longer complained if she left before he'd fallen asleep. Nor did he leave his room, asking for all the things he used to. Barbara had accepted Gordon's praise over this change, but she knew she couldn't really take credit for it. The truth was, Nicholas liked to be on his own now.

Her son had always been precocious. The teachers at his new nursery school seemed to agree, and they were professionals. Which surely meant that everyone else — Gordon's mother, the nurse, and that awful Glenda Williams — could be disregarded.

When Barbara reached the living room, the clearing up had been done, and Gordon sat in his easy chair, holding a baby bottle at an angle.

It was tilted too sharply; it would create gas. And that would mean more nighttime crying. You didn't need a parenting book to tell you that. Barbara averted her eyes.

Gordon spoke softly in the waning light. "We have to give her a name."

She didn't respond.

"People at the shop are asking. People in

town will start, too. And at Nicholas' school. Besides —" Gordon broke off. "She deserves a name. A special name, all her own."

Barbara kept her eyes fixed forward.

Peripherally, she saw Gordon rise. He passed so close by that Barbara could smell the tang of formula on his clothes. She wrinkled her nose.

The stairs sank beneath his weight as he trod them.

"Barbara," he said, pausing in the middle of the flight.

Tiny hiccups came from his direction. Periodic little clicks in the air, so regular and machine-like they didn't seem to be made by anything human.

"Can't you let yourself love her?" Gordon asked. "Just a little bit?"

The meal Barbara had so painstakingly prepared threatened to disgorge from her belly. Her mottled, pouching belly.

The moon appeared in the window over the stairs. After a moment, Gordon turned and continued up.

Barbara waited a long time to go upstairs herself. She wanted to be sure Gordon had fallen asleep so she could spend time checking on Nicholas, watch him sleep as she drew the covers over his body. But when she passed her hand across the top bunk, it touched no lump, no sleeping form.

Her heart caught in her chest. She rose on tiptoes, but even in the dim glow the night-light provided, it was clear that this bunk was empty.

A sparkler of thoughts momentarily blinded her.

Nicholas had decided to play the game after all. He'd somehow made it down on his own and was pretending the bottom bunk was a boat. Barbara bent over. But the blankets down there lay flat and undisturbed, the bed untouched since the day she had made it.

She spun around unsteadily, peering into unseen corners of the room. Nicholas had fallen, he'd gotten hurt —

The room was empty.

Barbara ran into the hallway. About to cry out for Gordon, something called her attention at the end of the hall. She drifted soundlessly, feet padding over the runner of carpet, in the direction of the spare bedroom.

Nicholas stood there, his little hands clasped like cuffs around the bars of the crib.

CHAPTER SEVENTEEN

The four of them climbed the stairs single file, an unlikely group of compatriots.

"I didn't see a computer downstairs," Nick remarked. "You must keep them in the bedrooms? Family like you has to have more than one computer."

"You don't know what kind of family we are," Ivy muttered.

An inner cymbal clanged — *you tell him, Ive* — but then Sandy saw Nick's shoulders level out, a single blade of bone. He turned around on the step, deftly checking his footing.

"I'm getting kind of sick of you," he said. "Are all kids today as nasty as you?" His tongue flicked between his teeth as if tasting something bad.

"Right," Sandy said. "It's the kids today who are bad."

Nick shifted his gaze to her. "Interesting comment," he said, like a teacher addressing his class in hell. "Care to elaborate?"

Sandy pressed her lips together.

"Mom?" Ivy spoke up. "What are you —"

"You want to see our computers?" Sandy interjected. "I'll show them to you."

Nick began to mount the steps again. "That's the kind of attitude I like."

They reached the top, Harlan positioning himself on the broad swath of landing with a burst breath of relief. The sleek wood steps, while wider and deeper than standard, weren't big enough to accommodate him comfortably.

Nick turned to Sandy. "I'll need your cellular phones, too." He seemed to have forgotten his desire for a nicotine fix.

"The signal isn't good here," Ivy said instantly. "And it's out now anyway. Because of the snow."

"I don't recall asking you about the weather," Nick replied, extending his hand.

After a moment, Ivy reached into her pocket and took out her phone.

"Where's yours?" Nick asked Sandy.

"I don't know." Sandy rarely kept hers on her. "Probably in my room. Along with my laptop."

"Harlan," Nick said. "Don't let either of them move."

Sandy parsed the command. Not *stay with*

them. Or even *keep your eyes on them.* Harlan was highly literal; he would do just as Nick commanded.

Nick returned, arms laden with a teetering stack of technology. "I'm assuming the princess has one of these?" he said, using his chin to indicate the slim sandwich of a laptop.

Someone capable of laying waste to their whole world should be ugly — hunched and gnomic. But Nick wasn't. He was a rough-looking, gritty, but appealing older man, and you could see that fact reflected in Ivy's posture, the way she jutted her chin before responding, "Yes. I've got a laptop."

Nothing could have horrified Sandy more.

"Okay, then," Nick said, giving an approving nod. "Shall we enter your chamber, princess?"

Ivy's room lay between the master bedroom and the stairway.

Nick edged in front of Sandy to go inside. He placed the cell phones and laptop on the floor, taking Ivy's computer off her desk and adding it to the accumulation.

Nick pointed. "Stamp on these, Harlan."

No sooner had Nick asked than Harlan lifted one enormous shod foot. He brought it down on each of the phones, then jumped on the laptops, until all the devices had been smashed into an eely mass of black shards.

The pounding echoed in Sandy's ears. Two long trenches had been dug in the floor.

Nick began stalking around, looking into corners, checking the windows. "No locks?" he asked over his shoulder.

A pang sealed Sandy's throat shut as she watched him move about. Because she'd realized that something was missing from Ivy's room: Mac. How could she have forgotten about him? Nick must have put their dog away somewhere. Alone.

"You should've spent some time considering how to keep the bad guys out," Nick added.

"No one's getting in through one of those windows," Ivy scoffed.

She was right. Ivy knew the way this house had been built, its back to a bluff that resisted even Ben's skilled efforts.

Nick took a step in Ivy's direction. "Well, good. Then you'll be safe up here." He turned toward Sandy. "Now say goodbye to the princess."

Sandy yanked her head up. "What? We're not splitting up. Remember? One big slumber party, you said." She and Ivy couldn't be apart right now. They had to stay close in order to snatch any opportunity for flight that might present itself. And if no opportunity appeared? Then being together would be even more important.

"I did say that," Nick agreed. "And I can understand why you'd feel misled."

"So why change the plan?" Sandy asked. "Sticking together is safest. And from up here, you can see all the way down to the road at the same time as you keep an eye on the weather —"

"My turn," Nick said, his voice a brittle wind.

Sandy ground to a halt.

"I want some insurance while we wait." Nick's gaze slid past Ivy. "A reason you might choose not to flee this place too quickly."

Sandy's hands folded, nails sharp enough to dig ditches in her palms, and her face went stony, Botoxed with hate. Ivy had taken a step back when Nick ordered the separation. She took another one, and another, until meeting the plane of Harlan's chest.

Harlan had been locked up for armed robbery. He wasn't a killer, Sandy told herself, or someone who had sick predilections better left unnamed. Still, franticness descended upon her at the thought of leaving Ivy alone with him. She felt as if she were on the top floor of a building, looking down as it collapsed beneath.

Nick studied her with something like understanding. "Harlan's not going to do a single thing except what I tell him to. And all I'm telling him to do is stay with the princess. If you keep bugging me, though, I might just have to change my directive."

Sandy felt her shoulders sag. Two escaped prisoners, and trusting them seemed her only option. Ivy stuck out her hand, and Sandy grabbed it.

"Mom," Ivy said softly.

Sandy's head snapped up. "Yes," she hissed. "What, sweetie, tell me!"

"You're pressing too hard."

Sandy looked down and saw Ivy's hand flaming red inside hers. She loosened her grip.

"Please, Ivy," she said. "Just hold on for a little while longer." The look in Ivy's eyes was heartbreaking, the same one she'd worn on the brink of her first day of school.

Nick clamped his hand around Sandy's arm, and pulled her into the hall. "No more stalling. You and me downstairs, Harlan and the princess up here."

"Okay," she muttered. She tried to wrench free. *"Okay."* She sent a reassuring glance toward Ivy, all the love that could be delivered in a look. "I'm going."

Harlan's hand grazed Ivy's bedroom door, the lightest of touches on a solid plank of wood. The door swung shut on its hinges before closing with a *click*.

CHAPTER EIGHTEEN

Ivy was alone again with Harlan. She could smell him, feel heat coming off him. He had lips as thick as sausages, and round, blank eyes. Ivy couldn't help shrinking away. Then she heard Darcy telling her that was the dumbest thing she could do. Harlan would know that she was scared, and maybe worse, disgusted by his presence. Ivy put her foot down, halting the backward step she had been in the midst of taking.

"It's okay," Harlan said softly.

Ivy jerked her head up. Waaay up. His big body filled her room like foam. The room she'd only just begun to think of as her own, bestowing on it a handful of personal items: the hopeful, colorful rug she'd made sure came from their old house, a photo that her dad had printed out of her and Melissa on the summit of Mount Marcy.

Now this room would never be hers. She could never rid it of this intruder's presence.

How was Mac doing? Was he okay all by himself? And oh God, what about her dad? But Ivy clamped down on that thought. The world blurred, and she scrubbed at her eyes with the backs of her hands.

She plunked herself onto her bed. It didn't matter, standing or sitting, she was still snail-sized in comparison to Harlan. Ivy lowered her head so that he wouldn't see how close she was to crying.

He took slow, plodding steps in her direction.

Ivy scooted backward on the bed. *Scooch,* she heard her mom say, and then she really did start to cry. How could it have been only a few hours ago that she'd been sitting next to her mother on this bed? And how could Ivy have refused to go down for dinner? If she just got the chance for them all to be together again, Ivy would eat dinner every night with her parents till she was twenty.

Harlan stood over her, and Ivy waited, as far back on her bed as she could go. If he sat down, Ivy was going to fall off. Try to scrunch underneath. He'd never reach her there — he was too huge. Big balls of his hands hung by his thighs, which were as wide around as silos. Ivy could hardly see past him into the rest of her room.

She swallowed.

"Why are you scared of me?" he asked.

"I'm not," she said, a stupid response, the first one that came to her lips.

"Yes, you are," he said, softly again. His eyes looked a little less empty, more aware.

He sat down, and the mattress sank almost to the floor.

Ivy didn't fall off. She was cemented into place.

"They're always scared," he said. "And they always think I don't know."

A slick of disgust coated Ivy's tongue. "Who?"

"Well," Harlan said at last. "Everyone." He lifted his arm, and it was long enough that all the way across the bed, his hand landed on hers.

Ivy muffled a little shriek. "Don't touch me!"

He looked down at the offending hand. "I didn't mean to!"

Ivy could no longer conceal her revulsion in the hopes of lulling Harlan. Things were colliding in her head with the force of cars piling up. She brought her hands to her ears to try and dull the impact.

The words she'd said to her mother earlier that night.

Her stupid, girly attempt to fight Nick in

the basement, flailing at him, hurling herself around, and only succeeding in lashing his face.

How ugly and swollen his foot was. He'd never be able to walk miles into the woods.

Another memory, from longer ago. When the school year had started, Ivy attended her first boy-girl slumber party. She'd expected an ordinary Saturday night with Melissa and Darcy, plus a few others. Hair, nails, popcorn, a movie. *Maybe* a few giggly texts to some boys they were crushing on, asking them to come over, accompanied by hoots and hands clapped over mouths, the curtains immediately drawn if anyone was dumb enough to take them up on it.

But when Ivy arrived, there were boys hanging out in the finished basement, twirling around on bar stools, slouched over on the couch.

Darcy had laughed at her. "No one has just girls at sleepovers anymore."

"Yeah," another faux friend added. "We're juniors now, you know."

When midnight crept around, they'd started playing a game called Hook Up, which went just about how it sounded. Maybe because Ivy hadn't been that into it, she was the last one chosen, by a wormy boy named Dave Parks who had a bristle of growth above his lip that he either liked or didn't know to shave. Ivy had kissed boys before and she wasn't worried about that part, even though Dave totally icked her out. But after pushing his slimy tongue into her mouth, which she tolerated for a while, Dave went to pull down the zipper on her jeans, and stuck his hand in her waistband. Ivy had begun to twist and turn in some weird dance, finally flinging herself free, and the boy's laughter had followed her the whole way out.

Now Harlan's hand was touching hers, and Ivy had no chance of getting loose. It was like a tree stump upon her.

"Please," Ivy said. The word broke and grated like glass in her mouth. "Please don't."

"Why are you crying?" he asked.

Ivy looked at him. "I . . . I don't know."

His big, rolling mouth changed, and after a second, Ivy realized he was trying to smile.

"I don't want to hurt you, you know," he said.

"What . . . what do you want, then?" Ivy asked.

Harlan's hand plopped down, hitting the mattress with enough force to rock them. "This, I guess."

"Our house?" Ivy demanded. Good. Let

'em have it.

"No." He looked frustrated. "This," he repeated. "What we're doing now."

"What are you doing?" Ivy ventured. She felt as perplexed as he did.

He took a breath, as if relieved to be on surer ground. "Whatever Nick tells me to."

Ivy wasn't sure it was a good idea to say the next thing that came to her mind. "Do you always do what Nick says?"

Harlan's face folded. "Nick's my friend."

That was too much. "He's a jerk!" Ivy burst out. "He grabbed me downstairs — hurt me even — and he did something terrible to —" She swiped at her eyes and nose, both of which were wet. "— to my —"

"Shh," he said, reaching out and lowering Ivy's hand with his own. She couldn't have resisted if she'd tried. "Don't do that."

Ivy's face smarted. It was a relief to stop trying to stem her tears and just let them flow.

"I've known Nick a long time," Harlan said. "You know how someone you know that long can be a friend even if they're not very nice to you?"

Ivy was silent. She didn't know what to say, and anyway, she'd figured something important out. It wasn't Harlan she had to worry about. It was Nick.

CHAPTER NINETEEN

A solid sentry of wood stood between Sandy and Ivy. The only way Sandy was able to cope with the space splitting them was to listen to the quiet place inside her, the therapist's assessing instinct, which said that unless ordered otherwise, Harlan didn't present a danger.

She felt Nick's dark presence behind her as they walked down the stairs.

"The snow really isn't that big a problem," Sandy said. "My husband takes groups out in it all the time."

"I'm sure he does," Nick muttered.

Encouraged, Sandy swung around. "And you seem to be walking just fine. You don't want to waste these hours while everyone's occupied clearing the roads."

"Of course I'm walking just fine!" Nick roared, and as he stepped, he stumbled. He recovered quickly, grabbing the twisting vine of rail and repositioning himself on a length of level wood. "Save your tricks for Harlan," he said. "They won't work on me."

Nick shoved her forward, making her lurch. Sandy's feet found the next stair and she stayed there a moment, waiting for her heart to stop thudding and her breath to return.

Things were silent as they began again to descend.

Then Nick spoke. "Come on. How long are we going to keep playing this game?"

His voice was a flicker, right at the edges of her consciousness. He leered at her like a reflection in a funhouse mirror. Sandy looked away.

Down below and through the kitchen lay the door to the basement. A few dozen feet, maybe a hundred at most, yet impossible to reach.

"Suit yourself," Nick said at last, and Sandy blanched at the lack of life in his tone. It was as if a computer were talking. He extended his arm, indicating that she should go. "After you."

Sandy edged around him. This time, Nick checked before shifting on the stair, making sure he had room. He followed a step behind.

As they reached the bottom, a series of notes sounded.

■ ■ ■ ■

"What the hell is that music?"

Sandy grinned humorlessly. "It's the phone. They don't just ring anymore. That's the landline."

Nick pushed past her. "I cut it. Downstairs."

Sandy's smile became a trifle more real. "You need a degree in engineering to be sure you're cutting the right thing these days. It's impossible to fix your own car anymore, too. Did you know that?"

Nick didn't answer.

The phone continued to play its lilting, upbeat song, a few bars over and over, interfering with thought. Possibilities burred in Sandy's mind, most of them stupid, immediately discarded. Nick began to walk forward, but Sandy stayed in place, thinking furiously.

"There aren't many people who call on that line," she said. "It won't be — it shouldn't be a problem. But if I don't pick up . . . well, it could be."

Nick let out an ugly laugh. "You forget I already know what a liar you are. Maybe someone's calling about the combo to your safe." He headed for the kitchen again.

"Please!" Sandy screamed. "I'm telling you the truth!"

The music abruptly cut off.

Sandy felt her wrist locked by Nick's hand, then he dragged her toward the kitchen. Sandy's feet skidded; she had to skip a step to keep up. Injured or not, Nick pulled her easily across the floor, stopping only when they came to the cordless phone on its section of counter.

Nick pointed to the green flashing light.

"Tell me what that means," he said. He lowered his face to hers and spoke into her ear. "And don't lie about it. If you do —" A puff of breath. "— I'll go back upstairs and tell Harlan to throw the princess out her window."

Sandy turned to him in horror.

Nick smiled blandly. "That'd be a fitting exit from the castle, wouldn't it?" His voice broke into a growl, and he spoke deliberately. "Now. What. Does. That. Light. Mean?"

Sandy's tone was brittle. If she allowed any emotion in, she feared she might break down completely. "It means we have a voice-mail."

Nick swiveled toward the staircase. "Oh, Harlan —" he called in singsong.

"A message," Sandy said hurriedly.

"Fine," Nick said, turning back. "We had those before I went in. They just looked different. Play it."

The hollow, disembodied voice that entered the kitchen was instantly recognizable, even though the caller didn't identify herself.

"This time it's pretty bad, Dr. Tremont."

Madeline insisted on calling Sandy *doctor* even though Sandy had explained many times that she was a social worker, not a psychologist or psychiatrist.

The message continued. "Gloria says she's trying to reach you, but your cell must be out. So I decided to try you this way. I hope you can call me back. Here's my number."

The airless voice recited it.

Sandy lifted a triumphant face to Nick. Never mind that a patient had her home number; she wasn't even all that surprised by that.

"See?" Sandy said. "I have to call her back."

"Who is it?" Nick asked. He was eyeing the cordless as if it were an infuriating insect. "And how the hell many ways are there to call someone these days?"

"A patient of mine," Sandy replied. "I can help her with her problem, and then everything will be fine. But if she doesn't hear from me . . ." Sandy let her voice trail off, hoping Nick would envision a scenario.

He leaned against the counter, arms folded across his chest. "Yeah? If she doesn't hear from you, what?" His face fractured into a smile. "She comes out here with an arsenal and mows down the criminals to save you?" Nick paused. "What kind of doctor are you anyway?"

"I'm not a doctor," Sandy muttered. "I'm a therapist."

"Ah," Nick said. He was sitting on the counter now, regarding her from above. "No wonder you went to work on Harlan. A head shrinker. Why am I not surprised by your choice of career?"

Sandy took a breath. "She may not send in the cavalry," she said, choosing words carefully, like stepping over rocks in a creek. "But she could call my boss again at the hospital." Gloria wasn't actually her boss, but that didn't matter. "And Gloria does know where I live. She might get concerned and drop by. Or send somebody."

Sandy closed her mouth and waited. The truth was that if Madeline pestered Gloria with too many more calls, the admin would tell her to scram until her next scheduled appointment. Gloria could keep patients at a distance like a bodyguard held off paparazzi. But again, Nick would have no way of knowing that.

He eased himself off the counter. Sandy flinched, anticipating a series of blows. Instead, Nick turned and placed the receiver in her quaking hand.

"Fine," he said. "Call her back."

Sandy looked at him.

"Go on, do it," he said. "It's not a trick. I'm not going to stop you."

Further hesitation would only give him the chance to change his mind. Sandy's fingers skidded over the face of the phone, slap-dash keying in a sequence to call up the number. Sandy hit the wrong one, had to stop and go back. She started over, pressing each button deliberately.

Nick lowered his hand onto hers. It felt strong enough to crush not only her fingers, but the phone she held too. Dark, inky tattoos began at his wrist, then twined up his forearms before disappearing beneath his sleeves.

"You'd better not try anything," he said.

Sandy nodded. Her mouth was woolly and dry.

"If you say anything that sounds even a little funny to my ears, the princess vacates the premises without making use of her door." Nick walked to the wide window above the kitchen sink and gazed out. "Man oh man, was she right." He whistled loudly. "The second floor must be thirty feet off the ground." Nick touched the glass with his palm, then gave a mock-shiver before turning around. "Oh, and let me listen in, will you?"

"I can put it on speaker," Sandy said faintly.

But for a few seconds her fingers trembled too hard to press anything. Instead, her gaze was fixed on the black void outside, imagining the sight of her daughter's body tumbling through all that space before breaking into pieces on the frozen ground.

CHAPTER TWENTY

Cut off from the rest of the world, without her phone or even her computer, Ivy felt as if she were stuck on one of the backcountry trips her father planned, where she was forbidden to bring any devices.

Not stuck. That wasn't the right word. Ivy actually enjoyed those trips. She used to anyway. Back in the days before Darcy and all the others except Melissa blurred into one shiny, skinny streak, practically interchangeable right down to the fact that they all looked down on Ivy.

She and Harlan were sitting on the floor now. Thank God. This felt a lot safer. Ivy had managed to locate a deck of cards in the bottom of some box that had never gotten unpacked. She had tried to teach Harlan Spades, but that hadn't worked out so well, and the sight of him getting frustrated had caused instant backtracking on Ivy's part.

"Go fish," she mumbled, unable to

masquerade her boredom. *What time was it? When was this night going to end?* How *was it going to end*? She shivered.

"You could put on a sweater," Harlan suggested.

Ivy got up and went over to her dresser.

Harlan looked happy, thrilled almost — as if he had figured something out and it hadn't been half so hard as he'd imagined — when she came back, zipping up a hoodie.

"How come you let Nick boss you around?" Ivy asked. She pushed her fanned-out cards onto the purple band of her rainbow rug.

Harlan lifted his head. His brows wriggled like caterpillars. "Nick's a lot smarter than me," he said at last.

"Huh," Ivy replied. "You know, I don't think so."

"You don't?"

Ivy shook her head, though she wasn't one hundred percent positive about that. In some ways, Harlan seemed more simple-minded and literal than the kids she babysat, although he showed flashes of knowing things deep down. And hadn't Nick been a little babyish himself, tantruming when Ivy refused to do what he wanted in the basement? He'd acted a lot cooler and smarter since coming upstairs, except when he saw the snow, but still; Ivy momentarily dismissed both captors with disgust. *Children,* she thought. So maybe Harlan could be manipulated, like a sugared-up preschooler. Without him even realizing what she was doing.

She'd have to get him to talk.

As if reading her thoughts — but he couldn't do that, could he? — Harlan said, "You look like someone I know."

"Yeah?" Ivy asked eagerly. "Who?"

He turned his head away momentarily. It was the size of a pot you put a houseplant in. A really *big* houseplant.

"Want to see something?" he asked.

Now he sounded almost shy, like this boy Ivy had known forever, since kindergarten anyway, but who only spoke to her once a year.

"How was your summer?" the boy always asked.

Darcy teased Ivy about it, saying how the boy's mother probably coached him at home. She would act out the whole scene, playing the mom in a whiny, nagging voice: "Why don't you just talk to the girl?" and then doing the boy: "Oh, yeah, right, what should I say?" Finally Darcy would sing out: "Just ask her how her summer was!"

Harlan began to shift his body around, messing up the cards Ivy had spread out. He took off one of his shoes, and Ivy frowned. The shoe came apart, and Harlan removed something, holding it out to her.

Ivy reached forward with a hand that felt too loose to grasp anything, as if all the bones inside it had dissolved. "What is this?" she asked, trying not to let her distaste show.

"That's my sister's teddy bear," he said. "Well, part of him. I never had a teddy bear. My daddy said I was too big to need one. But my sister didn't mind sharing."

Ivy looked down, the caramel-colored clump resolving into a tuft of fur. She bit her lip. "Is it your sister?" she asked. "Who I look like?"

Harlan matched her lip-biting gesture, revealing front teeth the size of stones. "You know things, too. Just like your mama."

"What?"

He took the piece of fur out of Ivy's hand, and reached up without rising so much as an inch off the floor. He tucked the clump under the sheet on her bed.

"Why was it — why was he in your shoe?" Ivy asked.

Harlan settled both hands in his cavernous lap. "He comes out after lights out and

277

goes back in before morning count."

"Lights out? Like at camp?"

Harlan wagged his head. "I never went to camp."

And they wouldn't really do morning count at camp anyway, would they? The truth was beginning to come to Ivy now, pieces jigsawing into place. She couldn't believe she hadn't put them together before. She really was dumb, just like Darcy said.

"Hey, look." Harlan pointed to his cards. "I have another match."

Ivy took the pair and placed it on the slim stack he had acquired.

"You met Nick in prison," she said, a figuring-things-out note in her voice. "That's why you're wearing those clothes." A short laugh escaped her; it didn't sound anything like normal laughter. "How the hell did you get to our house?" Cursing. Also not like her. "No wonder you have to walk to another country."

Harlan's face changed, grew smoldery and shut.

He doesn't want to talk about it, Ivy realized. Doesn't even like to think about it. Why? Because he can't stand the idea of being captured. She felt a flash of power, like a plug sparking.

Maybe if she made Harlan mad, some

kind of change would take place. Like shaking a stuck appliance until something popped loose.

"You think the police won't find you there?" Ivy asked. "They have the news in Canada too, you know." She sounded like Darcy when she talked to that shy boy, or any of the losers — Darcy's name for them, not hers — at school.

But unlike Darcy, Ivy instantly regretted her course of action.

Harlan rose off the floor, looming over her like a building. "The police aren't looking for us."

"No," Ivy said. "I'm sure they're not."

"I better ask Nick." Glowering, he lowered his hand.

Ivy cowered on the floor. Once she stood up, she wouldn't have any excuse for how insignificant she felt beside him.

Harlan thrust his arm at her impatiently.

Ivy stared upward until her neck began to ache.

They were at a standstill, except not a real standstill, because both of them knew how easily he could just pick her up, make Ivy do whatever he wanted.

Light swept across the windows from outside. Ivy twisted to see, and Harlan turned, too. Two far-off blue-white scoops, bright as spotlights. Or headlights.

Just about to make the turn onto their road, a car.

CHAPTER TWENTY-ONE

Making this call under Nick's direction entailed at least one or two ethical violations, but Sandy couldn't think about that right now. As if there were guidelines governing situations like this. Protecting your patient's confidentiality when a madman broke into your house.

The phone rang once in her ear, and Madeline picked up.

"Dr. Tremont! You're all right!"

Sandy looked up from the phone. Nick's gaze sat on her, heavy as rocks.

"Yes, Madeline," she said. "I'm fine."

"It's a good thing you called back," the girl said cheerily.

Madeline had turned twenty last year, but Sandy persisted in thinking of her as a young girl. It was part of the countertransference she talked about in supervision. Something in Madeline pulled for a caretaking response from Sandy.

"Is it?" Sandy said. "Why?" Trying to be neutral, to conduct therapy when the man who had taken her family prisoner was sitting on the opposite side of the kitchen, was proving to be something of a challenge. Take that, Dr. Phil.

"Well, I was worried," Madeline said. "You always call right back."

Sandy opened her mouth to respond, then hesitated.

Nick took a few deliberate steps across the room, planting his boots in front of Sandy, so close that she could see him breathe.

"I know," Sandy said, subduing her voice. "And I'm sorry that tonight I —"

Nick coughed, a warning rumble.

"I was about to come out to your house and check on you!" Madeline interrupted in that same high-pitched, oddly jolly tone.

Nick reached for the phone, but Sandy clutched it, shaking her head and shooting him an *I told you so* look. She tried to broadcast her thoughts. *Don't you hear the state she's in? If I can't talk her down, then we're getting a visitor.*

Nick lowered his hand.

"Why don't you tell me what's going on tonight?" Sandy suggested, all the while thinking madly. Did Madeline know where she lived? It was possible. The house Ben built had been small-town news, and the hospital had a rumor network more efficient than a class of gossipy sixth graders. Good God, Sandy thought. Imagine if Madeline had walked into this. How much trauma could one young life hold before it burst like a balloon?

Madeline had been talking. Sandy swerved to catch up.

"And then she" — a retching sound, a cry — "she didn't want me to tuck her in tonight!"

Dottie. They were talking about Madeline's little girl.

Madeline was crying full-force now. "She said — oh, Dr. Tremont, she said she could do it herself!"

Something inside Sandy went quiet and still. Nick's hovering presence faded until Sandy was focused solely on her client, as if they were sitting in a private office somewhere, discussing Madeline's palpable pain.

"Okay," Sandy said softly. "Yes. I understand."

"You do?" Madeline cried. "Because I sure don't!"

"I know, Madeline, but you're a young mother," Sandy said softly. "Remember?

We've talked about this. How parenting is a series of stages, and you have about a second to get used to the one that you're in before the next is upon you."

"This isn't a stage," Madeline burst out. "My child hates me! She doesn't love me anymore, she doesn't even want me to — oh God, I don't think I can stand this —"

"Madeline," Sandy interjected. "You can stop this before it spirals out of control, remember? Count inside your head. Practice your breathing."

Over the speaker, the sound of shaky breaths, in and out.

"What did you do when Dottie asked to put herself to sleep?" Sandy asked, knowing the words would cause a resurgence of pain, but hoping that by hearing them spoken out loud, the event would become a little more normalized.

"What could I do?" Madeline demanded. "I let her."

Sandy smiled. Despite everything, she felt a glimmer of pride for her client. "That's wonderful."

"Yeah, right," Madeline said. "It's just great that my baby is rejecting me."

"Dottie isn't rejecting you," Sandy said. "She's becoming a toddler. Taking stabs at independence. I know it feels bad to you, but as far as Dottie is concerned, she loves you even more now. Because you're showing her that you can let her do what she needs to."

Sandy hoped her words would buoy the young woman. For all her youth and wounded-bird quality, Madeline was smart, and intuitive, and resourceful. She'd found her way to a spot on the organic farm, created a life for herself and her daughter out of nothing.

"Dr. Tremont?" An anxious rise in her voice.

"Yes, Madeline. I'm here."

"I miss my mother." A sob traveled across the line. "I miss her so much."

The focused place Sandy had come to receded like a wave, sucked back into an endless ocean. Madeline's mother, whom therapy had revealed to be a skinty, disapproving woman, unable to give her daughter a sliver of praise for anything. Sandy took the phone from her ear. Nick's gaze seized hers, but he was the last person she could stand to look at right now. She turned around unsteadily, as if the even surface of the floor had begun to roll beneath her.

"Dr. Tremont?" Madeline said again.

Her voice seemed to come from far away. Time sloshed by in a fluid, unmarked rush.

Nick reached for the receiver, and Sandy reared back as if burned.

"It's terrible that your mother was killed," she said at last, all but panting. "But there are other ways to lose your mother —" The sentence sheared off, and Sandy had to start again. "Sometimes your mother can be right there and you still don't have her. So try to be glad that you were so close to yours before she died."

Silence over the phone.

Sandy bent over, spent. The line between judicious self-disclosure and too much information shared by a therapist was perhaps the vaguest and hardest to identify in the whole profession. Self-revelation could serve a therapeutic function. It could normalize, illuminate, connect. But Sandy knew that what she'd just said hadn't come out of a willingness to utilize an aspect of her own life to help a patient. Sandy had blurted those words out, hot and unexamined. Where had they been dredged up from?

Madeline's breathing was quieter now, though, and steady.

After a long moment, she said, "You're right, Dr. Tremont. I am lucky about that."

Sandy pulled herself back to the present. It felt like it took physical effort to do so, as if she had hauled herself up over the edge of a cliff.

"I think you'll be all right tonight, Madeline," she said. "And Dottie will, too."

"Thank you, Doctor," Madeline said. "I feel much better now —"

Nick took the phone and set it back in its cradle.

As his hand grazed hers, something let loose inside Sandy. Her knees gave a jog, and the final brick crumbled to dust in her mind. Sandy brought her hands up to her temples, pressing hard, but she couldn't halt the stampeding herd of memories.

Nick looked at her, an *aha* in his pale gray eyes. "So. Now we stop pretending?"

"No," Sandy said, still squeezing. "No, no, no . . ."

"Shut up!" Nick hissed.

There was a distant crunch of gravel, then the growl of an approaching car.

December 16, 1977

The Happy Learners Nursery School was housed in a low red building on an isolated road leading out of Cold Kettle. Barbara had balked at first, not wanting her little boy to be so far from home at only four years of age, even though the school was really just a few miles from the center of town as the crow flies. But there weren't many options for children before they started kindergarten. When Barbara had looked into the one other place, run by a good friend of Glenda Williams, the woman had eyed Nicholas oddly and accepted Barbara's application with a studied coolness. Barbara wouldn't have allowed Nicholas to spend his days in such a place for all the gold in California. If her son was going to enter school, then he would have to be treated with the same loving warmth Barbara provided.

Nicholas went to Happy Learners three

mornings a week, so Barbara had found it a little odd when the director invited her to drop by on a Thursday, one of the days Nicholas didn't attend. Not only her; Gordon had also been asked. Barbara arranged for Nicholas to stay with Glenda upon the director's suggestion that the little boy not come, another thing Barbara thought strange.

"Tell me again why I'm here," Gordon said, shifting uncomfortably on the rigid chair in the hall outside the director's office. It wasn't one of the children's seats, but Gordon still looked out of place in it — in this whole situation, in fact, like an adult playing at dolls. School, along with the rest of Nicholas' life, was Barbara's terrain. "Why did they want to see us both?"

"I'm not sure," Barbara replied. She twisted around in the seat she occupied, almost facing the wall so that she didn't have to look at the hall. Then something occurred to her. "Maybe they want to talk about skipping Nicholas ahead into kindergarten. That's why they asked us not to bring him along. So he wouldn't get, you know, a swelled head."

Gordon was distracted, studying the hallway.

Barbara continued to avert her eyes from

the spot where he kept a watchful eye.

The door to the director's office swung open, and Ms. Castleman stuck her head out.

The *Ms.* had impressed Barbara upon introduction — she felt a blend of interest and admiration for the women's libbers who were infiltrating Cold Kettle — though the director's political leanings were less important than the education her son was being given, of course. But Nicholas actually had a touch of the hippie himself, with those long locks of curls Barbara cut so sparingly. He fit right in here.

"Mr. and Mrs. Burgess? Won't you come in?" Ms. Castleman poked her head out a little farther, peering into the hall. "And bring your little girl, of course."

Gordon stood up and walked in the indicated direction, stooping down and offering one hand as he scooped up a toy with the other.

Barbara left him to the task, entering the office first.

"There are some playthings over there," Ms. Castleman said, pointing to a corner.

Barbara faced the director's desk resolutely, waiting to begin.

After a few moments spent fussing and

settling, Gordon came and took a seat beside her.

"Thank you for coming in," Ms. Castleman said to him. "We don't usually ask to see both parents, usually just the mother is fine. Your extra time is appreciated."

"That's all right," Barbara replied for both of them. "When it comes to Nicholas, we want to be here for whatever is needed."

"I'm glad to hear that," Ms. Castleman said. There was something careful in her words.

Barbara decided to spare the director any delay in deciding how to proceed.

"Ms. Castleman . . ." The title felt awkward, unseemly on her tongue. "I have an idea about why you wanted to see us."

Ms. Castleman sat forward. "You do?"

Barbara nodded eagerly.

Gordon had been checking behind him; now he turned and faced front again.

"It's about Nicholas and whether he should be here, isn't it?"

An expression of something like relief crossed Ms. Castleman's face. "Why, yes, Mrs. Burgess. I'm not sure how you knew — what you might've been told — but that's exactly the reason I called you both in today."

"We've been wondering the same thing,"

Barbara said. She snatched a quick look at Gordon, keeping her line of sight sideways so it wouldn't wander over to the play corner. "I have at least."

Ms. Castleman nodded. "And what is it that you've been wondering?"

"Why, whether Nicholas wouldn't be better off advancing more quickly," Barbara said. "To a kindergarten class where the other children will be — up to his level."

She hadn't realized how awkward it would be to put this into words, until silence cast a heavy shroud over the office.

Ms. Castleman aimed her gaze down toward her desk.

Gordon gave a cough. "That's not — this isn't why you brought us in here today, is it, Mrs. Castleman?"

Barbara frowned at him. "It's *Ms.* And what are you saying, Gor—"

Ms. Castleman shook her head. "No. I'm afraid it isn't."

"Well, what is the reason, then?" Barbara asked. She was accosted by the strangest urge to get up and leave. Just run right out of the office, the whole school, fetch Nicholas away from Glenda at the rectory, and never let these halls darken him again. "Is it because he's a little undersized? Because I've been working on that. He drinks milkshakes every day."

Ms. Castleman spoke stiffly, as if her words had just been cued. "We here at Happy Learners don't feel that your son is a suitable addition to our facility. We think that he would be better off someplace else." She took a breath before going on. "Less officially, I would like to tell you that I have been a nursery school director — and a teacher before that — for more than fifteen years. And from what Nicholas' instructor has told me, and what I took the opportunity to witness myself, I think that your son would benefit greatly from some sort of intervention." She paused. "A visit to a psychiatrist or a child psychologist would not be out of order."

"A psychiatrist!" Barbara burst out, so loudly and suddenly that there was a clatter from behind. Barbara remained in place, chest heaving, as Gordon got up and restored whatever order had been breached. Ms. Castleman sat there, watching, a perplexed expression on her face.

"What?" Barbara snapped. "Why are you looking at me like that?"

Ms. Castleman's cheeks fired. "I wasn't looking at you, Mrs. Burgess. In fact, I was just wondering . . ."

"What?" Barbara returned in the same

clipped tone as before. "Wondering what?"

Ms. Castleman shook her head before speaking in a great rush. "How you can have one child who's so well behaved and pleasant, when the other appears to be so greatly troubled." Her professional voice returned. "Perhaps that is for the doctor to get to the bottom of."

"We're not taking Nicholas to any head shrinker," Barbara answered. "He's gifted. That's why he can be moody while his sister is level, as you say. It will be the challenge of my life to help Nicholas direct his talents instead of being driven by them." That phrase had been in the book she'd read. "And I'm deeply sorry that you won't join me in that pursuit."

She stood up.

Ms. Castleman rose and put a hand out to stop her.

"Mrs. Burgess," she said. "I didn't say that your daughter was levelheaded. I said that she was sweet and well behaved. Just look at how she's putting those blocks together. Look at her smile."

Barbara stared steadfastly ahead at the director, who took a breath and went on.

"And Nicholas isn't only moody. For one thing, he's not achieving in an age-appropriate manner, learning letters or numbers with the rest of his class, nor even colors and shapes. And it has nothing to do with his size." Ms. Castleman paused as if waiting for a response. When none was forthcoming, she added, "Nicholas is the most unstable and roughly tempered child I've ever met."

Barbara felt a vein pulsing between her brows.

Gordon placed his hand on her arm, but Barbara shook him off. "He's stormy," she told the director. "As are most geniuses and artists."

"Mrs. Burgess!" Ms. Castleman burst out, raw exasperation now present in her tone. "It's not moodiness, it's not storminess, and it is most certainly not genius. Nicholas is violent. Do you know, I nearly lost another student after he attacked her in the classroom? The only way this child's mother agreed not to withdraw her daughter from my school is because I promised that the little girl would never again have to go near the boy who hurt her. The girl is having bad dreams every night." An expression of repugnance rolled across Ms. Castleman's face. "She had a perfectly round circle driven into the skin between her thumb and forefinger. It was put there by the hole punchers we use for making Christmas ornaments."

"Well," Barbara replied. "Perhaps you shouldn't allow weapons into your classroom."

Ms. Castleman was finally at a loss, standing behind her desk, mouth rounded and silent.

"But thank you for helping me to understand," Barbara said.

"Understand?" Ms. Castleman echoed. "Understand what?"

"How two children got into a tussle because your teacher cannot maintain control and you decided to scapegoat mine." Barbara whirled on her heels. "Good day, Ms. Castleman. All told I am glad we found out sooner rather than later that you don't have the skills or resources necessary to educate a child like Nicholas."

Barbara strode across the room without checking to see if Gordon was behind her.

Ms. Castleman spoke up as she reached the doorway. "Do you know what I noticed when I told you about the hole puncher?"

Barbara paused with her hand on the knob.

"You didn't seem surprised."

Gordon drove the station wagon to the end of the winding lane that led to the rectory.

He parked and got out, then busied himself with something in the backseat. Barbara strode across the lawn, stepping without particular care over the walkway flowerbeds to approach the front door.

Glenda answered her abrupt knock. "Back already? How did it go at the school?"

Barbara gave a rapid shake of her head. "How is Nicholas?"

Glenda gestured her inside. "Fine, just fine. Come on in. You look like you could do with a cup of tea."

Barbara was about to shake her head again when tears suddenly spilled over. "I want to go see Nicholas."

Glenda noticed her tears, which Barbara rued inwardly. She couldn't stand to be chided by one more person right now.

"You poor dear. Nicholas is perfectly fine. My youngest is taking care of him. He's the only one who never had anyone to babysit." She offered a smile of fond reflection, considering her brood. "You have yourself a cup of tea and relax."

There was a knock on the front door, then Gordon walked in.

Glenda smiled brightly in his direction. "Well, aren't you a sight for sore eyes. I bet you'll be just the thing to cheer Mama up."

Glenda walked over to the door and lifted

Gordon's burden into her own arms. She returned with her neck wreathed in a choking clasp. Glenda looked down with a smile, her hand stroking wisps of hair, and positioned herself in such a way that Barbara couldn't help but see what she carried.

Barbara blinked back the last of her tears and turned away. "No tea, Glenda, thank you. You said Nicholas is upstairs?"

Barbara heard murmurs as she left the room.

Gordon's voice, then Glenda asking, "Leave the school completely?"

Gordon said, "It's not as if she gave us much choice."

If she hadn't been headed upstairs to Nicholas, Barbara would have wound her arms around her husband's throat in a merciless hug, and squeezed the words right out of him.

A mewling cry began behind her. "Mama?"

Barbara's nerves felt like fur being rubbed the wrong way. She walked away from the sound. Glenda and Gordon spoke in similar soothing tones while Barbara mounted the stairs, and the cries grew muted.

In a back bedroom, Nicholas was sitting at a little table with Adam, a strapping boy of fourteen or fifteen who straddled a too small chair, a leftover from one of the many childhoods lived in this house.

Barbara stood in the doorway, barely allowing herself to breathe.

Nicholas sat straight and still in his chair while Adam laid cards out in front of him. They were Candy Land cards; Barbara recognized them from a set Nicholas had shredded for some art project. Squares of bright M&M colors: red, green, yellow, orange.

"Now which one is this?" Adam asked.

"Purple?" Nicholas guessed in his sweet piping voice.

Barbara's heart clutched with love.

Adam shook his head. "Try again," he said. "You're close. When you get real good at this, I'll tell you about the color wheel, and then you'll see just how close you were."

Nicholas squinted at the card. His little hands knotted in frustration, and his brows drew down. He was going to get upset; Barbara could feel it.

"Take your time," Adam said.

"I'm just thinking right now," Nicholas said.

"That's right," Adam said. "That's a good thing to do. Want me to give you a hint?"

"No." Nicholas caught the tip of his tongue between pearly teeth. "I can do it."

"I bet you can."

Barbara walked into the room. "Adam Williams! Don't you talk to him like that!"

Adam pushed backwards in the small seat, toppling it over. He stood up awkwardly. "Like — like what, Mrs. Burgess?"

"Why, sarcastically. Making him think he's not good at this." She looked down at her little boy. "Nicholas knows perfectly well what color that is."

Adam's face tangled in a frown. "I wasn't being sarcastic. I'm trying to help him learn his —"

"He doesn't need any help," Barbara said.

Nicholas was standing up now too, looking from his mother to Adam.

"Do you, Nicky?" Barbara asked.

Adam took a step away from the table, holding out his hands. "We were having fun, Mrs. Burgess. Nick has been learning a lot. He's a real good kid."

Barbara looked down at Nicholas. He tilted his face, gave her a smile that felt as if it were attached by cords to her heart.

Barbara crouched beside him. "It must be so hard for you."

"What, Mama?" He pitched on tiptoes, looking into her face. "What you mean?"

Barbara wrapped her arms around him. "So hard," she crooned. "To have to sit still

300

like that. And do silly, stupid exercises." Her voice slid into a singsong. Out of her peripheral vision, she saw Adam leave the room. "I remember what happened when you played with these at our house." She leaned over, still hugging Nicholas, and teetering in her crouch as she snagged a handful of cards from the little table. "Do you remember what you did?"

Nicholas looked at her. Then he looked at the cards.

Barbara's shoulders settled. She gave a nod, so small it hardly felt as if her head was moving. Nicholas closed his miniature fist around Barbara's hand, and she savored his touch, sitting back on her haunches.

Nicholas let out a wolfish howl then, hooking his little fingers. His nails dug divots into the cards as he began to tear each one into pieces. Though small for his age and slender, Nicholas didn't lack strength. He threw the scraps into the air, running back to the table for the rest. These Nicholas set upon with a vengeful rage, howling, ripping, tearing. And as the pieces of card stock fell around them like snow, Barbara rested, and watched her son be consumed by his desperate need and vision.

She wasn't sure how much time had passed.

Cards lay all around, obscuring the floor. Even the game board had been broken. The little table had joined the chair that fell over when Adam got up.

Nicholas' chest rose and fell, his body heated as he lay in Barbara's arms. His curls were tangled so badly, she was going to have to comb them out when he was asleep.

There were footsteps along the hall. A sucked-in breath from Glenda. Gordon's defeated sigh. "Nicholas, come here," his father said.

Nicholas roused himself enough to scream, "No!"

Barbara forced herself to stand, lifting Nicholas unsteadily and carrying him out of the room. "I'm sorry about the mess, Glenda. Adam chose quite an activity to do with my son. Perhaps you were right never to let that boy babysit."

There was the barest of pauses. "Barbara, I'm a pastor's wife," Glenda said. "I pray every night not to judge myself when I fail, and not to judge anyone else either."

"Someone should judge you," Barbara bit out. "Raising a great, big strapping boy who likes to torment little ones."

Glenda blanched.

Nicholas flung himself around in Barbara's grasp, nearly sending himself over the stair railing. Glenda reached out and repositioned him more safely in Barbara's arms.

"I have my limitations, Lord knows." She let out a sigh. "And I fear I may only be making things worse in this situation. For your child, perhaps, but certainly for mine. Right now Adam's so mad at himself, he can't stop pacing downstairs."

Barbara didn't respond as she began to trudge down the steps.

"Please don't bring your boy here again, Barbara," Glenda said. "May God bless and keep him. And that little girl of yours, too. Gordon, watch out for her. Watch out for them both."

Gordon gave a nod, then bent down. "Cassandra," he said. "Come to Daddy."

CHAPTER TWENTY-TWO

Ivy jumped to her feet. "Please," she said. "We have to go see who that is."

Harlan moved more slowly, but he too turned in the direction of the bedroom door. "Nick will take care of it."

Ivy ran back to the window, feet suddenly light with hope. One of her dad's sportsman friends, a lost hunter with a gun, maybe even the police.

Visoring her eyes, Ivy peered out. She could see only part of their driveway from this angle, but it was enough to reveal the rear portion of an SUV.

Everything inside her plummeted. Seconds ago, she'd sprinted on air; now it was as if both shoes had been sunk into cement. She couldn't believe he had actually come. She couldn't believe she had forgotten.

Well, said Darcy, inside Ivy's head, *a home invasion can be kinda distracting. And it's not like you ever had a boyfriend before.*

Even scared as she was, Ivy felt her ears grow hot. Cory wasn't her boyfriend.

Ivy couldn't let him walk into this. Not with Nick downstairs.

With a mad shriek, Ivy ran past Harlan. He moved clumsily enough that she made it into the hall. But sheer size allowed Harlan to catch up to her in two jerky steps, and then his hand settled around her arm. The force with which he pulled her back was staggering. Ivy felt her shoulder wrench in its socket. She flew through the air, coming down so hard at Harlan's feet that the wind was knocked out of her. She sat, holding on to her sore shoulder, and heaving and grasping for breath. She stared upwards with burning eyes.

"I'm sorry!" Harlan said. It almost looked like he was crying. "I told you I didn't want to hurt you!"

"That's my . . ." Ivy began as soon as she could speak. "It's my . . . that car."

Harlan shook his head, confused.

Ivy forced air down into her lungs. She took her hand off her throbbing shoulder. "I know that car. It's my friend's. I can't let Nick get there first."

Harlan's face broke into a relieved smile. "Nick isn't going to hurt anyone."

Ivy shook her head hopelessly. "Oh yeah? How about what he did to my dad?"

For the first time, Harlan looked doubtful. He pinched Ivy's hoodie between his thumb and forefinger, setting her back on her feet. Then he turned in the direction of the stairs.

Ivy could hear gravel being churned by tires now. At any minute that car would pull up, spelling safety and escape and freedom. But Harlan, standing beside her in the hall, was as big a barricade as the whole rest of the house. The whole rest of the world.

"Okay?" she whispered. "I can go?"

Now he was crying for sure. His tears were like the rest of him, big, like beads.

"I don't know," he said through them.

Nick appeared at the bottom of the stairway, gun hand extended. Ivy's mom moved into view slowly, like someone who'd been wakened out of a deep sleep.

Nick crooked his elbow around her mom's neck, pulling her forward. Ivy's mom went slack, allowing herself to be dragged.

"Mom!" Ivy screamed, and started downstairs.

"Harlan," came Nick's growl. "Stop her."

He stopped Ivy mid-step, the ledge of his hand holding her in place.

A car door slammed.

Ivy's stomach turned to ice water; she was going to puke.

"Kill those floodlights outside," Nick commanded. "Where's the switch?"

Ivy's mom looked around as if she weren't sure. It was like she was drunk or something.

"If you turn the lights out now, it'll only attract more attention!" Ivy shouted.

Keeping a hold of her mom, Nick craned his head upstairs.

Ivy fought to get free of Harlan, but it was no use. She might as well have been trying to shove ten boys off of her. And she couldn't figure out why her mom was acting like one of the special-needs kids in class, who couldn't follow instructions, or put five coherent words together.

"Plus our neighbors will wonder!" Ivy called down again. All things her mother should be saying. "They know we're supposed to be home!"

"Your neighbors," Nick scoffed. "All zero of them?"

He didn't know about the Nelsons, then.

The doorbell rang, a jarring clang.

Nick aimed the gun at her mom and spoke in a deadly, drilling voice. "You didn't get rid of that girl on the phone."

What girl? Had Melissa called? The way

this stupid house muffled sound, Ivy hadn't had a clue. Just like Cory standing on the porch right now wouldn't hear them even if they screamed.

"I did," Ivy's mom said dully. "It isn't her."

"I don't believe you." Nick lowered the gun to her mom's chest, and Ivy cried out.

"She's telling the truth!" she shouted. "It's my friend out there! He planned to come over earlier — before you even got here! Oh please, he doesn't have any idea!"

In the moment following Ivy's announcement, everything went completely still. When the doorbell rang again, it sounded an oddly cheerful chime in the silent house.

Nick squinted up the stairs. "Harlan," he said, "let her come down."

Ivy had been trying every which way to lose Harlan's shackling presence; but once she did, she hesitated. She shucked off her hoodie — stupidest, vainest act ever, but she didn't want Cory to see her in that ugly old thing — and tossed it on the floor. Starting downstairs, she didn't have the first idea of what she was going to do when she got there.

Nick met her midway, gripping her mother, who looked at Ivy with sightless eyes. Ivy nearly reached out and grabbed her. Partly to check whether her mom was okay, partly to hold on to her herself. But their position — the three of them on the stairs — was too precarious to make any sudden moves.

Nick broke into her thoughts. "That's your friend out there?"

Ivy nodded.

"You need to send him away."

Ivy nodded again.

"Your mother did a pretty good job with her friend," Nick went on.

What friend? Ivy looked at her mother. What was wrong with her anyway?

"I'm hoping you'll be as good," Nick continued. "Because if you try to tell your pal anything stupid, I will shoot him. Even if I have to fire through you to do it."

That snapped her mother out of it. She twisted in Nick's grasp so suddenly that she nearly hurled herself free. Nick pulled her up short by her hair and she let out a yowl of pain. Ivy wouldn't have imagined her mother capable of making such a sound, so wounded and young.

"Mom?" Ivy said in a small voice. "What's the matter with you?"

Her mother stilled in Nick's grasp and his grip on her hair loosened. She hung there, motionless.

"Calm down," Nick said, smiling. "I didn't say I was going to shoot her. Or her boy toy either. Just that I would if I have to. So long as the pretty princess behaves, nobody gets hurt." He paused, finally letting go of her mom, but keeping the gun trained on them both. "Can you do that, princess?"

Ivy nodded a third time, and brushed past Nick on the stairs.

The doorbell rang again, and Ivy jumped. From behind, she felt a metallic, unfeeling caress. The gun, against the small of her back.

"Princess," Nick said, and Ivy let out a little whimper. "I changed my mind. If you screw this up, I'm not going to kill you. I'm going to kill your mother."

Ivy couldn't bear to turn in her mom's direction, see her looking slumped and dumb, as if she hadn't even understood what Nick said.

From upstairs, Harlan called down encouragingly. "Just make him go away," he said. "And Nick won't do anything."

Ivy turned the doorknob.

Cory stood on the porch, legs planted wide, his gloved hands shoved into the pockets of his parka. Snow fell in a sheet

310

behind him. It was still coming down hard.

"Hey," he said. "Sorry it took me a while to get here."

Ivy stared at him. She wasn't sure her voice would work. Her jaw felt like it had rusted shut.

Cory spoke into the silence. "You were right. My folks were worried about the storm."

Ivy could feel the weight of all three people behind her. Not just Harlan's immense contribution, but also her mother, so hushed and weirdly stuporous, plus Nick and his gun.

"So you wanna go out?" Cory asked. "People will be by the Rock. I got snowshoes in my car." He inclined his head. Snow flew like darts through the air. "Nice weather for a trek."

A smile wobbled on Ivy's lips. On any other day, she would've had to inwardly marvel at the cliché. Her first chance with a boy, and he was just like her father.

Her dad. How could she have forgotten about her dad?

"Hey, are you all right?" Cory asked.

There was a warning cough behind her, a rumble that threatened to turn into a growl.

Cory cocked his head, trying to get a look inside the house.

Ivy spoke hurriedly. "I can't go out tonight. I'm sorry."

"Is it the weather?" Cory asked. " 'Cause I'd be glad to talk to your folks. That's them inside, right? Probably I should introduce myself."

Ivy looked at him.

"I mean . . . if we're gonna hang out or whatever." A hopeful smile appeared on his mouth.

Ivy's cheeks bloomed. Even anticipating the thrust of the gun against her — or worse, one explosive burst from it — she couldn't stop staring at Cory's mouth.

"Don't worry, I chained up. The beast is great on a night like this." He offered a grin, sticking his thumb in the direction of his Explorer.

How Ivy longed to be in it. The power of that engine, considerately left thrumming so that the interior would stay warm, could take her away from here so fast. Take all of them away. Ivy nearly made a run for it right then. Only movie images of bullets and spatters of blood flying, fleshy crimson against all the snow, stopped her.

"It's not that," Ivy said. "It's — my dad is sick."

Or hurt. Just not that word she couldn't think.

"Oh," Cory said, clearly confused. "Like, and you have to take care of him?"

What a dumb lie. Ivy wrapped her arms around herself, her body wracked by shivers.

Cory took a step forward. "Is he going to be all right, your dad? Hey, you want my coat?" He pulled the zipper down with awkward, puffy fingers, and began to shrug out of his parka.

"No —" Ivy started.

"He's not going to be okay?" Cory's face folded with concern.

"No, not that —" Ivy tried to push at the coat Cory was offering.

From behind her came a grunt, and then a barely audible *tick.*

The safety on the gun.

Cory first, then her mother.

Ivy's knees jolted. "Cory, look!" she said, almost crying. She would've cried if she hadn't thought it might alert Cory. "I don't want your coat, I don't want anything from you! My dad isn't even really sick." She let out a laugh that burned her throat, as if she'd just thrown up.

Cory began to frown.

"What I really want is for you to go. Okay?" Ivy took a step into the cold, away from the front door, as if a few feet could

313

deter a bullet. "I just want you to leave. I mean, I don't want us to go out. At all. Okay?"

Cory's coat was still thrust out. It fell to the ground as he stumbled backward across the slippery stone. "Sure, okay," he said, righting himself. "I just — I guess I misunderstood. Take care, Ivy. Hope your dad is —" He seemed to remember the lie and his face fired red despite the temperature. He turned and took the wide steps at a skid.

Leaving without his coat.

Ivy couldn't let him come back up here.

The lidless eye of the gun continued to probe from behind. Ivy pictured it tracking Cory across the snow like one of those red laser beams in a heist movie.

"Cory —" she called out, her voice hitching, breaking apart on the word.

Cory turned back, an expectant lift to his eyebrows, and Ivy hurled the parka. Cory bent and snatched it up. He threw himself into his car, grinding the gears and fishtailing as he swung the vehicle around.

Then he was gone.

Nick stepped out onto the porch. He squinted into the snow with an expression of fierce hatred. "Goddamn storm," he said.

As if it was personally setting out to upset

314

him. As if he hadn't just witnessed Ivy's display of cruelty and betrayal, far worse than any weather could be. Ivy was no better than one of the mean girls at school.

She stared down at the ground, blinking through a silver sheen. Her legs, her whole body, were entirely glued with white. Snowflakes ran down her face like tears.

"Get back inside now," Nick said after a while. "Good job."

Chapter Twenty-Three

Sandy stepped forward and took Ivy into her arms. The two of them like refugees, shock-stung, wordless.

Ivy stood like a post in Sandy's loose grasp, her head hanging, hands at her sides. There wasn't any tension in her body. It had all drained out onto the stone, become one with the snow when she'd sent that boy away.

Sandy hadn't even known her daughter had a boyfriend.

She hadn't known anything, least of all herself.

Nick didn't have to speak. She could feel him beside her, and she understood what he wanted her to do. How she hated understanding what he wanted her to do.

"Ivy," Sandy whispered. *Forgive me.* "You have to go back upstairs now."

Nick smiled.

Her daughter raised her head, but she

didn't look at Sandy. Her gaze was directed at a slant. Possibly it wasn't directed at all.

The cost of this night. Sandy was trained to recognize the signs, and she saw them all in Ivy. Shock. Dissociation. Trauma.

And, of course, even worse was coming.

"Are you — okay?" Sandy asked. It wasn't a therapist's question, neutral, unleading, aware that there was no such thing as *okay*. It was a mother's, who needed there to be. "Up there, I mean?"

She got no response.

"With Harlan," Sandy added.

Ivy's cloudy eyes cleared momentarily. "Yes. He's fine."

Sandy felt something give in her chest. "Oh, thank —"

Harlan's hand closed around Ivy's upper arm, and he began steering her upstairs, the two of them moving like one shambling beast.

"Ivy!" Sandy shouted.

Ivy paused, but didn't turn on the stairs.

"I'm sorry." Sandy lowered her head. Her tears made splotches on the floorboards. "I'm so, so sorry."

"It's okay, Mom," Ivy said woodenly. "It's not your fault."

Oh yes, it is, Sandy thought. She hadn't been talking about the boy.

317

■ ■ ■

With Ivy and Harlan out of sight, Sandy's mind was directed two floors away. Now that she knew Ivy was all right — physically at least — Ben was everywhere inside Sandy, in each thought, on the tip of her tongue, and even in her hands.

"Tell me your husband's name," Nick said.

Sandy flinched. He was able to read her as if she'd painted signs.

Nick straddled one corner of a high occasional table. It had been forged from the round base of a tree, silken, undulating wood.

He continued to eye her. "If you want to go see him, that is."

At that, Sandy lifted her head, though she didn't allow hope to spark. She knew who she was dealing with now.

"Come on," Nick said exasperatedly. "I thought we were going to stop this game of pretend. I saw your face back there in the kitchen just before the kid drove up." He paused. "Can't believe I didn't realize what was going on until then. What the hell happened? Did you just — forget?"

Not forget. That wasn't the right word.

You couldn't forget more than twenty years of your life unless you were amnesiac. But there were other defenses a fully functioning person could mount. And not even realize they were doing so until something — or someone — jolted them off the high tip of the spire on which they had built a fragile, careful life. Dissociation, compartmentalization, splitting. Sandy knew all the terms. Why had her patients never told her how unhelpful those words were, how much they missed of the real life, flesh-and-blood process?

What had really happened was that she'd amputated a part of herself. And after that part was gone, she never spoke about it, gave it no reference or mention. Ultimately she hadn't even thought about it, until it receded into a state where it felt more dreamlike than real.

The problem with dreams, though, was that you eventually woke up.

Nick's leer assailed her, knitting past and present into a single lurid tapestry.

"You'll really take me to my husband?" Sandy whispered.

"Maybe," Nick said lazily. "Maybe not."

A howl built like a twister inside Sandy. She imagined inhuman strength: throwing Nick off the table — their beloved find of a table, like a piece of the forest itself — and bringing the whole slab down upon his head.

Nick laughed. "Come on, Cass. One thing you've got to remember is that I don't exactly stick to my word."

Her energy unleashed itself in one drawn-out yell. "I told you not to call me that!"

Nick fiddled calmly with the cuff of his borrowed shirt, unmoved by her force. "Do you have a different name now?"

Sandy felt the two halves of her life collide with the power of a plane touching down. One moment she was airborne, in a state of roaring suspension, and the next she was on the ground, everything silent and calm around her.

"Sandy," she said at last. "I changed my name legally to Sandra. In college."

Nick set his ashy eyes upon her. "That works." He eased down off the table and walked in the direction of the kitchen archway. When he got there, he turned and looked back.

Sandy frowned, but she was already walking forward, tripping as she started to hurry.

At the entrance to the basement, Nick stopped her with the flat of one hand.

"I don't think we'll find your husband in any shape to do much," he said. "But just in case we do — remember, I've still got the gun. And no reason not to use it." Nick moved his palm to her shoulder and she cringed. "You should know that best of all. *Sandy.*"

She raised her eyes to Nick's lightless ones. Not for one second did she doubt him.

Her brother had always been the most dangerous person Sandy knew.

CHAPTER TWENTY-FOUR

The basement was big and dark and empty, a featureless, cavernous space, and it seemed at first that her husband — superhuman as always — must have not only survived the fall, but escaped. Gone for help. Someone might be on the way even now, as Sandy descended the steps.

Then her eyes began to adjust, and in the distance she saw the ladder of two-by-fours that Nick had pounded up over the exit door. The windows were slits a ways off the floor, too small for a man to crawl through.

Sandy entered the grayed-out space as if she were wading into the sea. Toward one side was a bricking of storage bins, high as a wall: items that had never gotten unpacked after their move, and other artifacts of family life. Her wrapping station, readied for the holidays, waited like a pageant just before the curtain rose.

Nick took a step beside her into the void.

As Sandy inched away from him, a narrow band of light captured her eyes, and she blinked. The light was coming from beneath the wine cellar door. A mound lay in front of the door, curved in on itself like a larva. Flashes of silver tape sparked, and Sandy started to run.

She skidded onto her knees like a ballplayer sliding into base. More sparks, and the grating of cement through her jeans. Sandy barely felt it. She crabbed forward, warning herself not to touch Ben's still form.

"Honey?" she whispered, from a few feet away.

Time passed without a reply or a single hint of motion. Too much time.

Sandy felt Nick standing over her, the weight of his satisfaction. She wanted to rise, grab her brother, and wrest away the gun, not caring whose body the bullet struck when it went off. It wouldn't matter if she got shot. Nick's preeminence had been established since before she was born. He had gotten everything, and if he'd stolen Ben from her, the one thing that had allowed Sandy to enter another life, then she didn't want to live.

But that life had given her Ivy. Sandy had to survive this. For Ivy.

From the concrete floor came a sound, a signal.

"San— ?" The single syllable emerged on a breathy wisp.

She looked down, and as the dim light gave way to a coherent form, Sandy saw Ben's eyes blink. She was beside him without being aware that she'd moved, extending one halting hand. Nick trailed her unhurriedly. Perhaps it hurt him to walk on his injured foot. Oh, how she hoped it hurt for him to walk.

"Ive?" Ben brought out, and Sandy bobbed her head.

Even in the low light, she could see relief flood his face. It was her turn then, and she mouthed, *McLean*?

Ben turned his head a fraction to the side, and Sandy raised her eyes to the wine cellar door. No noise came from the small room. But the light was turned on, which in an emergency just might have allowed McLean to endure a barrier of wood between him and his master.

Ben gave a single nod, corroborating her conclusion.

Joy frothed inside her, and Sandy burst out, "Oh, honey. Oh, thank God. You're okay. You're alive."

A rusty rumble registered late as an attempt at laughter.

"I'm — some," Ben said. "Some."

"Some," Sandy repeated. She didn't understand, and she didn't care. Ben was speaking more freely now, and that speech seemed to indicate a hold on life.

Ben couldn't move a hand or finger; both wrists were bound together. But somehow he communicated — a slight lift of one shoulder maybe — that she should wait.

"Nah — not good," Ben said. "But some . . ."

Sandy felt connections fire. "You're *something.* I get it. I get it. Oh my God, Ben, I'm so —" She broke off.

What had she been about to say? She was going to apologize and then Ben would want to know why, how was this her fault, and she couldn't tell him that now, when he'd just been given back to her. Sandy had kept half a lifetime from Ben, not consciously, but because her past could never be threaded with this present. She had walked away from that existence, and in doing so had lopped off a part of herself. It had been the right thing to do, a necessary surgery. Only now did the excision strike her as an appalling breach of trust. How had she not realized this before? She'd kept herself from thinking about that time so thoroughly that she had been able to deceive her own husband. Her shoulders bowed and she hid her face in her hands.

Ben tried to console her, but the effort clearly cost him. There was a gray, withered quality to his skin. Ben's normally vivid eyes were dim with pain. Sandy imagined him on a trek or climb, fallen from some great height, lying there and hoping help was on its way.

"My legs." Ben gestured downward with his chin. "They're pretty bad."

Sandy looked down, then away, her mind clouding with horror. She had been there when emergency units arrived at the hospital, but seeing her husband in similar straits made Sandy's throat seal up, a clutching, choking grasp.

She forced herself to look back. In a way, the binds Nick had applied were helping; the tape served as something of a splint along the ankles. But above each silvery wreath, Ben's bones no longer lay smoothly, seamlessly beneath the skin. Two jagged-edged pieces didn't line up; his jeans were tented with what had to be shards.

Sandy got to her feet, beseeching Nick. "Cut the tape. So I can take a look at his legs."

Ben lay on the floor, blinking silently,

depleted by his effort to communicate.

"Still inflating your own abilities, huh?" Nick said.

Sandy regarded Nick. He wanted to act as if he knew her — well, she knew him, too. And though he might not be about to let Ben go free, Nick had proven moveable in other respects. As had always been the case. As long as his aims and desires weren't thwarted, her brother tended to be a rather affable sort. He had come here to use them, because he believed everything and everybody was put there for his own benefit. But Nick didn't make people suffer.

Until the day came when he did. But Sandy wouldn't think about that right now.

She was good at that, she chided herself, blade-sharp. Not thinking about things.

One thing, though. Upon acknowledging the truth, the phantom itching in her hands had fled. Permanently, she sensed. Sandy glanced down at the tiny patches of scar tissue that remained, the crinkled texture of plastic wrap here and there among the healthy, healed skin.

Ben had asked about those scars, of course. But he'd accepted her explanation of a childhood accident. She herself hadn't thought further than that partial truth until now.

Her gaze darted around, envisioning ways to make her husband more comfortable.

"I need to get a blanket," she told Nick. "There's one in the laundry area. And water."

Nick squinted down at Ben. "Blanket, yes." He jerked his chin toward the washing machine and dryer. "Water, no."

Like they were bargaining, playing *Let's Make a Deal.* Everything and everyone had also always been a game to Nick.

Sandy opened her mouth, but Nick warded her off with one arm. "If your husband takes anything down, he's gonna choke when it comes back up." Nick shook his head. "We found him alive, Cass — or I guess I should say Sandy. Conscious even. Not bad for the fall he took. Tough son of a bitch, ain't he?"

Sandy looked down at her shattered husband on the floor.

"I think you should quit while you're ahead."

Sandy walked back to Ben with the softest quilt she could find, and one of his sleeping bags as well. The bag was rated to twenty below, and the two together should stave off shock.

Sandy squatted, arranging the folds

around Ben's body, taking care not to touch him. He was shivering, but his core radiated a reassuring heat. He was her husband, and she longed for him to fold her up in his arms until this night had passed, taking the storm that had come along with it. Sandy settled for placing her hand on the floor beside Ben. Spasmodic jolts and jitters began to subside as the material settled down, camouflaging the heap Ben made on the floor.

She was about to stand up when something in her husband's eyes told her not to go.

Sandy crouched down again. "What is it, honey?" she asked, softly, encouragingly.

"Why?"

"Why what, Ben?"

He paused to muster breath. "Why does." A sucked-in sip of air. "He keep. Calling you. Cass?" The last syllable, when it emerged, was strong and sure, the truest approximation of Ben's real voice yet.

"He doesn't know," Nick remarked blandly. "So that's how you've pulled this off." He extended one arm, taking in the whole of the basement.

Ben's gaze held Sandy's.

Love was a steel girder between them. You could walk across it, precariously high off the ground, yet be safe so long as you kept your balance.

That balance was threatened now. They were going to fall.

Nick spoke into the silence between them, soft as a caress. "Tell him, Cass."

Sandy didn't take her eyes off her husband.

"Tell him," Nick repeated, and his voice was no longer gentle. "Or I will."

Sandy closed her eyes. She wasn't sure if her husband would understand or even register her words; she could no longer tell anything from his pain-dulled face. But the truth was a watery rush inside her now. "I changed my name when I went to college. Just before you and I met."

Ben blinked.

"I used to be called Cassandra."

A solitary shake of the head, palpable confusion. "He —" Ben licked blood-encrusted lips, before starting again. "He knew you then?"

Sandy stared down at her husband. After a moment, she nodded.

"Like —" Again, Ben broke off, but after that, his voice became stronger. "A stalker? That's why he came here?"

Nick belted out a laugh. "I think you've got things a bit wrong down there. Care to correct him, Cass?" Nick paused. "I think it's okay for me to call you by your real name again now, isn't it? Since we're all *family*?"

Sandy slid her hands under the muffling blankets, searching for some part of Ben it might be safe to touch. "Nick isn't a stalker, honey." She fought to get the next words out. "He's my brother."

Ben's whole body jolted and the movement made him cry out.

Sandy laid her hands against his side, trying to still him. "I'm sorry." She didn't allow herself to cry. She didn't deserve the relief that would bring, for the two of them to cry together, for tears were now rolling out of Ben's eyes. When Sandy tried to blot the wetness with the tips of her fingers, Ben jerked away, ignoring the agony it must've caused him to move.

"You don't have a brother," he rasped. Then comprehension cleared the silt out of his vision. "You lied to me. The whole time we've been married? And then even after he came in —"

Sandy shook her head, fast and hard. "I didn't recognize him myself. I swear. It's like — I put up a wall between that life and my real one. It took a while for it to come down."

331

Disbelief bathed Ben's features, and Sandy tried again, though her first explanation had been the truer. "I haven't seen him in more than twenty years. He looks completely different. His hair is short —" She broke off, shuttering her eyes against the recollection of Nick's curls, which he used to keep groomed like a pet. How the girls had loved those curls. How their mother had.

Ben's face went stony, whether from pain or fury or both, and Sandy's voice began to climb, reaching for ever less relevant justifications. "He used to be so skinny! He must've spent a lot of time lifting weights in —"

Ben responded as if she'd said nothing. "You're relay—" The word split, fragmented in his mouth, though Sandy understood it. *Related.*

Nick spat a fat globule of saliva onto the concrete. "You got it."

Ben was himself once more now, betrayal and rage fueling him. He wrenched his shoulders back, throwing off the coverings.

"Honey, stop," Sandy cried. "You're going to hurt yourself."

Panting, stomach muscles visibly straining, and sweat mixing with the remnants of tears on his face, Ben made it into a seated position.

Nick took a step forward, though he seemed more to be observing the act than concerned by it.

"No," Ben growled. "*You* hurt me. And him —" Ben's wrists strained against their binds; he tossed his head back and forth like a dog, grunting with effort.

A cry escaped Sandy. "Honey, please, stop! I would never hurt you!"

Ben mustered all the force that resided in the top half of his body, angling his torso to try and lift it from the floor. But he only made it inches before dropping back down. There was a second's lag time as Ben sat there, blinking. Then pain contorted his face, and a helpless howl emerged before he got control and bellowed, "Get out of here, Sandy, or whoever you are —"

Nick's head turned back and forth between them as if he were watching a show.

He wanted them to keep battling; Sandy saw the desire lapping in her brother's eyes. He had come here for help in his escape, but would a side benefit be to bring Sandy's life down around her, enjoying the fireworks as it fell?

Nick had never given Sandy his time or attention. He'd ignored her, dismissed her, except on the rare occasions Sandy was forced into his consciousness. But that had been because Nick didn't just get the best of everything — he got everything, period. While Sandy now had so much. A house, a family, a life. At some point, especially if his escape was delayed much longer, would these penetrate Nick's self-absorption, become worthy of his notice?

Ben fought to subdue himself, an almost physical feat. His breathing leveled out and the expression on his face smoothed as if a roller had passed over it. A thin thread of blood unraveled from beneath the blanket as he lay back down. Something must have broken through.

Sandy remained on her hands and knees, unable to stem her tears.

"Enough," Nick said irritably.

He flashed out a hand, but Sandy ignored it. She crawled forward, stopping only when Ben twisted sideways, scaly pain covering his face.

Sandy sat back, and cold air filled the space between them. Ben lay with his legs as heavy and motionless as pipes. Only his back moved, curling in on itself.

Nick's shoulders hitched, and he took a restless look around. "Come on. It's freezing. And we've been down here long enough."

"Take care of Ivy." Ben spoke into the blanket pooled beneath him. "Can you do that? Can you keep her safe now?"

The question struck Sandy with the force of a slap. Ben was asking many things. Not only whether she could protect Ivy from Nick and Harlan, but whether she could do better by their daughter than she had for Ivy's first fifteen years, teach her honesty and bravery and truth.

She nodded once, then again.

Ben let his eyes close.

Sandy didn't see anger or even betrayal any longer in the dusky pools before they fell shut. Instead, Ben looked terrified. As if for the first time in his life, something was coming for him, and he was helpless to get away.

CHAPTER TWENTY-FIVE

Ivy trudged up the stairs, hearing Harlan breathe behind her. Harlan. What a stupid, hick name. She hadn't thought much about it until her mom had said it out loud. Nobody called Harlan belonged in their lives.

Ivy couldn't believe how he and Nick had so thoroughly laid waste to her life. What was she supposed to do at school now when she saw Cory?

Something squeezed deep below the place her furious thoughts resided. Something sickly scared that anger couldn't touch. Would she even go to school again? What was going to happen tonight?

She stooped and snatched up the hoodie she'd abandoned. How dumb she had been to take it off. What she'd done to Cory was a million times worse than wearing something lame.

They made it down the hall to her

bedroom. Harlan pushed the door open — a panel of wood so heavy Ivy herself had to apply muscle to budge it — and it flew backward, striking the wall with a *thud.*

Inside, Ivy flopped facedown on her bed as she'd done so many times when she'd been angry at her mother or father or both. All the fights they'd had seemed so stupid now, bits of dust and vapor that blew away as soon as you focused on them.

"You did good down there," Harlan told her.

Ivy lifted her face from her pillow. That disgusting tuft of fake fur sat beside it. She rolled in the opposite direction. Harlan was sitting on her wheelie desk chair. You couldn't even see the seat beneath him.

"I bet Nick is glad," he said.

"What do I care if that bastard is glad?" Ivy muttered.

Harlan's brows drew down. "Don't talk like that."

"Like what?" Ivy said, just as angry.

"Like that," he replied helplessly. "So ugly. You're a girl. Girls don't talk like that." A faint smile took hold of his mouth, lifting it like a hot air balloon.

"What kind of paternalistic crap is that?" Ivy said into her mattress. *"Free to Be You and Me* much? *Girls Can Be Anything?"*

"Patern . . ." His voice trailed off.

Suddenly Ivy hated herself. Playing mental games with someone whose mind she knew was . . . compromised. Ivy only knew these things because back in better days, her mom used to talk to her about the seventies and women's liberation. And now Ivy was no better than Darcy, darting like a butterfly around the special kids who were mainstreamed into their classes.

She got out of her sulky plunge, and sat with her legs crossed on her bed. "I'm sorry," she said. "I'm a —" She stopped before she cursed again. Hanging out with convicts was having an effect on her mouth. "Do you really think girls talk nicely?"

Harlan shrugged huge shoulders, and the gesture looked shy. "My sister did." He paused, then let loose with the longest burst of words Ivy had heard yet. "She used to always ask me first if she needed something, and she'd say please and thank you. I was pretty happy to have my kid sister around."

"Really?" Ivy said. "I like being an only."

He looked at her, a crevasse appearing on his brow.

"Child," she supplied, noting his confusion. "It gives my mom a lot of time to spend with me. We come from a long line of just one girl," Ivy added. "My mom's an only child, too."

Now Harlan looked even more confused.

"Anyway . . ." Ivy twisted the fringe on one of her decorative pillows. "How old is your sister?"

Harlan didn't answer.

Ivy set the pillow aside, and scooted forward. "I guess she's a grown-up. Unless she's a lot younger." She realized she wasn't really sure of Harlan's age. It could've been almost anything.

Harlan lifted his head slowly. It looked like it took effort to do it.

"Is something wrong?" Ivy asked.

"I just don't get . . ."

"Get what?" Ivy asked. She felt like when she was babysitting and the game had gone on too long.

"How your mom can be an *only* —" He broke off. "I like that word."

Ivy nodded.

After another moment or two, when Ivy was back to fiddling with the fringe, and almost back to lying facedown, contemplating the mess of her life, Harlan finally finished his question. "— when she has a brother?"

"My mom doesn't have a brother," Ivy said.

Harlan nodded. That huge head jogging

no less effortfully. "Sure she does."

Ivy looked down at her finger. It'd gotten cocooned in a length of fringe, and the skin was purpled and pulsing. "No," she said. "She doesn't."

"Then who's Nick?"

All the jagged edges, the pieces of her life that had never entirely added up, speared Ivy. She brought her head down into her hands, clenching her skull as if she could drive out this new knowledge. Even though it made everything suddenly make sense.

How her mother never talked about where she grew up, although from her dad Ivy knew it was a town just a little north of here. So why had they never visited? Ivy's mom didn't refer to her family either, even though Ivy had started to ask about them. As far as Ivy knew, she had no grandparents on her mother's side, but how was that even possible? It was like her mom had been dropped from the mother ship. Yet she knew this place, Wedeskyull, so well, and sometimes certain people in town seemed to know her. Ivy lifted her face out of her palms, and looked at Harlan sitting in her desk chair, and she knew he had told her the truth.

And hadn't Ivy sensed it for a while beneath the watery surface of their lives?

The realization had finally broken through tonight, when Ivy hurled her accusation. Her mom had been lying all right. In a million years, though, Ivy wouldn't have guessed it'd be about this.

Harlan was making a weird noise, almost like he was holding back laughter. As Ivy stared at him, the laugh broke free, throaty and wild.

"I'm sorry," he said. "I know it's not nice to laugh. It's just . . . I never . . . never . . ." He began to wind down, perhaps realizing that Ivy wasn't laughing, or even smiling. "You didn't know Nick was your uncle? Why did you think we came here tonight?"

Ivy shook her head. She was stuck on the uncle part. No wonder something about Nick had seemed familiar to her. They were *related.*

She shuddered.

She'd never had many relatives to speak of, just a grandfather she barely knew — he'd been sick for a long time before he died. And now the one she did have was a psychopathic convict. Who knew what he'd gone to prison for? Maybe for taking families hostage. Or worse.

Ivy's skin went crawly and angry hairs stood up along it. It wasn't just her uncle who had done that; it was her *mother's brother.* What made Ivy suspect that her mom was keeping a secret? She still couldn't say what had given it away. Little kids accepted whatever they had or didn't have, but as soon as Ivy had begun asking her mom questions about the past, there were holes that never got filled in.

She'd fallen into one of those holes, her and Cory.

And it was all her mother's fault.

Ivy went hollow, a husk with no creature inside it. The blankness her mom had put between them, everything unsaid and un-revealed, was all that she had left. She wasn't even mad at her mom. The frightening thing was that she didn't feel anything toward her at all.

After a while, Ivy became aware that her bed had sunk and Harlan was now sitting beside her. She turned chalky, dead eyes on him.

"Know why I was laughing before?" he asked.

"Haven't got a clue," Ivy said flatly.

"It's 'cause I never know anything first," he said. "Before someone else, I mean. Once someone told me, 'Even the dog knows what's going on before you do, Harlan.'"

Oh, how Ivy wanted her dog. Was Mac

okay down there? She didn't want him to be hungry, or thirsty, or have to go and not know what to do if he wasn't let out. It occurred to Ivy that Mac was the only member of her family she could really count on.

Harlan's face bunched up. "That was my daddy. He was the one who told me that."

Ivy frowned. That was mean enough — coming from a parent — that she figured she should say something even if she was still so mad that every muscle had clenched up inside her. But she couldn't think what.

From downstairs came a voice that should've been familiar, but sounded like it belonged to a total stranger. "Ivy! Come down here right now!" called her mother.

OCTOBER 5, 1987

Barbara caught a glimpse of herself, reflected in the window as she wrapped a scarf around her head. Perhaps it was the scarf — or more than that, the whole of what she acknowledged was a rather bygone look compared to the shoulder pads and mannish suits all the smart ladies were wearing these days — but Barbara's appearance took her by surprise.

How old she looked.

She paused for a moment, one hand halted in tucking up a tuft of hair. Was that really her face, as crenulated as a walnut, beneath its chiffon wrapping? Barbara had actually been feeling rather jaunty, setting out on errands by herself. She'd chosen her prettiest scarf, a recent birthday gift from Gordon, to wear. Yet the image in the window looked unsettlingly like her own mother, who'd always said that raising Barbara and her five sisters had destroyed her, hollowed her out until there was nothing left inside.

"Nicholas!" Barbara called in an unsteady voice. An old woman's voice. "I'm on my way. Make sure to keep an eye on things here. And do your homework."

Her son's voice sounded strong and sure where hers was not. "It's Nick, okay? And I always do, don't I?"

A smile lifted Barbara's mouth, imparting a feeling of restored vigor. This was one part of her life that had grown easier at least. She had time on her own now, and the ability to move about unencumbered. Nicholas — *Nick* — was fourteen, one of the cool kids at school, with friends who gave one another nicknames. He was more than responsible enough to hold down the fort.

"Yes, you do," she called back.

She looked at her reflection again, and felt a jolt of relief. Now she appeared almost girlish, flushed beneath the scarf, the pink fabric trembling on a current of air. Raising her son made Barbara feel young again. How sad for her mother that she'd been saddled with so many daughters, rendering motherhood a blood sport, girls trampling over her in their haste to grow up and become women themselves, one by one beating her into the ground.

■ ■ ■ ■

Barbara went to the grocery store, she went to the post office, then on a lark, she poked her head into the beauty parlor in town.

"Help you?" the woman behind the desk asked as the bells on the door jingled.

Barbara nearly backed right out again. She didn't recognize the woman now working here. She was young, not much more than a girl, and she had one of those terrible new hairstyles, scalp-short on one side, brushing her chin on the other.

But she gave Barbara such a bright smile that Barbara hesitated, and the girl let out a laugh. "Don't worry. I had my asymmetrical done downstate." She wrapped a piece from the longer side around one finger. "Shelia's here today and she'll cut your hair perfectly normal."

Barbara began unwrapping the scarf from her head. "I suppose I could do with a freshening up."

Shelia looked up from a chair where she was styling another customer.

"Want to wash her for me, Tiffany?" she asked, and the new girl stood up. She led Barbara back past the customer whose hair was being wound around curlers, and shook

346

out a smock as she waited for her to sit down.

Until her hair had been trimmed and she was sitting underneath the dryer, Barbara didn't realize who the other customer was.

Once she did, she deliberated whether to pretend she hadn't seen, continue flipping through out-of-date pages of *Family Circle,* or if she should say something.

There was no reason not to be friendly, she concluded at last. They had fallen out of touch, but that wasn't Barbara's fault, was it?

"Glenda," she said, leaning over to touch the woman on her smock. "How nice to see you."

The pastor's wife turned her head inside the plastic bubble. "Yes, Barbara, you, too," she replied in a way that gave Barbara the sense she might've known all along who was sitting beside her. "I hope you've been well?"

"Very well," Barbara replied. "And you? And the boys?"

Glenda glanced down at the no-less-out-of-date pages on her lap. "Well, thank you. Everyone's doing just fine." Then, as if she couldn't help herself, she added, "Adam's finishing up seminary this year."

"How nice for him," Barbara murmured.

347

She waited for Glenda to inquire in kind, but the silence went on until it bordered on rude.

Finally Glenda asked, "And your own two? How is your son and how is the darling Cassandra? I do get to see her from time to time. She's taken such an interest in youth group."

"Has she?" Barbara replied. Her mouth had gone tight, as if she were trying to hold a pebble between her lips. "Well, Nicholas is doing wonderfully. Nick, I mean," she added with a merry trill. "We finally found a school that can keep up with him."

They had kept Nicholas out of both nursery school and kindergarten in the end — too constraining — and when his first and second grade teachers had proved lackluster at best, hunted for a facility that would provide what all the scholars called for these days. Child-centered education. Curricula that acknowledged each student's unique gifts, instead of trying to place them in a set mold.

"Yes, I heard," Glenda murmured. "That military school in Wedeskyull."

"Prep school," Barbara corrected. "It's been wonderful. Expensive — but then, we only have the one child who really requires an enhanced education."

Glenda set her magazine aside, and twisted around to lift up the hood. Curls clustered like grapes on her head, each glistening with moisture.

Shelia hurried over, administering a quick pat. "You're still a little damp, hon," she said. "Give it ten more minutes?"

"No," Glenda replied. "I don't believe I will." She pressed a fold of bills into Shelia's hand and walked out of the shop.

At the house, Barbara began lugging in her purchases, tossing her new, lighter sheath of hair as she set things down. She had run late in town, meandering around after her appointment at the beauty parlor, and darkness was already starting to fall. Barbara was just returning for the last, considering calling out to Nicholas for help, when she heard raised voices that made her hurry back out to the car.

Best to leave the children to their argument. Gordon was always saying that Barbara intervened too much and that kids needed to be allowed a fair fight.

Inside again, she nudged bags with her knee from the hallway toward the kitchen.

"Do 'em better than that," came her son's voice, loud enough to carry. "Mama'll ream you out if you leave all that grease on 'em."

349

There was a reply that Barbara didn't quite hear.

"See that speck?" said Nicholas.

Barbara felt a clamp of annoyance. Could the child not even learn to keep house?

"Here," Nicholas said helpfully. "Try this."

There was a scream, so high-pitched and sudden that Barbara knew she could delay no longer. She stooped to pick up two of the heaviest bags, before making her way into the kitchen.

"Nicholas?" she called out. "Nick, I mean? Look at me, I got my hair cut —"

Nicholas spun around at the sink. "I don't know what happened, Mama. She was doing the washing and then she just started screaming."

Barbara's gaze flicked to the sink. Cassandra was standing on a stool, arms thrust out before her. They were as stiff as a length of rebar, flaming a livid red. Cassandra clawed at her skin as if she intended to peel it off, still letting out those frightful shrieks. Barbara walked closer. In addition to a bottle of dish soap on the porcelain surround, there was an open jar of lye.

Barbara turned off the hot water and moved Cassandra's arms underneath the cold, taking care not to touch the skin until it was rinsed clean. Whether from the effect of the lye, or because the child really had stripped off her own skin, the pieces had a blotchy, bubbled appearance.

"Nicholas," Barbara said. "Get me the butter out of the fridge."

Nicholas had been leaning back against the counter, but did as he was told, turning and bringing over a tub. Barbara tried to smear the fat on the reddened flesh, but the skin was loose in places, and the child's screams began anew. Barbara had to settle for dabbing pieces of butter on wherever they would stick.

"Why ever did you think to use lye?" she asked after she had done the best job she could.

Cassandra raised her face. The skin on it appeared almost as red and swollen as that on her arms. "I — I didn't, Mama."

Barbara flinched.

Nicholas took a step away from the counter. He'd stayed here all this time, concerned for his sister.

Barbara sent him a small smile. "Next time, perhaps, you'll do housework as I teach you."

"I tried," Cassandra whimpered. "Nick said it wasn't good enough."

"That doesn't mean you should use lye."

351

"I didn't," Cassandra said again. "Nick —"

Barbara turned on her so suddenly that Cassandra slipped off the stool. She fought to regain her balance without use of her arms.

"Mama," she cried. "My arms don't look right, do they? Do they look okay to you, Mama? They hurt so bad."

"It's okay, Cass," Nicholas said. "They'll get better."

Cassandra's shoulders sank, and after a moment she nodded.

Barbara followed Nicholas' gaze. "Your brother's right. They just need time to heal."

There was a heavy beat of footsteps, and Barbara, Nicholas, and Cassandra all looked up at once. No one had heard Gordon arrive.

"Darling," Barbara said. "I'm afraid I don't have dinner on just yet —"

"What happened?" Gordon demanded. He took a single step forward and lifted up Cassandra, his big hands wrapping her waist so that her arms could stay thrust out, untouched. "Oh sweet Lord, baby, what happened to your hands?"

Cassandra began to screech once more, sounds that made you clap your hands over your ears. Barbara barely heard Gordon begin to comfort Cassandra in singsong.

"Okay, it's okay, baby. We're going to get you help."

Car keys clamped between his teeth, Gordon held Cassandra aloft as he ran with her toward the front door.

"It hurts, Daddy!" came a bracing cry, like cold water thrown.

"I know it does, baby. I know. But it's always worse at night. Trust me, this is going to be much better in the morning. Things are always hardest at night."

It was two a.m. when Gordon returned from the hospital in Wedeskyull. Cassandra hadn't required specialized treatment at another unit, or even overnight observation.

"Only second degree," Barbara said, once Gordon had come back downstairs, having gotten the girl settled. He sat down in his chair, across from Barbara on the couch. But he didn't speak or even look at her, and Barbara felt compelled to go on. "It could've been worse."

"Grease," Gordon said. "It's the worst thing you can do for a burn."

"Imagine that," Barbara said, robotically.

Gordon's forearms lay along his thighs, his hands fisted. He lifted his head and regarded her in the lampless dark. "How did it happen?"

Barbara looked away. "I don't know why she decided to use the lye."

"She did," Gordon said. "Cassandra?"

"That's right," Barbara replied. "Well, I wasn't there, of course. I had about a million errands to run today," she added merrily. "But Cassandra was the one washing dishes. Nicholas — did you know we are to call him Nick now, darling? — said something about trying to get off some very tough grease."

Gordon looked down at his lap. After a long moment, he nodded. "I think I've figured out what to do."

Barbara was barely listening. "What to do?" she repeated.

Gordon linked his fingers together. "We've got to give Nick an outlet for his aggression."

Her husband said the name as if he had long since made the switch, as if somehow Barbara had missed something essential in their son's growth and development.

She responded less rotely. "Nicholas isn't aggressive!"

She couldn't see enough to make out the expression on Gordon's face, but she sensed her husband sitting there in the dark, his hunched-over form and fast, irregular

354

breathing.

"It's what my father did when I was a kid, getting into fights, not caring much about anything." Gordon braced his hands on his knees and stood up. "Funny as it sounds, it was probably the thing that gave me the most reverence for life."

Barbara felt suddenly consumed by a pressing need to see. She leaned over and flicked on a lamp, and the room flooded with brightness. The bulb illuminated pieces of furniture, the walls that contained them, and each shadowed entry into other parts of the house.

Shielding his eyes against the sudden flash of light, Gordon said, "I'm going to teach Nick how to hunt."

Chapter Twenty-Six

Carolyn Mills was washing up after dinner when she became aware of a noise on the dirt road outside. It happened sometimes, an encroachment, even way out here on a piece of acreage that had been in her husband's family for generations, bordered by state land. Danny was responsible for the road himself, plowing it, but also laying in fresh gravel after the spring runoff washed the old away. Tasks that to Carolyn were novel and new were for Danny like taking a shower or sweeping the floors. Up here you maintained the road. In the Connecticut suburb where she'd grown up, you took care of yourself and your house, although Carolyn's family had had a cleaning woman for the latter. Actually, they had people for the former, too: performing mani-pedis, waxing stray hairs while coiffing ones they meant to keep.

This noise didn't belong to a car; there

was no rumble of an engine. And though a light snow was falling, there wasn't enough accumulation to merit a shoveling yet. Danny must be in the living room, with the paper and his pipe.

Carolyn called out to him, setting aside her sponge.

"Hunter gone astray, I'm thinking," Danny said, rising from his chair by the woodstove.

In addition to coming from a completely different background, Danny was also almost twenty years older than she. How her family had blanched when perennially single Carolyn had gone for a ski weekend with girlfriends — women who weren't single, who had left behind husbands and even children — and simply never come back.

Eventually her family had rallied, attending the small wedding she and Danny hosted up here. Her husband loved this land, and would never think of traveling out of state to take part in some white and flowery occasion beneath a tent.

"This late? With weather up there on the mountain?" Carolyn asked, indicating the occlusion of the moon outside. Even she knew this was no night for hunting.

Danny gave a shrug she had learned to

read. It said: *Who knows what folks from downstate get up to?* "Let's see if he needs any help."

He walked past her toward the mudroom. But when Danny drew the side door open, there was nobody to be seen.

Her husband stepped outside, coatless in the cold. The temperature hardly seemed to affect him, but when he came back inside he rubbed the sleeves of his shirt up and down, shaking his head. Snow drifted down like confetti.

"No one there," he said.

And still those sounds, a slow sliding along the dirt, almost a rasp.

"It's coming from in front," Carolyn noted.

They went to look. With the lamps on, it was impossible to see more than a few inches through the window, so Danny opened the door, and they squinted out into the flakes.

Only Carolyn wasted time on a gasp.

One of the reasons she'd fallen so deeply and surely in love with Danny was his air of take-charge capability. Nothing was beyond him. Carolyn had been taking one final run when she'd lost a ski and badly strained her ankle. She was hovering mid-slope, trying to decide whether to try and wedge her one ski back on, or hobble down in her boots — maybe even take the slope butt-first, so badly was her ankle beginning to swell in its constraining cuff — when Danny swooped down amongst the moguls, landing a perfect Christie beside her. Instantly, he assessed the situation, and just as fast, he was skiing her downhill, somehow managing to tow her equipment along. Nobody had to go back up the mountain for so much as a pole. Carolyn had known then and there that she'd never leave this man's side.

He told her to go get the phone, and Carolyn cursed the paralysis that always beset her when trouble came. Even she could intuit that this situation was much more dire than the one she had faced on the slopes, and it had landed literally at their front door, in a house that was lost in the woods and a thickening layer of snow.

Carolyn turned and ran, praying the landline hadn't gone out, while Danny ducked outside. Racing back with the phone, Carolyn watched him from the window. She could see quick questions being mouthed, and a brisk examination performed when he was met with nothing besides a blank stare. Danny seemed to decide that it was safer to take the woman in his arms than task her with walking one more step. She was wearing the oddest coat: black on one side, beige in front.

Danny strode back into the house, his back barely bent beneath the burden he carried. His arms were streaked with something dark. Not dirt. Carolyn drew in stifled breath again. That coat wasn't two-toned; it was soaked through with blood.

"Call the police," Danny said. "Number's on the fridge."

Her husband was practically law enforcement in this town himself, lifelong friends with the old chief of police, and an advisor of sorts to the new.

She dashed back into the kitchen, hunting for the right magnet on the refrigerator.

Danny laid the woman on the couch, and Carolyn heard her rake in a breath. "Man . . . took my car . . . stabbed me . . ."

"Shh," Danny told her. "Lie still now. You're going to be all right."

Carolyn came and handed him the phone.

"Chief," he said once the call had gone through. "It's Mills. Got a woman just walked up out of nowhere. She's hurt bad. Lost a lot of blood."

A pause.

"Forgot all about the 911," Danny said. "Sorry about that, Chief."

Carolyn bent over the woman. Her eyes

were closed and her skin had gone waxy.

"Blankets," Danny said.

Carolyn went and fetched an afghan, draping it over the woman's prone form. The sudden weight of the cloth must've disturbed her, for the woman began to writhe on the couch. Blood that had clotted renewed its flow.

"Long," the woman panted. "Hill." A great sucking intake of air. "Road."

Danny looked up from the phone, while Carolyn's hand stilled in the pressure she was applying.

"Long Hill Road, she's saying," Danny said into the phone. "Maybe she lives there, wants her family notified —"

The woman's body began to jerk on the couch, rising high, then slapping down against the cushions, as if she were possessed.

"Danny!" Carolyn shrieked, trying to hold her.

Danny dropped the phone and the police chief's disembodied voice floated out.

"Keep her calm, Mills," he said. "I'm sending a bus and two of my men to you while I go check things out on Long Hill. I heard about that road once already from my officer tonight. And you know how I feel about coincidences."

CHAPTER TWENTY-SEVEN

"What is that infernal noise?" Nick demanded. "It sounds like hissing."

Sandy felt herself sinking down, becoming infant-soft and trapped again. *Infernal* was the word their mother used to describe Sandy as a child. Only then she'd been Cassandra. Cassandra with her infernal crying, her infernal curiosity, her infernal demands.

If she let herself become Cassandra again, she would never get them out of this.

She straightened the rod of her back. Swallowed around a stone lodged in her throat. Then she went to look through the sliding doors that let out onto the yard, wiping away a circle of vapor on the glass before squinting outside.

"It's sleet," she said after a moment. "The snow must be letting up." Sandy took a breath, then glanced back at her brother. "Were you in prison so long you lost your north country?"

Nick regarded her coolly. That chill used to be the harbinger of Nick's cruelest intent. He'd looked at her that way just before he took out the lye.

But now Sandy stared back, her fear transformed in the wake of Ben's learning the truth. Sandy had been terrified for most of her life, but with this chasm opened up between her and Ben, she realized she'd been scared of the wrong thing.

"It should stop soon," Sandy went on. "You'll want to get out there ahead of it."

"I told you not to try your shrink tricks on me," Nick muttered. But he was studying the window while hope lit his gray gaze. He reached down and touched his lower leg.

"Why are you doing that?" Sandy asked boldly. "Didn't my husband hurt your foot?"

"My leg bothers me when the weather's bad," Nick said. "Call this my way of checking on the storm."

Sandy hadn't been prepared for that. No amount of strength strapped on like athletic gear, extra padding to protect the flesh within, would enable her to tolerate that memory.

Nick seemed to sense her queasy pang, and aimed a smile at her. "We should bulk up before heading out. What are you gonna fix?"

The thought of preparing her brother a meal repulsed Sandy. Their mother had always waited on Nick, but Sandy had been called upon for the usual chores of childhood, not to mention a fair amount of cleaning up after her brother, until she simply began staying away from the house.

"Harlan will be hungry, too. Make extra." Nick broke into a throaty chuckle. "A lot extra."

Everything inside Sandy felt tightly coiled, like an animal ready to pounce.

"And then tell him and the princess to come down."

The order galvanized her. Sandy found an ovenproof crock that had been judged safe enough to remain behind and dumped some sauce into it, placing the makeshift contraption on a burner. She located a few flimsy plastic utensils in a picnic basket in the pantry, and put them on the table, before crossing to the stairs and calling out to Ivy.

Nick joined her there. "Would you be so kind as to put on the news?" he asked with elaborate politeness. "I want an update."

Sandy grabbed the remote from a chest in front of one of the couches, and lit up the flat screen. The cable was out — or had been cut by Nick, more likely — but after a few seconds of fiddling, and a return to basics, the local channel came in amidst a ghost of static.

The weather report was being broadcast, although the sound quality was terrible, cutting in and out. "The first snowstorm of the season . . ." said the announcer. There was a series of grainy hisses as the audio blurped off and on. ". . . blow over as fast as it came in." Sandy practically let out a cheer. Back to lip-reading until the announcer's commentary grew audible in spurts. ". . . up to *hiss* feet of accumulation in the higher altitudes, with *hiss* less lower down *hiss* temperatures rising throughout the *hiss* to a balmy thirty-eight degrees." A final clear burst of words, which should've especially pleased the weatherman since he seemed quite proud of them. "Old Man Winter, you may be just getting started, but for now, you're a lot of hot air."

The weather map switched to a shot of newly filled salt trucks, while a roster of game cancellations scrolled across the screen. Then the screen changed to footage of construction on a small bridge. A female newscaster, her coat and muffler blown about by a sudden shock of snow, shouted, "Now for the latest on tonight's breaking news."

Nick pushed Sandy aside to step closer to the TV, but at that moment the flurry of static broke into a buzzing swarm, and audio was completely lost. Hand thrust out, Nick stalked toward the television. The static grew louder, its rush filling the room. Nick ran a hand along the sleek black frame, looking madly around. "How the hell do you get this noise to stop?"

Sandy picked up the remote and pressed Mute. An acrid smell began to drift in from the kitchen, stinging her nose, and she hurried toward it.

Nick strode over to the windows and checked them before lowering himself into a chair. His head twitched nervously, gaze flicking this way and that.

Sandy scraped noodles from their earlier dinner into two bowls, plunking one down in front of Nick. The sauce had charred and blistered in spots, but she supposed it had to compare favorably with prison fare. At the least it would present a distraction from that news story.

Nick twirled a clump of pasta with the plastic fork, but didn't raise it to his mouth. "Didn't the route your husband laid out take us down?"

Sandy gave a nod, frantic and fast.

Nick set his forkful back in the bowl, and

stared off into space.

"Lower altitudes," Sandy murmured. "They said there'd be less accumulation."

"I heard what they said," Nick muttered. Then, without so much as shifting in his seat, he raised his voice. "Hey, Harlan. Good news."

Sandy looked toward the archway, where Harlan and Ivy had appeared. Sandy was about to rush to her daughter, but when she spared another glance, she stopped.

Because, somehow, Ivy knew.

Harlan must have told her; it was the only way. Sandy had the mad urge to rush forward, squeeze the breath from this mountain of a man who not only served as her brother's muscle — allowing him to wreak havoc as surely as their mother had — but who had also cut the last fraying thread between her and Ivy.

Harlan nudged Ivy, just a tap, but enough to make her lurch and step into the kitchen. Ivy looked around the room, her eyes gray and bleak. They were Nick's eyes, at least in this light. How had Sandy never let herself see that before?

She snatched a peek outside before walking up to Ivy. "Listen to me," she hissed while Nick picked up his fork again. Harlan wedged himself into a chair and lifted his own meal, studying its contents. The bowl looked like a teacup in his hand. "I know that you know."

Ivy's gaze continued to circle.

Sandy leaned forward, grasping Ivy's slim arms, and ignoring the way Ivy stood like a broom handle in her hold. "But they're leaving, Ive. They're going to go now, for real! And once they do, everything will return to normal."

Still Ivy wouldn't look at her.

"No." Sandy shook her head. "Not normal. That isn't what I meant. I mean that we can sort everything out. We'll talk about this. We'll talk about everything."

Ivy wrenched herself free of Sandy's hands, and looked back toward the living room, where images continued to shadow across the TV screen.

Nick and Harlan both set to their meals.

Sandy had always lied to Ben. She'd justified it by telling herself that they weren't big lies; these were about the definition of white lies or fibs. Like if business was slow for Off Road during mud season, Sandy would downgrade the sum on their propane bill. Or when she hadn't insisted that Ivy tell Ben about her failing grade earlier-this-evening-slash-a-whole-lifetime-ago. Sandy lied so often that it had become a habit, a way to survive everyday worries and stressors and hassles, the lubrication of a shared life. But now she realized that these small lies had been possible only because their entire relationship was built upon one tremendous, overarching deception. And although Sandy didn't take those same liberties with Ivy, a similar faulty foundation lay beneath the two of them.

At the table, Harlan was digging in with gusto, while Nick shoveled up one forkful after another, swallowing them down unchewed.

" 'S good," Harlan remarked, his mouth full.

"Honey?" Sandy said to Ivy. "Why don't you go get the packs and put them by the door? Gather up all the outerwear too, please."

Ivy didn't make a move. Instead, she opened her mouth, and posed a slow, defiant question. "Why were you watching that weird old-fashioned kind of TV?"

Sandy responded, keeping her answer deliberately vague. "It was the news, honey. We wanted to check on things before they go."

It took Ivy only a moment to parse the statement. Sandy watched as its meaning came clear. *No,* she thought, the word a tiny pinprick in her mind. *Ivy, please. Just keep quiet.*

But it was too late. Ivy was angry in a way she never had been before. This wasn't the resentful petulance of a teenager, but the legitimate rage of a young woman who had every right to feel betrayed. As Ivy's fury unfurled like the petals of a carnivorous plant, Sandy knew she was about to witness the implosion of the last chance they had.

"Oh," Ivy said. "That's right. My *uncle's* been in jail." The word seemed to blister on her tongue.

Nick looked over at Ivy in the midst of slurping up a strand of pasta.

"He doesn't know that nobody gets their news on TV anymore," Ivy continued. "And you haven't filled him in, have you, Mom?"

Sandy held up a desperate hand, warning Ivy, pleading with her, but Nick sent her a look that tripped her back a step.

"We all know that's not your way," Ivy went on. "To tell people the crucial stuff they really need to know."

Nick pushed back his plate, studying Ivy with a look of intent alertness.

Ivy faced him. "What you were watching wasn't news," she went on, emitting a dry, husky laugh. "It was olds."

Sandy's mouth was so woolly, she could hardly speak. "The television is fine for local."

Ivy shook her head. "You couldn't even hear on that thing."

"Is there something that we could hear on better?" Nick asked. "And get tonight's stories?" There was a thrum beneath his mild tone, like a railroad track just before the train came roaring along.

"You get news online now!" Ivy burst out, wielding the scrap of knowledge like a weapon. "For all you know, the police are waiting for you at the bottom of our road."

Harlan turned a panicked face to Nick, anguish grouping his features together into one sodden mass.

Ivy huffed in satisfaction. "Too bad you smashed all of our computers."

Nick nodded sagely. "That is too bad."

Sandy was suddenly filled with a seething hatred and rage, directed not at her brother, still less at Ivy's perfidy, but at herself.

A slow smile rose on Nick's face. "What to do, what to do?"

For the first time, doubt entered Ivy's eyes. She looked at Sandy.

Sandy turned away, feeling fright and desperation overtake her. *Oh, baby girl. They were about to go. You've put us all back in*

371

danger just to lash out at me.

She heard Ivy speak as if from a distance. "I mean, probably not for local, my mom's right about that. I meant more for national stories —"

"Ivy," Sandy said quickly. "Don't lie to him. It will only make him —"

"Oh, you're a fine one to talk!" Ivy shrieked, so suddenly that Sandy jumped.

Nick moved into the space between them. His step seemed sturdy enough now. Maybe he could even get on Ben's boots.

"It's okay!" he said heartily, as if someone had inadvertently offended him and he was brushing it off to be polite. He flashed a smile at Sandy. "Don't blame the pretty princess. She's a smart girl to suggest we double check."

Sandy stared at him.

"Come on." Nick paused to chuck Ivy beneath her chin, ignoring it when she flinched. "I bet it won't be too hard to find a computer. Let's go visit those neighbors you told me about."

Ego

Nick stood in the hall, staring at the front door. It was a slab made out of some dark red wood that looked as if it were bleeding. Three hours in this place and he hated it more than the cell he used to occupy. The only thing that would be better than never having to see this house again would be watching it burn to the ground. How his sister, who'd always been the pond scum of the family, wound up living here was beyond him.

She'd done it by lying, Nick realized. By disavowing him. As if *he* were the loser.

His fingers bore down in the borrowed gloves he was pulling on.

He was borrowing from Cassie, when he was the one who was entitled to this life. To some life at least. The injustice of it made him want to cry out, fling things around, destroy them.

His foot was in bad shape. He was going

to have to walk down to the neighbors in his shoes, which would mean they'd get soaked. He'd just have to hope that a little more time would allow him to cram on that pair of boots. If the swelling didn't recede, he would force his foot in. He had always been able to tough out an injury — he'd once gotten shivved during a fight and hadn't even known it till blood loss caused him to black out — although lately he'd been working to become more aware of his body. *Mindfulness* had been the word the prison counselor used. Well, mindfulness was for shit. Mindfulness was making his foot throb like a bad tooth.

It wasn't supposed to go like this. Back when he'd begun considering his escape, he'd envisioned such a smooth, clear path. His sister lived at the edge of great wilderness, land that would swallow him and Harlan whole, allow them to disappear. Even better, Cassie had a husband whose knowledge and skills would equip them. It was as if it had all been set up expressly for him, like the rest of Nick's charmed life, steered by some divine hand. Right up until the day he got sent to prison.

So what had happened? Things had gone wrong, but Nick couldn't quite make out how. First Cassie's bull of a husband, responsible for the monstrous thing Nick's foot had become. Nick felt a muddy red hatred toward him, tied only partly to the bruised pulp of his foot. Then there was the snow, and now even technology seemed out to get him. Why did the television have to stop giving the news?

The princess was the one piece of this whole night that was turning out to help. She kept serving up things he could use — like the existence of the neighbors — and warning him away from things that might trip him up.

Maybe everything would start to fall into place again for Nick. He would get an update on the search while they waited out the storm. The snow would stop falling just as he learned where the police were looking, any necessary retooling of their route, or areas they'd better steer clear of. Nick gave an experimental wiggle of his toes. He thought the injury might be resolving — either that or he was losing sensation.

Before he'd gone inside, things used to happen around Nick and he wouldn't have any idea why. Someone would tick him off, then suddenly he'd get mad, and then there would be chaos, the whole damn scene shot to shit while Nick just stood there, wondering what had caused the first piece to break.

It was like this yellow buzzing through which he couldn't think or hear or see. Like a beehive inside him.

In prison he'd learned to subdue its hum. To stop and take a look around, decide on his best course of action. That strategy had enabled him to build up to work duty, a job on the outs. And it was what would ensure that the night from here on out would go well, too. He just had to make sure to keep calm, act and consider things methodically.

The search should be pulled back quickly. If he and Harlan hadn't been located within the first few hours, law enforcement wisdom would have that they were probably out of reach.

Nick realized the princess could become his best form of traction. But he kept the knowledge buried — he didn't want Cassie forewarned, on her guard where he and the princess were concerned. Another bonus: the cops would give any group the princess was traveling with the royal treatment, wouldn't they? No shoot-out or helicopter ambush from above.

Nick peered through one of the windows beside the door. The precipitation actually seemed a little lighter, as if thinned by the sheer power of his desire. Nick looked over his shoulder, hunting Harlan, who was standing in the entrance to the kitchen.

"Bring them here," he ordered.

Harlan pushed his two captives forward, and something inside Nick eased. How greatly Nick depended on his cellie. Not his cellie, his friend — even more than that. Harlan was truer with him than Nick's own mother had been. Harlan said things like they were. He asked Nick for what he really needed. If only everyone could be like Harlan.

Changing locations would introduce complexity, of course, but Harlan could take care of any potential complications. Nobody risked defiance when he was around.

The opening to the kitchen was blotted out by Harlan, who kept a hold of both Cassie and her kid. Nick smiled at them. "Almost forgot something."

"Yeah," the princess said in that nasty voice of hers. "Our coats."

Nick retained his smile. "Nope. Your father."

He was pleased by the effect of his words. They jolted the princess out of her stance. Her knees jerked, and she might've gone down completely if Harlan hadn't yanked her up.

Words spilled from her mouth. "Is he all right? My dad?"

Nick grinned. "I don't know that *all right* is the phrase I'd use." He pivoted again. "What would you say, sis?"

Silence spread itself out. Nick realized for the first time just how the quiet pressed in from outside. Enough snow had accumulated that the falling flakes landed on a muffling blanket. The wind had stopped. There were no human noises at the moment, and no animal ones either. Not so much as a single bird cry. Despite the heat in the house, Nick went cold. Out there, under a blank, anonymous sky, nobody cared whether you lived or died. Scratch that. His sister and the princess would probably be all too happy if he were dead.

He took a few steps toward the kitchen. A pleasant numbness was spreading through his foot, as if it were already sunk outside into a wafting drift of snow. Nick grabbed Cassie. "Come on. We'd better go deliver some last minute instructions."

After telling Harlan to stay behind with the princess, Nick headed for the flight of basement stairs, Cassie trip-stepping along beside him.

He had a feeling what they would find down here; Nick had stalked enough animals through the woods, hunting with his father, to recognize the effect of pain that severe. Far worse than anything Nick had been through tonight. Warmth suffused him as he imagined Cassie getting her next glimpse of her husband.

But when they found him, lying in the same spot where they'd left him, he was alive. The sight filled Nick with a clawing rage. This guy was like a fucking Timex watch.

Cassie whimpered, and Nick had to work not to turn the anger against her. He felt like he was holding back a freight train. Cassie had no clue how lucky she was, the bullets she kept dodging. This perfect charmed life of hers had cast a spell over everything. Her house stood, her husband survived. Even the princess still seemed plucky.

"Shut up," Nick told Cassie.

He crouched, and thrust his finger into the meat of the man's thigh. The man's body curled up like one of those bugs that went hard and round when you poked it. There was a moan, almost too low to hear.

Nick leaned down and spoke into the man's ear. "Listen up."

Cassie opened her mouth, then closed it.

"I have a few things of yours. Your gun and your binoculars. Also, your wife and your daughter." Nick grinned up at Cassie.

"We're going to be gone for a little while. There are no more phones, there's nothing left in your house. Still, if you try to summon help — if you so much as tap on the ceiling — I'll be watching and I'll see you do it. I will know. Sis, want to tell him?"

Cassie's words came out of some distant valley whose echo carried toward Nick. Once before, he had heard his sister beg a person not to die. "Please, Ben. Hold on. Oh, please just hold on a little while longer."

"You see, it turns out I have a bit of a temper," Nick explained. "And I broke something that your lovely daughter was kind enough to remind me that we need."

Nick reached down to the man's leg and stuck his finger in forcefully again. He felt the place where the bones shifted and ground together. And he watched the man pass out, his face and body almost completely unchanged, eyes still staring upwards, but something ineffable indicating the loss of conscious resolve.

Cassie clamped her hand against her mouth. As if this were bad. Seeing her tough and stringy husband laid out would be nothing compared to the departure of the dewy princess.

He looked back down at her husband. "Is that clear?"

No response from the floor.

Nick got up and faced Cassie. "I'd say we're good."

He grabbed the back of his sister's shirt and pulled her toward the stairs.

"Good," Nick said, when they returned. Harlan had gotten dressed; he was sweaty and overheating in the warm house. The kid's coat hung open on her. "Looks like everyone is ready for a trip." He indicated a coat draped over the couch, and Cassie leaned to pick it up.

"This is how the next part is going to go," Nick said. "I've got the gun, and I've got Harlan."

"Nick?" Harlan said.

Nick wasn't quite able to quash impatience. "Yeah?"

"I left — something upstairs. Can I get it before we go?"

"What are you doing, moving in here?" Nick said.

Harlan shook his great head. "I'm not moving in. You said this was just going to be for a little while. To get a few things we needed."

"That's right. I did."

"But see, I put something down on the bed —"

Nick interrupted him. "Is it really important to you, Harlan?"

Harlan nodded. "Yeah, Nick. It's real important."

"Something you like a lot?"

Harlan nodded quickly again.

"Something you love even?"

Another nod.

Nick nodded back. Then he yelled, "No, you cannot go upstairs!"

Harlan lowered his head. His shoulders dropped, and his back slumped. On the few occasions when Nick shouted at him, Harlan almost seemed like a normal-sized person.

Nick continued as if there'd been no pause. "In other words, I have more than enough ammo to make sure we all arrive at the bottom of the road," he said. "If we do, and if everyone plays their part, then you two don't get hurt."

Cassie spoke up. "We don't get hurt. What about our neighbors?"

Nick shrugged. "We'll deal with them when we get there."

The princess regained her nasty tone. "Like it'd be a real loss if you did anything to the Nelsons."

Cassie frowned. She reached out a hand in her kid's direction, but the princess backed away. Nick felt a smile build. Their mother had hated Cassie, and from the looks of things, her kid didn't have much use for her either. Maybe the princess would even prefer it in Canada.

"OK?" Nick brought his hands together. "We ready to go?"

CHAPTER TWENTY-EIGHT

The snow lightened momentarily as they left, flakes falling through the night like stars. Sandy walked behind Nick, while Ivy kept her distance as much as Harlan would allow. Despite the sad and straggly group they made, the sudden burst of freedom, no walls penning them in, made Sandy feel as if she were on one of Ben's expeditions.

Ben.

A weight settled over her like slowly draping cloth. Her husband was going to die. Sandy had seen that look in people's eyes at the hospital when she'd had counseling to do on the medical side. The ties that kept a person tethered to the earth were many, but Ben's were being snipped one by one. He was already partway gone.

Tears traveled down her raw, cold cheeks, and she savagely wiped them away.

Nick had taken everything from her, starting with their mother's love. Now he had her husband, and he wanted their daughter. Sandy had seen that desire, molten inside him, when they'd been in the basement.

But then, she had been living on borrowed time ever since she'd left home and made a life for herself here. How had she dared to think otherwise? You could never really escape the past; she told people that all the time in therapy. And sure enough, hers had caught up with her like an unwelcome visitor. She should've been expecting it. *Hello again. Did you think you could leave me?*

Sandy stopped in place, letting the cold gather around her. Her legs felt too weak to hold her up, and she leaned against the ridged bark of a tree. Snow had clotted in the crevices, and she tilted her face, welcoming the burn upon her bare skin.

She deserved to suffer for what she had allowed to happen to Ben, to them all. Bile stung the back of her throat. Her punishment would be a lifetime without her husband, who had given her so much, shown her a different way to live. Sandy didn't want to go on without him. How easy it would be to stay here, sink down into a mindless, frozen death. But she didn't have the luxury of escape. She had Ivy, and no matter what, she wasn't going to let Nick take her. Mourning Ben and all that they had lost would have to come later.

Sandy turned to give her house one last look. It rose up as if hewn out of the sheer rock face of the cliff behind it. The wind began to blow, and veils of snow gave way to a glow of yellow lamplight. Sandy's body shook inside her coat. She leaned over and zipped it to the neck, pulling on her hood as well.

Nick had reached the woods by their winding length of drive. He was walking almost normally now, a slight hesitation before he set his right foot down the only sign of injury. Sandy couldn't tell if the improvement helped or hindered them. He would be able to swap shoes for boots as soon as the weather let up, then set out on the trek he believed would carry him and Harlan to freedom. But would a weakened Nick be easier to oppose if it came to a fight? Or would such a state render him more of a threat, like a wounded animal?

"Get a move on it," Nick called over the plaintive wind. "I don't like us all exposed out here." He looked up at the blank, howling sky before starting forward again.

If Sandy ran, Nick would shoot her, and she couldn't leave Ivy alone. There was nowhere to go anyway. It was all but wilderness out here; there was no source of help.

And weren't they going toward help of some sort? Although Sandy couldn't imagine drawing her neighbors into this disaster. She was already responsible for a wide swath of damage tonight.

Her passivity assailed her. Was she merely going to bide her time, guard Ivy until Nick and Harlan left on their own? Or did she know better now than to count on Nick for anything?

She wasn't Cassie any longer, a tiny mouse in her brother's batting paws.

Nick's shoes made a series of dark, staring eyes through the otherwise untracked white. Sandy meandered slowly along in their trail, refusing to hurry.

Their driveway took them within sight of the Macmillans' darkened camp, its road bisected by twin tire tracks, then veered sharply for another half mile or so. A ways off at the bottom, you could catch a glimpse of the Nelsons' smaller home, a log cabin built from a kit.

Nick marched along as if he were leading a parade, snow dotting his borrowed coat, shoes sending up additional clods.

Sandy fell back, hoping to get a word in with Ivy.

The wan paleness of her daughter's face

frightened Sandy when Ivy finally caught up to her, slowly and as if against her will. Harlan formed a consuming shadow behind them, blocking out sight of the night sky and the forked fingers of trees.

"Honey," Sandy said, softly so as not to be heard.

Ivy raised hooded eyes to her.

"It's going to be okay."

Ivy gave her a smile completely devoid of mirth. *Yeah, right,* that smile said.

Sandy stepped close to her daughter. "Listen to me," she hissed, clenching a fistful of Ivy's open coat. "And zip up."

A smile that looked a trifle more genuine appeared on Ivy's face, seeming to catch her off guard. The teeth on her zipper sealed together as Ivy pulled up a clump of lift tickets, affixed during happier outdoor excursions.

"I'm not just saying so," Sandy continued. "I lied to you in one big way, I admit that. But other than that —" Sandy turned aside, feeling tears start to swell. "Aside from that first lie, it was always important to me to be straight with you, Ive. I didn't butter you up, or trick you, or tell little fibs. Other people — Dad even — yes. But not you. I'm not even entirely sure why."

The ends of Ivy's hair had gotten caught

in her coat collar. Sandy went to lift them out, but Ivy brushed her away.

"Yeah?" she said. "How is Dad, then?" A pulse in Ivy's throat, visible even through the moonless dark. "Is he going to be okay?"

Sandy stared down at the ground. The snow topped her shoes, and speckled the legs of her jeans. A falsehood was there on the tip of her tongue, as slippery as candy. How comforting it would be to protect Ivy right now, or think that she was. If all of this had never happened, if Nick and Harlan hadn't come, would the tumult and challenges of Ivy's encroaching adulthood have led Sandy to treat her much as she did Ben? Telling white lies, settling for shortcuts in the same automatic, taken-for-granted way?

"Mom?"

Sandy stepped up to the brink of reality, and when she spoke it felt more like jumping.

"He's hurt, honey," she said. "Dad broke both his legs pretty badly. But he's alive. He's in the basement."

Ivy's brows lifted. "So's Mac."

For just a moment, hope sparked between them.

Then Sandy's arm was grasped rudely, and she found herself stumbling as Nick pulled her into deeper drifts of snow.

■ ■ ■ ■

They stood in a loose pack amongst a stand of snow-clogged trees to the left of the log cabin. The wind stirred and flakes spattered their faces, obscuring sight. Snow started coming down hard again, and they all moved deeper into the trees.

"So, you just want to use their computer, right?" Sandy's voice startled a crow, which flew off with a *caw* and great beating of wings.

Nick turned to her. "To be perfectly honest, Cass —"

Ivy winced and demanded, "Does he have to keep calling you that?"

Nick ignored her. "— I don't think there's any way to get what I want and preserve the Joneses over here." He glanced at the cabin, which Ben had called by turns *cozy, diminutive,* and a *squalid little shack,* as the relationship between the two families devolved. "It's all right," Nick added in a musing tone. "I don't think they were really keeping up anyway."

Alarm shot through Sandy as she pictured the silver gleam of gun tucked inside Nick's sock.

"No," she said. "You can't kill our —" Her

lips clamped down. *You can't* had always been the worst pairing of words to say to Nick. Like a red flag in front of a bull.

"I can," Nick said flatly. He turned to Ivy. *"Cass."*

Sandy took his arm and spoke with a rocking cadence to her tone. "Look, you have the gun, you can do anything, you can do whatever you want."

It was as if Nick's face had been waxed. A smooth pallor of satisfaction slid over his features. Snowflakes melted, dripping down.

"But why don't you let me try one thing?" Sandy suggested. "It's unlikely that anyone would hear screams or gunfire on a night like tonight, but it is just this side of possible." She watched her brother carefully, gauging, assessing. "You don't want anything out of the ordinary called in. The police are already on alert."

"What are you proposing?" he asked.

Sandy swallowed. "That I just talk to them. You know. Neighbor to neighbor."

CHAPTER TWENTY-NINE

Sandy found a scarf thrust deep into the pocket of her coat, wintered over from last season, and gave it to Ivy to wind around her face. "I won't be long," she whispered, trying not to mind when Ivy didn't answer. Sandy walked forward, kicking up clumps.

The cabin's steps had been swept at least once, but were frosted with snow that had fallen since. Sandy's shoes left feathery footprints as she hurried to the door and knocked.

Where Ben had installed a pull forged from hammered iron, shipped in from a metalworker who lived in Montana, the Nelsons had a cheap chrome knob purchased at a Lowe's or Home Depot downstate. Sandy shuddered in the steely air. She suddenly hated herself, hated them all. Why had she and Ben decided to build a grand lodge up here instead of being content with the life they had built with each other in town?

An answer came from deep inside her, and she couldn't help but take a reflexive step away from where Nick waited.

Because it made you feel like you left all that behind.

But a big house couldn't do that. The higher she'd climbed, the closer Nick got. Or maybe it was that he'd been there all along.

Anita Nelson pulled the door open with an unwelcoming frown. Biding herself not to look over her shoulder at the others, Sandy asked if she could come in.

"Come in?" Anita said. "What, did the pipes burst up at that castle of yours? Mountain living suddenly feel a little more real?"

"Anita," Sandy said wearily. "I come from Cold Kettle." She hadn't said those words to anyone in twenty years. "Please stop treating me like I used to own a bakery in Brooklyn."

"Well." Anita sniffed. "Your husband doesn't come from Cold Kettle. He fits the bakery bill pretty well."

At the mention of Ben, Sandy's vision blurred.

Anita seemed to catch sight of it.

"What's wrong?" she asked, a trifle less ir-

393

ritably. "Is somebody sick? Or hurt?"

Only the worst enemies would fail to come together over a medical emergency in the mountains. Time was too short, and the consequences too potentially dire. But another lie had scrambled together in Sandy's brain, better than an injury. It was just outrageous enough to have a chance of working.

"I did something really stupid," she said, confession working itself into her tone. Old habits died hard. There was something almost soothing to Sandy about lying again, like slipping on a comfortable old robe.

"Anita? Who's there?" It was Hark Nelson's voice from inside the cabin. He walked up behind his wife, dwarfing her form, though he would still be no match for Harlan. He too frowned upon seeing Sandy. "What do you want?"

"Quiet," Anita told him. She gave Sandy a grudging nod.

"It was childish of me," Sandy explained. "But I found this reality show."

The story fell from her mouth as easily as the accumulating snow. If she could get the Nelsons to vacate their property, Nick could break in and have access to anything he wanted. While Sandy would have access to things, too. This home hadn't been rid of its

394

household weapons.

"It's called Nasty Neighbors," Sandy went on.

The Nelsons frowned in unison now.

"I told them our story. Gave your information," she added. "They're going to come out here tonight to interview you."

It was absurd, of course — a television crew arriving unannounced, during a storm — but hadn't TV in fact become completely ridiculous these days? Any chance to find someone willing to prostrate herself, anything for a story.

Sure enough, Anita said, "They're coming out here?"

"To interview us?" asked Hark.

Sandy nodded, watching for the expected distaste to paint their faces. Adirondack people were interior, private. The notion of airing dirty laundry to anyone, let alone strangers, should provoke an instant recoiling.

"They want to hear your side of the story," she explained. "There'll be a camera crew and everything." Now was not the time to check whether the others were continuing to stay hidden, or if Nick was growing impatient, but it felt as if it took chains to keep from turning her head. Sandy went on rapidly. "I think you should leave, just for tonight. Believe me, I regret the whole thing now. I don't want you subjected to bright lights and microphones."

Hark stepped outside, even more alarmed than she'd imagined by the idea of outsiders — from television, no less — encroaching on his home.

"I mean, get your coats first," Sandy said. "And then just go to the motel on the highway. The crew will come and not find you here and probably never air the segment at all."

The story sounded relatively plausible to her worried mind. Not bad anyway, given the options, and Hark and Anita did seem to be going for it. Sandy allowed herself a shallow breath of relief, the barest glimpse over her shoulder.

Everyone was still well concealed.

Hark faced her, glaring. "You called the media? Let 'em come. I'd love to tell 'em what happens when Fifth Avenue meets honest, hardworking folk."

Sandy felt something slide away inside her.

"Nice try, Cass," Nick said, shouldering his way out of the woods. Bringing the gun into view, he motioned for the Nelsons to back into their cabin. Nick jerked his head, calling Harlan and Ivy forward. "But I've always found honesty to be the best policy.

Haven't you?"

Nick kept the gun trained on Hark while Harlan made an awkward shuffle onto the porch. During the moment his wife was unguarded, Hark shouted, "Anita! Get my —"

Anita's gaze flew to a cabinet that stood by the entryway; just as fast, she took a step toward it.

"Harlan," Nick growled, and Harlan crossed the porch in one step.

"Grab him," Nick ordered.

Hark let out a high, unexpected yelp as Harlan's enormous hand encircled his throat. The man's eyes bulged and a terrifying blue started to stain his cheeks.

"Harlan," Nick said, gun keeping Anita in check. "Loosen up a little."

Harlan did, and Hark sagged in his hold.

"Let him sit," Nick commanded.

The room was too small and crowded for men of their size to walk in tandem. Harlan knocked over a chair, and a plate fell to the floor in his wake as he sat Hark down.

Nick jerked his chin toward Anita and she went to take a seat beside her husband.

"I think you can both see that fighting is the wrong approach," Nick said. He waited until Anita and Hark nodded. "The good news is that there's no need to fight."

Sandy had gone to stand next to Ivy, the gun cabinet tantalizingly within reach.

"Get away from there," Nick said, and Sandy let out a breath. It was easier in some ways to be told what to do. Less thinking. Less risk.

She tried to nudge Ivy closer to the kitchen table, but her daughter shrank from her touch.

Nick turned back to the twosome on their folding chairs. "As these two lovely ladies will tell you, nothing bad has to happen tonight. So long as you do what I want."

Hark finally regained his breath, bracing his throat with one hand. "And what is it that you want?"

"Just stay there." Nick looked at Harlan. "If either of you so much as coughs funny, Harlan will snap your wife's neck with one hand while he holds you down with the other. Is that clear?"

Hark looked as if he were trying to nod, but could not.

"I'll take that as a yes," Nick said. "I need something on your computer, but the princess can help me with that." He turned to Ivy with an expression of confidence in his eyes.

Ivy nodded, and the sight made Sandy

want to take her daughter and shake her. *No,* she screamed silently. *Please don't you be cowed by him, too!*

Only, how could Ivy not be? Nick had taken five people captive tonight, including Ivy's unstoppable father.

Ivy wouldn't look at Sandy anyway. She'd sooner follow Nick's lead than turn to the mother who'd betrayed her. Sandy couldn't send any sort of message, not a single note of reassurance. How did you make up for a lie that had lasted a lifetime?

"Can you tell me where your computer is?" Nick asked politely.

Hark let go of his throat, and pointed toward the living room. Five oblong bruises made a peacock's tail against his flesh. "In there."

Anita started to rise — some automatic reflex of hospitality — and Harlan took a step in her direction.

"Anita!" That high note of alarm again before Hark's voice gave out and he erupted in a cough. "Sit down!" he begged once he could speak.

"Actually, go fix some coffee," Nick corrected as he turned. "And make it strong."

Anita walked over to turn a light on under the kettle.

"Can I help?" Sandy asked her.

Anita's glance took in her husband, who sat slumped in his chair, gingerly touching his neck. Harlan stood over him.

"I think you've done quite enough already," Anita said, then added, "Would you like some coffee?"

Sandy looked into the living room. Ivy was skidding the mouse over a pad, displaying different windows on a desktop computer for Nick as if she were helping one of the kids she babysat with his homework.

"You know?" Sandy said. "I actually would."

Anita opened a cupboard and took out a jar of instant coffee.

"Can I get a cup?" Hark let out a grinding cough. "Be good on my throat."

Anita nodded. She lifted down a bouquet of mismatched mugs from the cupboard.

"No coffee except for Nick," Harlan said, looking at Sandy through bleary eyes. "Think I can't guess what hot coffee would do if you threw it in my face?"

The idea actually hadn't occurred to Sandy, and she realized she'd better start thinking in different terms. Hark clearly was. Upon hearing the refusal, he squeezed his hands into frustrated fists, eyes set at a point right above Harlan's belly.

Anita twisted a knob on her stove, dulling the electric coil before the kettle could start to shriek, then came back and took her seat at the oilcloth-covered table, a foodless version of the world's strangest dinner party.

Hark was staring at Sandy. "Level with me," he said, low.

In addition to appearing frightened, Sandy noticed that Hark also looked unwell. His face was ashen, his throat stubbled with straw-like bits of beard. It came back to Sandy then — how Hark's aggressive resistance toward their construction had begun to wane during a resurgence of some type of cancer.

"How much trouble are we in?" Hark's gaze flicked toward his gun cabinet, the sheer curtain that hung over the window of the back door, and his truck parked outside.

"I think we're in the kind of trouble we can get out of," Sandy said. "They want to get away clean. That's it."

Hark gave a single nod, although doubt tapped a finger on Sandy. The thoughts she'd had in the basement were starting to seep in again, rising like floodwater. Beneath Nick's rational plan to escape lived a completely unchecked urge to see Sandy taken down. And even if Nick could deprive himself of that, was he really going to leave behind witnesses?

But what would Hark have done if Sandy shared any of that? Instead of voicing her fears, she asked, "Hark? Are you on any sort of medication? Painkillers, I mean."

He frowned. "I've got some Oxy, sure. Why do you ask?"

Sandy looked to where Harlan stood, standing guard. She couldn't tell if he was listening, much less following, but she gave a straight answer. "His foot is hurt." Sandy pointed toward Nick in the living room. "If you could spare a few pills, it might help us once we leave here."

Hark dug around in his shirt pocket, coming out with an amber vial. "You can have the whole damn bottle."

"You sure?" Sandy asked. Hark obviously kept his pills close at hand. But she was already closing her fingers over the offering. These would make the Advil Nick had taken seem like Smarties, subduing any residual pain, and dulling resistance when he went to switch his shoes for boots. Oxycontin could also produce softening in mood-related ways, resulting in a more malleable, easier-to-manipulate Nick. The snow would become less of a threat, the trek would seem more manageable.

A flash came from the direction of the living room. Someone had turned on the TV, an old-fashioned box kind on a stand.

Anita lifted her head straight up, addressing Harlan. "Can I hold my husband's hand?"

Harlan shifted his body to check, but Nick was intent on both screens. Finally Harlan said, "Can't see any harm in that."

Anita scooted over in her chair and Hark leaned across the table until they were close enough to touch. Their hands came together like magnets.

Watching them, Sandy's eyes spilled over. That simple, elemental connection between husband and wife. Had hers been lost, was it dying now on a cold basement floor, without Sandy there to share the final moments?

The barker voices of anchors and reporters penetrated the room while tears ran down Sandy's face. After some time, she became aware of Anita looking at her.

"I knew I didn't want you moving up here," she said.

Sandy looked at her, outrage soldering her tears.

Anita stared back, until the humor contained in her statement began to leak through. Sandy shook her head, suppressing a faint peal of laughter. She wondered if, in a different life, the two of them might actually have gotten on quite well. Anita stretched her free hand across the table, and after a moment, Sandy took it.

"Coffee ready?" Nick asked, entering the kitchen with Ivy at his heels.

"I'll get it," Sandy offered. She rolled the tablet she had managed to eject between her fingers. Just one shouldn't do much more than take the edge off. She wanted Nick comfortable enough to leave, but not so comfortable that he lost his motivation.

Sandy could feel Anita's eyes on her as she crossed to the yellow flecked counter. Sandy poured hot water over a hill of instant, then let the pill drop from where it had stuck to her sweat-slicked palm, swirling the mug around to dissolve both powder and grinds. The medication's effect would be concentrated because it wasn't being swallowed whole; Sandy remembered that from work. Something about a time-release mechanism.

Nick took the coffee from her, inclining his head in a position of exaggerated thanks. "We're good," he said, drinking deeply. He seemed to be barely suppressing glee, his mouth trembling to stay level, fist half-raised to pump the air. "No coverage on . . ."

"Online," Ivy supplied in a pseudo-helpful tone.

Nick's smile evaporated like a drop of water on a hot stove. "On the computer. That's what I meant to say, princess."

Ivy kept her eyes aimed away and Sandy also studiously avoided everybody's gaze. What Nick was saying had to be impossible — the escape of two convicts would have made it to the police website, blogs, possibly even CNN — but it struck Sandy that Nick had been in prison for twenty-plus years. He would have had limited access to the net, if any at all. Little idea how to conduct a search, while Ivy would be perfectly able to make it just look as if she were doing one.

Nick drained the mug, then gestured them all to their feet. "And get a load of this."

Hark, Anita, and Sandy trooped into the living room, bookended by Harlan. Ivy was allowed to remain behind, and Sandy's thoughts went to the gun cabinet again: how tempting it was, how much worse it might make things.

Nick leaned forward, rotating the knob on the television. The image for channel twelve was cloudy, but the sound came in clear. The earlier weather story cycled before they heard, "No further update on the capture of three escaped convicts. Police are warning residents of Elizabethtown and the area around Route 9 near Wedeskyull to be on their guard."

A pretty, plastic anchorwoman chirped in conclusion: "The convicts are still on the loose. Do not open your doors to strangers. Do not . . ."

"What?" Harlan said. "That's where the roadwork was. That's where we did the job."

"They got nothing," Nick said triumphantly. "Haven't found the car — they might not even know we hitched a ride. And they think there's three of us." He shone a radiant smile upon everyone assembled. "Even the new freaking media you've got can't stop me."

A pause as everyone studied the living room floor.

"You know what?" Nick said. "I think it's time for us to go."

CHAPTER THIRTY

After Tim Lurcquer took the call from Daniel Mills, he sat in his car for a minute or two, staring at the windshield as heat gusted through the vents.

Long Hill Road.

And a woman, showing up injured, having staggered out of the woods.

Because her car had been taken?

A strong wind was kicking everything around. The windshield wipers couldn't keep up and the glass filmed with snow. Tim flicked the lever by the wheel, skipping the wipers into a more frenetic beat. Then he turned to Mandy in the passenger seat. "Tell me again what you learned after the initial report came in."

A computer thrust itself out of the dash. Mandy tapped the screen to get it going. "About the prison break?" she asked.

New on the job, and the first female the Wedeskyull force had ever employed,

Mandy showed potential, although she'd clearly watched too many cop shows and was in this for the drama as much as anything else. Which was a fine but short-lived motivation, in Tim's experience. A lot of cops started out that way. One real crime scene and it changed pretty quick.

"The escape took place off prison grounds." Mandy pointed to the screen, split now to display two different photos. "That's Harlan Parker on the left."

Tim nodded.

"In for multiple counts of armed robbery," Mandy went on. "Parker's not the ringleader; he drives the getaway car or holds a gun on the hostages. But he's the only one who's served time. His partner never got nabbed."

She even spoke like a character on TV.

"He's a big guy," Mandy concluded. "Huge."

Tim studied the blurred picture. "And the other guy?"

"Nicholas Burgess," Mandy said promptly. "He's from Cold Kettle. Still has family in the area. He's in for murder one, a really grisly —"

"Go back," Tim said, ignoring her palpable excitement at the crime. "To the family in the area. That took some looking

408

into, didn't it?"

He'd assigned Mandy the task of rooting out anything she could find when the report about the escape had first come in. If she wanted drama, he was happy to oblige.

Mandy started flipping pages on her notepad. Too much of the pad was filled up for such a short time on the job. Like other newbies, she tended to write down anything and everything with no filter for what was likely to wind up being important.

"Mom's still in Cold Kettle," Mandy said. "But he also has a sister, married, surname Tremont, living on Long Hill Road."

"That's what I thought I remembered you saying." Tim put the car in Drive, tires spinning for a moment before gaining traction in the snow.

Mandy's thoroughness and diligence, combined with GPS, led Tim to a small, unnumbered road that in all the years he'd spent in these parts — a lifetime so far — he couldn't remember seeing, then a long drive that laddered up a mountainside.

They passed a tiny, lit-up cabin, but Mandy shook her head when Tim started to brake.

"It's that one," she said, pointing. "Up there."

Tim was taken by rare surprise. He kept himself from muttering out loud. Vacationers had been coming up to the Adirondacks since the turn of the last century, imposing their great camps on the land. But their descendants would've rehabilitated the family lodge rather than constructing a new, shiny version of it. People who built houses like this one were hard for Tim to wrap his head around; brightly colored rain-forest creatures who bore no resemblance to any animals he knew. Living here, but not from here, submitting to north country conditions by choice instead of lack thereof.

They passed a camp, sprawled across a half-acre of land, dying a slow death. Unoccupied, it looked like, although the field in front showed the recent cuts of a snowmobile, not entirely filled in yet. Kids probably, exploring. Not the best night to enter the wilderness, but since when did kids choose the best night for anything?

The tires of the patrol car sent up a wake of snow as Tim pulled into a circular section of drive at the top of the hill.

"Chief?" Mandy said. "Can I ask what we're doing here?"

She was eyeing the house with the same emotion Tim had sought to hide. Something akin to awe.

"We're here on a hunch," Tim replied, opening his door and climbing out. Snow pelted him like BB shot. "If it proves out, I'll explain my thinking." He drew the brim of his hat down to keep the snow from dashing his face, and looked across the roof of the car to Mandy. "This is as good a time as any to learn that if half of the job is driven by rules, the other half should be steered by your gut."

Walking through the untouched drifts to a stone deck at the front of the house, Tim looked for hollows signifying footprints, but if there were any, they'd been obscured by fresh snowfall.

Mandy followed. She knocked first, Tim happy to let her take the lead. When nobody answered, he took a turn, pounding his fist against the wood.

Tim turned and looked around, the wind and the snow limiting sight. "Notice anything?"

"The lights in the house are on," Mandy said, "but no one seems to be home."

"And there are two cars," Tim said, pointing. To the right, a Jeep and a late model sedan were buried to their hubcaps.

"What can we do?" Mandy said. "That might be strange, but if no one comes to the door, we aren't allowed to go in."

Tim eyed her. "One thing to know about Wedeskyull," he said, reaching down to the fancy metal pull and squeezing with his gloved hand, "is that nobody locks their doors."

The door swung open, letting out a breath of welcome, heated air.

"Hello?" Tim called. "Anybody home?" He looked at Mandy. "Come on. Let's give a shout to make sure."

In addition to warmth, the house breathed cooking smells.

Spaghetti. Or pizza.

"Mr. and Mrs. Tremont?" he called out. "Hello? Anybody home? This is the chief of police." He walked toward a high, carved archway, still calling, indicating to Mandy that she should take a look around the rest of the first floor.

In the kitchen, the remains of a meal were spread out.

"Hello?" Tim said, the sound of his voice loud in the empty room.

Too empty. Not only unpeopled, but —

Tim frowned, looking around.

He didn't want either himself or anyone on his force to pursue practices like these — a search with no probable cause — but something about the scene gave him pause.

He crossed to the stove, where a jug or urn of some sort sat on one of the many burners. Tim bent over and took a look. Tomato sauce. But what a strange way to heat something up.

So now it's a crime to use the wrong cooking implement?

Tim squared his fists on his hips, adjusting his belt. He made a mental note to check for cross-country ski or snowshoe tracks in the fields, although the snow had been coming down hard enough that any trail was likely to be blanked out already. Maybe the Tremonts had been the ones on that snowmobile.

He turned once more in the enormous space. His gaze took in a pair of sliding glass doors, huge walk-in pantry, an entrance to what must be the basement, and food and water bowls for a dog. Idly, he opened a cupboard door, drew out a drawer.

Mandy walked back in with a shrug. "Everything checks out. No signs of disturbance."

Tim pulled open another drawer. "There's something weird about this kitchen."

"Yeah," Mandy said. "It cost more than my whole house."

"That and every single drawer is empty." Tim circled the room, looking down, looking up. "That fancy pot ring doesn't have any pots hanging from it."

Mandy followed his gaze.

Tim walked across the floor — swept clean, and made out of some ultra slick, mottled substance he'd never seen before — not thinking, trying to empty his mind. It was how hunches usually resolved. In a state of non-thought, impressions aggregating until they formed a coherent picture. Tim squinted through the window above the sink. A black-and-yellow snowmobile had landed like a wasp to the left of the old camp.

Tim crossed the room to the basement entrance.

"Did you hear that?" he asked, his hand on the doorknob.

"What?" Mandy said. "I didn't hear anything."

Tim hadn't either really. He paused before the now open door. The barest of noises, so faint as to not even count as sound.

Mandy watched as Tim took the first stair, her face open, curious. "Chief Lurcquer? You going down there?"

Whatever Tim did now would become part of this young officer's breed of policing. And Tim had seen what lay down this particular road. Where it led, what it turned people into. How it made them do things until they were no better than the criminals they locked up, unfit to take care of the people they were charged with protecting.

Everything was dark below, and silent. Tim turned and climbed back up.

"I'll call in our location to dispatch," he said, unclasping his radio from his belt. "And then let's go see who's home at that other residence."

"You have a problem out there?" asked his dispatcher. "Want your men at the ready?"

Tim glanced at Mandy to see if she'd taken offense at the *men*. Something else to put a protocol in place for. Changing times.

"Negative," he said. "I got nothing. Just a kitchen that doesn't look right to me."

The radio crackled. "The wife got you doing the cooking these days, Chief?"

Tim gestured to Mandy and they walked back through the bulk of the downstairs, pulled open that soaring door, and stepped outside into the snowfall.

"Negatory on that, too," he said before signing off.

November 13, 1988

Barbara stood by the front door, waiting for Gordon to get home with Nicholas. She'd expected them back earlier, and had been standing in her heels long enough that her feet had started to hurt. She kicked off her shoes and rubbed the ball of each foot.

It was a late autumn twilight, purple and blue. Not enough light at this hour for them to be out there, doing what they were doing. Barbara walked across the house, shouting upstairs crossly. "Cassandra! Are you on the phone?"

"No, Mama," came the response. "And we have call-waiting now, remember?"

Barbara returned to her perch by the door. A glossy pickup was just turning into the drive — the wood-paneled station wagon junked for parts years ago — and Barbara let out a relieved breath. She grabbed her coat, slipped her shoes back on, and hurried outside, the ache in her feet forgotten.

Nicholas let himself down from the truck, his boot on the runner, not tall enough yet to step out at one go. He never wound up gaining much weight either, although his slightness didn't seem to pose any sort of encumbrance in his life. Then again, could anything possibly encumber Nicholas? Barbara walked forward, about to pull him into her arms, when something stopped her. Not the blood that dabbed Nicholas' camouflage jacket, but the look in his eyes.

"Nicholas?" she said on a high, piping note.

Her son turned away.

Gordon climbed out of the truck. "Nick's got some washing up to do."

Barbara watched Nicholas trudge into the house, not bothering to kick off his boots. Upstairs, a light signaled the occupancy of the spare bedroom. If Barbara could've transferred the poisonous brew from Nicholas' face into that glowing room, she would've done so in a heartbeat.

She looked around for Gordon.

He had gone into the barn. The generator rumbled and the lights kicked on. Barbara took another look around, noticing the kill for the first time. In the truck bed, a six-pointed buck. Two rifles lay on the rack on the roof. Gordon walked back outside, wiping his hands on a rag.

"I'd better go after Nicholas," Barbara said.

Gordon reached for her arm. "Might be best to leave him be."

Barbara looked down at her coat. Despite the rag, her husband had left blackish smears on the light-colored wool.

"Look what you've done," she protested. She tried to tug loose, but uncharacteristically, Gordon resisted.

Finally, he freed her. "I think you should give the boy some space."

Barbara was halfway to the house, but something in Gordon's voice — or maybe it was his demeanor, the unexpected way he'd held on to her arm — made her return.

"Why?" she asked. "What happened?"

Gordon looked up at a pocked moon rising. "Nick wouldn't let me field dress the kill. That's why I brought the deer home intact. Gonna make a helluva mess in the barn."

Barbara squinted in the deepening dusk, trying to make out the buck. Even fallen, he was a beauty, large and muscled, angled head still proud.

Gordon's voice drifted forth again. "He said the strangest thing."

Barbara felt as if a cold wind were rushing

through her. Whatever Nicholas had said, she didn't want to hear it. She lifted her head slowly, finding Gordon's eyes in the descending dark.

Her husband dropped his face into his red-smeared palms.

"Gordon?" Barbara said faintly. "Are you — are you crying?"

He looked up swiftly. Blood lent his cheek a clownish streak. "He told me that I'd better not cut the deer. Because once I did, I wouldn't be able to stop."

Gordon's eyes changed focus then.

Barbara turned around in her heels to see what he might be looking at.

Nicholas stood in the entrance to the house. The moonlight gave his shadow an odd, lurching cast as he took a few steps into the dooryard, an oblong box thrust forward in his hands.

"Is this for me?" he asked.

Gordon reached for the box. "It was, son," he said. "But I can hold on to it for now. Why don't you go on back inside? Let me finish up out here."

Nicholas turned in the direction of the deer. "You need my help to get that bad boy off the truck, Dad."

The tone made Barbara blanch. It was her

419

boy's voice — light, humorous, warm — but at the same time it wasn't. There were depths beneath that statement, as if the words were only a thin skin of air over an alive and pulsing world. Barbara had always known Nicholas was smarter than she was, that there would come a day when she wouldn't understand all that was going on in his mind. She just couldn't believe that day had come so soon.

Gordon flinched as if he had heard the same thing.

"Besides," Nicholas said. "I want to see what's in the box. I want to see what you got for me, Dad."

Barbara turned back, an encouraging smile painted on her face. "Go on, Gordon," she said. "Let Nicholas see his present." She stepped close to her son, touching him on the shoulder. "I'd like to know what's in the box myself."

Gordon's mouth set in a thin, firm line.

Nicholas lifted the lid. "Oh wow."

"What is it, darling?" Barbara asked, and looked.

"Just lookee, Mama," Nicholas said happily. "It's a knife."

Gordon stared down at the dirt of the dooryard, hands linked behind his back. "I bought it before we went out today, son.

But if you're not going to hunt anymore, then I can return this, and get you something else." He looked up. "Anything you want. Maybe some new records? We could even talk about a car for next year."

Barbara frowned. They had both been in agreement that a car was out of the question. Gordon felt it was too extravagant a gift, and Barbara worried that Nicholas might get hurt, especially if his friends encouraged him to drive recklessly.

Nicholas studied the knife in its nest of padding. The handle looked to be made out of bone, stripped clean and smooth, its silver blade reflected in the moonlight. Nick lifted his arms, raising the box toward the sky.

Barbara spoke. "You don't want that, do you?"

Ivory lit Nicholas' features while he gazed upwards. He was so beautiful, like a statue carved out of marble. Barbara's throat clutched. She moved in her son's direction, pulled as the tide was now being pulled, many hundreds of miles away, by the very same moon.

"You're better than the men around here," she said softly. "There are great things you're going to do, that you're destined for."

A cloud slid across the sky, blotting out

the moon.

Nicholas pulled the blade free, letting the box it had come in fall to the ground. He ran to the pickup, lowered the tailgate, and hoisted himself inside. Then he threw himself onto the dead animal, burying his face in its wiry coat. It looked at first as if he were sobbing, remorse and regret, into the stricken creature's flesh. But then the stabbing motion of his hand revealed itself.

Barbara let out a terrible cry, like the high, manic whistle of some faraway wind. She ran forward herself, arms flailing, stumbling in her heels, and climbed into the truck bed. Her knees smarted as she crawled toward Nicholas. Barbara gathered her boy into her arms, holding on to his hand, trying to stop it, so that for a second it seemed they were both driving the knife, again and again and again, into the deer's belly.

Back inside the house, Barbara saw Cassandra bolt down the stairs. The girl entered the kitchen, its door swinging shut behind her.

Barbara stilled just outside. A column of light shone from underneath the doorjamb. She blinked at its brightness.

"Daddy?" Cassandra said. "What's wrong?"

The rush of water through the pipes signaled that the shower was on. Nicholas upstairs, cleaning up. Barbara turned around so that she could go dole out towels and soap.

"It's going to be okay," Cassandra said then. "Things always seem worse at night, remember?"

Minutes meted themselves out.

"Nick was scared," Gordon said at last. "But not of me. I mean, he said that he was, that he didn't want me to start cutting. But really, I think he was scared of himself."

Another long, clawing silence.

"It's like what happened with your hands did something to him. Took the safety off. And today out there, hunting the deer, he had to ask for it to be put back on."

"You knew?" Cassandra whispered. "You knew he hurt my hands?"

Oh, for God's sake, Barbara almost said. She was pushing at the kitchen door when Gordon's voice stopped her.

"I do now, sweetheart," he said heavily.

"He's going to kill somebody someday," Cassandra said after a while. "Not a deer. A person. You know that too, don't you, Daddy?"

Barbara let the kitchen door fall shut, making sure it didn't brush audibly against

the jamb. She reached down and slipped off
her shoes. Quietly, on tiptoes, she backed
away toward the stairs.

CHAPTER THIRTY-ONE

"Harlan, get me a knife from the kitchen."

Sandy's heart galloped upon hearing the command. She whirled around.

Hark and Anita lay facedown on the shoe-abraded rug on the floor in front of their shabby couch.

"Just for a little while," Nick was saying as he wielded the roll of duct tape. "Once my friend and I are good and gone, Cassie — um, *Sandy* — here will come back and free you." He smiled down at his captives, a light lifting of his lips that looked more menacing than a scowl. "That's what neighbors are for, huh?"

Tape, Sandy thought. *He just wants to contain them for a while.*

The medication didn't seem to be having any effect. Perhaps it was too soon. Or perhaps Nick was so fueled by adrenaline that it would've taken a boatload of pills to subdue him.

"Harlan," Nick said. "A little help here."

Harlan edged by Sandy, handing Nick a short, sharp knife and placing one of his boots upon Hark to hold him in place. The expression on Harlan's face was wide and placid. His boot covered most of Hark's back.

Suddenly, Nick paused, sticky lengths of tape dangling from his teeth. His back had straightened and his eyes gone wide, ears all but pricked. Sandy shot a look around, wondering what he was responding to. The kitchen drawer where Harlan had gotten the knife snagged her attention. It hung open, a tempting silver array inside, blades and teeth and tines.

Sandy took a step in that direction, already picturing her choice of weapon, and what she would do with it. Nick first. His throat. She couldn't waste time on warning or an ambivalent attempt. With Nick gone, the threat Harlan posed would disperse like sand blown into the wind.

Sandy squinted as she drew closer. There were other knives in the drawer, and what looked like skewers of some sort.

"Harlan," Nick said. "Take hold of my sister."

It was as if she'd been given the ability to fly. One moment Sandy was contemplating a move of desperate brutality, the next she was in Harlan's arms and hovering above the floor.

"And then all of you shut up," Nick added.

He stayed quiet, breathing, listening.

With a single slice to the pieces of tape he'd applied, Nick set Hark and Anita free. Sandy frowned, watching her brother help them both into sitting positions.

Only then did she hear what her thwarted attempt to pilfer a weapon had made her miss.

Outside, the twin thud of boots.

"Listen up and listen up good," Nick said. "I think we can all agree that if I wanted to kill you or your wife, I would've done it by now, right?"

Hark and Anita twisted to look over their shoulders at the door.

Nick got down on his hands and knees and crawled forward until he was close enough that his spittle flew into their faces. "I said, listen to me!" They both jumped, and Nick went on without a hitch. "If I wanted to hurt you, I would've done it. I'm good with the gun." He touched the knife to Hark's throat, who sat stone-like, refusing to wince.

It wasn't true — their father had actually

once called Nick a clumsy shot, impatient and unstill — but Sandy couldn't see what difference that made at such close range.

"Put her down," Nick told Harlan.

The first thing Sandy did was scan the room for Ivy.

Her daughter turned away from her.

Nick spoke again to Hark. "Be perfectly calm while you get rid of whoever's here." A beat. "With no suspicions raised. Just act like this was a normal night while you say bye-bye." Nick got to his feet, brushing off his hands. "And in case you get the idea to make a run for it, signal or anything, I think I'll keep your wife by my side for a little extra insurance."

Anita's shoulders sloped. Her husband reached out to her.

"I can shoot her and Cassie while Harlan disembowels the kid," Nick said. "All before your guests even make it into the house."

Anita shut her eyes and a slow tear slipped out. Hark released his wife. "I won't let that happen," he said, and Sandy felt her own eyes fill at his vow.

"Oh, and just one more thing." Nick handed over his coat, indicating that Hark should put it on, then held up a scarf. He wound the length of wool around Hark's neck, dressing him like a child.

When Hark frowned, Nick pointed to his own bare neck in explanation.

"Yours looks a little sore," he said. "I think we should make sure that no one has any reason to worry about you."

They huddled in a tiny, under-the-staircase bathroom; Nick, Sandy, Ivy, and Anita. Harlan couldn't fit, so Nick placed him in the mudroom, which looked out onto a back field, now hillocked over with snow.

Letting the cramped conditions serve as excuse, Sandy edged closer to her daughter. It was a relief to feel the slim wand of Ivy's body beside her, warm and alive. But then Ivy took half a step away, all the small room would allow, and chill air filled the space between them.

Nick nudged the door open so that they could hear what was going on outside.

"Sorry to barge in on you like this, Mr. Nelson," a male voice said.

"Not a problem, Chief."

The police were here. Every muscle inside Sandy coiled and tensed.

Nick laid a hand on her arm, heated as an iron brand.

"You headed out somewhere?" asked the chief.

A minute pause, not long enough to be

noticed.

"Just want to keep on top of my plowing," Hark said.

Silence, maybe a nod in response.

"Tell you why we came," the chief went on. "This is Officer Bishop, by the way. She's new to these parts and to the force."

"Welcome," Hark said after a longer pause.

"Thank you," came a youngish-sounding woman's voice.

I'll shoot both her and Cassie while Harlan disembowels the kid.

"Anyhow . . ." Throat clearing. "I just paid a visit to your new neighbors. The Tremonts, right? Up there on the hill."

"That's right," Hark said.

"Mind if I ask you a couple of questions about them?"

After a moment, " 'Course not, Chief."

At some point, Nick's hand had dropped from her arm. Sandy now stood unimpeded. And by taking that step away from her, Ivy had wound up closest to the door.

Sandy ticked off the steps in her head.

Shove Ivy and Anita out and onto the floor. Bolt through the doorway herself, screaming for the police and for everybody to get down.

"Have you seen them tonight?" the chief said.

"Can't say as I have," Hark replied swiftly.

Swiftly enough that it might raise suspicion, put the officers on alert. The distances in this space were minute. If Sandy acted fast, the risk would be slight.

"Would they usually be home at this hour?" the chief asked.

"Can't say that either," Hark replied in a tone that commanded finality. "We really don't know them all that —" Then he changed course. "Actually, they do often go out at night."

"That right?" the chief said.

"Into town maybe," Hark concluded with faint dismissal. "For dinner."

After his initial stumbles, this delivery was Oscar-worthy, composed of shielded dislike blended with mountain manners.

"One more question," the chief said, "and I'll leave you to your night."

The gun wasn't near her now. Nick held it pressed against Anita. Sandy made sure that even her eyes remained still as she went through the steps. No barely perceptible twitch of her body would reveal what she intended.

Hark gave a grunt of agreement.

And then Nick's voice wound a silky scarf

around Sandy's ear. "Sure you want to try it?"

It was as if the blood in her veins solidified, cementing her in place.

"When we're all so close to going free?" Nick went on at a whisper.

Sandy's shoulder sagged, admitting defeat. How had he known?

The chief said, "Can you think of any reason why the Tremonts would've emptied out their kitchen?"

This time the silence went on and on, long enough to wear thin.

Sandy's flesh broke into prickles and she reached involuntarily for Ivy's dangling hand, which her daughter snatched away without a sound.

Finally Hark supplied, "They just finished moving in." He sped up, relief palpable in his tone. "Maybe they haven't unpacked everything yet."

"Makes sense," the chief said. "Thanks for your time. And good luck with the plowing."

Boots then, in retreat.

Nick reached for the powder room door, and Sandy and Ivy and Anita all crowded forward.

When the chief's voice sounded next, it

came from farther away. "Almost forgot to ask."

Nick halted, and the three of them stumbled against the hard rack of his spine.

"What's that?" Hark asked.

"How many cars do the Tremonts have?"

Sandy saw her own feeling of confusion mirrored on Anita's face, although Ivy seemed unaware, folded so deeply into herself that the goings-on around her didn't make an impact.

And then the chief's meaning came clear. He had gone to their house first — that's how he knew they weren't home. So he'd seen both cars there. And Hark had said they were out.

Anita took a step around Nick into the doorway.

A vicious scrawl transformed Nick's face, and he drove the gun toward Anita in a warning strike. But she had gotten some distance away, and the gun didn't quite make contact.

Sandy suppressed a scream. She grabbed Ivy — never mind her daughter's resistance — and shoved her deep into the powder room, away from the chaos of Nick and Anita and the gun at the entrance. Ivy's hip and shoulder banged against the tile wall, and her mouth opened in an O of outrage before shutting soundlessly.

Nick's hand moved in a blur, the safety making an audible *snick*. Nick sighted on Anita, who had come to an instant stop as if a line were pulling her up short.

"Three," she sang out.

There was silence from the kitchen.

Anita bent over, gasping for breath.

"Mrs. Nelson?" called the chief. "That you?"

"I'm sorry, Chief." Anita snatched a towel from a bar by the sink, and braced her hand against the powder room doorway. "I'm just doing a little cleaning back here."

Nick touched the snout of the gun to Anita's neck.

Ivy sucked in a breath.

"You were asking about the Tremonts?" Anita trilled in a pleasant voice that made her husband's earlier performance sound like a kid in a grade school play. "They have three cars."

Hark rallied then. "As if anybody needs three cars." He let out a snort. "Those people get rich off the backs of folks who come up here on the weekends."

The declaration seemed to lend a final needed note of authenticity.

"Ah," the chief said. "That explains a lot."

"The wealthy are strange," added the

younger cop.

"You can say that again," Nick muttered under his breath.

Boots clopped off once more. This time Nick waited until the door clicked shut and the sound of the car engine had died out.

Then he came out clapping.

"Excellent job, both of you," he said. "Now give me back my coat, and then you can resume your marks." He laughed at his own joke before pulling open the door to the mudroom.

Harlan reentered the house, and the group moved back to the living room, Ivy still keeping her distance. As soon as Hark and Anita drew close enough, they embraced as if their bodies were braided. Then they both got down on the floor untold.

"Not on the rug," Nick told them, and they shifted onto the wooden floorboards, wriggling over until their shoulders touched.

Nick uttered instructions, and Harlan yanked Hark's arms back. Rolling him about as easily as if he were moving a broomstick, Harlan bound both wrists together, then did Hark's ankles before moving on to Anita.

"Their mouths, too," Nick said, and Harlan pulled up on Hark's and Anita's hair, lifting their heads off the floor at the same time, and applying silver rectangles to their mouths.

"Now move them back," Nick said in a voice that almost sounded kind. "Close to each other. Like they wanted to be."

Harlan straightened effortfully. "I'm tired, Nick," he complained. "I'm all worn out."

It took more work for Nick to move the pair than if Harlan had done it, but Nick nudged both bound forms over until they were touching.

Anita's eyes flashed gratitude as she nestled against her husband.

Kneeling, Nick put the gun to the back of Hark's head and shot him. His body thrashed a few times, like a fish on a dock. It had settled beside Anita's by the time Nick killed her, too.

CHAPTER THIRTY-TWO

When the shots were fired, Ivy felt her own body buck as if she had been hit. The stupidest, most babyish phrase kept circling around in her head like a gnat. *But you promised.* She stared at Nick, at her uncle — that disgusting, piece of shit monster was her uncle — until her eyes ran and she couldn't see him anymore.

She blinked, and saw that he was gazing at her, too.

He did a loop-de-loop with the gun, and it wound up aimed at Ivy. Her mother tried to step between them, but Nick pushed her aside.

A torrent of words spilled out of Ivy's mouth. "But they were just going to lie there! They're all taped up! They couldn't stop you!"

Nick scoffed as mercilessly as Darcy ever had. "Oh, come on. You don't think that man planned to make trouble for me first chance he got?"

Ivy's lip trembled so hard that she bit it. "You didn't have to kill them."

It seemed impossible that the Nelsons were dead. It was only after Ivy had opened and shut her eyes a few times to clear her vision that she saw wreaths of blood around their heads.

Except the blood didn't look real either. It was like out of a movie. At any minute the Nelsons would jump to their feet — Ivy ignored the troublesome interference of the tape as she allowed herself to slip into her fantasy — and their performance would be complimented. Even better than the one they had put on for the police chief.

Again, Ivy's eyes blurred. Mr. and Mrs. Nelson had done what they were told. They had thought they were going to live.

She swiped at her face hard enough that it hurt. Back at the house, Ivy had spoken so callously about the idea of Nick hurting the Nelsons, who were annoying, did nothing but give her parents grief. Like that'd be a real loss, she had said. Something like that.

But Ivy had had no clue what someone getting hurt really meant, what it would be like to see people die. She stared at the terrible sight on the floor, trying to freeze herself inside.

"That's the thing, princess," Nick told her, flicking one hand at the bodies. "I didn't have to. I just decided to. I can do whatever I want." He paused. "Bet you used to think the same thing about yourself."

"I never thought I was anything like you," Ivy spit out. "Not *anything.*"

Nick regarded her. "Well, maybe the princess does have a few brains in her head after all. Because it's true. We're not alike. Nobody's like me."

Ivy looked away.

"I'm not subject to the same rules other people are," Nick went on. "I live outside all of that." His voice grew louder. "I do what I want, or don't do it, say what I want, or don't say it —" He leaned closer, eyes red-rimmed, spittle sizzling on his lips. "— do nothing, do everything, and you know what?"

Ivy began to back away.

"It doesn't matter!" Nick shouted. "You get that, princess? Whatever I do, it will never, ever —" He broke off for a moment, panting. "— fucking matter!"

Nick walked off toward the fireplace, his breath coming in heaves and hitches. He punched the mantel with enough force that ashes flew up from the grate in a hazy film. When Nick withdrew his hand, it left behind a spatter of red.

Ivy became aware of her mother, watching her with a weight of sorrow in her eyes. She stepped forward tentatively, like Ivy was a prickle bush or something.

Ivy drew in a shuddering breath. And then she walked into her mother's arms.

Her mother tilted her head forward until it touched Ivy's.

"It's not okay," Ivy said. "It's not okay. It's not okay." She couldn't stop saying it.

"No," said her mom at last. "It's not."

A shushing noise came from behind, and they parted to see Harlan dragging both bodies off by the scruff of their collars, one in each hand.

Nick kicked the rug over a few feet to cover the bloodstains on the floor.

He had planned everything out, right down to making the Nelsons not lie on the rug.

"What do they say about more hands making less work?" Nick asked. "I'd say that one Harlan makes a lot less work."

Ivy wiped a swampy brew of tears against her mother's shirt and looked up.

There came a terrible bellow, so loud it shook the room. It was as if a dinosaur was dying. "Niiiiick!"

Even utterly unflappable Nick started, though he quickly smoothed out his features.

He aimed a finger trigger-style in their direction. "You two stay there."

Nick headed toward the mudroom. Cold air shot in from that direction. Harlan must have gone outside and left the door ajar.

Her mother looked at her with a heated, intense gaze. Ivy frowned. *What?* she mouthed.

But it hit her. Harlan was outside, in the rear fields, occupied with both bodies. Ivy's heart gave a lurch, but she couldn't let herself think about the poor Nelsons right now. Because Nick had gone after Harlan, telling Ivy and her mom to stay. And why should they listen to him?

Ivy twisted around to look at the front door. Then the kitchen door, which opened onto a spot higher on the road. All she and her mom had to do was run up the remaining length to their driveway. And Ivy still had the keys to her mom's car. She withdrew them from her pocket, looking down in wonder, stifling their clink.

Her mother's face broke into a curve of sheer joy. She closed her hand over the clump of keys. "How on earth did you get —" She broke off with a quick shake of her head, pocketing the ring. Then she grabbed Ivy and moved them both in the direction of the kitchen.

Soundlessly, her mother drew open the door.

Outside, the snow had ceased coming down in great muffling curtains, giving way to sporadic spurts of flakes. Black branches pitchforked the sky.

She and her mom would send help for her dad. If he even needed it. Part of Ivy didn't believe that her dad was really up there, staying put because he was hurt. More likely he had gotten away, but didn't know where they were. He would never guess they had gone over to the Nelsons. It struck Ivy then, a sunny blip of hope. Maybe her dad had sent the police.

Her mother spoke in a whisper from behind. "Walk or run?"

Ivy understood the dilemma immediately. Should they go fast, put every ounce they had into it, or attempt to make as little noise as possible, scurrying along, trying to stick behind trees?

"I say aim for speed," she whispered back.

They launched into an all-out sprint, taking the stoop steps, then hitting the road and swerving to avoid a wall of snow the police car had left behind. Their shoes beat flat the accumulation on the road, and a wave of white flew up behind them. The snow that was still falling made it hard to see. Ivy slapped at the flakes as if they were bugs, trying to keep her gaze focused.

She and her mom moved at an identical pace, white puffs coming from their mouths, though her mom's breaths sounded louder. Suddenly her mom thrust one hand out to the right, and Ivy nodded, understanding. The field at the back of the Nelsons' house where Nick and Harlan had gone lay that way. The road crossed right beside it, and so would Ivy and her mom.

Ivy jerked her head to the side, trying to make eye contact with her mother through the scatter of snow and her heaving breaths. She was panting now, too. She'd never run this fast in her life. But maybe they should slow down, move off course, even belly-crawl for this portion. That stretch of field was so wide, and they'd be completely open to it.

It was too late, both she and her mom were moving too fast to pause. They seemed to duck instinctively, running with their backs almost horizontal, and then they were past the juncture at which they'd been exposed.

Ivy felt a swell of laughter build. She could

see the lights of her house now. She had never been so happy to see its huge, hulking form. She pushed on, passing her mother, covering the final distance to the cars.

Her mom's — the one she had the keys for — was partially buried.

Ivy's knees sagged and she fought not to fall.

It would be difficult to get the door open against the weight of snow that had accumulated against it.

How could she not have realized? The snow had begun falling hours ago. If this had been a normal night, her dad would've gotten the shovels and scrapers out of the basement, maybe completed one pass with the plow.

Tears made tiny divots of melt as Ivy went down on her knees and began to claw up great armfuls of snow, throwing them behind her. Crusted clumps slid down her coat sleeves, but Ivy hardly even felt their burn as she dug and dug and dug. Powdery masses blew over her: the wind sending back almost as much as she shifted. Her mom joined her, throwing herself onto the hood and using her hands to clear the windshield.

Ivy crawled across the uneven ground to begin scooping out the other two tires.

"I think I can get out now!" her mother panted. She battled with the passenger door, tugging it open against the remaining white, and all but shoving Ivy inside.

In a headlong rush, her mom ran around to the driver's side.

Ivy saw him before her mother did.

Nick, lunging through the snow, kicking up mounds before him, and panting as he fought to catch up.

CHAPTER THIRTY-THREE

Nick skidded to a stop at the car, and his face cinched with sudden pain.

Good, Ivy thought savagely. She had never been so glad to see anyone suffer.

Nick leaned over, elbows on the hood as he tried to catch his breath. After a second he brought both fists down, hard enough that despite the padding of his gloves, the metal clanged in the night.

Harlan was nowhere to be seen. It occurred to Ivy that between her and her mom, they might be able to get past Nick. He didn't seem quite as strong or sure anymore.

Her mother dropped onto the front seat. "Move out of the way," she called through the open door. "Or I'll run you down like a piece of roadkill." Ivy could see her mom's face in the rearview mirror, wobbly, as if she didn't have control of the muscles. "Ivy, put on your seatbelt."

Ivy did.

The sky spat snow as if it were disgusted with Nick, too.

Nick's gaze swerved around; it looked almost panicked. "You'll never —" He was still breathing hard. "— get through this snow."

"Watch me." Ivy's mom slammed the door shut. She moved a trembling hand in the direction of her pocket. Then she looked down and frowned.

Through the windshield, Nick's features became distorted by the snow. Only when his gaze honed in on a spot some distance away did a layer of calm slide over his face. He strolled forward, favoring one foot before speeding up.

Her mother was up and out of the car like an arrow shot from a bow. She dove, but Nick got there before she did, and thrust his hand into the area they'd cleared, where the ring of keys had fallen.

Her mom's hands slapped the ground and a powder puff of snow rose up.

"Get up," Nick said, jamming the keys into his coat. "And get the princess out of the car. Now, while I'm in a forgiving mood."

Nick led them back down to the Nelsons'

cabin. Ivy took one last glance at the curved sickle that led out to Long Hill Road, cleared by Mr. Nelson earlier. Hopelessness assailed her, as blank and empty as the snow.

She stopped short when they got to the rear of the cabin, screening her eyes. Lamps from the house floodlit the field, but what Ivy was seeing had to be impossible. The portion of ground she and her mother stood before had become something out of a Disney movie. Ugly white snow all turned a pretty candy color by some fairy godmother's wand to take away the horror of the night.

Then Ivy realized what she was really seeing, and she let out a long, spiraling cry. "Oh noooo —"

The Nelsons' bodies were under there; their blood had tinged the snow. This must've been what got Harlan so upset.

Ivy's legs wouldn't hold her up, only she couldn't, wouldn't fall onto that terrible spread of pink. In her mind, it became much bigger than the streaks by the Nelsons' heads: endless acres of rosy snow. Ivy twisted around, hunting for someplace, anyplace safe to go.

"Now," Nick said conversationally. He grabbed the handle of a snow shovel that had been stuck deep into a drift. By Harlan probably; Nick had to work to get it loose. "Which of you ladies will go first? Because we've clearly got a visibility problem here. Not to mention some time pressure."

He looked skyward, and it came to Ivy why. She imagined the helicopter pulsing through the air, she pictured the pilot — no, the *cops* inside the bubble, knowing which direction to start searching in because they'd spotted this horrible stained snow on the ground.

Her mother rushed Nick, flinging herself at him in one fierce, fluid motion. She let out a scream, a dread, wonderful sound. "Let! Her! Go!"

Nick held her back with the tips of his gloved fingers.

But Ivy's mom surged forward. "Please! Harlan is obviously done for, too!"

Ivy hadn't seen him till then. Harlan sitting, rocking, by a heap of snow he'd dug up, his body like a huge, quivering pile of its own.

"Let Harlan go inside with Ivy!" Her mother screamed and the wind joined her. "I'll do it, you monster, I'll finish your dirty work!"

"You know what, Cass?" he said. "That's not a half-bad idea." He jerked his head at Harlan, who got to his feet. "Take the princess inside. And don't let her go anywhere."

Harlan led Ivy back across the blessedly white sea toward the Nelsons' cabin, their faces lowered against the wind and dwindling flakes of snow.

Harlan followed Nick's instructions, guiding and guarding Ivy, but unlike the time they'd spent together in her room, he seemed unwilling to talk or be drawn out. Ivy curled up on the frayed couch, while Harlan sat in a worn armchair that barely contained him. His fists rested on his thighs as he looked glumly off at a fireplace whose powdery cone of ashes had long since stopped providing any warmth.

After some unmarked span of time, Nick and her mother came back in. Her mom's body was wracked with shivers; it was as if she had a high fever. Ivy jumped up and snatched a knitted blanket from the back of the couch. She took off her mother's damp coat and gloves and wrapped her up like a geisha or Native American woman or something.

Her mom gave Ivy a nod to acknowledge the act, blinking down at her new garb, then went back to those electrified shakes. Ivy drifted over to the uncomfortable couch again.

Nick spoke up. "Harlan. Enough delay. That took twice as long without you."

Harlan just sat there, his wet clothes sticking to him. He too was shivering hard; the armchair looked like it was convulsing.

Nick eyed him, crossing the distance to the chair. "We're going. Now."

"You promised," Harlan said. "Back in the car. You promised not to, but then you went ahead and did, and now everything's all shot to —"

Nick's voice changed then. Instead of issuing orders, he spoke in a low, level tone, almost like the one Ivy's mom sometimes used. He must've said something about promises, because Harlan shouted, "That's rules! That's rules are made to be broken. But you know what? You shouldn't break those either!"

Ivy crossed the room to check on her mom. Her mother's trembling had lessened, and she seemed to be staring off at something Ivy couldn't see.

Ivy said the first thing that came into her head. "Great. If those two start freaking out on each other, they'll never take us back to our house."

"No," her mom said. "They won't."

Ivy had already started to go on, say any random thing just to keep her mother talking, but as her reply registered, Ivy stopped and asked, "They won't what?"

"Ivy." Her mom shed the blanket, let it fall to the floor. "We can't leave this up to them."

Ivy wrapped her arms around herself, bearing down to suppress panic. But it was the strangest thing. Scared as she was — scared as her mother obviously was, with everything unknown and uncertain before them — Ivy felt like the two of them had never been this close before in her life.

When she grabbed Ivy's hands, her mother's skin was the pale blue of skim milk, as if even the blood inside her ran cold. "I think I know," her mom said, "who might be able to help."

CHAPTER THIRTY-FOUR

Nick had killed Hark and Anita without seeming to think twice about it. Sandy wondered whether he had planned to do so all along, worried about leaving loose ends, or if he had pulled the trigger on a whim. As a child, hurting people didn't cost Nick anything because he'd never had to pay for his actions. Their mother had glossed over them, or looked the other way. Even when Nick went to prison, their mother maintained that a miscarriage of justice had transpired, and Nick was spared disapprobation from the only person whose condemnation might've mattered. It seemed clear to Sandy now that she had entered the profession she had in order to try and understand the warped workings of this dynamic, which had stolen so much from her.

She wasn't going to let it take anything more.

Nick, leaning over, was about level with Harlan, who had crammed his body into an armchair, shoulders hunched, his back like the hull of a ship. Nick continued to address him with uncharacteristic patience.

On the other side of the room, an object sat in clear sight. An old-fashioned, corded phone, the last to go out in a storm.

Sandy traced a slow, wandering path in its direction, keeping an eye on the men. Harlan's eyebrows had descended like storm clouds, but he was listening to Nick. Only the pull of the phone unhooked Sandy's gaze from the sight. Harlan brought out a quality in Nick that she wouldn't have believed could be there. Not just tolerance, but something approaching affection.

Sandy arrived at the phone stand, and picked up the receiver. There was a nervous burr in her stomach, and her hands fluttered like moths.

Getting the police back here would be pointless. The police had already come, and gone.

While Sandy had been outside, throwing fresh white shovelfuls of snow over the heaps stained with red, she'd thought about her conversation earlier that night with Madeline. Sandy's behavior during the call was comprehensible to her now; she had been sitting perched atop a volcano. Beneath the dome was her refusal to recognize her own brother when he'd arrived.

Still, Sandy would've regretted her unprofessional outburst except that it had reminded her of something. Or someone.

She pressed down on the checkerboard of keys, hard enough to stamp each one on her fingertip. The numbers were imprinted on her mind from a lifetime ago. She feared the squawks they made would be overheard, but when she looked up, Nick was still talking.

Dull, droning rings began to fill Sandy's ear.

Her messy self-disclosure. The conflict with which Madeline had been struggling in therapy. Death, and loss, and loss that didn't come from death.

In bits in her head, the cobbled-together pieces of a plan.

The voice that picked up was one she hadn't heard in over two decades.

"Nick is here," Sandy said. Three small words, low enough that they were probably hard to make out, yet clashed like cymbals across the whole world.

Sandy couldn't bear to listen any longer; even just the sound of the breaths on the other end of the line was too dread, and too familiar.

She nestled the phone back in its cradle, realizing that she was rubbing the scar on her wrist. The wound had been deep, but still, Sandy had always counted herself lucky.

If Nick's knife had succeeded in striking that final time, its target had been her throat.

Sandy swiveled, one hand over her lurching heart. Ivy knelt backward on the sofa, watching her.

Harlan began to unfold his body, getting up out of the chair. He gave her brother a nod, eclipsing Nick's head with his own.

He had acquiesced, would be Nick's foot soldier once more.

Unless the grenade Sandy had thrown actually went off.

Because once Nick reached a certain point, there was only one person who'd ever succeeded in pulling him back.

April 19, 1991

Barbara heard the high, lilting voice in the living room, and frowning, she went in to check. It wouldn't be Cassandra. Cassandra never got home this early these days, doing God-knows-what at school or elsewhere till dinnertime or later.

With high school graduation bearing down, Nicholas had found it hard to decide on a direction. He had so many talents and strengths. And he hadn't applied to college because he couldn't find one where the caliber of student matched his own. Barbara hadn't pushed because she was in no hurry to see Nicholas leave home. But one of these days, he was going to choose to do something, and Barbara would have to let him, of course. That was the greatest challenge of motherhood: letting your fledgling fly away.

Her son stood by the front door, a girl beside him.

This one was dressed in one of those formfitting tops — bodysuits, Cassandra called them — that seemed to provide the wearer little more than skin cover, and an excuse to go braless. It was only April, the snow still sitting in shady pockets along the roads, and yet this girl's skirt twitched up around her thighs.

Nicholas wore his hair even longer these days, in looping curls that Barbara loved. But he dressed nicely for a teenager: clean jeans and freshly washed tee shirts — well, Barbara did his laundry, to be strictly honest — that hung casually on his skinny frame.

Barbara felt her lips drawstring in. "Nicholas?"

Her son switched his gaze to her, and everything else vanished. It was as if the sun had come out from behind a cloud.

"Mama," Nick said. "Meet Jennifer."

"Jessica," said the girl.

Clouds descended again, disturbing her basking. Barbara frowned at the girl.

"That's right," Nicholas said. "Jessica. We're going upstairs."

"Upstairs?" Barbara echoed. "To do what?"

"What do you think?" Nicholas called back.

He headed for the stairway, the girl trailing behind him, giggling, their hands linked.

"Homework," Nicholas added.

"But you haven't got any books!"

The girl giggled again, but the sound was a little less bright.

Barbara flailed desperately for some form of delay. "Wouldn't you like a snack first?" she proposed. "Juice or soda and some sandwiches?"

"Nick," the girl said, slowing her tread. "I am a little hungry."

"I am too," Nicholas replied, and he pulled the girl's hand hard enough that she tripped on the first stair.

Barbara slapped ham onto bread, and splashed soda into glasses, until the mess she was making caught her eye. Crumbs, and smudges of mustard, amidst puddles of melting ice. If she was going to distract Nicholas and his guest, she would have to do better than this. She forcibly slowed down, straightening the slices of bread and cutting her results into neat triangles, then adding a parcel of cookies. She set everything on a tray, which she lofted as she trooped upstairs.

She could hear noises by the time she reached the second floor hallway.

Moist and fleshy, paired with the susurrant slide of fabric.

Barbara set the tray soundlessly down on the floor outside Nicholas' room. The door had been left ajar, a generous slice exposing the portion of bed on which her beautiful son lay.

"You have, like, the most gorgeous hair," said the girl.

She got quiet after that, suctiony sounds ensuing. The tacky bodysuit was tugged aside, exposing high scoops of breasts. The girl was braless, just as Barbara had suspected.

Nicholas lowered his hand, and Barbara bit back a breath.

"Nick, don't," the girl said.

She placed one of her hands on Nicholas' bare waist, holding him away. His pearly skin, sullied by this girl's touch.

"Come on, Jen," said Nicholas.

"Jess."

"That's what I meant," Nicholas said, a smile in his voice.

They both got quiet again, then the girl said, "Who's Jen?"

"Jesus!" Nicholas exclaimed. "She's nobody."

More silence, or if there were sounds, they were muffled.

"Can we take it a little slower?" the girl said.

Her tone was sweet, cajoling, but it made Barbara feel tissuey and dry inside.

Nicholas rolled his body out of view. The stifled grunts coming from the room were louder now.

"Nick, no. Nick! Let's stop. Let's wait. I want to know who Jen is —"

"She's just a girl," Nicholas said, his voice low although still audible. "Who didn't give me anywhere near as hard a time as you."

Barbara's gaze flicked to the tray. It was as good a time as any for an interruption, and she raised her hand to knock.

A high-pitched yelp made her jump. Her foot kicked the tray, and a tumbler fell over, sending out a geyser of soda.

Barbara peered into the slit of open space.

The girl had scooted all the way back on the bed, and was trying to tug up the sleeves of that infernal suit. But the tight fabric was resisting her efforts, and Nicholas was sitting back on his heels, grinning as any boy would over such a ridiculous display.

"Barbara?"

She whirled to see Gordon. What time was it? How long had Nicholas and the girl spent tussling on his bed?

"What are you doing? What's going on in

461

Nick's bedroom?"

"Nothing," Barbara said quickly. "Nicholas just has a friend over —"

"A friend?" Gordon repeated. "I heard screams."

He pushed past her, shoe coming down in a sodden patch on the runner of carpet. The soda, sinking in.

Her husband yanked Nicholas up by one arm, nearly hurling him across the room, and Barbara let out a little scream of her own. "Gordon! What are you doing to him?"

"To him?" Gordon roared. "What am I doing to him?"

He bent down and snatched up a fistful of fabric. The girl's skirt, small enough to fit in one hand; underwear; socks. Gordon tossed the clothes onto the bed, turning his head aside.

"Get dressed," he said to the girl.

"Get your own girl, Dad," Nicholas said from across the room. "This one's mine."

"I am not!" the girl shrieked.

Her face was a red, mottled mess. How ugly she looked now, Barbara thought. The girl tried to tug on her clothes, but bent over before she could do up the clasp on her skirt, sobbing.

Gordon kept his head averted. At last he said, "Can I call someone for you?"

But the girl only shook her head, then — clutching her shoes, the flaps of her skirt flying open — ran as fast as she could from the room.

Gordon left the bedroom first, his head bent.

Nicholas walked after him, his slow, plodding steps like a bell tolling out the hours.

Barbara stayed behind, using the bathroom sponge to wipe up the soda on the rug. Out of the corner of her eye, she saw the two of them huddled at the top of the stairs.

"This has to stop, son," Gordon said. "With the girls. One of these days, you're going to get yourself arrested."

Nicholas' face turned match-quick in Barbara's direction, and she felt her lips curl in a reflexive smile.

"Oh, Gordon," she said. "If the police start interfering with kids and their kissing games, we may as well move to Russia."

Gordon frowned, while Nicholas turned slowly, arduously away. How tired her boy must be, defending himself from that girl's incessant questioning, and now having to deal with his father's brand of stubborn humorlessness.

"If Chief Weathers ever does get in touch

with Nicholas," Barbara went on in a light trill, "it will probably be to give him a medal, or the keys to the city."

"For what?" Gordon said. "Flunking high school?"

Barbara ignored him.

"Mama?" Nicholas said. There was something dark and unsettling in his eyes.

"Yes, Nicky?" Barbara said, a baby name from long ago. Her own eyes began to fill.

"You don't think there's anything the police could do to me?"

Barbara gazed up at her son, and saw how scared he looked, raw and vulnerable in a way that he never had, even as a baby.

"Oh, Nicky," she said. "Of course not."

"Really?" he asked. "No matter what I did?"

Gordon, lingering by the stairway, turned his head.

"Of course not," Barbara said again. "What do you mean? Whatever would you do?"

"I don't know," Nicholas said. "Anything."

"No, I don't," Barbara said, firmly to counteract the tremble in her son's tone. "You don't have to worry, Nicky."

There was a long silence. "Okay, then," Nicholas said at last. "Okay."

He turned and followed his father

downstairs.

Barbara sat there, her attempts to reassure her son circling over and over in her head, along with the rasp of the now dry sponge on the carpet. And she wondered why the voice that filled her ears was her mother's, saying what had always been truest about Barbara. That, despite her best efforts and hardest work, she couldn't ever hope for anything except to fail.

Barbara stopped cleaning and placed both hands over her ears, but even that didn't fully block out the sound of the voices drifting upstairs like smoke.

"Where did you get that?" Gordon asked. "We haven't gone hunting since —"

Nicholas broke in. "I kept everything you gave me, Dad."

Barbara let herself take just the slightest sip of relieved air. There was the Nicholas she knew. Loving. True. Then she heard the echo of the tense he had used. *Kept*. Not *keep*.

She looked down at the carpet. The stain was gone, the patch she had cleaned bright against the shoe-trodden area around it.

"I love this knife!" Nicholas said, his voice carrying much too far. That was a rebel yell, an Indian cry, not a declaration of feeling. "And I love you!"

The front door banged, and Barbara got up, trancelike, unblinking as she walked.

From the stairway, she heard Cassandra shriek. "Daddy! No! Nick! Stop it! Stop!"

Barbara descended the last step, and saw the reason for the screams.

Gordon and Nicholas stood close enough to embrace, both peering down at the bone-smooth handle of a knife, which protruded from Gordon's chest. Blood seethed from a slit in his shirt.

Gordon opened his mouth to speak, a wondering expression on his face, but only air came out, and a little spool of blood. Gordon's knees sagged, and he went down.

"Daddy!" Cassandra screamed again. She ran to her father, her arms extended. Nicholas pulled the knife free, and Cassandra got in the way of the blade. The tip flicked against her wrist. "Daddy, no!"

Cassandra shoved Nicholas hard enough that he let out a yell. The knife whipped about as he stumbled, right into his perfect, carved calf.

Barbara walked on stilt legs to the wall phone. She picked up the receiver.

"Chief Weathers," she said into it. "This is Barbara Burgess up in Cold Kettle. Can you send an ambulance? My husband has had an accident."

Nicholas and Cassandra were tangled together on the floor like a pair of puppies. Nicholas withdrew the knife from his leg, not even noticing the spout of blood that accompanied his action. Her son had always been strong, and good with pain. Once a terrible boy had bullied Nicholas, assaulted him, really, claiming that Nicky had done something to the boy's sister. When Nicholas had taken out a knife to try and defend himself, the boy had punched him right in the head. Nicholas had walked three miles all the way home, eyes goggled, a grapefruit-sized swelling on his scalp, and it turned out that he'd been given a concussion.

Her son had always been tough.

Now he raised the knife again. Barbara's vision was muddy; she couldn't tell exactly who or what that blade was poised to hit. But Gordon threw himself forward, falling over on his side as he tried frantically to reach for the knife.

"Nicky," Barbara said weakly. "Don't."

The blue of Gordon's eyes rolled back, and stayed that way, just as his son's hand finally stilled.

CHAPTER THIRTY-FIVE

The snow finally stopped for good as they all left the Nelsons' cabin. Sandy looked up at the sky, which stared back blankly, and she shivered. Would Nick and Harlan leave now, execute Nick's stated design from the start? A murky reality began pulling at Sandy from behind: one that said that even if this could've ended easily once, the time for that was gone.

Although Nick was walking confidently now, leading their tired clump at a good clip. There seemed an urgency to his step as he mounted the road back to the house. Nick held the gun in his gloved hand, keeping it handy.

The moon finally showed itself in the opaque sky, and Harlan cast a shambling shadow across the roadbed. Sandy was less afraid of the gun Nick palmed than she was of Harlan. Bullets could miss, or be dodged, or survived. Whereas Harlan, shuffling along next to Ivy, was unavoidable.

How could Sandy set Harlan against Nick, help him to start making his own decisions? If she could do that, it would be an explosive weapon on its own. She needed another pill or two inside Nick, so the effects of the drug would obscure her machinations.

She trotted forward, snow entering the cuffs of her jeans. Sandy nudged Ivy, and the two of them quickened their pace. Conversation between Nick and Harlan drifted over on a cold current of air.

"We'll take it slow," Nick said. "We can make it in three days. Or four."

Sandy let Ivy drift ahead, camouflaging her daughter's departure with her own body.

"I don't know if I can make it at all!" Snow on the ground flew in response to Harlan's exhalation, and he snuffled in miserably. "All that country out there. We're gonna get lost. Or die."

All Harlan would've had to do was reach down, encircle Nick's neck with one of his hands. He could have broken it with a single squeeze, changed this whole situation with the twitch of one limb. But Harlan had no idea. His was a mental prison, keeping him from acting.

"We're not going to die," Nick said. "I won't let that happen."

Harlan plodded along uphill. "That's what my daddy said. Before I got caught that last time. We both knew I was facing life. 'I won't let you get caught,' he said. And look what happened."

"Out here I can make sure he never tells you what to do again," Nick said, his tone a brutal razor. "But not if we go back. What if your daddy got locked up too? Likelihood seems pretty high without you to help him out on jobs. You might even have to share a cell."

Sandy tried to minimize the fluffs of snow she kicked up, the white puffs of air she emitted. She leveled out her breathing and her tread. Ivy had almost gained the steps of the front porch, and Sandy was just behind.

Harlan's head bowed, his tears striking the snow in patches large enough to blotch. Nick patted his back, losing his hand amongst the folds of cloth.

Sandy took off. Snow cascaded up in waves, blowing into her mouth, her nose, her eyes as she ran. The porch was before her now; she would take the stairs at a leap, push Ivy ahead of her into the house. They could barricade themselves inside, lock Nick and Harlan out —

"Ivy!" she bellowed. "Get inside —"

A bullet clapped the air, and Sandy stumbled, almost went down in the snow. When she righted herself, the first thing she saw was Ivy, ducking behind one of the stone pillars beside the porch steps, a cornice of white concealing her.

Sandy turned around, hunting the source of the shot.

Nick stood a few yards away, gun aimed at the sky.

"That one was a warning," he said. "The next shot will hit the princess in the spine. You'll be feeding her through a tube for the rest of her life. Or yours."

Barnacles of snow had crusted Sandy's wrists when she went down. They were beginning to melt, bitter, burning pustules.

"Now move along," Nick said. "It's almost time for us to set out."

Back in the house, Sandy gathered her daughter into her arms, rubbing her up and down, trying to erase the shivers. Ivy squeezed back, clinging to her.

Nick took off his shoes and tossed them aside, brushing a layer of snow off the lower legs of his pants. He looked around, then pulled on the pair of Hi-Tecs he hadn't been able to get on before. But his air of satisfaction vanished when he began to examine

Harlan. Nick let out a horse snort of frustration. He had clearly kept their departure in mind while outside, but Harlan had wallowed in the snow during the burial of the Nelsons, sat down and rolled around in his distress. Now he was soaked head to toe.

"Dry, not wet, Harlan." Nick's voice began to climb. "We have to be dry, not wet, remember?"

Harlan shook his head, then stopped and began to nod.

Nick released the wet expanse of Harlan's shirt bunched up in his grip. Freed, Harlan took a step back, nearly bumping into Ivy, who pirouetted.

"You're going to go upstairs with Harlan, give him a quilt or something to wrap around himself," Nick informed Ivy. "Then throw down his clothes."

Sandy made sure not to let her gaze rest on Nick as Harlan and Ivy departed. She didn't want him to see in her eyes the chance he had just given her. Instead, she reached into her pocket and took out Hark's medicine bottle.

"What's that?" Nick said.

Sandy could provoke ire in Nick in any one of a dozen ways if she said the wrong thing. "Pain medicine. I thought it might help with your foot —"

A spark of suspicion on Nick's face. Whether from the effects of the one Oxycontin sprinkled in his coffee, or due to excitement over their imminent departure, Nick's foot was clearly behaving now, and Sandy couldn't let her brother think that she was trying to dose him.

She changed direction. "— or, you know, if something unexpected happens out there. Just add it to the first aid kit Ivy gave you in case of emergencies."

Nick's face cleared. "Thanks," he said, his tone perhaps the most authentic she had ever heard from him. Pocketing the pills, he said, "That was good thinking."

"Mom!" Ivy shouted. "Here are the clothes!"

The garments fell to the floor in a small mountain. Sandy scooped up the mound, then headed for the basement stairs. Nick strode after her, grabbing her by the collar with one hand.

Sandy broke free. In the basement was Ben, and Sandy couldn't let him lie there for one more second, broken and discarded like her father had been after his last breath expired, and her mother had rocked Nick in her arms, comforting him while they waited for the police.

"You wanted me to dry the clothes,"

Sandy said, flinging open the basement door. Her shoes clattered on the treads.

"Not all by yourself," Nick drawled. "Plus, you forgot something." He held out one of Harlan's socks, the length of cloth dangling to his elbow.

Sandy reached for it, and Nick snatched his hand back.

"Suit yourself," Sandy snapped, starting forward again.

Nick grabbed her from behind, and Sandy went down hard, her shoulders hitting the lip of one stair, head banging against another.

"Me first," he said.

Nick hauled her up a few steps, but it didn't matter.

Sandy had reached the middle of the flight, far enough down to see.

Ben no longer lay there.

CHAPTER THIRTY-SIX

Hope crested inside Sandy. Her shoulders ached from striking the stairs, and her skull felt knocked about as well, but Sandy was only faintly aware of both injuries.

She turned to Nick, making sure to mask her discovery. "Actually, you know what? We don't have to go down there at all."

"No?" Nick replied. "You going to dry Harlan's clothes on the line?"

He sounded normal, just like Ivy had when she threw down the clothes. "Of course not," Sandy said, striking a note of casual ease. "But the better dryer is upstairs. It gets the load done much faster."

Nick regarded her. "Something you might've mentioned before," he said, then added, "You have better and worse dryers?" He shook his head. "Rich people really are nuts."

Sandy allowed him the sharp smile at her expense.

When her back was to him, she smiled, too.

"So where is this *better* dryer?" Nick asked once they'd reached the second floor.

Again, Sandy endured his mirthless grin, wondering what was behind this brotherly banter. Jubilance at his imminent exodus? Or did Nick have some additional idea in his top hat of tricks, a final goodbye ploy?

She needed a failsafe, a plan of her own.

The dryer up here was actually a much worse one, part of a mini stackable unit for quick washes or single items when they didn't want to troop all the way down to the basement. The excess suddenly struck Sandy as egregious. Why would anybody need two places to do laundry in the same house?

But being upstairs would allow whatever Ben might've set into motion to proceed.

"Dryer's in here." Sandy pointed to two louvered doors. "I'll take care of it."

Harlan's outfit would more than fill the compact drum, but Sandy would just have to overstuff it and hope for the best.

"Holy shit," Nick said, crossing into the bathroom. "Look at this thing. It's bigger than the one for my whole block."

Sandy looked up, and an idea grabbed

her. "Yeah, I know it's a little much." Don't sound braggy in any way, she cautioned herself, or remind Nick of what he doesn't have. Tempt him with something, but make him think he had the idea to take it. "Did you see the shower?"

When Nick responded, his voice came from farther away, and it echoed. "It's the size of a whole damn room."

"Right," Sandy called back, injecting a rueful note. *No one needs such a thing. How stupid and blind and greedy we were.* Then Sandy added, "Dryer's started. It'll run for about ten minutes now. The clothes weren't that wet."

That was a palpable lie; even a single shirt couldn't dry in ten minutes. Plus, Harlan's outfit had been soaked. But let Nick believe they had some super space-age appliance to suck the moisture out of clothes. Sandy didn't need for Harlan's clothes to emerge toasty; she just needed a few minutes to talk to him.

Nick didn't respond. Sandy wished she had gotten him to down a few pills, she could've used their cotton muffling effects on her side. Her hands clenched, holding on to the side of the louvered door. "You probably haven't gotten a bathroom to yourself in a while."

477

Her brother's voice drifted back. "Maybe I should rinse off while the clothes spin," he called, and Sandy's mouth went so dry with urging that she couldn't answer. "Take the first shower alone I've had in twenty-four years."

"Sure," Sandy said, the word emerging as a nearly inaudible hiss. "That's a good —"

Then her brother was before her, his eyes like twin spears, anything normal or friendly gone from his mien. "Idea?" he said. "Was that the word you were going for?"

Sandy stared back at him, a slat on the door cutting into her palm.

"What'd you think, that I would just have a leisurely soak? While you tried in some other half-assed way to screw me over? Don't forget who invaded whose house," Nick said, edging closer, into her space. "I own this palace, I own your kid, I even own a part of you."

He flicked a finger toward the twist of scar tissue on her wrist and Sandy recoiled.

"Anyway, a shower's not what I need." He looked down at himself. "Where can I find some waterproof pants? There'll be a foot of snow on the ground for the rest of the night."

Sandy swallowed, regrouping. She could still snag a minute or two. She'd just have to work fast. "You can take Ben's softshells. They're the best ones he's got; he keeps them in his closet." She gestured toward the master bedroom. "Harlan will have to make do with trash bags and duct tape. We just don't have anything that will fit him."

Nick nodded, considering. Then he sauntered off down the hall.

As soon as he was gone, Sandy entered Ivy's bedroom.

Harlan lay swathed in blankets. Like an enormous emperor, comfortable and overindulged, except that Harlan was more like a slave. He was stroking Ivy's pillow for some reason, or maybe it was an object on the pillow.

Ivy sat on the floor beside her bed, looking impossibly small below Harlan.

"You were right," Sandy said, and both Harlan and Ivy looked up.

"Mom?" Ivy said. "What's happening? Where's —"

"It's freezing out there," Sandy interrupted. "And the countryside is massive."

Shirtless, Harlan lifted himself on the enormous bulb of his elbow and peered at her.

"You'll never make it all the way to Canada," Sandy went on. "My husband

479

does this for a living, and even he wouldn't take anyone out on such a trek."

Ivy was fiddling with the edge of her dust ruffle. "Mom? What are you telling him —"

Sandy put one hand out to stay her. "Nick isn't going to be able to protect you out there." She paused for the revelation, the startling truth she hoped Harlan on some level already knew. "But you don't need him to. You can protect yourself. You just have to stop Nick first."

Harlan's pale gaze held hers.

"You can do it, Harlan." Sandy spoke slowly and quietly to optimize the chances of Harlan comprehending. "You can keep Nick from taking you out into that endless wilderness. And you can prevent whatever harm he intends to do here before he goes."

Ivy's head jerked up at that.

Sandy tried to telegraph reassurance for her daughter along with the words she had to say next. "He means to hurt us, Harlan. In one way or another. I think you know that. Nick's hurt a lot of people tonight."

Harlan nodded, once, then twice. "But I can't do anything about it."

"Oh, sure you can," Sandy said softly. It was the statement she made to patients who were just about ready to take some leap, make a change they were realizing they'd always had in them. "You can stop him, Harlan. You always could."

Ivy craned her head, watching Sandy with an expression she hadn't worn in years.

"No, I can't," Harlan said, his voice leaden with disbelief. He lay back down, pulling a length of fabric tight against him.

"You can!" Ivy interjected. "I've been watching you this whole time. I saw how you didn't want the Nelsons —" Ivy's voice hitched, and she smoothed it. "For them to be hurt. You have morals, Harlan. You know the difference between right and wrong."

Harlan's eyes stayed shaded, doubting. He twisted his hands, the section of blanket he held disappearing in his grasp.

"Think about your sister," Ivy added in a hush. "She knows you, Harlan. And she thinks you're good, and kind, and strong."

And with those words, Sandy knew the change had come. When Nick returned, he would find himself facing the solid wall of their objection.

Sandy gathered breath. "All you have to do is stand up —"

Harlan got up from the bed, disentangling the blankets around him.

"— and walk over to Nick," Sandy said. Literal. She had to remember how literal Harlan could be. "Then stay with him, and keep him in one place —"

Harlan rose to his full height while Ivy remained seated on the floor, her head at his knees. Harlan tucked one of the quilts around his massive form, toga-style.

"— so that I can get help. Medical help for my husband," Sandy went on in the same level tone. "He's going to die otherwise." Sandy sought to catch Ivy's gaze, trying to impart the knowledge that this was at least half manipulative strategy on her part. "And I know you don't want for that to happen."

Harlan's features bunched, and he shook his head.

Sandy could sense Nick behind her in the doorway now, but she didn't flinch, or look, or even remark upon his presence. She simply stared up at Harlan, breath caught in her throat.

Two long steps took Harlan away from the bed to arrive at Sandy's side.

Then one more, and he reached Nick.

CHAPTER THIRTY-SEVEN

"What's going on here?" Nick asked brightly.

He was clad from collarbone to ankles in the slick, supple fabric of Ben's softshells. The garments would keep him dry, and warm at temperatures as low as twenty-five degrees. He didn't deserve such comfort, and Sandy's fingers ground against the palms of her hands.

Harlan scrubbed his face. "I don't want to go, Nick. It's too far. And it's too cold out."

Nick glared at him. "We already covered this, Harlan. We're going. I'm sweating like a pig in these things, and the dryer must be just about done. Let's get everything ready."

Nothing.

"I'm telling you what to do!" Nick said, and his voice pitched on the last word.

Harlan shook his head back and forth. "Not this time, Nick."

Nick stuck one arm out, trying to elbow

his way past Harlan, but Harlan clamped down on Nick's arm with the vise of his fingers.

Sandy wanted to let out a cheer. She snuck a peek at Ivy.

Nick fought to get free, but he was locked by Harlan's grip. Nick put his other hand against Harlan's chest and shoved, but even muscled as he was, Nick couldn't budge him. He balled his hand into a fist and went for Harlan's throat, but Harlan rose on tiptoes, getting out of the way. Then he wrapped his left arm around Nick's waist, and lifted him clear off the floor.

"Okay!" Nick cried. "Put me down. I said, put me down, Harlan."

Harlan resettled Nick on the floor, keeping a hold of his forearm.

Nick seemed to regain control then, reaching into his pocket and drawing out Hark's vial. He shook two pills into his hand. "Do these things calm you down?" Without waiting for an answer, Nick placed both in his mouth and tossed his head back to swallow them. "I suppose you have a better plan?" he asked Harlan.

Harlan thrust the barrel of his thumb in Sandy's direction. "She's going to get help for the man you threw down the stairs. Otherwise he's going to die."

Nick's mouth lifted in a smile. "Ah. I see. My sister is going to call for help."

Harlan nodded.

"On the landline, assuming it still works. And assuming an ambulance can get up here, which it probably will because the storm has passed." A weighty pause before his final assertion. "Plus, the police car that comes with it will have a plow."

Harlan stopped in the middle of another nod. "Police car?"

"The police come when the paramedics are called," Nick responded. "Did it occur to you that my sister is trying to get us both thrown back in prison?"

Harlan's brows drew together, and he frowned in Sandy's direction.

"No!" she said. "That's not —"

"*No* the police aren't going to come?" Nick said, peering around Harlan's bulk to lock eyes with her. "Or *no* you're not trying to get us thrown back in prison?"

"Both —" Sandy began. "I mean —"

"Mom," Ivy said. "Don't lie to him. Please don't lie."

Sandy sensed the rubble of Harlan's resolve before them now. There was nothing she could say or do to restore it, and breath left her body in a snaking hiss.

"Harlan," Nick said. "My sister is telling

you what to do just like your daddy always did. But I'm trying to help figure out what's best for you. I'm trying to make sure you stay free."

The long plank of Harlan's shoulders sank. "I just don't want you to hurt anybody anymore, Nick. I just don't want anyone else to get hurt."

Nick tested the strength of Harlan's hold, then wrenched himself loose. "Well, that's great news. Because I don't want anyone else to get hurt either," Nick said. "And they're not going to. In fact, everything will be pretty simple from here on out."

He brushed off the arm Harlan had clamped, his satisfaction apparent. "You go downstairs and make yourself some leg coverings out of Hefty bags and duct tape." He tapped the pair he wore. "Like this."

Harlan nodded.

"Oh, and take the princess with you," Nick added. "Make sure she has supplies and a pack, too. The princess knows where to find everything."

"How come?" Harlan asked.

Nick mimed surprise. "Didn't I tell you? She's coming with us. Just a little extra motivation for my sister not to send anyone after us." Her brother's gaze found Sandy's, and he gave a pretend shudder. "Police and

486

their weapons. Chases on foot never seem
to end very well."

CHAPTER THIRTY-EIGHT

So this was the final trick Nick meant to pull out of his hat. Of course he would never leave Sandy standing. He was going to cut her off at the knees, the heart, the soul.

Nick spoke again to Harlan. "Sound okay? Because I'd like things to be more equal between us from now on, Harlan. I'd like to know you approve of this plan."

Harlan eyed him, but not warily. Gratitude filled his expression, a degree of joy.

"And I think you and the princess have come to really understand each other," Nick concluded. "Like each other even."

At last, Harlan gave a great nod. "I was worried you were going to hurt one of them."

"Nah," Nick said, transferring his gaze to Sandy. "Just a nice walk through the woods."

In the moments spent talking, Ivy had frozen in place. Only her eyes danced about wildly, and when Harlan's hand landed on her, she screamed.

Harlan frowned.

Sandy tried to get between him and Ivy, but Harlan was too big an obstacle: shoulders the size of boulders, torso like a tank. When Sandy attempted to move to Ivy's other side, Harlan took one sidling step, and he was there, too.

"Please!" Ivy cried. "Let me stay with my mom!"

Harlan looked down at her, and his expression creased with hurt and bewilderment. "But — you said I was good. Remember?"

Ivy began pulling against Harlan, and he looked down at her arm as if it might come off in his grasp. He let go, and Ivy dropped to the floor.

Harlan rubbed his eyes. "I thought you weren't scared of me anymore."

Ivy let her head fall back, her hair grazing the rug. "I'm not, Harlan. I'm not. I just — it's just that I want to stay here."

Harlan turned to look at Nick.

Nick gave a somber shake of his head. "Do you trust me, Harlan?"

There was no hesitation before his reply rumbled forth. "Of course I do, Nick. You're the best friend I ever had."

Something took hold of Nick's face then. For a second, he was the one to hesitate, and his voice creaked when he used it. "Then pick up the princess and take her downstairs. Make sure she packs everything she'll need. We want her to stay warm out there, don't we?"

Harlan bent over and scooped up Ivy.

Nick stretched out his arm as Harlan went by. He had trouble reaching Harlan's shoulder, so the caress landed nearer to his back. Harlan paused, and the two men stood there, linked.

"I need a pick-me-up from that suite or hotel room or whatever the hell they call their bedroom," Nick said gruffly. "That medicine I took sure works fast."

Cradling Ivy in his arms, Harlan walked out into the hall.

"You stay here," Nick ordered Sandy. "I don't want you talking to Harlan anymore."

Sandy gave him a nod. Smooth acquiescence never raised Nick's suspicions; he just accepted it as his due. Wondering what the effects of a total of three Oxycontin in his system would be, Sandy dropped down on Ivy's bed and tried to make herself look settled.

As soon as Nick left, Sandy yanked open the door to Ivy's closet so hard that her

490

shoulder wrenched in its socket. She had to beat Harlan to the stairs.

Ben's system of closets, made extra-generous in size by virtue of the connected passages between them. By pushing through the clothes that hung on Ivy's rod, Sandy emerged in a column of space beside the shelves of linens in the hall.

She cracked open the door, and looked out.

From down the hall came the tang of tobacco, and a faint drift of smoke. Nick had found Ben's stash of cigars.

From behind the louvered doors across the hall, Sandy could hear the muffled pounding of the dryer, Harlan's clothes a sodden mass clumped inside instead of spinning free. They would never dry like that. But it didn't matter; Sandy couldn't let things reach the point where Harlan was putting them on.

There he was, moving slowly along the hall, weighed down by the freight in his arms more than he would've been otherwise because Ivy had made herself dead weight.

The two of them passed so close to the closet that Sandy could have reached out and touched her daughter's listless, dangling legs.

491

She stepped into the hall.

Ivy's head hung, and her eyes stared blankly. Harlan set her down when they reached the top of the stairs. He adjusted the billowing quilt he was wrapped in, and then he and Ivy started forward together again.

The staircase was unique, a staggering feat of architecture, appearing to float in space but for its dagger of railing, forged out of branches, twisting and alive. The flight didn't quite meet code, but there were ways around the regulations so long as you got the right builder. Each broad plank was held aloft by seemingly nothing. The steps generous, more than large enough to contain two people. But not when one of them was the size of Harlan.

Sandy took the first step behind Harlan and Ivy. She wasn't sure what she was intending; she wasn't intending anything at all.

Ivy leaned back to see who was there, and Harlan did the same. But he was so big, and unused to these stairs. His foot got tangled in the hem of the quilt and he strayed overly close to one side, nothing beyond it but open space.

He was going to lead Ivy off into the wilderness. Harlan didn't even understand why that would be so bad. There was so much he didn't understand. And so much he would do, if it came at Nick's behest.

Ivy reached out, trying to steady Harlan, who hadn't yet gotten his balance. If Harlan clutched back, he might pull Ivy over the side. Acting on instinct, to make sure her daughter didn't get latched onto, Sandy pulled Ivy onto the higher stair she herself occupied. The two of them were too close together then, and Sandy switched places.

Her body clipped Harlan's unsteady form. It should've been like ramming a mountain, except that this mountain had already half slid off the face of the earth.

Harlan fought to free himself from the bundling cloth. He got one hand out in time to grab the railing, but the wood split beneath the force of his grip. Harlan teetered, arms windmilling over empty air, and then his immense weight carried the rest of him sideways.

He had time to give Sandy, who stood so near, a look of understanding, and remorse, and not the slightest hint of blame.

Then he fell.

When Harlan landed, the whole house shook.

Sandy grabbed Ivy, making sure she wasn't

destabilized by the impact, the aftershocks rising up from the floor. But Ivy broke free and raced downstairs to Harlan.

Nick emerged from the master bedroom, walking a bit unsteadily and stinking of smoke. "What the hell was that noise?" he demanded. His voice slurred and the *zzz* sounds ran together.

It took him a second to register the mass at the bottom of the stairs, and by then Ivy had reached the first floor.

They let out yowls of identical voltage and pain.

Nick stumbled as he went forward, and wound up sprawled out for a second on the floor.

Sandy's gaze whipped from Nick at the top of the staircase to Ivy below.

"Ivy!" she screamed. "The front door! Now! Go!"

CHAPTER THIRTY-NINE

"It's okay," Ivy said when she got to Harlan. She dropped down beside him. "You're going to be fine."

But he wasn't. Harlan had landed flat on his back, and his head had smashed like a vase. A wreath of red haloed it, spreading out across the floor.

"I never hurt anybody," Harlan told Ivy. "Not once on any job."

She nodded, only partially clear on what he was talking about. But what did she think Harlan had gotten locked up for? You didn't go to jail for being huge.

He angled his head, and more blood spilled out. He was trying to look down at his arm. "That's funny," he said. "Hard as I try, I can't move my hand."

"Shh," Ivy said helplessly. She tucked the blanket over him, making sure Harlan was covered.

"I wanted to hold yours," he said.

Ivy seized up his enormous hand, as many of his fingers as she could grip at once.

"He never gave me any of the money," Harlan said. "I just held the gun or drove the car." A great sigh of breath, sufficient to stir Ivy's hair. "I always did what my daddy told me."

Ivy's eyes welled. She bore down on Harlan's fingers, which he didn't seem to feel. There was something so terribly sad in his words. Even if Harlan didn't know it.

"Ivy?"

Ivy used her free hand to blot her face.

"Will you get Charley for me?" he said. "I'd sure like to . . ."

"Charley?" Ivy echoed. But she knew, and was already starting to rise.

Something changed in Harlan's eyes, Ivy couldn't have said what, and after a moment, no more breaths arrived to riffle her hair.

Ivy leapt for the stairs, aware of how little time she had. There might be no time left at all, but she was still going to do what Harlan asked. The little clump of fur his sister gave him sat next to her pillow; she had watched Harlan caressing it when he lay on her bed.

From the top of the flight, her mother let out a warning owl screech. Words accompanied it in an unconnected string. "No, Ivy, get out, now, go . . ."

But Ivy wasn't listening, so intent was she on getting what Harlan wanted.

She passed Nick on the steps, going up, and hardly even recognized him.

Her mother grabbed her at the top and then they were inside Ivy's room. Ivy snatched the bedraggled bit of fur in her fist, and turned back toward the door.

Her mother shoved it shut.

"Mom!" Ivy cried out. "Please! I have to give this to Harlan!" She revealed the bit of fur as if showing what she held would have any chance of helping.

"It's too late," her mother whispered.

Ivy shook her head back and forth. "No, it's not too late, it's not, he can't be dead, he can't! You killed him!" Her voice rose higher and higher, spiraling up toward the ceiling, and on the last cluster of words, it broke into a wordless shriek that threatened never to end.

Her mother slapped her across the face.

Ivy's head snapped back and her mother's hand skidded off it in a sloppy mess of tears.

They stared at each other, Ivy seeing the shock she felt reflected in her mother's eyes.

"I'm sorry," her mom said jaggedly. "I'm so sorry, Ivy."

Ivy had no idea what she was apologizing for. For hitting Ivy for the first time in her life? Or for pushing Harlan over the stairs?

"I didn't mean to," her mother said, and the statement could've applied to either. "I mean, I didn't want to." Her mother took in a rattling breath. "I didn't want to have to."

Ivy dropped her head, looking at a spot on her carpet that had turned wet and darkened. At last she gave a single nod.

"Ivy," her mother said, seizing Ivy's hand and closing it over the piece of fur. "It's too late for Harlan. But it isn't too late for us."

Ivy shook her head. "I can't," she said. "I can't go on trying stupid plans that don't work and only end up with people dead." She sank to the floor, wrapping her arms around her shins and beginning to rock.

Her mother bent over her. "Do you know why I named you *Ivy*?"

"She was a character in a book you liked," Ivy replied tonelessly.

"Well, yes," her mother said, placing her palms on Ivy's knees. "But the book wasn't really the reason for your name. Not the most important one anyway."

Ivy looked up.

"*Ivy* stands for connection." Her mother's fingers mimed twining strands of vine. "And that was you, Ive. From the moment I laid eyes on you, we were so connected. We were just so —" Her mom's voice split. "— incredibly connected."

Ivy had been furious with her mother for lying to her all her life. Those lies had led in some twisted, tormented way to these deaths. Mr. and Mrs. Nelson's. Harlan's. Maybe even — Ivy swallowed back a thick, gelatinous sob — her father's. But now she understood that her mom hadn't been lying exactly, or if she was, she'd mainly lied to herself. By blocking things out.

And Ivy had done the same thing after her father had been pushed down the basement stairs. Because it had been too scary to consider. Too hard. And what else explained the secrets her mother had shielded besides that same avoidance of pain?

Ivy was more like her mother than she had ever let herself realize. And more glad about it now than she'd felt in a long time.

Pressure built behind her eyes, but she didn't let the tears fall. Instead, she slid Harlan's clump of fur inside her pocket and got to her feet, realizing that for this one brief moment, a mere splinter of time, she could look right into her mother's eyes.

"What do you think we should do?" Ivy asked.

■ ■ ■ ■

They turned as one, taking in the circumference of the room.

There came a sodden thud of footsteps.

Noise didn't carry from one room to another in this house. Nick must be right outside her bedroom.

Ivy could hear him walking now, stalk-stiff, sliding his feet along in a shambling gait.

Her heavy door moved an inch or two, swinging slowly as if the person trying to open it lacked strength.

When Nick appeared in the frame, he looked less than human. His features were contorted with fury, his eyes smoldering bits of ember, red-rimmed and sullen.

"Give me the princess," he said, like a robot, or a machine.

Ivy's mother stepped in front of the doorway. "No," she said.

"Your choice," Nick said in a voice thick as clay. "She's going to die no matter what. You both are. But if I have to fight you for the princess, then I promise, her death is going to make Harlan's look pretty."

Terror overtook Ivy and if her mother hadn't been holding on to her, she would've broken into a run, gone tearing around the room like a panicked hamster in a cage.

Another sound penetrated then.

Like the throttle of an engine. Or a dog getting ready to attack.

CHAPTER FORTY

Tim stopped at home for a quick bite to eat between shifts, taking a few minutes to catch his wife up on what was happening. The visit he'd paid to the empty house on Long Hill Road. A K9 unit summoned from downstate. Items retrieved from the prison cells and given to the dogs to scent. Finally Tim mentioned the woman who had been admitted to the hospital having lost nearly a pint of blood, a likely victim of the escaped cons, although she'd been in no condition to give a report. Tim had left Mandy back at the barracks to identify the woman's missing vehicle, and phone in a description.

The staties were the ones setting up roadblocks and directing the search in a radius around the bridge, but since the escape had taken place within town limits, Tim felt a lingering responsibility. He'd stationed two of his men at the search area, and they'd already radioed to say that their presence didn't seem exactly welcome.

Tim drummed his fingers on the kitchen counter. If the cons were in the car belonging to the injured woman, then they were hundreds of miles away by now. He accepted the sandwich his wife had wrapped up in foil. She handed him a to-go cup filled with black coffee, holding a plate of cookies beside it.

Tim took one. "Are these really chocolate chip?" he asked. "Or did you slip zucchini mash into them?"

Liz shook her head, biting back a smile that hit him right in the chest. She was smiling more often now. For a while, he thought he'd never see her smile again.

Tim wished that he could stay. Let their gazes take hold, move them in the direction of the stairs. They would go up, and the kids would be fast asleep, digesting all those extra servings of veggies. While he and Liz would stay awake for hours. Tim had never been so short on sleep in his life as he was in the year since he had gotten married. They were making up for lost time.

"Tim?" Liz interrupted his thoughts. "Are you going to check that house on Long Hill again now, or later?"

Tim took a deep drink from the scalding cup of coffee.

Liz's fingers began stroking his skin, doing a quiet dance over and between his own fingers, and across his palm. She had magic hands.

"Because we both know you're going back," Liz went on. "The only question is whether it will be before or after you check in with the state police, who don't know this town anywhere near as well as you do."

Tim stayed there a moment, caught in her grasp. Then he loosened her hold on his hand.

"Before," he said.

Liz topped off Tim's coffee with some fresh from the pot.

"Coincidences," he added, shrugging into his coat. "Escaped con, sister's got an empty house. And do you know what's bugging me most of all? The couple I visited." He consulted the pad in his breast pocket. "Hark and Anita Nelson. Why did neither of them ask why I wanted to know about their neighbors? It was like they'd been expecting me."

The skin between Liz's brows, with its lingering touch of summer sun, puckered in a frown. "Mountain people living way out there," she said. "They're not the kind to ask."

Tim leaned to rub away the frown with

504

one hand while he reached for his belt with the other. "You're right," he said. "Most hunches are just air and worry."

Liz hesitated. "We both know some hunches are worth following."

Tim rapped the counter with his fist, a brief gesture of goodbye, and Liz went to open the door. In the aftermath of the storm, the night had grown startlingly clear, the air like black glass, and the sky shot through with stars. Tim pointed the keyless remote and the headlights flashed on the patrol car.

NOVEMBER 11, 2015

For twenty-four long years, Barbara had enacted the same routine every Wednesday, week in, week out, until the time mounded up like a pile of ash. Hundreds and hundreds of lost gray days, blown away into the wind as if they were nothing.

Without her son, life didn't mean living, it just meant existence.

Barbara paused by the mirror on the living room wall before she left, checking that the silver strands in her hair weren't too frazzled, and that twin streaks of pink colored her lips. She didn't know if it mattered to Nicholas, but it did to her. She wanted to present a semblance of the mother she had been to him, and would've continued to be had she only been allowed. As she peered into the glass, she wondered how long it had been since she'd last given herself a good once-over. Not last Wednesday surely, nor the one before that, or any of the others in recent memory. When was it that she had gone so completely gray?

Barbara went outside into the low light of morning, and climbed into the truck. It had been Gordon's before he'd died. Barbara hadn't changed vehicles, or done a thing to the house except clean it — and that sparingly — since Nicholas had gone away.

The route she drove took her along bare, desolate roads, stretches that led out to the flat midsection of the state if you followed them long enough. Soon this entire landscape would be obliterated by snow.

The prison wasn't far out of Wedeskyull, but it was distant enough. They didn't build prisons right in the middle of town; instead they sat them in wild places Barbara never would've ventured if she'd had a choice in the matter. She had seen a mountain lion on one of these roads once. It had run out in front of her truck in a desperate race after some type of prey, its plate-sized paws scrabbling to turn itself around just before Barbara would have hit it. She'd pulled over to the side of the road, placing a hand on her heaving heart, and looked up at the steep slope the cat had climbed. They'd stared at each other for a while, the cat from its perch on the hilltop, Barbara in the cab of the truck. The cat's eyes held the same look of pure, deadened frustration that Barbara knew must fill her own every day.

In the beginning, when she'd been making this drive, she'd petitioned the state for Nicholas to be allowed to leave, go on special outings, even if they only took place on Wednesdays. Once that request was refused, Barbara asked for extra visiting hours. But that too was turned down. Barbara supposed she shouldn't have been surprised. Nicholas' lawyer had utterly botched the case, and the judge clearly had a vendetta against them. His words still carried a tinny echo and the drop of his gavel rang out, haunting Barbara's sleepless nights.

Her testimony had been the last for the defense. She hadn't listened much to the prosecution's case, and she barely noticed when the jury was sent away to make their decision.

They had come back in under an hour.

"In light of the mother's testimony, this can't be considered a capital or first degree murder case," the judge reminded everyone, once the verdict was handed down.

Barbara had been sitting on a hard ridge of pew, feeling every pore and divot in the wood. Upon hearing the judge's words, she let her bottom shift just a little. Never mind that head-up-their-ass jury. The judge at least knew how to listen. Now she and Nicholas would be going home, and this nightmare would be over. Perhaps they would leave Cold Kettle. Their house contained so many memories, images of the dreadful accident in which Nicholas had struck his father instead of the meat Gordon must've been preparing to butcher. Barbara had found a hind quarter processed by Thiele. Had it already been lugged to the kitchen, or had Barbara opened the deep freeze, hefted the package in her arms, then dropped it on the counter with an exhalation of sheer exertion? She couldn't remember, and thus hadn't lied under oath. All she could clearly recall was unwrapping the deer meat from its slick plastic casing and leaving it to sit in a cranberry stain much like the one on the floor.

But the judge had gone on then. "However, given the portrait of the defendant's escalating instances of violence, which we heard about from several young female witnesses, his own lack of emotion or remorse, and especially due to the horrific nature of the crime of patricide, I am going to apply the maximum sentence this seat allows me."

The ridge of pew spiked Barbara and she let out a small shriek.

"Order," the judge commanded.

The bailiff took a warning step forward. Barbara had come nose to nose with this bailiff many a time during the last several weeks.

"I sentence the defendant to forty years in prison," the judge said, and Barbara's shriek rose to a high, circling scream, like a whirlpool; she was going to get sucked in. Her shouts echoed off the courtroom's tall windows and climbed all the way to the concave sweep of tiles that made up the ceiling above.

She was carried out of the courtroom, still clawing behind her for Nicholas.

In a narrow stretch of hallway, gray-walled and linoleum-floored, Barbara handed over her purse and keys, and endured the indecency of being patted down.

"Satisfied?" she asked the female guard. "I doubt my own mama knew me better."

Barbara had been thinking a lot about her mother lately. How differently might her life have gone if her mother had been different as well? It was a thought Barbara usually clamped down on, squeezing the life out of before it could squeeze out hers.

The guard ignored her question, waving her through with a frown.

"Have you come to your senses yet?" Barbara snapped back over her shoulder. "Realized that my son deserves some respect around here?"

She was surprised when the guard responded. Usually they didn't. Barbara squinted into the woman's unlovely face. She didn't recognize this one.

"Your boy's finally making some headway, lady," the guard said. "Why don't you shut your trap before you mess things up for him all over again?"

Another guard stepped out of a small, glass-enclosed room and took hold of the first's arm. "Sorry, ma'am," the second guard said. "She hasn't been here that long. She doesn't know she's not supposed to talk to you."

"I may be new," the first guard muttered, "but I know when someone's blowing smoke up her boy's ass instead of just letting him grow the hell up."

The buzzer on the door blared, stunning as an alarm, and Barbara was moved along.

She took a seat, straightening the hem of her skirt, and aiming a bright smile at Nicholas. It wouldn't do to let him see her upset.

Only Barbara's stranglehold on optimism, the belief that everything would get straightened out and proper justice handed down soon, had allowed Nicholas to survive in prison.

"How are you, Nicky?" she asked. She almost always used the nickname now. It was a small morsel of comfort she could give her son within these walls.

It was so difficult to get used to seeing him like this. The transformation had taken place over the course of many years, but that hadn't made it any easier to witness. First, Nicholas' head was shorn of those beautiful, lush curls, turned into a toothbrush bristle of spikes. Then her slight, fragile boy had started to put on bulk and muscle. Last came all the dreadful inking Barbara still couldn't stand to look at, even though he'd told her that one of the dark, twining strands hidden beneath his shirt read *Mama.*

Nicholas sat in the seat across from her, assuming a position of ease. "I'm good."

Barbara wasn't sure she had heard correctly. But her son was grinning, an expression she hadn't seen on his face in years. Decades.

"Well, that's —" She broke off, had to start again. "That's wonderful. I'm so glad to hear it." She paused, then dropped her voice. "Did you learn something? About your case from that new lawyer I found?"

Nicholas looked annoyed. "No, I didn't. You want to know what I learned?"

Barbara gazed at him. "Of course," she said after a minute. "Of course I do."

Nicholas leaned forward, speaking low. "I learned how to play thc game, Mama."

The guard standing in the corner of the room let out a cough and fingered his belt.

"Sorry, Officer." Nicholas sat back, and the guard resumed his stance.

Barbara looked down at her lap. This visit wasn't going as the hundreds of others had, but she couldn't say exactly what was different, or whether it was a bad thing or not.

Nicholas spoke again. "Why didn't you ever teach me how to play the game?"

"I don't know what you're talking about," Barbara replied.

Nicholas shifted in the chair so abruptly that it rocked. "No. I guess you don't."

"Nicky," Barbara pleaded. "I only tried to do what was best for you. You know that, don't you? I gave you support and praise and recognition. All the things the young moms today say are so important. I wanted you to be happy. That's all."

"You didn't give me the most important

thing of all," Nicholas said.

"I'm sorry," Barbara said automatically. Always before, whenever Nicholas blamed her for something, she had tried to take responsibility. Swiftly, so he couldn't be angry at her. But for some reason, it felt harder today to tuck his complaint away beneath a blanket of apology. "What was that? The most important thing?"

Nicholas stared unblinkingly at her across the table. When he spoke, it was quietly, almost under his breath. "Cassie's still with her sportsman husband, right? In that big place you told me about, up on the mountain?"

That busybody Glenda Williams had made it her business to deliver updates on Cassandra. She'd even seen fit to place a slice of newspaper in Barbara's mailbox once with a photograph of a gigantic house perched high on a hill, and an article about it to boot.

Barbara gave Nicholas a nod as if the conversation were simply continuing, making some sort of sense, instead of flinging her around like a child on a carnival ride.

And then she thought she understood. "I know how unfair that is, Nicky. You're the one who deserves that house. And so much more. It all got taken from you."

Nicholas seemed to consider this, staring at her levelly so that for the first time since she'd been making these visits, Barbara became aware of exactly where she was, in a sealed container, locked away with a legion of men who had done terrible, violent things.

"Maybe it wasn't what I didn't get," her son said, scrubbing the short brush on his head.

There was some gray in there, Barbara realized with a sharp intake of breath.

"Maybe it was what I got," he said.

"You got everything!" Barbara exclaimed, a note of outraged pique in her voice that she couldn't remember ever applying to her son. "Everything I had to give!"

After a long time, Nicholas broke their stare. "I love you, Mama."

"Oh, Nicky." Relief coursed through her, and she began to cry. In all the years she had loved and devoted herself to her son, she didn't know if she'd ever heard him say those words before. "I love you, too —"

"I thought you should know that," he said.

"Five minutes," the guard intoned from his point of remove.

"Nicky?" Barbara said. "Is anything the matter? You're not — you're not sick, are you?"

"No, Mama. I told you, I'm doing real well in here."

"Oh," Barbara said. "Well, that's . . . good."

Nicholas offered an odd, sad smile. "Is it? You're happy about that?"

"Of course I am," she said, giving the words thrust.

"Good," Nicholas said, still with that peculiar note in his voice. "Because I wouldn't want you to be disappointed in me."

"Nicky! I could never be disappointed in you."

It had occurred to her, during the dark days and years that had accumulated without Gordon, or Cassandra, and especially without her beloved boy: what if she had pulled back just a little, changed course the slightest bit? She might have; in the chill, dull light of retrospect, possible places stood out. But parenting Nicholas had been such a slalom ride for her. From the moment her sweet, beautiful son tumbled into her life, Barbara had been overcome. Nicholas pulled her along like a river, and Barbara had been helpless ever to stop.

"No," Nicholas said. "You couldn't, could you?"

He was agreeing that she'd succeeded in her mission of motherhood. The one thing Barbara had most hoped to provide her son with was overarching love and approval.

So why did Nicholas' response sound so much like damnation?

CHAPTER FORTY-ONE

Sandy acted on brute instinct, flying forward and throwing her body against the immense door. Her full weight against the wood was enough to ram it shut. She and Ben had both thought it wise not to install a lock on a teenager's door, a decision whose pointlessness Sandy now understood. Hardware wasn't the only way to keep a person out. It wasn't even the mightiest.

Still, Nick was at least temporarily barred outside.

With McLean there, holding him in check?

That had to have been their dog, although Sandy had never heard Mac growl like that in all the time he had been a part of their family. She could picture the standoff, though: McLean a length of fur-covered muscle, Nick more than half beast himself now, his teeth bared to meet McLean's fangs, eyes crackled with reddish threads.

"Mom," Ivy whispered.

Sandy twisted to look at her daughter. One of the windows was cracked open, a knife blade of frigid air entering through it.

"I can get down from here," Ivy said in a low voice. She gestured outside.

"Ivy, no," Sandy said. "There's no way. We're thirty feet off the ground."

Her gaze flicked to the door before she cast it back toward the slitted window.

Her daughter peered beneath the raised glass. "It's no worse than some of the climbs I've done with Dad," she said. "I really think I can do it."

It was different from any climb Ivy had done with Ben, and Sandy knew it. But she also knew they had no other choice. Nick was going to kill Ivy as soon as he got the chance. Harlan was dead, and so Nick would destroy the one person who meant the most to Sandy.

She shoved the window the rest of the way up, letting a breath of cold, frosty air into the room. Then she grabbed a hoodie from Ivy's floor, zipping it around her daughter.

"In or out?" she asked, her voice splintering on the final word. The game they'd always played, offered in the hopes of delivering Ivy a few extra shards of strength.

But Ivy seemed to have strength enough on her own, standing straight and tall, level with Sandy so that they could look right into each other's eyes. Sandy felt an electrocuting jolt of pride.

"Out," her daughter whispered.

Ivy hoisted one leg over the sill, then brought the other up as well. She looked down, assessing the route with the same focus Sandy had seen Ben apply countless times.

Ivy lowered herself, executing a precise flip of her body so that she dangled with her chest against the clapboards.

The last thing Sandy saw was Ivy's fingers letting go of the sill.

A gunshot split the silence in the hall. There was a high, shrieking yelp, then a skitter of claws and a *thud*.

Sandy let out a scream before clapping her hand over her mouth. She tore her head back around to the window. Had Ivy heard that? Nothing would make her more likely to fall, lose all focus, than the thought of something happening to their dog.

The bedroom door heaved open on its massive hinges.

"Your dog's dead," Nick announced. "I splattered his brains all over the wall."

Sandy felt the familiar quake at her brother's fury, his careless wrath, shiver through her. "He ran away," she said. "I heard him."

Nick jeered at her. "You always were a sucker, Cass," he said, gun held loosely by his thigh. "You could never admit she wasn't ever going to change."

Sandy fought desperately to see into the hall, to check on Mac and also to buy time, give Ivy every possible minute to get away.

"Mama, I mean," Nick went on. "I may be high as a kite right now, but I'm still sharp enough to wonder why you loved her so much when she never gave a damn about you."

The words hit Sandy like an iron weight; she staggered.

Nick aimed a sloppy grin at her. "Know what you did when you changed your name?"

Sandy bore down. If it would prolong the moment when Nick noticed Ivy's absence, she could stand any cruelty, even the truth flung right in her face.

"You cut off the part I called you by."

Cassandra. Sandra. He was right.

Nick jabbed the gun in her direction, and Sandy reeled back.

But Nick only laughed. "Don't worry. A bullet's not going to be the way you die." He leaned forward and grabbed Sandy's arm, his fingers like drill bits boring into her skin. "I want you to know what it feels like to live after the princess is gone."

He took a look around, as if the question was just now occurring. "Where is she?"

Sandy raised her face, eyes trembly with their need not to look, not to show him.

Nick grabbed for Sandy's wrist again and the spiral of scar tissue on it split. "I got a piece of you all those years ago," he bit out. "I'll always know you better than anybody else."

He made his way over to the window, and looked down. Then he turned back around with an expression of blank and terrible calm on his face. Sandy pushed in front of him, peering out herself. But she didn't see anything. Ivy had gotten down already. She must have.

"Just remember," Sandy said. "You took out a piece of yourself in the process."

Nick's fingers fumbled for the wound on his leg, landing some ways north.

Sandy had moved so fast toward their father that momentum had carried the blade into Nick's own flesh. That had been part of their mother's testimony: why would Nick have injured himself if the whole thing hadn't been a terrible accident?

Reading her again, Nick said, "Bet you

wish it had been me instead of Dad."

He sounded almost hurt.

Nick nudged Sandy into the hall. There was no blood here, and no sign of Mac. Still, Sandy's legs felt faulty, unequal to the task of bearing her along. She hadn't seen anything amiss when she looked out the window, but something besides the effect of the drugs had to explain Nick's unrushed breeze, why he wasn't running outside to halt Ivy's flight.

"Didn't you ever think about it, Cass?" Nick asked. He came to a stop in the hallway as if he'd forgotten what they were doing there.

"Think about what?" Sandy said, desperate to stall, give Ivy time to get away.

"If it'd been me who died," Nick replied vaguely. "Or not even that. What if we'd just held — what would you call them — different positions? In the family, I mean. Like if you and me somehow traded places. You got what I did, and I got everything from you."

It was a funny way to put it because Sandy would've said that she didn't get anything at all. But it struck her now that, in reality, she'd been the lucky one. All the love, and false belief, and expectation their mother lavished upon Nick had bowed and broken him. No one could stand up under such weight.

She lifted her head and looked at her brother. This version of Nick seemed almost workable, someone she might even be able to reason with.

Or beat outside.

Sandy put on a burst of speed, taking the stairs at a run and ignoring the voids on either side. Nick trailed her, but Harlan's body amidst its folds of quilt presented an obstacle at the bottom, too massive to skirt around.

"You took him from me," Nick said, pointing unsteadily. "And so you know what comes next? I get to take everything from you."

The front door blew open, creating a wind they felt all the way at the stairs.

Nick and Sandy looked around, then at each other, Nick's gaze vacant in comparison to Sandy's needle-sharp alertness.

The voice that called out was high and brittle as shale, uniquely recognizable to them both.

"Nicky?" it said.

CHAPTER FORTY-TWO

The wooden part of the house would be the toughest. The boards were sleek and stained smooth, impossible to get a grip on or even a toehold. Ivy realized this as she hung beneath her window, feeling with her feet. The good news was that the boards also made up the shortest portion of her descent. They had been used on the upper area of the house, while a stone foundation made up most of the first floor. If Ivy could just slide for a bit, then stop herself, she'd have a ready-made climbing wall.

But this, the smooth and silky segment of boards, was what her father called the dead zone. The place where a climber could enter an uncontrolled descent. Ivy felt her heart pattering in her chest. She was hardly aware of the temperature, so fast was the blood coursing inside her. But her reddened fingers gave the cold away. Ivy wouldn't be able to rely on dexterity from her hands for very long.

She had to get down, and fast. But speed was the enemy of a climb.

Ivy glanced through her window one last time, clinging with all her might to the side of the house. She could see her mother still standing there. Then Nick appeared behind her and Ivy's hold went instantly slick. She felt herself start to slip.

Wedging her knees into a crevice between the boards, Ivy was able to slow herself enough to gain some control. Taking a deep breath, and channeling her father's focus and his confidence, she sank into her descent. Climbers focused on three spots. One in front, one above, and one below. Anywhere else and you had the recipe for a mistake.

The wooden boards were terribly smooth, but they delivered one advantage Ivy hadn't expected. They were relatively soft, more so than rock anyway. She was aiming for a large hump of stone. It protruded enough that she would practically be able to stand upright on it so long as she didn't miss. Still, Ivy quickly figured out that this plan would've been physically impossible — she was going too fast — except that as she slid, she was able to dig her fingertips a tiny bit into the side of the house, slowing her pace.

Wind shrieked around her, commanding her to stop. The snow had ceased falling, but the wind stirred what lay on the ground into blinding cyclones. Ivy couldn't let go with either hand, and the snow stung her face. She didn't need to see, though; a descent like this was all about sense memory. Ivy had imprinted the location of that rock on her brain and she trusted her feet to know what to do when it appeared.

One final claw at the boards — a splinter shooting deep beneath her nail and the ensuing scream lost beneath the wind — and she was there. The rock seemed to come up and catch her feet like a holster. Ivy flattened her body against the house, chest heaving, the solidity of stone a temporary platform while she rested. She exhaled a long, pent-up breath, suddenly aware of the cold slicing deep into her core. Her cheeks and the tip of her nose felt like iron.

The worst part was over, though. Ivy broke one of her father's rules, tilting to look all the way down at the snow-heaped ground. She identified the next likely rock. Once she gained that one, she would be able to hold on with her hands — frozen as they were — in addition to her feet. After that, this climb would be a piece of cake.

■ ■ ■ ■

Her dad always said that half of the game was mental toughness, but as Ivy maneuvered, she couldn't stop her mind from wandering. Where was Nick now? He could be waiting for her on the ground, and Ivy bit down on a jolt of panic. If she let fear overtake her, she wouldn't reach the bottom, simple as the remainder of this route was. She distracted herself by considering where she would run as soon as she was on land again.

The Macmillans were hardly ever home, although Ivy supposed she could break into their place. Probably such a thing would be excused under these circumstances; their camp was falling apart anyway. The Nelsons' cabin was also an option, but Ivy didn't know if she'd be able to make herself go in there again. Especially since the Randalls lived just a mile or so away, and might even be home. Ivy babysat for their toddler, and she often walked to their house. She was going to be so ecstatic to be free, fueled and heated by adrenaline, that Ivy figured she might get all the way to town. She could go anywhere so long as she was unshackled from Nick.

Ivy found her next hold, then let go of the rough piece of rock she gripped. Thank God her father had insisted on a real rock foundation instead of the stone-facing he scoffed at on other people's houses. This was easier than many sections of peak she'd hiked with her dad. Her foot felt for a spot as she continued inchworming her way down. Ivy could make out craggy surfaces on the rocks, peer into dimples that provided holds. The recently emerged moon illuminated her way, and she experienced a giddy sense of triumph. In just a few feet, she would be able to jump the rest of the way down. Then she would run and run and run and maybe never stop.

A gust of wind sent a spatter of snow at her face, and Ivy let go with one hand to wipe away the wet. She didn't even need both hands. Her foot felt for its next perch; found it and lodged securely. Ivy took in a bracing breath of air, letting snow particles dance on her tongue.

It seemed like she was hardly climbing. She had entered the zone her father always talked about, where the rock had become an extension of her body. The fact that she clung to the side of their house in order to escape a madman didn't matter. She was the climb and the climb was her.

Then her foot caught a jutting piece of rock.

Her father had taken such pride in this house.

"Look at them," he'd told Ivy's mother on the morning a dump truck spilled a pile of glowing gold- and purple- and smoke-colored rocks next to the hulking skeleton of their house-in-progress. "Every single one is different. Look at the irregularities in that stone."

It was one of those irregularities that had snagged Ivy's foot. Her stiff and freezing fingers flailed, but they couldn't curl tightly enough to catch hold. The stones in this section were glazed with ice, impossible to get any sort of grip on. Ivy's body tilted at a pitch; she felt the initial rush, followed by the total unrestrained terror of freefall. She bounced, hitting the bigger rocks with enough force to make her cry out, before landing in a crumpled vee on the ground.

Ivy was on her feet again and running before the cold of the earth had penetrated. The snow must have blanketed her fall, cushioning her from the worst of the impact.

But it hadn't blanketed it completely. Shock or adrenaline or something triggered her to run; she made it perhaps a quarter of a mile before she started to slow. It took Ivy a few more loping steps to realize how badly she was injured.

Something started to come apart in her ankle — some essential part she needed, although Ivy couldn't have said what it was — as she continued to drag herself across the unlevel ground.

Ivy dropped to her knees then, and crawled.

Now she felt the cold. And the damp. Moisture seeped through the legs of her jeans and turned her hands into clumsy things, mechanisms whose works were breaking down. Ivy lifted up her fists and brought them onto the ground like blocks of wood. She pulled herself forward a few more feet; then she could no longer manage even that.

She fell, belly-down. Snow poofed up around her.

Ivy reached down to her ankle, halting, hesitating, but snatched her hand back too late. She was punished for daring to touch her own body. Ivy lay there, panting, sweating despite the snow.

Her ankle must've shattered inside her. Because something had torn open the skin. Her hand, when Ivy squinted at it, was painted black as birds' wings.

A thick overlay of terror descended. She had escaped Nick only to do far worse damage to herself out here. How much distance had she covered? How would anyone find her, even if there was somebody to look? It was hard to tell where she was, with the land encapsulated by snow. Though Ivy had a feeling that in her current state, it would've been hard to determine where she was even if the earth and grass had been exposed in one naked sweep.

She couldn't scream, or even wave to give her location away.

Ghostly white trunks of birches surrounded her; Ivy looked up at their limbs. Otherwise, she couldn't see much of anything. Not her house, or the Macmillans' camp, and not, thank God, that protruding spear of bone.

She let her head fall, surprised by how warm the snow felt, like a down comforter.

She was near the creek.

Ivy could hear the hiss and sizzle of the water now. How had she gotten all the way back here, almost to their property line?

She turned her face toward the constant, white-noise rush of water. The creek writhed a few yards away, moving like a great, black snake.

How good that water would feel on her ankle.

The hills above her were shrouded in white. Snow cloaked everything, even the pain in her leg. If only her mother were here. Ivy wished she could see her mother, appearing out of the veils of white. She thought she did see her for a moment, or maybe that was someone else, or perhaps no one at all, just a dream fathomed from the pieces of Ivy's pain-altered mind.

A silence settled, so profound it seemed not to be of the living. It was the quiet of the dead, or nearly so, and Ivy felt herself pulled along by that rolling water to a place where no sound lived nor ever would again.

EXIT

Nick wasn't sure where the packs had gotten to, although it didn't seem to matter much anymore. Finding that gear would be like grabbing a rope once you'd already fallen off the cliff. It was too late for his plan to work out. A feeling Nick had never experienced before, not even the day he'd learned he was going inside, sank over him. There'd always been an air of unreality to everything that happened to Nick, and to all that he did. This moment, with his mother standing in that great canyon of an entryway, and his sister about to lose everybody she loved, was in some ways the realest he had ever known. It split the cocoon of medication that had sealed itself around him. Or that his sister had sealed around him? That idea hadn't occurred to Nick until now, and it triggered a smoky, howling rage.

He thumbed the cap off the bottle and

downed another pill.

Harlan was dead and that beehive was back, filling Nick's mind with a furious cloud of activity, an electric, jangling hum. He needed Harlan. Harlan had kept him alive more than once inside. Tonight too, probably. He knew Cassie's husband would have killed him if Harlan hadn't been around. But it wasn't only reliance on Harlan's size and ability to intimidate that made it impossible for Nick to get his head around this bitter new reality.

He loved Harlan.

Harlan belonged to Nick.

He was going to strip Cassie bare, like peeling bark off a tree, leave her shivering and raw. First, he'd do away with her husband, assuming he still managed to draw breath. Then that freak-eyed mutt of a dog, who had scampered off like a bug when Nick raised the gun, although Nick was pretty sure he'd at least wounded him. He could hit a moving target.

And finally, Cassie's precious, pretty daughter.

The princess was lying broken and battered in the snow. No kid could manage a climb like that — he didn't care who her father was — and plus, Nick had seen when she started to fall. His vision had been fuzzy thcn, but it was clearing, as if the fuse lit by Harlan's death had finally ignited. The sight of the princess sliding down the side of the house came back to him as clearly as if Nick were watching it on TV. He felt as if he could've finished off the whole bottle of pills and remained clearheaded and focused.

Nick checked the number of bullets in the gun, then made sure the knife he'd taken from the neighbors was still jammed into his coat pocket. His father's slaughter had been a bloody mess, but in prison Nick had learned the value of neat, execution-style killings.

The princess wasn't going to get one of those, though. She deserved better.

Or worse.

And he would make his mother watch.

His mother had missed most of the action when Nick killed his father. Maybe that was why she'd been able to say what she did in court. This time, Nick would make sure she caught every last moment, in all its stark reality, no Technicolor or special effects. The screams would be real enough to blister her ears; she'd taste the metal of splashed blood.

His mother called out uncertainly once again.

Nick sent Cassie a wicked grin, then pushed past her into the hall. "Mama," he said. "So glad you found us."

"Nicholas?" she said. "What are you doing here?"

Her voice sounded uncomprehending, as if Nick had somehow teleported out of prison. Or as if she were the one on meds. But at last she seemed to put the pieces together.

"Why didn't you come home?" she said.

Nick felt his lips curl. "Sure," he said. "Trade one prison for another."

Pain flickered in his mother's eyes. She appeared to notice Cassie for the first time. "Cassandra? Is this why you called me?"

Cassie's face was white and unseeing.

Nick barked a laugh. "So that's how you knew to come." He turned toward Cassie. "Still looking to Mama to save you, huh? When will you finally get it through your head that she's never going to do it? She doesn't even want to."

Cassie's knees gave a jolt, but Nick kept her on her feet. He took his mother by the elbow, prodding her along, too.

"Come on," he said, displaying his weapon. "We've got to see a man about a gun."

His mother reached down and touched him on the hand. "I'm going to let you kids

537

do this by yourselves." She smiled at him. "While I take a look around this beautiful house."

Nick smiled back. "Don't be silly, Mama. Of course you're coming with us." He paused. "We couldn't do it without you."

He led them both in the direction of the basement. Cassie appeared calmer now, and Nick had no idea why. She could've been in shock, but that didn't seem to be it. Cassie didn't trip or stumble. Her breath came regularly, and her arms hung loosely by her sides. They reached the stairs and started to descend, Cassie's footing sure.

Nick was seized by a savage impulse to kick her legs out from under her.

"Nicky?" his mother said at the bottom. "It's such a cold night. I'd love a cup of tea."

There was a teething inside him, a gnawing that no tea would damp. Nick gestured with the gun, and his mother looked quickly away.

"Walk," Nick said.

His mother took a few steps forward. Nick crossed in front of her, heading for the spot where Cassie's husband had last been seen.

He no longer lay there.

Cassie came to a stop, arms folded across her chest.

Nick wasn't sure if he was imagining the smugness and triumph on her face, but he pictured bringing the butt end of the gun down on her nose. Smashing it, sending slivers of cartilage into her brain. He had to hold on with both hands — as if gripping the side of a mountain — to the real goal. He wanted Cassie to be the last woman standing. To view her world in chunks and pieces around her, as if an atom bomb had detonated inside her palace of a house. Then he would kill her.

Nick craned his neck, looking around the dark, shadowed basement. He squinted, still having just the slightest bit of trouble seeing. Had he taken another pill, had he possibly downed the whole bottle? He couldn't remember.

A sliver of light on the floor appeared like a wavering line, and Nick stumped in its direction. The door was unlatched, and understanding dawned.

Nick felt a smile ride up his face. "At least now we know the answer to that infernal song." The words he'd been meaning to say skidded away from him, and Nick clutched at them. "Who let the dog out?"

He entered the small room. Inside lay Cassie's husband. The guy had squirmed or wriggled his way over here, then got the door open using — what? His shoulder, maybe his chin? With a spike of satisfaction, Nick imagined how torturous the journey must've been. And for what purpose? To let out some mangy pet who had run away, tail between his legs, as soon as Nick faced off with him?

His mother gave a shriek that grated on Nick's ears. "My goodness. Who is that man?"

Cassie began to rush forward, but Nick placed the gun against her ear, or as close to it as he could get. His fingers felt clumsy and somehow thick, as if he were wearing gloves. "Back off," he intoned heavily.

"He's dead," she said. "Oh, please just leave him alone, he's dead, he's dead, he's —"

"Shut up," Nick growled. He twisted to look over his shoulder. His mother was strolling away as if they were in a goddamned park instead of a concrete basement.

Cassie took another step forward, and again Nick held her at bay.

"You're right, I'm sure." In his ears it sounded like he'd said *shore.* He must've taken another pill. Hopefully not more than one; he still had work to do here. Who let the dog out. Scooby-Doo. There was meaning there, some connection, but Nick couldn't grasp it. "But I'd better check."

Cassie grabbed his arm, and Nick prized off her fingers. He reached down, deliberately feeling for the scar on his leg, and gave it a lethal twist. Pain arced into his consciousness, and with it came clarity.

"Not that I don't appreciate this moment of sisterly affection," Nick said. "But I've got business to take care of." He crouched, putting two fingers upon the man's neck, then let out a whistling breath. The guy had a pulse, faint but consistent, like the flutter of insect wings.

Cassie's sob was audible. Still squatting, Nick looked up at her. Cassie had hardly cried the day he'd killed their father, even though Nick knew she loved him. That wasn't why Nick had killed their dad, though. He'd done it because his father saw through him. Even a fatal stab wound wasn't enough to carve that knowledge out.

"Your husband sure can hang on," Nick remarked. "He deserves a death worthy of a — well, of a first class lingerer." He stared up at the lightbulb on the ceiling, blinking blurrily.

"Please," Cassie whispered. "I'll do anything."

His mother's voice sailed out from the

cavernous space on the other side of the house. "Look at these lovely wrappings! Someone's getting ready for Christmas."

Nick stared at Cassie. If he hadn't done it already, now was the time to uncap that bottle, swallow the contents so that they could pull him away like an animal dragged off its prey. At this point, he would welcome it.

"No," he muttered. "Not yet you won't. But we'll find the princess, and then I bet you'll be ready to make good on that promise."

He turned away from Cassie, placing the muzzle of the gun snug against her husband's belly. Wall-hard it was, ripples delineating each set of muscles.

Fighting weakness in his hands, holding on tight to the grip with both of them, Nick pulled the trigger, and the bullet exploded out of the gun.

Now Cassie was in shock more severe than any mood alteration Nick was experiencing. Her eyes had gone big and staring, and her fingers splayed out around the railing as she tried to make it back up the basement stairs. She fell a few times, going down onto her knees. Nick managed to stay straighter, nudging her upright with the snout of the gun.

The two of them stood poised at the entrance to the kitchen.

There was a light trip of footsteps from behind and his mother arrived at the top. "You'd better go now, don't you think, Nicky?" she asked, and Nick blinked at her, confused.

"You must have so much to do," she went on. "Interviews for jobs. People longing to see you. I can't wait to hear all that you get up to."

Nick's head bowed in a nod. He chambered the next round in the gun, although he could no longer remember who the bullet was meant for.

He turned around in place, then walked blindly toward the rest of the house.

The dog. The dog was supposed to be next.

But his mother had left the front door ajar when she came inside.

The possibility of failure kept hitting Nick anew. Like when he'd first gone inside and every morning he'd wake up with no idea where he was, disbelieving even once he saw the walls, the chrome toilet/sink combo, his thin and stinking mattress. For years, Nick had gotten written up, lost privileges, spent time on the SHU, because he went tearing around in fits, beating up his cellie before they'd given him Harlan, every time reality hit him. The idea that he wouldn't get what he wanted had always been a bit unfathomable to Nick.

"Goddamnit," he roared. "Didn't somebody tell me that mutt won't go anywhere on his own?"

The dog had gotten away.

The pretty princess wouldn't.

He dragged the front door open. Nick prodded Cassie with the gun, forcing her outside. He didn't care where his mother was anymore. He and Cassie ran in a sickle shape around the house, arriving at the window where the princess had climbed out.

Cassie got there first, looking down at the ground, her chest and shoulders heaving.

The princess had made it farther than Nick had thought she would. His mental calculations seemed hazy, and he was finding it difficult to run, although at least he no longer felt the slow, lethargic beat of the injury in his foot. It was the snow that was slowing him down then, pasting the soles of his boots to the earth.

Still, the story of the princess' journey was hard to miss, told in footprints and deep pockmarks in the snow. There was a smooth, honed area a ways up ahead where she must have begun to pull herself along.

Nick followed the punctures, looking down to find the next one, then slip-sliding along beside it. He was in no hurry, and to tell the truth, he didn't feel like he could've hurried if he'd tried. It was okay, though. He knew what tracks looked like when an animal had dragged itself away to die.

The creek surged, drowning out whatever sounds the snow didn't silence.

Cassie clawed at him, trying to pull him back, make him stop.

They skidded to a halt by a deep, dark cradle of white. A scooped-out section that could easily have contained a body. Except a body wasn't there.

The footsteps they had been tracking, small ones made by light little shoes, had ceased abruptly. But larger shoeprints pierced the snow after that.

Cassie's cry carried up to the sky, loud even over the churn and froth of the water. Relief, joy, hope. Goddamned ever-present hope that Nick couldn't kill in her no matter what he did.

Understanding came to him in smashed-up bits and pieces. He was smart. Just not as smart as his mother had always led him to bclicve.

The heavy breathing he'd heard in the SUV they had stolen, not his own, not the woman's, and not precisely in time with Harlan's great breaths either. The hunched shape Nick had spotted in the back of the vehicle.

He had thought the newscaster had been wrong, an idiot when she made her pronouncement. But Nick had been the idiot.

Three convicts had escaped.

CHAPTER FORTY-THREE

By the time the man arrived, Ivy had sunk into the accumulated snow, a thin pasting of white all over her body. She didn't know how she had been spotted. Ivy had become one with the landscape, just as she was one with the rock before her fall. Her disastrous fall. But she had been seen, she must have been, because Ivy felt herself picked up, then held aloft as whoever he was plodded along, his feet sending up clouds of snow with every step.

At first Ivy tried to fight, or at least protest. But her fists were so feeble, striking with the force of ping-pong balls. The man grasped both of them, holding on until she'd quieted.

Some part of her didn't think this was real. It was a fantasy borne of unspeakable pain, a kind of death-throes vision. Ivy's own personal version of the light everyone claimed to see, which in her case included an old man with wiry white twists of hair covering his hatless head and creases gouged deep into his dark face.

"How did you . . . why did you . . ." Ivy didn't recognize the sound of her own voice. She didn't believe she could make noises like that.

"Hush now," the man said. "Save your breath."

He trudged forward, not toward her house, but in the direction of a faint yellow glow that filtered through the branches of snow-clogged trees.

He held her in his arms like an infant. Ivy let her head fall back, dragged down by the weight of her hair. Her body was wracked with shivers, and a whimper of pain escaped her.

The man looked at her, the whites of his eyes shining. "You listen to me," he said fiercely. "You listen to me as we walk. And you don't go nowhere. You understand?"

No, Ivy didn't understand. How could she possibly go anywhere when she was lying in the sling of this man's arms? But then she thought maybe she did know what he meant.

She was shaking so hard that the man had trouble hanging on to her; twice he staggered and almost went down on his knees.

The snow had turned the whole world blank. Ivy herself was blanking out, breathing so shallowly that the cold air shocked her when it scraped against her throat. She jolted, and the world swam back into view for a moment before receding again.

The old man began to talk, making his voice loud, peering down at her instead of looking where they were going.

"Started out walking, but I turned back," he told her. "Didn't get more than a few miles or so 'fore the snow got bad. Figured the police maybe might come here, so I wandered around a while, trying to find it again. In the end it was hard to miss, big place, all lit up like a castle."

His words yanked her out of the white.

"Got no hat, no gloves, no matches even. And that's not all I don't got."

Ivy tried to lift her neck, and couldn't. But doing so made her feel the temperature for the first time in what seemed like a while. "Wuh —"

"Hush now," the man said again. "We almost there."

Almost where? They weren't anywhere. Just two drifting forms through a featureless landscape, walking nowhere, except maybe to heaven.

"I don't think Harlan's got it neither," the

man said.

Ivy thought she might've hallucinated the word. It shot a burning dart through her head. How did this man know Harlan? Was he part of the same dark and dismal place Harlan had come from, which had been brought to Ivy's house, her life, sent her out through her bedroom window to fall through the night?

"Harlan's —" Tears began to seep from her eyes. They were beastly hot against her nice, cool skin. "He's . . ."

"I know what he is," the man said, hard and final.

And then Ivy realized where they were.

At the Macmillans' camp. That was where the soft burr of lights had come from. Smoke lifted from the chimney and was carried away, the same color gray as the sky.

The man laid Ivy gently on a mat before the front door. Then he sat down, his back to the wall of the house. His shoulders quaked; he fought to take in breath.

"Thought I would like it," he panted. "Being free." Another arduous intake of air. "Turns out maybe I don't."

"Cold," Ivy answered, or maybe she hadn't said it out loud, for the man didn't seem to hear anything.

He looked at her, eyes still gleaming, his

skin silhouetted against the snow. This man was of the night as she had been of the rock.

"Don't got many years left," he said. "Think I'd like to spend them where I know how."

Then he twisted around, lifted his hand, and thumped on the door.

The borders around the man's body had turned fuzzy. Everything faded until all Ivy wanted was this one last piece of information.

The answer came to her, borne on a cold current of air.

"They call me Old-School."

CHAPTER FORTY-FOUR

Twenty-four years ago, Sandy's mother had asked her not to testify in court. Only Sandy hadn't been Sandy then. That wouldn't become her name for a few more years.

Her mother hadn't spoken to her much in the aftermath of her father's death. The words she had said the morning they were setting out to see Nick's lawyer had been among the first.

"He's going to ask if you have anything to say, Cassandra," her mother said. "But I don't think you saw anything. If you did, you couldn't possibly remember it right."

Sandy felt her back bow upon being given the command. It was delivered creakily because her mother hadn't used her voice in so long. Sandy had never realized before how rarely her mother spoke when Nick wasn't around.

She had been looking forward to the start of the trial like other kids anticipated summer vacation or graduation. There was no escaping the truth now. Nick's monstrousness would be described to a jury who would hand down justice. A judge would mete out the punishment that had been missing for so long.

Only what was her mother asking Sandy to do? Good God, what was her mother going to do in court herself?

"You can't make me not tell what happened," Sandy had replied.

Her mother's eyes were like chips of stone. "Maybe not," she said. "But I can tell everyone that you're a liar when you say whatever foolishness you have in mind."

Sandy felt pressure build inside her chest. She offered the only thing she had left.

"If I don't get to talk in court, I won't come back here," she said. "You won't see me again. Not unless you come find me. And we both speak the truth."

Her mother wasn't even listening by the end.

She had begun to smile as soon as Sandy spoke.

Sandy hadn't been able to make good on her threat, at least not right away. She was fifteen and had nowhere to go, although it occurred to her from time to time that Glenda Williams might have taken her in.

But instead of pursuing that, Sandy had set her sights on school and achieving a straight-A average. She had graduated early and gone to college downstate with a full scholarship. She met Ben, and if his dream hadn't been to start a guide service and live the life of an outdoorsman in the high peaks, she wouldn't have settled anywhere near this close to Cold Kettle.

Her mother had never come to find her, of course.

Until tonight.

Sandy raced after Nick, who seemed to be having trouble navigating the uneven hummocks of snow, following marks that had to lead to Ivy. Sandy had no idea who might've saved her daughter, whose footprints these were. But she couldn't let Nick find him.

Cold clenched Sandy. She blinked particles out of her snow-encrusted eyelashes. Nick ran ahead, the lead in some dreadful race.

But he was running strangely, blockily and relatively slow. His pace allowed Sandy to catch up.

She put on a burst of speed, maneuvering over hillocks of snow. Sheer rage seemed to spur Nick on, giving him momentum. He moved like an unbridled animal, emitting vaporous puffs from his nose, sweat shiny upon his face despite the temperature.

At a flash of light, Sandy spared a glance behind her. Back at her house, the front door stood open, and her mother was stepping outside, coat clutched around her. She spotted Sandy and Nick, and began to trudge in their direction.

Her voice drifted over on a faint gust of wind. "My goodness! You don't have much in that kitchen of yours, do you?" A pause, then another cry. "Nicky! Where are you going?"

The prints on the ground changed direction, and Nick careened away. Sandy had let herself be distracted for a second, and she damned the part of her that still opened like a bud every time her mother appeared.

But while seeing her mother for the first time back at the house had been like a physical blow, now Sandy recovered from the sight quickly, picking up her pace again without so much as a stumble. Because she knew. Her mother had eyes only for Nick, and Sandy was but a chink in the wall of her feeling. Nothing had changed. And nothing ever would.

The knowledge, putrid and buried for so long, was somehow liberating. It was like the moment you finally allowed yourself to be sick, then lay back afterward, panting and sweaty and emptied.

Sandy charged forward, Nick almost close enough to touch. Another advantage she had: she knew where they were headed. These footprints led to the Macmillans' camp.

As they approached, the front door on the structure swung open, and someone stepped out onto the sagging porch. One of the Macmillan descendants. It had to be.

"Hey!" the guy called. "Are you from the big house? I just found this girl on my —"

There was a momentary delay, Nick nearly tripping before he shouted back, "Thank God. She's my daughter. Can you send her out?"

Sandy was near enough that she could see how young the man standing there was. Too young to hear the husky thrum in Nick's throat, or to understand the madness it implied. The guy took a few steps across the uneven boards on the porch.

"Dude, I don't think I can do that," he called out. "I hate to tell you this, but she's hurt pretty bad. I just called for an ambulance —"

Sandy's mind tore through possibilities. If she screamed at him, he might not understand, or listen. Certainly he didn't seem to sense anything off about the situation yet. If she could just get there before Nick, then she could blow past the guy, barricade them all inside —

Some instinct, or maybe it was the sight of Nick, now neck and neck beside her, drove out the capacity for rational weighing, and Sandy began to scream. "Get back! Inside your house! Close the door and lock it!"

"Huh?" the guy called. "What did you —"

A bullet screamed through the air.

The young man's face bore an expression of faint perplexity as he went down on his knees, then tumbled over.

Nick made the front steps a slash of a second before Sandy got there, and leapt.

There was a blur from behind, or to the side; it seemed to be everywhere at once. Sandy's first thought was that a deer, tawny and white, was running inexpressibly fast to catch up with Nick. But then she realized the animal was too small for a deer. It was Mac, moving with such swiftness and grace, he seemed winged.

The dog erupted in a volley of barking, bristles of fur standing on end as he dove.

For a single heart-stopping and joyful moment he was a puppy again, or maybe the puppy he'd never gotten a chance to be, scattering snow with his snout, shaking himself off in midair.

Then he seized Nick's calf and sank his teeth deep into the flesh.

Nick let out a shriek of rage and agony, and the gun went flying. He kicked, but Mac hung on, his jaw locked. Nick made it onto the first step with one foot, but the other sank into the snow, and he stumbled backwards, trying to rid his body of the clinging dog. One leg kept kicking, the other hopping to maintain Nick's balance, so that he looked like a dybbuk, a dancing devil, or maybe simply an out-of-control, tantruming boy.

Mac's forelegs and even his lips on Nick's leg trembled as he fought to keep hold. You would have had to know their dog, been there after his rescue, overseen the long climb back from a life of abuse, to realize that Mac had never before rallied such force and such strength, and probably never would again; that, no matter what happened tonight, whether they all lived or died at Nick's hands, Sandy was getting to witness McLean's last great stand.

When Mac grabbed hold of Nick's leg, the gun had sailed free, landing in the snow. Now Nick pulled out the knife he'd taken

from the Nelsons', the handle a sleek extension of his rolled fist. He twisted around
behind him, stabbing viciously at the dog,
and Sandy let out a long, blistering scream.
"Mac! Runnnnnnnn!"

The dog turned, love and comprehension
both in his strangely beautiful pair of eyes,
one dark, one the liquid of a clear daytime
sky.

Mac let go, and did as he'd been told.

He wasn't as nimble as he'd been just moments ago, and his paws stuck once in a
drift, sending him face-first into the snow.
But he made it out of Nick's reach. McLean
found the woods and entered them like a
snowy shadow.

Nick spun on one foot to face Sandy. The
other leg leaked blood. It looked black in
the night, as did the holes Mac's fangs had
drilled in the pants Nick wore.

Their mother had nearly caught up to
them. The sheet of snow where the gun had
landed lay in front of her, its presence
revealed by a dark well.

Nick lunged forward with the knife, but
he didn't seem able to aim precisely and
Sandy felt only a whicker of air from its
blade.

"Nicky," came their mother's voice. "What
is going on out here?"

"Not shore," Nick said, or that's what it sounded like, as he pogostepped in Sandy's direction, holding the knife thrust out at an awkward angle. With a rasp, it slashed the fabric of their mother's coat, and then her arm. Barbara looked down as if she wasn't certain what had made that sound, still less what might be causing her to bleed.

Then it was as if a curtain came up, and everything onstage was exposed for their mother to see. Shock and pain transformed her, widening her eyes and twisting the skin on her face into a thready web of crevices and wrinkles. Her mouth opened, forming a small, dark cave.

There was a hard, wrinkled pit inside Sandy that felt glad. Surely the sight of her own blood flowing would make their mother finally start to feel.

Instead her eyelids came down, pressing into the gray hollows beneath, and she uttered one word, in the tone of voice someone would use to chastise a child who'd just spilled juice. "Nicky!" She made a *tsk*ing noise with her tongue as she walked forward, arms outstretched as if she hoped to draw Nick into a bloodied embrace.

Nick ignored her, coming for Sandy in an ungainly lurch that seemed no less menacing for its imprecision.

Their mother was going to pass right by the gun.

"Mama," Sandy pleaded. "You're bleeding! Do something!"

Their mother continued to take light, tripping steps through the snow, impervious to the red dots now stippling it.

"Mama," Sandy said again.

Nick grew distracted by the pattern of their mother's blood, his eyes perfectly round, glassy in the darkness as he stared at the ground, and a second was shaved off his wild lunging with the knife.

Their mother looked up, a paralyzing toxin of futility and regret and hatred freezing her features. She touched the blood now matting the cloth of her coat. "And just what is it that you would like me to do, Cassandra?" She turned back toward Nick.

Sandy plunged her hand deep into the snow. She withdrew a hunk of icy metal.

As Nick limped toward her, blinking to clear his vision so that this time he could drive home the blade, Sandy sighted on him.

"This," she said, through a scrim of tears so hot they felt like flames.

And she fired the gun.

CHAPTER FORTY-FIVE

The police chief arrived with a plow that sent up a high wake of white, clearing the road for the ambulance that came next, gunning its engine and lunging up the road. Two police cars followed, cutting through the blackened night like fins, their light bars spinning in a kaleidoscope of red and blue, while their sirens let out a long, wailing cry.

Eight people jumped out onto the snow.

Sandy stood on the Macmillans' porch. "Please!" she cried. "Over here! My daughter's hurt! And this boy!"

A medic swerved in her direction, black medi-kit banging against his leg as he ran.

"My husband's in the basement of that house," Sandy shouted again, pointing.

But she couldn't help dropping her head in defeat when a second medic headed in that direction. She knew Ben couldn't possibly have survived. Only the thought of Ivy enabled Sandy to move forward again.

■ ■ ■ ■

She held on to Ivy's startlingly chilled hand without letting go.

The Macmillan boy had been led off to the ambulance, gauze applied to his shoulder, more terrified than gravely injured.

Nick wasn't a good shot after all. Just like their father had said.

Sandy felt tears slide down her face, for him, for Ben, for them all.

A medic tended to Ivy, who passed in and out of consciousness while she was wrapped in an emergency blanket and her ankle immobilized. But her vital signs were fine, the medic assured Sandy. Ivy would recover.

Her mother's wound had stopped bleeding by the time it was examined.

Sandy followed her daughter to the ambulance, which stood parked on the long, curving road that ran between the two properties. She caught a glimpse of an old black man walking over to one of the police cars. He pulled open its rear door, and quietly, without looking around for anyone, lowered himself down and took a seat inside.

From her own house came a noise that split the night: the irritated sound of tearing, clawed-apart wood.

Then the other medic burst out of the now-open underground level.

"I'm gonna need that gurney!" he shouted. "Get the DOA off of it now!"

Nick's corpse was lifted aside, and the gurney shoved forward.

In a swirl of events, Sandy watched the gurney rolled carefully back out again, with a different body upon it. But this one wasn't dead. Instead it was wrapped in a second emergency blanket, its face concealed by a bulbous, insectile mask.

The medic who accompanied the gurney leaned over, hands pressing down hard as he said, "I'll apply pressure now, sir. You did great. Just great. Now let me take over."

Sandy snatched one look over her shoulder at Ivy, being loaded into the ambulance.

Then she began to take the frozen moguls of snow at a leap, racing toward her husband.

JANUARY–JULY 2016

With even less to fill her days, lacking the semblance of routine and the bright spot of her Wednesday prison visits, Barbara took to driving the same route that had brought her to her son at the end. Once, she left her car near the cabin with the *For Sale* sign on it, and trudged through the woods alongside an endless road. There were enough fir trees with laden boughs, and snow-draped, hulking boulders surrounding the house that nobody saw Barbara approach. She reached the place soundlessly, and stayed hidden, observing the people who moved about inside.

At first, Barbara didn't dare risk such a trip again. But as the months passed, she found herself beckoned back. She wanted to see them.

The man on his crutches, his right leg encased by some contraption from ankle to thigh. When Barbara had arrived during the boundless maw of that sucking, swallowing winter, the man had worn two such contraptions, and he had been in a wheelchair.

But now it was summer, and he had come a long way.

They all had. Barbara never even looked at the divot of skin on her arm anymore, like a new and girlish dimple.

And the daughter, too. She bore a resemblance to how Barbara used to appear, a long, long time ago. There were class pictures from that period, which helped Barbara to recall, and also scant memories of a mirror they had before her mother removed every glass from the house, declaring that she wasn't going to have six girls preening themselves around her. This one called Ivy looked different from Barbara in only one respect: she walked with a glitch in her step. Barbara, at sixty-three, was lighter and easier on her feet than the girl, and during the first of her visits, that fact had given Barbara a jaundiced sense of satisfaction.

She had a boyfriend, Ivy did.

He came up the long driveway in a new car now, too big and fancy for any child, or any grown-up either, for that matter. Though sometimes Barbara regretted not giving Nicholas his own car. Maybe if Nicholas had gotten that, everything would've been different.

The boy climbed out and joined in the meal the family was eating on their enormous covered porch. God knew what it must cost to construct such an arena-sized expanse of stone. The food being served on the glossy wooden table looked expensive, too.

After some time, when Barbara had grown sore from sitting on her haunches, parting the branches of a tree with stiff fingers, the boy and the girl prepared to leave.

The father asked them their plans.

Cassandra gave Ivy a look that made Barbara want to grab hold of something and tear it apart. How could a mother look at her daughter that way, with eyes so full of love and adoration that they overflowed?

"That's really where you guys will be?" Cassandra said. "All night, honey?"

The girl pranced across the stone — that snag in her step, but still, prancing — and said, "All night, Mom. Unless if we go over to Brian's — his parents aren't home this week — but I promise I won't drink, even if everybody else is. And I'll call for a ride."

The boyfriend let out a guffaw. "Man. No secrets in the Tremont family."

Cassandra's hand reached for the man's, like a missile finding its target, and the man said, "You got that right, Cory."

And then Cassandra and the man laughed, great, blooming laughs, louder than the joke really warranted — Barbara didn't get what was so funny actually — and they both watched as the boy helped the girl down the stairs, even though she really didn't need much help, not anymore.

Barbara watched too, from amidst her stand of broad, leafy trees, leaning against the scabby bark of a trunk for both conceal-ment and support.

The next time she crouched in back of the house, behind a rock whose nooks and crags she studied as voices floated her way. And as the weeks wore on, Barbara risked ad-ditional visits. Finding that she wanted to feel more a part of things, she began to crawl forward on the ground, below eye level. She wasn't noticed, and so she drew close enough to sit beside the forged metal latticework that encircled the porch, almost as if she were a guest at the party.

Cassandra and the man would linger outside on those soft, peachy nights when their daughter had gone off, and the sun seemed incapable of sinking. They had an old dog, who lay on the hot, baking stone beside them, occasionally blinking one milky blue eye and snuffing in gratitude as they dropped pieces of food down to him, charred meat and bits of roll.

The dog was aware of Barbara — he lifted his head and sniffed — but her presence didn't appear to bother him, and Barbara took that as a sign.

Maybe she belonged here too, just a little bit.

She liked listening to the conversations Cassandra and the man had. So intimate and understanding. Those qualities didn't enrage her as they had in the beginning. And as the summer passed, Barbara decided to make one final trip, as if aware that both the year and her time would soon be growing short.

Cassandra's voice traveled out over the fields.

"I know I've said this before," she said. "But I didn't keep anything from you, Ben — I kept it from myself." She wrapped her arms around herself as if she were cold despite the balmy temperature. Cassandra had always been the most vexing and illogical child. "If you don't think about something for long enough, it begins to go away. Or gets buried by the passage of time."

Her husband studied her across the table.

"I didn't want to be that person anymore.

I wanted to be someone . . . I wanted to be worthy of you." And for some inexplicable reason, Cassandra put her face down in the cupped bowl of her hands.

Her husband began quietly stroking her arm. "Worthy of *me*?"

Cassandra looked up.

"Oh, Ben, you know how you are. You're strong — good God, but you're strong — and you're moral and good-hearted. But you see things one way. If ever I hadn't been that way . . . I mean, look what happened when you wanted to move up here and I didn't."

After a moment the man said, "We moved up here."

They both chanced a smile.

"Right," Cassandra said.

"I'm not strong," the man said, his smile fading. "I can barely walk." A long pause before his next words. "I'd say you're the strong one."

The irregular oblong of wood wasn't even, like a table was supposed to be. Cassandra laid her arms across its short end.

"How many bones broken?" she replied. "And how close did that bullet come to hitting your spleen? A fraction of an inch and you might not even be . . . ." Cassandra compressed her lips and stopped speaking.

The man looked away from her to gaze out over the land. Far off in the distance, now pared down to a speck, was the retreating car that carried their daughter.

"It's the nights," he said at last. "The nights are still hard."

His hand found Cassandra's and they came together like links on a chain.

Barbara awaited Cassandra's response, watching these people, who had taken away the only person who'd ever mattered to her, put a stop to his reign on her heart and her life.

And for just a moment, as brief and fleeting as warmth in Wedeskyull, she was glad.

ACKNOWLEDGMENTS

Dana Isaacson deserves mention first and foremost. Dana is the wizard-behind-the-curtain of my editing team, and I am grateful every day that I have never had to publish a book without his sharp eye, keen ear for dialogue, and visionary sense of pace. There was also that eleventh hour, live-action editing session on the phone that is one of the most amazing revision experiences I've ever had. If Anita Nelson's moment in the powder room gets your heart pounding during this story, you have Dana to thank. And for a whole lot more besides.

Everyone at Penguin Random House/ Ballantine deserves huge thanks. For adding their wisdom to this book, Kim Hovey, Mark Tavani, and Jennifer Hershey deserve special mention. To everyone at the helm of this ship, I am humbled and honored to be on it with you.

Anne Speyer, I miss you terrifically, but

am so glad to have been left in the able, enthusiastic hands of Elana Seplow-Jolley.

To Pam Feinstein, and to Jennifer Rodriguez and every single eagle-eyed person in the production department, my jaw drops at what you catch, smooth, and polish. Thank you for making my story into the book readers hold in their hands.

All of my covers have been designed by the incomparable Marietta Anastassatos, and I've heard their praises sung at every book event I've done. And that's saying something — I do a lot of events. But the cover for the original publisher's edition of this book is to my mind a tour de force. I've never seen anything like it . . . and I read a lot of books. For that special sort of genius that helps you judge a book by its cover, my hat is off to Marietta.

Thank you, Rachel Kind, for bringing this book to readers across the ocean. To know that my stories live in places I have not yet traveled to myself is a unique thrill.

Bookstores are near and dear to my heart, as many of you know, and the bridge Maggie Oberrender helped build between them and this novel is something for which I'll always be grateful.

You also may know that I go on very long book tours. While 20,000 miles of driving and 200 events might be a bit over the top, Michelle Jasmine and Poonam Mantha handled their portion so seamlessly, I wish four-month tours would just become standard already so that every event could go so smoothly. Thanks go to Michelle, Poonam, and Alexandra Kent for sending books to every corner of this country, and making people happy for months after my release.

Speaking of publicity, every author should have the town book criers at JKS Communications involved in their releases. Not only does JKS know how to spread the word to just the right people, event sites, and media outlets, but Julie Schoerke, Marissa Curnutte, Samantha Lien, Chelsea Apple, Mike Matesich, and Angelle Barbazon have the most important traits imaginable in this business: passion for books and love for authors and readers.

I would not be where I am in life without two groups of people so special, it's hard to know how to describe them — even for a writer. Booksellers, you are keeping alive a precious resource in our country, the face-to-face in a virtual world, and a treasure chest in each community. One day I will thank each and every one of you in acknowledgments that will become a book in its own right. For now, the welcome you have extended me, my family, and my novels is something that inspires me to write my heart out every day. I can't wait to see you all again.

And librarians, thank you for the wealth you give readers every day. It is measured by something greater than coins. You made me rich as a child, and I hope to be able to repay you and your patrons for years to come.

Book bloggers do virtually what booksellers do in person. I am so grateful to this passionate, creative community. Thank you, bloggers, for your reviews, interviews, and the spotlight you shine on great reads. Five deserve particularly special props — and an immediate subscription to their blogs: Allison Hiltz, Tamara Welch, Rhiannon Johnson, Kristin Thorvaldsen, and Helen Barlow.

Author and consummate writing teacher, Les Edgerton, challenged every assumption and clichéd view of prison I had, grounding me in a greater reality. If any mistakes were made, the fault lies with me, not his spot-on tutelage.

Writers need other writers. I am lucky enough to be part of four superb writing organizations, and I recommend you join them all, as a writer, reader, fan, or all three. International Thriller Writers is the most supportive and exciting group I've come across. Sisters in Crime is the most nurturing and clever — the Mavens of Mayhem, Triangle SinC, Border Crimes/Kansas City, and Heart of Texas chapters all deserve special mention, as does SinC National in Lawrence, Kansas, where the whole organization began. Mystery Writers of America is the most rich in tradition. I also have a special spot for Charles Salzberg and everyone at the New York Writers Workshop, which has helped far more people get published than its regional reach would suggest — including yours truly.

Speaking of writers, online groups also rule the day. The Crime Scene Writers are there whenever an author needs a reality check, or wants to ask how this or that wacky scenario could progress. Chris Norbury helped me figure out what Ben would tell his captors in this novel. That Chris became a supporter in real life (that is, Minnesota) too is icing on an already tasty cake. Members of the Cozy Café — Savvy, Judy (those baked goods!), Sara, Derek, Lori, Windy, and Katherine — I wish you all words and pages and success. The ITW Debut Authors Forum came in at the tail end of this book — and I hope to have them for many more.

Lauren Sweet, freelance editor extraordinaire, provided her always incisive read, and made sure everyone got into the cars that they were supposed to. When it comes to French toast sticks and dead bodies, we all need Lauren.

Violet Snow, Anique Taylor, and Simona David, I so enjoy our Wednesday Writer lunches, and appreciate your hearts and your support.

Three mystery publications deserve to be read far and wide, and thanked. To John and Shannon Raab at *Suspense Magazine,* my thanks for a publication filled with articles you can't find anywhere else, the fun conversation at ThrillerFest, and one of the honors of my career thus far. Anthony Franze and Jeff Ayers at The Big Thrill, you keep the content riveting — and the in-person get-togethers, too. Jon and Ruth Jordan of *Crimespree Magazine,* not only do you pick great toys for the kids, but I also can't get enough of your thoughtful, in-depth pieces.

On the road with me — in spirit and live on the radio once every week — was Authors on the Air host, Pam Stack. As an author, you may already know Pam. And as a reader, you're going to want to know her. She features the best of the best on her show, and as a relative newbie I was honored to be included.

The novel you've just read was written in two houses I lived in, but which don't belong to me. I am grateful for both homes-away-from-home. John Strauss, thank you for your third-floor aerie — and the desk that migrated up the road with me. Kevin Lanier, thank you for the window on the creek, which became a window into the world of this book.

People always wonder how we lived life on the road for so long. I say that it's easy — no housework! But for sure it's made even easier by the people who extended their homes and their welcome. We got to stay in places of beauty, interest, and warmth . . . from a Victorian B&B to a writer's retreat house, a mansion by a lake to a wood-and-stone expanse perched on a mountain (and seemingly carved out of it). Perry and Nancy Adair, Melanie Bragg, Carla and Tim Buckley, Gary and Stacie Parkes, Karen Pullen, Bryan Robinson and Jamey McCullers, Dan and Lisa Scheiderman, and Tina and James Whittle, thank you for giving the whole family a place to rest during our very long time on the road. I also have to thank the geniuses behind Airbnb and their hosts for their contribution to making possible this nomadic life.

We spent memorable afternoons and evenings, talking about words and art and life over great food, with Patricia Albrecht and Bruce Miller at their cabin in the woods; Stacy and Ron Allen, who found the best apple crullers; Christina and Tony Carrini, who traveled a long way to Queens; Sally and Don Goldenbaum, whose pool and ribs can't be beat; Jen and Brett Grigsby, who offered respite in Vermont; Judy Hogan, whose farm gave us a living meal; Lynne Kote, who put together an elegant pre-event dinner; Kevin, Robin, and Collette Lanier who served up real Texas BBQ, with a swimming lesson; and Rebecca Suskind-Davis for lunch and hugs in Seattle.

Another way we pull this off is thanks to writerly friends who set up events from afar. Barbara DeMarco-Barrett in Corona Del Mar; Diane Beirne at the historic and elegant Women's Club of Richmond; Greg Bogard at La Grande Middle School; Marjorie Brody, who championed me at not one but three Austin-area events; Bobbi Chukran, who introduced me to a fantastic new-to-me bookseller — and took me for BBQ; Connie di Marco, who knew my event schedule better than I did — and shared every bit of it; Timothy Domick of Centenary College; Seán Dwyer and the Red Wheelbarrow Writers; Donna Figurski at a beautiful library in Surprise, Arizona; Windy Lynn Harris, Susan Pohlman, and the women of Phoenix; Kay Kendall and the rest of the chocolate lovers in Houston; Cara Lopez Lee and the Denver Woman's Press Club . . . you all made me feel at home and I thank you.

Thanks to fellow authors who paired for events with me all across the country. Whether you're a fan of mysteries, women's fiction, magical realism, or thrillers, the following is a tantalizing list of must-reads. Carla Buckley, you are the best partner in crime, and the Thelma to my Louise (or vice versa?). Kelly Braffet, Peg Brantley, John Clement (on air), Robin Devereaux-Nelson, Reed Farrel Coleman, Shalanna Collins, Lala Corriere, Donna Fletcher Crow, Richard Cunningham, Annette Dashofy, John Dixon, Brian Freeman, Karolyn Graham, Elizabeth Heiter, Naomi Hirahara, Cynthia Lott, Matthew Quinn Martin, Jamie Mason, Rick Murcer, Dennis Palumbo, Lori Rader-Day, Bryan Robinson, M. J. Rose, Robert Rotstein, Charles Salzberg, A. J. Scudiere, Michael Sears, Julia Spencer-Fleming, Earl

Staggs, Lauren Sweet, Wendy Tyson, Therese Walsh, and Tina Whittle, thank you for coming out and proving that nothing beats an author event.

There is a writer who inspired me as a child and gave me a moment I never dared hope for as a new author. To the incomparable Queen of Suspense, Mary Higgins Clark herself, the judges, and everyone at MWA and Simon & Schuster who did me the honor of giving my first novel the Mary Higgins Clark Award, my deepest thanks.

Book clubs have welcomed my books onto their rosters, and me into their midst. Huge thanks go to Linda Dewberry and her book club at Orca Books; the Bookstore Plus book club; Nikki Bonnani and the Killer Coffee Club; Eleanor Siegel and the Riviera Readers; Janice Kmetz and the Deep River book club; Mary Jane Weber's book club; Dee Abrams and the Mystery Lover's Book Club; Julie Schroeder's book club; Tanya Seaward and the OHHA book club in Morristown, New Jersey; Let's Talk Murder in Rocky Hill, Connecticut; June Kosier's book club; and last but never least, the King of Prussia book club.

I hope that everyone who just read this book fell a little bit in love with McLean. To the booksellers at McLean & Eakin in Petoskey, Michigan, for giving Mac's real-life counterpart, Edie, a home and a home away from home, and to rescue dogs everywhere . . . you are all heroes to me.

Finally, no book is complete until I thank my family. My parents, Alan and Madelyn; my brother, Ezra; brother-in-law, James; and sister, Kari, knew this dream long before it was realized. Special thanks go to my mom for reading and for event catering fit for royals, and my dad for reading and his ribs. Thanks also to Shirley Frank for tidbits at my launch party, and another very welcome read.

Josh, Sophie, and Caleb make it all possible, and I mean that literally. They are navigating and cheering, and being their interesting, entertaining, and loving selves at home and on the road. Thank you, dear ones, for sharing my dream, and allowing me to share in yours.

ABOUT THE AUTHOR

Jenny Milchman lives in the Hudson Valley with her husband and two children. She is the author of *Cover of Snow, Ruin Falls,* and *As Night Falls.*